Yours Truly, YOUR HUSBAND FOR LIFE

JANAE JAMES

Copyright © 2023 by Janae James.

Library of Congress Control Number:		2023907956
ISBN:	Hardcover	978-1-6698-7581-9
	Softcover	978-1-6698-7580-2
	eBook	978-1-6698-7579-6

All rights reserved. No part of this book may be reproduced or transmitted in any form or by any means, electronic or mechanical, including photocopying, recording, or by any information storage and retrieval system, without permission in writing from the copyright owner.

Any people depicted in stock imagery provided by Getty Images are models, and such images are being used for illustrative purposes only.
Certain stock imagery © Getty Images.

Print information available on the last page.

Rev. date: 10/17/2023

To order additional copies of this book, contact:
Xlibris
844-714-8691
www.Xlibris.com
Orders@Xlibris.com
847212

We've all had relationships that we know we held on to for way too long, or even some that we never should have entered in the first place! The question I am asked time and time again, "How the hell did you end up marrying a jailbird?" Not just writing, kickin' it, passing time, like full-blown fell in love and had a whole jail wedding! I was raised in a two-parent nuclear family and maintained either merit roll or honor roll from elementary to high school. I went to college straight from high school and graduated with a bachelor's degree. Yes, I became a single parent shortly after graduation, but I had a plan for my life, so I went back to school when my babies were five years and one year old, and earned my master's degree in childhood education in December of 2006.

I moved to Charlotte in August 2007. My baby girl had turned four the day we left Buffalo. Poor baby spent her whole birthday on the road. (For birthday number six we went all out to make it up to her!) I was full of ambition and excited to take on the role of teacher in my very own classroom. But I wasn't prepared for such a drastic change, being a single parent in a new city, with no family and friends, and taking on the responsibility of educating twenty children. I was beyond overwhelmed. I cried a few times. I wasn't Superwoman as I thought. I struggled to balance it all, and somehow I survived my first and second years teaching fourth grade. Then I was laid off in June 2009. I gave 150 percent to my job and there wasn't enough of me left to guess. It simply wasn't enough. I decided that moving back to Buffalo would be my best bet. I applied for teaching jobs back in New York and even landed an interview by phone, which didn't go too well. Honestly, I don't think I put forth a lot of effort in that interview because I love everything about the South. My mother constantly pressured me and secretly pressured the kids, pleading for us to move back. But Charlotte felt like home. So I made up my mind that Charlotte was home, and I was here to stay.

Sometime in late winter of 2010, my best friend asked if I could write a letter to the parole board on her brother's behalf for his upcoming parole hearing in March. Of course I would help the family out even though I knew very little about him, I knew my bestie/sister. She sent him a copy of the letter for his records, and unfortunately for him, his parole was denied. He asked her who I was and she told him her best friend. Her brother told her to tell me he wanted to marry me. When she called me and told me that, we had a good laugh about it. I told her hell naw, but tell him to holla at me when he gets out 'cuz brotha was fine! The hormones and naughty side of me thinking after all those years in jail, *sure*, we can link when you come home! However, I asked her for his address, and decided I would write him a letter and we can get an early start on the "hey, how you doing" part. This is where our story begins.

April 2, 2010

Hi Jarelle,

 I actually love the name Bryan but Brooklyn calls you Jarelle, so I will too for now. I didn't want to start this letter with the standard "how you been," "what's up," or "what's going on," but it's been so long since I wrote a letter, and since we really haven't officially met, I can bore you by talking about me! Lol. it really was no problem for me to write the letter for you. I really admire the relationship you have with your little sister. I have an older brother, and I love him but we've never been close like that. So I would do anything I could to help her and help you.
 So about me, as far as the basics, I'm thirty-three turning thirty-four on June 1. Gemini of course, but I'm told I'm not a typical Gemini like my hot-tempered brother. I have a six-year-old daughter (Justine) and an eleven-year-old son (Jordan). I want another child, but I gave myself a deadline of thirty-five to have more. And that time is close, so if it doesn't happen it's not the end of the world, but it would be nice. I lived in Buffalo all my life and moved to Charlotte in August 2007. It was such a hard decision because I was going alone with my kids and had no family or friends there. My mom pressured me (and still does) to please stay, and made me feel so guilty, but I needed to do it. And I felt guilty taking the kids from their dad, but at the same time I needed to get away from him. Not because of abuse or anything, but the back and forth and lies and babies, etc. But more importantly, I needed to prove to myself that I could make it, and I was starting a new teaching career.

Fast forward two and a half years later, I taught fourth grade for two years. Spent a summer in Buffalo giving it one last try with my kids' father (summer '08), which didn't work, and was laid off in June 2009. Been looking for work ever since, so in the meantime I started at a Girl Scout troop and have got to spend so much more time with my kids volunteering at their school and being home when they get off the bus. It's been a blessing, so I try to focus on the positive. But money is tight, so I can't wait to get back to work. I'm not sure if teaching is meant for me, so I'm trying to listen to God more and let him guide me where I need to be.

That's a very brief intro about me, but I don't want to bore you any longer. As far as looks, I'm five foot six with brown skin like medium complexion, black hair to my shoulders, thick (full-figured) but how I like to say a large hourglass LOL. Basically a well-proportioned big girl, considered very attractive, but I seem to attract the wrong guys! Since I've been here in Charlotte I have officially scratched South Carolina off my list of potential men to date because three out of three have been idiots! But not giving up.

Brooklyn told me you wanted to marry me. I told her you are probably looking at me like the saltine cracker in Eddie Murphy's *Raw* when the girl held out then finally gave him some, and he said, "Damn, is that a Ritz?" LOL! I have had droughts but can't imagine what it's been like for you, but I definitely know I am a Ritz with the cheese and other toppings! I know you were probably joking with Brooklyn about marrying me, but I would really like to get to know you better, so it's about time for you to get up out of there. I'll be praying for you, and in the meantime I'm looking forward to getting a letter from you. I hope you're not laughing at my print, but I just don't write in cursive. Takes too long for me! And I've seen your pictures, damn! You definitely got it going on, which I'm sure you know. But anyway, Jarelle, I can't wait to hear back from you. And my hand is tired. Bye for now. Chat with you soon.

Your newest friend,
Janae James

April 8, 2010

Dearest Janae,

    May this letter find you and your family in the best of health and blessed. First and foremost, I would like it if you called me Bryan as my name, 'cause I think it's kinda hot myself (Lol). And we have officially met, as soon as I said your name I blew breath into something that could be if only patience is practiced. And please never consider your conversation boring. 'Cause if we didn't communicate, how could we build a solid foundation to stand on? As you very well know by now, I was denied parole for the last time, meaning once this year is done I have one year left before I come home. And I want to thank you personally for the beautiful letter you wrote. It inspired me to know who you are! As far as my sister goes, that's my rock and shining armor, and she means more to me at times than the air I breathe! Words can't come close to what she means to me, and I'm looking for a wife with those same qualities. Are you that spirit I need to connect with? I'm thirty-nine. I will be forty this year, but as you can see, I take care of my body and constantly seek knowledge! I'm a Virgo. I have two daughters, Alexis (eighteen) and Cheryl (sixteen and a half). I would love a son also if God decides to deal me those cards! I'm glad to hear you're a determined and goal-oriented woman, and I think that's sexy and attractive. You're supposed to always want the best for yourself and your children at all times. I'm very happy to hear that you're an educator. We need more black teachers because they are not teaching our kids what they need to know (devils) that is! Where's the Girl Scout cookies (Lol). That's good you're mentoring young women. That's a special gift. That's real special when you say you're learning to listen to God more and let him guide me where you need to be. I feel the same way, although sometimes I get discouraged when dealing with where I'm at and the things I go through.

As far as describing yourself, I like what I hear, 'cause that means you like to eat. And I love a woman who's not scared to put on a few pounds, 'cause I'm a great cook. I know about the outside, what about the inside? Your heart, what inspires you who once your short and long-term goals were you looking for in a man? 'Cause three out of three doesn't sound good, maybe you're trying to compare the past when you should be concentrating on the future? And I was dead serious when I told my sister I want to marry you. Your letter alone sealed the deal. Between my sister and the letter, I have to meet you and <u>begin</u> the <u>process</u> of <u>becoming one</u>, even if I have to start in here! That's good you have droughts, 'cause your body is a temple, and you just don't put anything in a temple. But as for me, I would make love to you mentally, physically, and spiritually from the balls of your feet to the follicles on your scalp!

And as far as crackers go, I like Graham crackers, 'cause brown sugar is better than white any day! That answers your question. I wasn't joking, and I look forward to getting to know you better. And I'll pray for us, that sounds better. And it would be a pleasure to continue to communicate and grow with you from friends to wherever we allow it to create. And no, I'm not laughing at your writing. I think it's cute. And thanks for the compliment. Beauty is as beauty does! Well, I can't wait to hear back from you. In the meantime, take care of yourself and your kids. And please don't settle for less. Aim high. Please tell my sister no more tears now, we good. We on a countdown. And I love her and waiting to hear from her! Until our spirits meet again, I'll see you soon!

Your future husband,
Bryan Edwards

PS: Please send me some pictures of you so we both can look at each other!

April 12, 2010

Hi Bryan,

 I was so happy to get a letter from you so fast! Honestly, when I checked the mail I was sort of expecting it and hoping for it at the same time. I'm glad to know you are in good spirits about having to go through one more year. It's hard for me to picture or imagine because I really never met anyone in your situation before. I will probably be asking you a lot of straightforward or blunt questions as we get to know more about each other. I don't want to be judgmental or overbearing, but this whole situation is so new to me and I want to go in with my eyes wide open. In the past I made the mistake of not speaking up when things bother me, or being afraid of offending someone or having him upset with me, etcetera. Carrying all those bags weighs you down, and I have gone through enough to learn to stop and drop some of those bags as I go through life's journey.

 So you're a Virgo! My closest friend in Buffalo is a Virgo, and I get along with that sign pretty good. I'm a Gemini, which I think I told you, June 1. You have to tell me your birthday too so I can send you some type of care package. Please tell me you don't smoke because I won't contribute to that habit and my son has asthma. I actually have two boxes of Girl Scout cookies left, Do-Si-Dos and Tagalongs. Both have peanut butter, so if you're not allergic, I can send them to you. I guess you can send a list of the things I am allowed to send you so we don't get in trouble!

 About me, I definitely wear my heart on my sleeve. I brake for animals, and thank goodness, have never hit anything yet! When I get a house I plan to have two dogs, one big and one small, cute, little one! Right now we have a bunny. She is an absolute doll. My daughter is just like me, sensitive when it comes to animals. Every time the ASPCA commercial comes on she's like, "Mommy, call the number. Hurry up, all the poor little kitty." My son jokes that if we opened an animal hospital we would be crying too much to care for the animals! LOL. I'm always overly optimistic, and never really believe that some people's true intentions are really foul. I have a save-the-world attitude—hard as hell right now because so many things are wrong with the economy and environment but change is coming eventually.

When I first moved to North Carolina, I thought I was well on my way to meeting my goals. I had my degree, starting a new job, and all I needed was to meet a man, get married, buy a house, and have my third baby. After teaching for a few months I was like, "Oh my god! I did not sign up for this! It was an unbelievable amount of work on top of being in a new city and away from family and friends. Now I'm not so sure that's my true passion. The second year of teaching was easier than the first, but it still made me question if this is my calling. I know I want to work with children, but I'm just being still right now, trying to listen to God. I always said if teaching didn't work out I would love to be a nurse. I still want to get married, buy a house, get my two dogs, and have a baby. I'm considering going back to school. For now I just focus on my own kids, Girl Scouts, and trying to learn more about myself. I recently let go of a huge bird and dealing with my kids' father, and I kept hearing over and over in my head, "A lesson learned will be repeated," and I knew he was not in my future. So as far as goals, my whole way of thinking has changed. I've grown a lot, and have a lot more to do because I want to find a career that satisfies my spirit. I'm just being still and listening and praying. You know, you came into my life at an interesting time. I'll go into detail about that in another letter, but I'm so flattered about how you feel about a potential us. I'm a very patient person sometimes for the wrong reasons, but I understand sometimes that other times I take risks and dive in, like when I relocated. A definite plus about our current situation would be communication. We can learn so much about each other that when we meet in person it would be like we've known each other for years. But then I look at my long-term goals. What about yours? The system is so biased and unfair to those with a criminal record. What are your plans when you first get out? How will you conquer those discriminatory issues to support yourself or a family? I know it will be challenging but not impossible. Do you have hobbies or skills and talents that could lead to a career? Are there training programs that you can enroll in while you are there? These are things I think about and hope have a positive outcome.

When I think about what I'm looking for in a man, I realize I've been compromising too long. I feel like since I'm a total package, my man needs to be too. Strong mentally and physically, able to express himself to me, love kids, like to travel, know how to be polite, no money to put someone in their place (even me if I'm trippin' LOL), affectionate, and know how to kiss. Outgoing and a homebody, honest, driven, and ambitious. Not just settling when things are down but reshuffling the deck, looking at the problem from another angle, and trying again! Sexy. I want him to be the first person I think about when I wake up, and dream about him at night. Sounds like a lot, but I've waited this long, so I deserve it! LOL. Besides, I'm giving everything I'm asking for and it's only fair!

I'm sleeping now, and we'll have so many letters exchanged over time. I'm glad you're my new friend. Can't wait for letter number two. Hope you like the pics!

Sincerely,

Janae James
Xoxo

April 14, 2010

Dear Bryan,

Hellooo! Here I am writing letter number three and still have number two in my purse. But I will make it to the post office tomorrow and mail them separately to pass the time. I guess by now you must be the master of patience!

Since I can't base this letter on a reply from you, I can go into more detail about me and my family. So I'll talk to you about my babies. Jordan just turned eleven in February. He is so incredibly smart but lazy. For example, he scored very high in math and science with very little effort but hates to read. He did end up falling in love with a book called *Wringer* last year. He liked it so much, I bought it for him. Then an author came to visit their school and read a chapter from his book, and Jordan begged me to buy it. So any book that makes him want to read, I get it because he hates reading! Me, on the other hand, I love, love, love to read. Especially Black authors. Sister Souljah's book *The Coldest Winter Ever* is my favorite, and I like Stephen King's books too.

I'm assuming you all have a library in there, so do you like to read too? Or I'm getting off-topic. Back to my son. He has a selfish streak like my brother and his uncle on his dad's side. And can hold a mean grudge, so I'm always talking to him about that and to be a better big brother. He has a hard time being the oldest because he doesn't understand that his punishments are going to be tougher than his little sister's because she is still learning and she admires him so much and follows behind him. Or I explained to him that I had to learn by doing when he was younger, so he's almost like the guinea pig, so I may have disciplined him one way when he was younger but my daughter may have gotten a lighter punishment. But on the other hand, he don't let nobody mess with his little sister! The way it's supposed to be. I guess he feels he is the only one that can harass her! LOL. That's my Jordan.

Now, Justine is my baby girl. Six years old, so, so smart in school. She's already reading over fifty words per minute, and the goal for first grade is forty by year's end. She looks just like me with dimples. She is very sensitive, like will cry watching *Animal Planet*, and disciplining her, I admit, is harder because she has waterfall tears! Only newborn I ever saw with tears from birth! She has such a warm, caring heart, and wants to save every stray animal. She's overly concerned with her friends liking her, which I have to break her out of because clutches are no joke, especially in middle school. She adores Jordan, and even when he is mean she is quick to forgive. He holds on to grudges a lot longer than her!

Justine loves junk food and hates vegetables, even corn! I make smoothies for her with spinach and carrots to make sure she gets her veggies in. I love cooking for Jordan, he's a hearty eater that has a big appetite. Justine will love spaghetti one day then pick at it the next. But I love to cook and love to bake, and I'm good at both. My kids are complete opposites and complement each other as well. They're both smart, both slept through the night as infants by three months old. I could go on for days about how great they are and how much they drive me insane! But I'm thankful they know how to act in public, I can take them anywhere, and living in a new city, I had to train them at nine and five years old about being home, so when it's necessary I am at ease. All that unpaid overtime as a teacher, sometimes had to leave them alone. Being unemployed financially is a burden, but it's been such a blessing. I have lunch with them at school, volunteer at the school, go to all the assemblies and programs, all the things my mom could never do because of work and I couldn't do previously. So I focus on the positive.

Well, that's all for now, I can't wait for your next letter!

Janae
Xoxo

April 16, 2010

Dear Bryan,

I hope you've been in good spirits this week. Here I am writing letter number four, finally mailed number two yesterday, and number three is in my purse! You'll probably appreciate the fact that I love to write more than anyone. My kids' father, I'm sure, hates my letters because they were always about how I wasn't happy, why can't he just be with me and stop messing around, please spend more time with me, blah blah blah! LOL. Why do we women hang on so damn hard when we know it's going nowhere? I started writing a book when I was pregnant with my daughter and picked up on some more during the summer 2008. I haven't written anything since, and now would be a perfect time, being off work. I think I'm going to jump into that. Feed now. I need to be motivated and inspired to get the creative juices flowing, and writing you is getting me back into the writing group, so thanks!

Right now I'm at the auto shop getting my crank shift or sensor done. I swear I have had the worst financial luck lately. Just paid a speeding ticket (my first and last hopefully). Got my laptop repaired for a work-from-home job that ended up falling through, so that was $224 is wasted. The car will cost me $180. The little bit of tax refund money I was hanging on to is officially gone! But all those expenses could have come up in like August when I seem to always be broke, so I still have to be grateful I was even able to pay those.

And I'm so glad I booked our cruise as soon as I got my tax money. Three days in the Bahamas, April 29 to May 2! Not sure if I wrote that in letter number two or number three. This will be my fourth cruise. For my first I went in November of 2000. JetBlue had just come out and I won round-trip airfare to Florida. I was like, I don't know anyone in Florida. Me and the kids' father were on again off again and he was broke, so my mom suggested I go on a cruise. Her and my dad had already been on two or three by then. So I went to a travel agent on my birthday. I had a lot of fun despite being alone. Some couples in groups saw me alone and welcomed me into their group, so it was cool.

My second cruise was in October 2001, a month after 9/11, so you know airport security was crazy. Then like two days before I got a crazy urinary tract infection, probably from not drinking enough, and I was in such pain I thought I would have to cancel. Luckily after medicine, it went away instantly. I met a girl right away who was alone too, and we both had sons the same age. So we hung out the whole time, and I had a lot more fun then.

The third time around (still single—no, really, still hanging on to empty hopes). I decided to take Jordan at age six. Justine was barely two, and I didn't want to spend the extra when she would barely remember. He had such a blast at Camp Carnival and being able to eat whatever and the beautiful blue water and so much to see and do. He's fun to hang around with and such a clown! And can draw his ass off! He's working on doing living things more in drawings, but inanimate objects like cars, boats, and houses—he is off the hook!

So now cruise number four will be the three of us. Justine is so excited, and Jordan because he knows what to expect, has her all pumped up. I'll be sure to send plenty of pics. Who knows, maybe cruise number five will be with you. I love spending time with my kids, and going alone was fun, but it's nothing like being with that special someone. It was so fun when me and Jordan went. On the last night, I don't know what we ate but we were blowing up that little room. It was bad! I was feeling bad for whoever had to clean our room because smells tend to linger in closed-up rooms.

You'll learn about me. Sometimes I'm kind of blunt, and I have a big sense of humor and I love to laugh. It's fun learning about myself since moving from Buffalo and being away from friends and family, particularly the kids' father. I always felt constrained, like I couldn't be around him like he was always judging my actions. But honestly, for years I was telling myself that I've invested so many years trying to make it work, and we have two kids that I have to stick it out and wait until he realizes it don't get better than me! Mind you, when we met he had two other kids. Jordan was number three, then got bumped to number five. Justine is number nine, and there are twelve in total. So I've put up with a lot. Sorry if I talk about it a lot, but for me it's all part of the healing process and reminding myself what I have endured and sacrificed in trying to make us fit and work. But honestly, we were never compatible. Eight baby mamas and no one has been able to keep him, that's a losing battle! It was hard to accept, but finally it's sinking in.

The great thing about being single is it is stress free and I can "find myself," because I've been lost for years. I do what's best for me and my kids and no longer worry about their dad's input as much, even my mom. She wants me to move back to New York so badly but I'm happy here. Honestly, I think she rather me not get a job and be forced back to Buffalo broke. Now, I would understand her point if she was that type of grandma who always had the kids, took them places, etc. She is not! I had to go through the third degree to get her to babysit. She favors my son over my daughter, and she complains that they are too loud, and fuss at every little thing they do. I know she loves them, and we drove to Buffalo at least a dozen times since moving here, which is a lot of miles on my car. But my parents have yet to come to Charlotte. It's always an excuse, but they did go on another cruise last year. My mom came into a settlement, which I thought would be a perfect time to visit, but they chose a cruise. So when I say it's all about me and the kids, I mean it! My last drive to Buffalo was right after Christmas, and at least their dad has come to visit a few times because I always want them to have a great relationship with him. But I won't be making that drive anytime soon! Ten to eleven hours alone, the kids can't help, it sucks. Plus, I want my car to last. Three more payments and I officially own it. Woohoo!

Okay, they are still working on my car and my wrist is tired. I write very fast, though. I did all this in exactly one hour. I may start typing them instead if you don't mind so that I don't get carpal tunnel in my hands and wrists! LOL. I hope they don't try to find any more problems with my car. It's a 2000 Oldsmobile Intrigue, my baby! I try to keep it well maintained.

So in one of your next letters tell me all your favorites: food, movies, TV, color, books. Do you get to see TV on a regular basis, or movies? I have a very large movie collection. What are your short-term goals when you get out, and long-term goals? Well, now I'm going to read my book, so I'll be writing you soon!

Sincerely,
Janae J.

April 21, 2010

Greetings Janae,

 First and foremost, I hope this letter reaches you and your family in the best of health and blessed! Thank you for considering my feelings for being strong, sometimes it's more mental than emotional when dealing with slavery and prison. And that's amazing that you never met someone in my situation before. That means I can be your first in many other meaningful situations. You can ask all the questions you want, I don't mind 'cuz I have nothing to hide. Just keep an open mind, and you will discover something that's been missing in your life. And I want you to speak your mind when things offend you or upset you 'cuz we can't have a understanding without being understood. One thing I don't want you to do is compare me with the past 'cuz I'm incomparable to anything you ever had!

 Yes, I'm a Virgo. My birthday is September 6, and I think our spirits will combine in time. As far as smoking, I did here and there but not to the point I buy them, so you don't have to worry. I love my body too much to continue to poison it. And I'm sorry to hear your son has asthma! As far as a care package, that would be sweet of you 'cuz I definitely lost some pounds being in this box. And I will send you a list of things I can have at the end of this letter. But wait until I'm at the new jail next month to send anything.

 Yes, I do like peanut butter cookies (Girl Scout or whatever). I'm definitely an animal lover, especially dogs, big dogs (rottweilers, mastiff . . .). That's cute your daughter loves the SPCA. Maybe she wants to be a veterinarian. It's a good salary. It's alright to be optimistic, but you do have to keep in mind that the world is not perfect and you must continue to maneuver through the obstacles put in front of us. That's what shapes our being. And we must not wait on change but initiate it 'cuz success needs no explanation and failure needs no alibi!

And I know what your intentions were when you moved to North Carolina, but life doesn't always go in chronological order. We have to arrange first what's more important and what's pure fantasy. And to keep from second-guessing yourself. Sometimes it's good to brainstorm on what you want out of life instead of diving into regret later or the choice you've made! And to listen to God is to take the first step, and he'll take two. So if nursing is what you want to do instead of teaching, then pray for and achieve it. But remember, you're at an age where being established is right around the corner!

I'm not sorry it didn't work with your children's father. That just gives me an opportunity to do right what he has done wrong! I'm glad to hear you're patient, but you said it for the wrong reasons. Please explain? And there's nothing wrong with taking risks 'cuz without them a lot of people wouldn't have an identity! That's right, a definite plus about our situation is communicating as well your good days and bad, your struggles and your triumphs. One thing about me is I'm not scared to struggle, and I'm embracing adversity. I know the system is biased, but that's no excuse to use that as a crutch.

What I will do when I get out is thank the Lord for carrying me through, then I will make a schedule for the program I must complete intertwined with a job search. I will conquer the discriminatory issues with a great support group consisting of family, church, and most of all, hopefully you! My hobbies consist of music, reading, bowling, and cooking. One of my talents that can lead to a career is cooking and for which I have a certified Department of Labor certificate. I'm well-versed in carpentry, also my oratorical skills are at a level where I'm thinking of becoming a drug counselor or working with the juvenile system for young men! And I have no problem expressing what I want, and I love myself so I have no problem showing or sharing love. And I'm not a package. I'm the business that creates the package!

I love kids and travel. I definitely know when to be aggressive and affectionate, and being put in one's place is a two-way street that I embrace but I don't believe in physical abuse or verbal! About kissing, I'll let you judge when the time permits itself! I'm not one to settle, and I won't allow my better half to settle either. But one thing I know for sure if and when we intertwine, I have no doubt that you will go to bed thinking of me and waking up thanking God for me! And that's all I ask is equality, being equal in all ways.

Well, I'll leave for now only to return later. Remember, never goodbye, always see you later. I'm glad to be your new friend. It's a good feeling to feel. Take care of yourself, and I look forward to your next letter. And I love the pics, but I know you have some recent ones also?

Sincerely
Bryan Edwards
xoxo

PS: Before I write this list of the things I like or can have in my package, never forsake your needs or kids' needs when you tend to my wants and needs because I come secondary to them and you! And anything else you think I want. Remember, I can have 35 lbs., so please wait until you send it. And remember, wait until after the fourth of May, then you will know where my new jail is. Also, you don't have to send the full 35 lbs., whatever you send I'm over grateful!

April 24, 2010

Hi Bryan!

So glad to finally hear from you. I'm trying to give you time to catch up 'cuz I know I bombarded you with a bunch of letters. This one will be shorter. I promised the nation point I'm sitting here cracking up at Comedy Central. I love stand-up comedy when they funny. Today Jordan went to a birthday party at a paintball field. I've got to try that one day, it looks so fun. But he got blasted and got a mean welt on his chest right near the nipple! So me and Justine went and got ice cream and I washed her hair. I know, boring, right? But it rained this evening, so overall pretty boring.

I'm glad you are not a smoker. I've only dated a smoker once, and the smell just annoys me. Jordan's asthma is pretty well maintained but he's allergic to peanuts, which sucks! I love peanut butter in dessert, cookies, candy bars, etc. All taste ten times better with peanut butter. Justine can eat it but she's like, on Jordan's team, and doesn't eat it just because he can't. But I eat it, just not too close to him. I thought he would outgrow it but it's not happening, oh well.

Yes, I'm still debating the whole going back to school thing. It's a good time to go with my kids being a little older, but I haven't felt that strong desire yet, so I'm just waiting. When I say I'm to patient that was more during the time when I was waiting and hoping the kids' dad would settle with me, but I think I explained that in detail in one of my earlier letters. What I learned is that one person doubling their effort to make something happen cannot compensate for the other's lack of effort.

I'm glad you have plans and seem to have many avenues to try out once you are released. Mentoring juveniles would be awesome with your background. The best teachers are those who are former students! We share a lot of similarities with hobbies, and your snack list sounds like what's in my cabinets! And yes, I have recent pictures, but I look the same in those that have been developed. I have lots on my computer and in my phone that just needs to be printed, so yes, I will send more soon.

So you're a coffee person? I'm definitely more a tea person. What does hermetically sealed mean as far as cheese? And can you have home-baked goods? And Cheez-Its are so much better than Cheese Nips! People don't realize that! LOL.

Okay, I said this would be short since this is my fifth letter and I've only gotten two from you so far. I really need to give you an opportunity to catch up and get situated in your new location. Why are you being moved?

Well, our cruise is in five days. I am so excited! Can't wait to send you pics and tell you all about it. Looking forward to letter number three from you. I'll be patiently waiting!

Sincerely,
Janae James
Xoxo

April 29, 2010

Dear Janae

Yes, I'm in good spirits this week. Not just you sending me letters 'cuz that's a good thing, but also this is my last week in the box! So the next time you write me it will be a new address 'cuz I'll be at another jail, so don't send no more letters here until I send you the new address or Brooklyn gives it to you first.

That's okay if your children's father don't like your letters. You're not with him anymore, are you? I know you love him, but are you still in love with him? The reason why women hang on so long is because in your vision things will always be alright until adversity constantly hits you in the face. Meaning nine times out of ten things go right in a relationship until sex is exchanged, especially if sex happened early in the game. Then when children come into the game, for some men that's their security card to start trying to conquer something else. And sometimes love makes us naive to things that are right in our face, but we choose to ignore!

I'm glad writing me has sparked your creative juices. I'm sorry to hear that your car is giving you problems and your financial luck is down. What are you doing to get your financial stats back up? You know you got to get out there and make it happen 'cuz nothing comes to a sleeper but dreams! LOL.

I'm very happy to hear that you are on your cruise with the kids. I hope you're enjoying yourself and taking a lot of pictures for me. That's good to hear that Jordan can draw. Maybe he could draw something for me and I'll hang it up! I'm glad you're blunt because I'm very blunt myself. I believe in being that way 'cuz if you don't express yourself freely it stunts your growth! Just 'cuz you have kids doesn't automatically mean you're soulmates and you're supposed to be together forever. God puts people in each other's lives at the craziest times to see what we teach and learn from one another, where bonds are made and broken depending on the individual. That's what shapes a person's character. And to have all those children by different women, why would you still be with him after your first child? That's insanity to continue to do the same thing over and over thinking it's going to be a different outcome. You have to realize that you will never be able to change a person that can't change themselves. It will stunt your growth, and you will miss your blessing!

As far as your mother, I don't know her, but it will be her loss if you don't feel she wants to participate in your children's life because I regret not being able to see my daughters turn into women. The time you lose you can never get back. For some, regret will kill you. Then for some people, they sometimes have a way of trying to stagnate other family members' growth and development to where you will always be dependent. Remember if your heart is filled with faith then you can't fear! And last but not least, don't allow your children's father to use them to get to you, to play with your emotions 'cuz it seems like you're still vulnerable!

If you feel like typing your letters, feel free. Communication comes in different levels of understanding. My favorite foods are chicken wings, pizza, fried fish, spaghetti, and lasagna. My favorite baked goods are cheesecakes, chocolate chip cookies, peanut butter cookies, and German sweet chocolate cake. Movies: Black films that deal with reality (family, relationships, Black women and men's plight) comedies, and a little drama. I love sports and the news. Favorite color is Carolina blue and lavender. Books, romance (reality), espionage, history. And yes, I see TV on a regular, but I like to read more and also I meditate a lot.

My short-term goals are to seek and maintain employment and secure a bank account 'cuz I'm definitely about a dollar. I'm a go-getter, far from lazy! Long-term is to be established on a couple of rentals, enjoy myself with my better half, travel, and make sure my daughters are secure and my nieces and nephews are headed for greatness and success. And last, make sure my sister has everything she deserves for always being there for me through thick and thin! And that, my dear Janae, is the end of another fact-finding journey.

One more thing, whatever comes out my mouth is my word and my word is my bond. And before I break my bond I'd rather die, I said that to say whatever I say I'm going to do, I do, and I mean it. All I ask from you is you stand by that law, also 'cuz over my life I've been sold a lot of illusions by people I gave my all too. So you are going to have to work for my heart just like I will work for your heart and trust 'cuz the only women I trust in this world are my grandmother and my sister. I pray you can change that!

That's all for now, only to return in another envelope, so until then may your day be blessed and filled with success.

I'm sorry, so sloppy! I was trying to hurry to get you a letter before you left! I hope you enjoyed your card!

Sincerely,

Bryan Edwards

May 1, 2010

Hi Janae

    I hope this letter finds you having enjoyed your cruise with your children, I just wanted you to have something in your mailbox on your return instead of bills! It's actually 1:00 a.m. Sunday morning my last day in the box. I'll be going to a new jail Monday morning, so don't write any more letters to this address. I'll write you with the new one. And you don't bombard me with letters 'cuz I enjoyed them as well as getting to know you. Life is too short for you to cut a letter short, so express yourself as much as you want.

    I've always wanted to experience paintball, I hope Jordan's chest is all right. That was nice of you and your daughter to go get ice cream! While I love peanuts too, but that's good Justine looks out for her brother like that. And yes, you did express you're patient. You have to also realize children interpret and understand what's going on in their environment long before parents usually think they do, so the only thing that you should double your effort for is to compensate for knowing you did your best and how you're moving on and focusing on the growth and development of your children and yourself!

    And yes, the best teachers are those who are former students as long as you're real with yourself and not in denial! I'm glad we like the same snacks and hobbies. That's good to know that more pictures are coming. I'm a coffee and tea person, especially the Celestial fruit teas. Hermetically sealed means like what the sliced cheese comes in, and the cookies can't be in resealable packages, meaning like the way Oreos open up now where you can reseal it. And yes, Cheez-Its are the bomb, especially the new all three cheeses in one box. I wish I could have home-baked foods, but nope they have to be store-bought 'cuz people put drugs in the middle of things!

Well, I hope I caught up with the letters. I never want you to feel deprived of the things you enjoy! I'm moving to a new place 'cuz this one I'm in is awful, and I'm trying to get closer to home. Well, until I see you again in another letter. I'll see you later, and now I'll be waiting . . .

Sincerely,
Bryan Edwards
Xoxo

May 2, 2010

Dearest Bryan,

Thank you so much for the card! I never get Mother's Day cards, so it was a special treat. And sorry, but you were a day late and a dollar short in trying to get a letter to me before we left! We left on April 29 and came back Sunday early evening. The drive from Florida was a mean thing. No AC in my car, and it was in the mid-nineties most of the drive. But oh, we had a great time! But today it was back to making my own bed cooking my own food, no morning cocktails, and no more pampering! LOL. But getting another letter today was a special treat. It's like us talking on the phone then you put me on hold and I'm waiting,

waiting, waiting for you to come back to the phone! I know that sounds silly. I'm always making up corny analogies! So I guess this letter will be in my purse until I hear from you again, so you may get lucky and get two. I'll include pictures in my next letter. I took about 150 pictures on the cruise! The kids had so much fun, and we ate way too much. Breakfast was at eight thirty, again at ten thirty; lunch at twelve thirty, again at three; and dinner twice. Everywhere you go there's food and it's awesome. You have to go on a cruise as soon as you get out!

And no, I'm not in love with Quincy, but yes, I still love him. I know in my heart and soul that we have no future. But as I stated in a previous letter, I felt like I had invested so much time that I had to just keep waiting until he came around. It's even embarrassing because my friends and family watch the situation and see all the kids and wonder what the hell I am thinking. It almost became like a contest because everyone is like, ain't no way he's going to ever settle down with one woman, and I was out to prove that I'm such a good woman that I am the baby mama who beat all the others out and came out on top, and I would compare my best attributes to these other women. It sounds ridiculous, I know. And the hardest part is that I've never had a truly committed relationship. I met Que when I was twenty. We dated briefly, then at the mall one day I busted him giving some chick his phone number, so I ended it right there. Then stupid me one day called him up for a booty call. This went on and off for several months, then I got pregnant. Jordan was born when I was twenty-two, so we weren't even together. So you're right when sex happens too early and kids, men are like having their cake and eating it too.

As time passed I fell in love, and he did what he wanted but always knew not to piss me off too much to make me let go. I dated other guys in between but never really let anyone in because I didn't want to risk falling in love with another man because I knew that I would eventually choose myself. There was one guy when Jordan was about one-and-a-half to two, who was nice and I wouldn't give him the time of day, then Que did something real stupid, so I was like okay, maybe I should relax a little and give the other guy a chance. We started hanging out and chilling, and I was reluctant to get intimate. He, in the meantime, had a girl on and off, then she got pregnant but they were broke up at this time. We finally were intimate, and I was like wow, this guy is so nice, and I was thinking it was finally over with Que. Nope, he decided he felt guilty (mind you, the Monday after we spent the whole weekend together) about leaving his pregnant ex, so he told me he was going to work it out for the baby's sake. That really hurt me, so of course I went back to Old Faithful.

Even though Que wasn't faithful, he was familiar, and my self-esteem was too low to try to venture out again. Fast forward to 2003, Justine was born, then in 2006 I met this guy, Donald, online. He lived in Orlando, and I was thinking ain't no way. But we instantly clicked and he was mad cool. He flew up to see me a month later, and after that first visit, I was like Quincy who?? He was a gentleman in every way. We had so much fun and did so much, and he treated me so differently than Que ever had. It was amazing. To this day I thank him for showing me a new side to having a boyfriend, and teaching me how a man is supposed to treat a woman.

But all that glitters ain't gold. Our plan was to relocate to Charlotte in July 2007. I was already planning to move and he had been wanting to leave Florida, so we figured we'd get a place together. He flew up to Buffalo about six weeks after the first visit—another great visit. We talked on the phone every night since it was long distance, and for six months I didn't give Que the time of day. I was in love with Donald. But he was supposed to come in May 2007 for my graduation with my master's degree. I had bought the ticket for him and his son, and he was going to reimburse me half. But he was procrastinating on sending his half unlike the last time. I realized graduation weekend was Mother's Day weekend, then he started trying to get out of coming, claiming he was broke and didn't like traveling with no money. I was like, you staying with me so it's not like you need a lot. Then I get an email the next day from his GIRLFRIEND/baby mama. She found the flight plans in his email account and told me her man and her son would not be coming to see me! I was devastated and felt so stupid and played. Que happened to pop up that night to bring something for the kids, and I broke my six months of not thinking about him. I just wanted to forget the pain, but that would bring on a new set of problems dealing with him again.

So it's a shame for me to say, I've never had a monogamous, loving, serious two-sided relationship except for my senior year of high school boyfriend. It's embarrassing to admit because I look at me like why can't I get this right? A lot of times I figured I just couldn't do better. So after Donald I still moved to Charlotte, and then Que started showing me attention. He was shocked that I really went through with moving. So I ended up driving home like five times my first year away from home, so even the distance didn't break his hold on me. Then I spent the summer of 2008 in Buffalo and prayed to God if it's not meant to be with Que please give me a sign. And he gave me a sign all right. So he had baby number twelve on the way with some girl and was still with his so-called ex (not the baby mama). He denied it all of course, but it was all true.

So, Bryan, I don't blame you if you think I'm still vulnerable when it comes to Quincy. I know it's over and I know he will still make attempts to keep me close. He does it now, calling and texting, but I pray for strength. And luckily we both broke, so I won't be going to Buffalo anytime soon or he coming here. But I also pray for strength to not hinder my life anymore and keep that burden away from me. I look forward to someday having a real relationship, being loved the right way, and giving it in return. I've been blocking God's blessings for years hanging on to a relationship that never existed, and I'm ready for my cup to runneth over! LOL.

This is why I am so grateful for being able to take it so slow with you and really get to know one another without the complication of being intimate too soon. And like I said before, I've never met someone in your situation before (for that many years) and the idea of possibly beginning a relationship this way is very new to me, exciting and scary because I asked myself am I again putting myself on hold for a man? Or is this God's way of telling me to take a break and enjoy getting to know you better? Or what if I meet someone out here who sounds like the perfect guy? There are so many questions, but the only thing I'm sure of at this moment is the excitement I have by checking the mailbox and hoping to have a letter from you. I guess one day at a time is the only way to do things. But one thing you can be sure of, I am honest and loyal and have never cheated on a man before despite being cheated on.

And I stand by the man I'm with through thick and thin. And I plan to be open and honest with you every step of our journey of friendship and whatever else develops.

Wow, didn't expect to write this much, and I didn't answer all of your questions/comments in this letter, so I will end it here and continue once I get your new address. Take care for now, and I look forward to our next communication!

Yours truly,
Janae
Xoxo

May 6, 2010

Dear Janae

I hope you enjoyed your trip with the kids and all. I'm just writing you a little short kite to give you the new address that's on the envelope. I'm right outside of Albany, New York. I've caught up with the letters, so now the ball is in your court, so I should be hearing from you soon. Until then, may God continue to bless you and the kids!

Sincerely yours,
Bryan
xoxo

PS: Here's the address in case you forget.
Great Meadow Correctional Facility
Box 51
Comstock, New York 12821 - 0051

May 8, 2010

Hi Bryan,

You have finally caught up with me and the letters! But I have a finished letter to you in my purse just waiting for your new address. Brooklyn said she would email it to me, so I have to remind her. I should not have started a letter tonight because I'm already sleepy. I started braiding my hair, planning on being done by tonight, but I've been procrastinating all day. Justine was sick from Tuesday to Thursday night with fevers. Don't know if she caught something on the boat, so she missed two days of school and slept with me, which means I got no sleep, so my body is sort of catching up on sleep still.

So how have you been feeling? I didn't realize you were in the box writing me, so it must be a huge relief. So is that like solitary confinement? I watch *Lockup Raw* sometimes and wonder what it's like where you are. Some of those stories are off the hook! Jordan loves to draw, so I'm sure he would like to send you a picture. And I got the car fixed, so except for the AC, it's running great. Two more payments and it's officially mine! Woohoo!

I don't have any plans for Mother's Day tomorrow. I was going to go to church, but not done with my hair. And I really want to just chill and have the kids on their best behavior, and maybe take them to the pool. I had planned on mailing my mom an eight-by-ten picture of Jordan in his scouting uniform, but it wouldn't have got there in time. So I'm just going to mail it on Monday. I used to feel so guilty about moving and taking her grandbabies away. She has to regret all the times when she didn't want to be bothered keeping them, but I've driven home at least a dozen times, so I'm making the situation better. But it's their turn to come here.

When I worked at HSBC, I worked every Saturday for the first year. And every Saturday I struggled to find someone to watch Jordan My mom was available but refused. When I went back to school, I had class two to three nights per week, depending on the semester. My aunt, the kids' cousin, their dad, and briefly this other woman kept the kids for me. My mom was available but refused! When she actually kept them overnight, I always had to get them early. I know she loves them, but it's a control thing with her. She wants to dictate when, how long to keep them, but my being here takes that control away. Hopefully they will visit soon!

Fell asleep...

5/9/10

    I talked a lot to Brooklyn last night and today. I can't imagine how difficult Mother's Day is for you all, which is why I'm always racking my brain trying to figure out how to make things 100 percent with my mom. There are so, so, so many layers I've covered up over the past twenty-two years. Sometimes I feel like letting it all out, but that would be a tsunami wave of emotions and issues, and you know black folks' model of "if it didn't kill you, you're fine, for we don't air our dirty laundry" or "what goes on in this house stays in this house." I was never physically or sexually abused, nothing that bad, but my childhood was rough. Other times I think I turned out fine, so let the past be the past and just work on the future. Okay, enough with the serious crap!

    Tomorrow (Monday) is day one of Jordan's final exams. Math is over two days, one day reading, and one day science. I bought him a card of encouragement, and he always does very well. A four is the highest you can get, three is good, two is not passing, and one is well below average. He always gets fours in math and three in reading. I challenged him to get all fours and he will get a Nintendo DSi. Fifth grade also takes a science exam, but he absolutely loves science and does very well. So if he slows down and takes his time with reading, I will have to figure out how to get him that DSi! Between me, their dad, my parents, and his mom, I know we can make it happen. Justine was moved into the accelerated group for the last semester, so I'm very proud of both of my smart babies!

    OMG, I'm looking at your favorites. We like a lot of the same things. Italian food, wings (flat pieces, of course). Chocolate chip cookies from scratch are my true weakness! I love Tyler Perry movies and plays. I don't really have a favorite color, but I love how canary yellow looks against my skin. I like colors depending on my mood. My living room walls are burnt orange. If I had a house, every room would have a theme and be different colors. Can't have all that freedom in apartments. Speaking of lavender, my first boyfriend junior year was an asshole! He was my first. I was always shy, so I decided to be bold and buy matching bras and panties in lavender. So I tell him on the phone when I was on my way to his house, and he was like, "Yuck, I hate lavender!" He was ignorant and somewhat disrespectful, but I wouldn't dare say anything back because at that time no one was taking any interest in me (wasn't cool to date the big girl back then), so I don't with it until I found out he was cheating. I wasn't about to share him! It was so much easier to walk away from a cheating man before I had kids. And baby daddies know the hole they have and use it to their advantage. You know, being laid off for almost a year has been such a year of self-discovery for me, and I'm loving my new attitude and outlook on life, and my tolerance for BS is extremely low!

As far as my finances, I just accepted a work-from-home customer service job so that at least for the summer I don't have to worry about summer camp for the kids, and I really want to get into my book. The pay is terrible, but I don't have to worry about gas as much. I will start braiding hair again for extra money and try to get a teaching job for the 2010–2011 school year. Right now I don't qualify for food stamps. My unemployment exceeds the maximum amount by $90 a month, so with this new job, I will qualify, which will help tremendously with the kids being home all summer. No more breakfast and lunch from school! Lol. The new job starts on my birthday, June 1, and hopefully it will just be temporary to get this book written and start a new fulfilling job in the fall.

Well, it's quite late now and I'm volunteering to proctor the exams next week, so I need to go to bed. I know it's after midnight, but I actually enjoy writing you. And I'm also wondering if I have scared you off yet? I just wanted to be open and honest, and hope you do the same so that when we finally meet we will feel like we have known each other for years! So goodnight for now, even though you'll probably be reading this during the day! I'll be patiently waiting on your next letter . . . !

Sincerely,
Janae James
Xoxo

May 11, 2010

Hey Bryan,

    Oh no, you are not caught up with letters, mister! The last two were very short, so they don't count. LOL, I'm just teasing you. I actually got your address from Brooklyn this morning, so I had put two letters in the mail, then got your very short letter with the new address today. But it's fine. I wonder how many letters will be exchanged between us over the next year!
    I'm watching *Star Trek: Next Generation* right now when I should be braiding my hair. Usually when I do my own hair I take about a week, but when I do someone else's I can do it in about eight hours. As I'm braiding and wearing scarves over my unbraided hair, I get people asking about getting their hair done, so it helps me get new clients. The annoying part is that most won't call, and there are so many braiding shops here in the South that they can charge cheaper prices. I don't like braiding a lot, but it helps financially.

Fell asleep . . .

5/12/10

    Well, so much for my new job! I think I wrote you too many letters back to back, so if I already said this, sorry. I accepted a work-from-home job but the pay is much less than my unemployment and I was debating back and forth. Anyway, for the first thirty days you can't miss any time, and I found out this morning that Jordan's graduation is June 8 at 1:30 p.m. So I emailed the place to see if maybe I could take an extended lunch, like 12:00 p.m.–3:00 p.m., and they said no, attendance is 100 percent mandatory. So I had to pass that job up. Then today was day two of proctoring for the exam. I was put in a fourth-grade class (the grade I taught), and watching the kids take the test, I was just flooded with emotion and I realized I really do want to try teaching again.

I can't base teaching on the school I was at. The school was under restructuring, meaning we weren't making AYP (adequate yearly progress) and were in danger of the state taking over. So a new principal was brought in my second year. My first year was very difficult because teaching is a job you learn by doing. All the college education in the world can't prepare you, and Title I schools are typically Black and Hispanic, poor kids who perform low. So I survived the first year, and I told you before, with moving and baby daddy issues and teaching it was awful. But I have to thank Que because he convinced me not to resign in October because I was just like I did not relocate 700 miles to be this stressed! But my principal liked me and they were willing to work with me. But the second year, a new principal was brought in and her only objective was getting scores up. Math class was grouped by ability, five classes, and I got the lowest scoring kids. They were half ESL and learning disabled, and couldn't even subtract by borrowing! I've always been a whiz in math, and I don't see math the way struggling students do, so it was even more difficult. Then my observations were only done in math class, where I struggled to teach. I wasn't given help until like February, and the kids still did poorly. Then when budget cuts were announced, they said low-performing teachers would be laid off first. So my job was based on three, thirty-minute classroom observations in math only, even though we teach reading, writing, science, and social studies.

And that's how I lost my job. But the worst part is that it's public knowledge who the laid-off teachers were, so getting a teaching job is a bigger challenge. I had several interviews for a teaching job and no offers yet, so it's very frustrating. But I'm not giving up! I'm actually going to talk to the kids' principal because I volunteer so much at their school and everyone knows me. I'm hoping he has a vacancy for next year. It's all about networking!

Well, I'm still not done with my hair! But I got a big chunk done today, so tomorrow after the EOGs (exams) I will finish up and go get these cruise pictures developed. I'll take pics of my hair too so that you can see your girl got skills! LOL. Braided hair is the best for the summer for me. My own hair is so thick, it takes a lot of effort to flat iron it. And we like going swimming, and swim caps are a waste of time to me. Plus, when I go to the gym my hair sweats sometimes, and the curls fall. So with braids, I can still wash it and just go! I get fussed at all because I'll wear wigs too, and people say, "Your hair is that long and thick, why do you wear fake hair?" I just say it's easier for my lifestyle, and I love how braids look. And you can style them anyway.

It's very late and I'm sleepy again, plus once this is mailed that will be three letters and one card to you, plus pictures, and I need to let you get somewhat caught up! And your Mother's Day card was the only one I got (except the beautiful ones the kids made by hand), so thank you again. Can you take pictures? Brooklyn emailed me some and I have one, but another would be nice. How tall are you, by the way?

Okay, I'm going to bed for real, so take care of yourself and I'll do the same. Tata for now!

Sincerely,
Janae
Xoxo

May 16, 2010

Dearest Bryan,

How you doin' (in my Wendy Williams voice!)? I'm sitting here on a Sunday night missing you. No letter from you yesterday, and since there is no mail on Sunday, I have to hope for a letter tomorrow, which I better have! I mailed you four envelopes this week, which I guess will almost be like a housewarming gift for your final residence before you come home.

Speaking of home, I don't know if it's premature to be asking this, but at the same time if we may potentially have a future together, then it's something I need to know. I live in Charlotte (Matthews is like Cheektowaga to Buffalo) and you are in New York. I know your family is in Buffalo, and since it's been so long since you've seen your girls and grandparents, what are your residence plans when you get out? I know you'll spend a lot of time with your family reconnecting and all, but after that, do you plan to remain in Buffalo? I love living here in the South, and I miss my family but I feel established here in North Carolina. The kids are in great schools. I have my Girl Scout troop (still no job!). But overall, if I had to choose I'd prefer to stay because so far there is no compelling reason for me to move back. I always said for the right job I'd move back, and I almost moved back thinking that would help me and Quincy work better (duh, when I lived there it didn't work! LOL). So the idea of moving is not my favorite. Since we are very early on, I'm not expecting you to say your plan to relocate here, but if we get closer what would you do? I almost don't think it would be fair to expect you because I feel like you have so much lost time to make up. But also you need to move forward, and long-distance relationships just don't always work. That's been on my mind lately, and as we say, we need to speak our minds and communicate and always be open and honest with each other!

I hope you enjoyed the pictures. I tried to send a variety and now you can see my babies! See how much they look like their beautiful mommy? LOL. Jordan looks more like their dad, and watching Justine is like looking in a mirror twenty-seven years back. And she has two left feet just like I did. She hates to be reminded of how clumsy she is, so I try to be sensitive about that. But she trips over everything!

I'm getting sleepy, so I'm going to stop here and hopefully tomorrow after checking the mail I will continue with responses to you!

5/17/10

On my way to take out the trash and to the mailbox . . .

Okay, I am disappointed! I got my electric bill, two credit card statements, and a catalogue—no letter from you! But I'm not going to trip because the earliest you would have gotten any of my letters would have been this past Thursday, the thirteenth. And you did say in your last, extremely brief, letter that the ball was in my court. You would have to be a speed writer to ever write a letter and get it in the mail the same day. Wishful thinking on my part, LOL, so no, I'm not mad.

In the evening . . .

Wow, what a day. I may have the most exciting news. One of my ex co-workers has to move back to New York due to family issues. She and her husband bought a three-bedroom, two-bathroom house last year, an HUD home because teachers get 50 percent off HUD homes (too bad I got laid off so fast!). But you have to stay in the home for thirty-six months, and they've only been there for twelve months, so they were going to just pay the mortgage as a loss and have a friend send them their mail. So I asked her if she considered renting, and she was willing to rent the house for $450 just to cover the mortgage. I am paying $669 for a two-bedroom apartment and can get a whole house with a yard, driveway, and shed, and the house is on a dead-end cul-de-sac, for $219 less! Yes, Charlotte is a bit higher than Buffalo, and it was hard going from $269 all-included rent living in Langfield to the rent amount here, and even harder for my mother to comprehend!

The only downside is she lives on the other side of town, not as great schools. The gym is not nearby, and I really like my area. But her street is quiet and tucked into a lot of trees, and the kids love it! It's perfect for us, but about twenty to twenty-five minutes from where we are now. Not happy about the school, but if I can figure out a way to keep Matthew's schools, maybe by being car riders and we will move. And my Girl Scout troop meets near Matthews. But I also only have two more car payments, so I can potentially save $455 per month starting in July, so the extra gas up taking the kids to school, the gym, and Girl Scouts would be worth it.

I'm just not feeling the new schools! I called their current school and asked about the move. The secretary said if I change the address on the computer then their school would have to change. Meaning if I don't change it how will they ever know? And Kathryn said the only thing I'd have to do is get a PO box for my mail since they are supposed to be living there and mail her letters to her on a weekly basis. I'm very excited about the possibility. Apartment living is so irritating, having to share space! I've been wanting a house forever! A house that size could easily rent for $700 a month. I would need to stay in the house for two years to satisfy her HUD agreement unless they can sell it. Their house has been on the market since late January with no luck, so if I rent she will take it off the market. If I find a job near their school it will be the final piece fit in the puzzle.

(fell asleep)

5/18/10

Tuesday and still no letter from you! I hope you have a good reason and this letter is not getting mailed until I get one from you, so ha! I went to BOSU class at the gym. Not sure if you heard of it, but it's almost like step aerobics, but instead it's like a dome that is cushiony so it's easier on the joints but works your core much more because of balance. Well, the first time I went I was stumbling all over the place. Today I was doing pretty good and got a little cocky. Next thing you know I tripped over my pant leg, not the BOSU, and fell! I had to laugh at myself because I wasn't hurt but I cuffed the pants to my knees for the rest of the class, LOL.

So I talked to the school about moving and keeping the kids at Crown Point and Mint Hill Middle. The principal is cool as heck. He told me just don't change my address with the school so that it's not changed on the computer. The extra driving will be worth it for my kids to go to a better school and our own bedrooms and space. I like their class because it's a nice racial mix. Charlotte schools tend to be very segregated, all Black, some all White, some Black/Mexican poor schools, etc. Justine's class has white, black, Hispanic, and Asian. I hate schools where it's all white with like one black child in the class. I went to Waterfront in Buffalo and it was a nice racial balance. When I was a freshman in college, I went to Fredonia and I was always the only Black student in my class is, which I never liked.

Oh, I got an email from that second interview for the work-from-home job. Didn't get the job, but honestly I am relieved. I mean, damn, $8 an hour! I was making that ten years ago when I first started at the bank. Just means something better is coming along. The interviewer was asking way too many technical questions for a job that was barely above minimum wage. Such a slap in the face. I was making almost $40,000 a year to go down that much. This recession sucks big time!

5/19/10

Wednesday, still no letter! But Brooklyn did tell me you are probably out of stamps. Actually, so am I, but now you can get stamps from the ATM machine at Wachovia Bank, which is awesome. But it's no telling when I'll be mailing this out. I go to Wachovia every Monday for my unemployment. Jordan got his EOG scores today. He got a four in math and science, which is excellent. But only a two in reading, so he has to retake next week. He has <u>never</u> failed reading, so I'm like what the fuck! I'm mad at him, his teacher, and myself most of all! I know it's his least favorite subject, so last year when he was in fourth grade and I was teaching for it I would always bring reading comprehension sheets home and have him do those. He <u>hated</u> that, and always complained that no one else in his class had extra work! I told him that's the reward of being a teacher's child, and he got a three on the reading EOG. So with me being home all year, I could have been working with him. Then I'm pissed at his teacher because it's her job to teach him, and he's been getting A's and B's all year in reading, and to fail the exam doesn't quite add up! And he rarely has reading homework. I guess I'm not mad at Jordan after all because he wants that Nintendo DSi <u>badly</u> and I know he did his best. He was almost in tears, so I know he did his best. So I will be tutoring him all week and we can prepare for the retest next week.

As for me, I did a body pump class this morning and Zumba this evening. Yes, I was getting it in! A little sore but feeling great. I found some private Christian schools online with job postings, so I hurried up and applied. One for a fourth-grade job, which I am very qualified for. So feeling optimistic! Tomorrow is the Girl Scout volunteer dinner/awards. I was nominated for the Green Hornet Award for an outstanding new leader. I worked hard this year, so I'm very hopeful. I know you'll get this letter after the fact, but please pray for Jordan and his retest, and me for a teaching job and the award! Hey, I deserve it! LOL. Hopefully my next letter will be full of good news!

I hope you are settling well in your new facility. Why are you closer to Albany instead of Buffalo? And when is your sentence officially going to be finished? When do you get out? Will it be limited (house arrest, travel restrictions, etc.) or will you be totally free?

I'm going to officially stop this letter here because as you can see, this letter is quite long! And I don't want to keep beginning each page with "Still no letter . . ." I know it will come eventually, and my free time for the upcoming days will be focused on getting Jordan ready for his exam. I hope all has been well with you, and hopefully will hear from you soon!

Yours truly,
Janae
Xoxo

May 17, 2010

Dearest Janae,

 You're very welcome for your card. I wish it could have been more 'cuz you deserve, just for being a black woman for one and for teaching other mothers' children, which is something we don't have enough of. And it wasn't so much that I was laid on the letter. I made the effort, and that's what makes it worth the energy. Despite the lack of AC, I'm happy you all enjoyed yourselves. I can't wait to see the pictures. It's also a special treat to receive letters from you also 'cuz it shows you're also making an effort to see this friendship blossom. And your analogies are not silly. You're just expressing yourself, and I embrace that as well as look forward to it.

 I know you still love Quincy, and of course you have a history as well as children with him. But you don't strike me as a rebound woman, and he's not uplifting you. He's stagnating your progress, your mind, and your spirit to be the best woman you can be, as well as a mother. 'Cuz your children are very attentive to the surroundings that they occupy without us realizing, and the ways and actions both of you partake and they grow accustomed to it, and to replicate what Mommy and Daddy are doing as they grow older. Also, a form of insanity is to keep doing the same things over and over again thinking it's going to be different when you know logically it's not. That's very unhealthy for you and the kids. And the worst thing you can do as a woman for your growth and development is to compare yourself to other women, 'cuz then you start second-guessing yourself, which leads to making rash decisions you know you're going to regret sooner or a later. And that not only affects you but your children also. If you don't love yourself enough to stop mental abuse—'cuz that's what I see he's doing—then you and he will stunt your growth.

And the reason you haven't had a committed relationship is 'cuz you're settling for less, being that he's playing on you being naive to bullshit game and love for convenience. 'Cuz once he gets what he wants, he's gone. Your relationship wasn't based on love. From what you told me, it was based on sex! And sex is not love, it's only an expression, not a commitment. Until you're through being used and broken down mentally and spiritually, you're going to self-destruct to where your blessings are going to pass you by.

I'm willing to give you my all 'cuz I believe in you just by what my sister has told me about you and your constant efforts to educate me about yourself. But I'm not anyone's fool, nor will I become one for the simple fact I've been burnt to the point I've missed some very important years of my life as well as my daughters'. I pray for you, for us, for your children 'cuz I've asked God to bring someone into my life so that I may learn to love a woman for who she is, what she can become, and what we can create through knowledge, wisdom, and understanding. And then you wrote that letter for my parole board, and that touched me like you would never imagine!

I don't want to make love to what's between your legs first, I want to make love to your heart, your spirit, your being an educated black woman with aspirations, goals, morals! And about this being scary and new, you took a chance on an illusion of love. Oh, well, I'm not a mirage. I'm being so real that I'm scared, scared that maybe you don't want someone who's committed to learn how to love again for all the right reasons. Or are you accustomed to fake or just being the baby mother instead of a wife in the future? And if you did meet someone out there, I'm not a bitter or selfish person that wouldn't want to stagnate your happiness if it shall play that way. But I don't put energy into what if! I believe that anything worth having is worth working for! Faith without believing is just a myth.

And don't tell me you're honest and loyal. Continue to show me 'cuz people told me that my whole life but only if you show me! Living in the old 'cuz the new is in front of you, but in order to have, you have to want. So take your time 'cuz I am.

And last but not least, please don't compare me to Quincy. Not that you have, but I'm incomparable. And I know what I want. Are you ready?

Well, miss, it's 2:00 a.m. and I must depart, only to return again. May you have a blessed night. I hope you read this letter with an open mind 'cuz I'll never tear you down, only put you on a pedestal to where you should be, where you reap all the praises a woman deserves!

Sincerely yours,
Bryan Jarelle Edwards

PS: There's one right behind this, so watch out!

May 18, 2010

Dearest Janae,

I'm glad you started a letter while you were sleepy, I feel honored that you chose me over sleep for a moment. I pray that Justine feels better. I would love to see you with braids. You have to take pictures. As far as myself, I'm blessed. And yes, it is a huge relief to be out of the box. And yes, it is solitary confinement. And yes, it's like *Lockup Raw* but worse 'cuz you don't see what happens when they cut the cameras off. But I survived and put that behind me.

I'm very happy that you're close to owning your car outright. You deserve it!

You don't have to feel guilty about making decisions to better you and your kids' life. Your mother can't live your life and you can't live hers. You can't second-guess progress. You have to have faith in yourself. A lot of people live miserable lives 'cuz they always worry about what other people think, when they make the moves other people are scared to make. It is difficult at times on Mother's Day for me, but I haven't given myself time to mourn yet. 'Cuz if I do, I'm scared someone will detect my vulnerability and try to catch me at a low point and provoke violence, and I'm no pushover. So I'll wait until I'm free, and hopefully you'll be there to share that with me. You can't make things 100 percent right with your mom. Only thing you can do is love her 100 percent and pray for her wrongs and rights. But I do like that about what goes on in the house stays in the house. That's a real I stand by!

Tell the kids I wish them blessings in passing their exams. I'm sure they'll do great, especially with a great teacher such as yourself. Yes, we seem to have a lot of the same likes and I'm pretty sure dislikes, but that remains to be seen and heard. Let's get something out in the open. Mature men don't like full-figured women 'cuz they don't know how to love them from head to toe. I love full-figured women as long as you're healthy and you're not abusing food and you keep yourself sexy. 'Cuz I know how to love you. I know what you need. Are you going to let me give it to you is the million-dollar question. I don't think your tolerance for bullshit is low enough yet 'cuz you won't just say it. You will not only live it, but it will be implemented in your daily rituals! 'Cuz that line you just said about baby daddies know the hold they have and take advantage is a crock of shit. Only if you allow it, become accustomed to it!

I'm happy you found a little job to keep you out. And now you and me are on the subject of finances. I don't want a package until a couple of months so you can get you right. I can wait. It's not important to me right now. I'm also happy to see you have side hustles. That means you're about a dollar, and that's a very good trait!

I'm also up late reading your letters 'cuz I like when it's quiet and I can absorb what you're writing. Also, I hope you're reading my letters very closely. I'm opening to you 'cuz I believe in you, but I need you to believe in yourself also! And to answer your question, no, you haven't scared me off, nor will you. And I will be honest with you at all times. I don't know no other way. And I feel like I know you already honestly, but I know it's so much more to come. So I'll end this for now in order for you to continue to get your thoughts squared away, so you and I can give each other some more! So goodnight for now and sweet dreams. Until next time.

Sincerely yours,
Bryan Jarelle Edwards
Xoxo

May 20, 2010

Hey Janae,

Hope this letter finds you and family enjoying the summer and what goes along with. I'm very happy that you're back to practicing your cursive writing. It definitely put a smile on my face. And I was laughing, I admit. I pray the kids pass their exams with flying colors. I love the pictures, but two things first. Why is it more pictures of the ship than you? And why did you take a faraway picture with your bikini on? You don't want me to see what you working with? I know you have more pictures, so I'll be waiting! LOL. You look real sexy with braids. I have the picture right in front of my desk. And what is the tattoo on your chest? And on your arm? I have two on my chest. My grandparents over my heart and the twenty-third Psalm over my right side. And yes, I'm caught up on letters. It takes four days from this jail. Way slower than the other, so don't think you're beating me! LOL. And there's no telling how many cards and letters and pictures will be exchanged on my end, but I know I won't stop. Will you? And yes, they take pictures here. Soon as I make a little money I'll buy some picture tickets and send you some.

Do you know how to cut men's hair and beards? 'Cuz I do, and I'm very good, I must say. You know I rock a baldy. Can I trust you with a razor? LOL. That's good that you do here 'cuz that's constant money. And so they have a lot of shops down there. Quality always be quantity, and judging from what I'm looking at in the picture, you got skills. And don't get the big head either. LOL. You're blessed. Don't sweat that job that couldn't understand your son's graduation. It's their loss, not yours.

It's also sad that the school judged you on only two short classes. That sounds biased if you ask me. On top of that, they had learning disabilities, so that was basically doomed from the start. You were never really given an opportunity to show your skills. And don't worry about what's public knowledge. God's not going to give you more than you can bear, but you have to keep pushing. I'm rooting for you! Let me tell you right now, you don't need no wigs. You have hair, let it down. Do what it do! I would love to see you in the gym 'cuz I work out almost every day. Serious workout, no Jane Fonda. LOL. I've been getting on my sister about working out, but she's hard-headed. But that will change once I come home. She's not too old for me to put her over my knee. LOL. And you better not tell her I said that. I know how close you two are!

I'm happy in a crazy way that I'm the only one that sent you a Mother's Day card. That should let you know that before you start going backward again. I'm pretty sure you know what I'm talking about, so I won't harp on that subject. So I'll move on! But please know that I won't forget what's important to such things as that as well as small things. I just want to let you know when I love, I love 100 percent, not 50 percent. With me it's either you're in or you're out. There's no room for in between 'cuz when you leave gaps that's when bullshit tries to occupy that space!

I'm six foot two, 230 lb. solid with a little fat to even it out. Another thing about me that you don't know you sent me a picture. I like exotic fish and aquariums.

And what pictures did Brooklyn send you of me? I hope she caught the good sides of me. Oh, wait a minute. All my sides are good. LOL.

Well, girlfriend, ya man is about to take it down for the night. I just wanted to have something in your mailbox that you cherished instead of bills. And even if you do have more letters sent to me, there's nothing wrong with a woman leading as long as you're going to elevate me to constant elevation. So for now, take care of yourself and I'll do the same. Ta-ta right back at you!

Sincerely yours
Bryan
Xoxo

PS: I'll be waiting for those pictures I asked for, and please don't hold back. I know I got a woman in you, and I'm going to earn loving every inch of you if you allow me to!

May 21, 2010

Hello sweetie,

You totally made my day! Two letters on the same day! Once you get the letter that precedes this you'll know that I was checking the mailbox every day, just waiting and being unnecessarily impatient. Yes, I was tripping. LOL.

And my first set of good news, I received the Green Hornet Award for an outstanding new leader for Girl Scouts at the summation point. It feels good to have my efforts recognized. And thank you again for the card, and it was the only card I got. Did get a text message from Quincy, and I don't even get disappointed anymore. I know I do a great job with my babies, and I don't need a nod of approval from him. And know I will never compare you to him or any man. Just the communication we have together is more than he has ever done in that area. I just appreciate our new relationship slowly forming because I've never gotten to know a man on a deeper level as this without the pressure of sex or being intimate too prematurely. It is exciting!

I know the kids look to their parents as the main role models in their lives. And I know I was doing a serious injustice to them by having this make-believe and on-again, off-again thing with their dad. I talked to them frankly about the situation and actually explained to them the way things were was not what I want for me or them when they got older. But that's a lesson learned, and I'm no longer looking back on what could have been. I feel great about the future. Yes, I was stagnant for years, but some people go through the "stupid phase" longer than others. And I had convinced myself that I <u>had</u> to make it work so that the kids would have both parents. But I realize as Dr. Phil says, kids would rather come from a broken home than be in a broken home, or something like that. I'm so grateful that you are willing to take a chance on us. And you're right if it's worth having, it will take work and effort.

Yes, I read all of your letters thoroughly multiple times. I keep them in a binder in chronological order and it makes me smile. Wouldn't it be cute to put our letters together as a book and publish it? Kind of like an inspiration to others, like how friendship can blossom into so much more because we were patient and communicated it, and we're always open, honest, and optimistic! Except my letters are much longer than yours! But I am a Gemini and truly have the gift of gab!

I'm still in disbelief about how you said being in there is worse than *Lockup Raw* once the cameras are off. It hurts hearing that, but I'm glad you are a survivor. And as you said before, the countdown has begun. And I'm sure the US Postal Service is appreciating us right about now!

Jordan is doing very good with reviews so far. I'm confident he will pass with a three, but if he gets a four that would be awesome! I need to make him read much more. His stamina and desire for reading are low, so those long passages on the exam intimidate him.

I talked to my mom yesterday. I was so excited about the three-bedroom house I told her that idea! She starts telling me how newspapers and TV are saying Buffalo is the place to be and all the so-called new apartment buildings are being constructed and how people are hiring like crazy. So I asked who was hiring. Geico and other customer service jobs! I'm not uprooting the kids for a doggone customer service job! So as excited as I am, she says to keep my options open and just apply. She will never get it, so I don't waste the energy. As her siblings turned eighteen they moved to California and she was stuck in Buffalo, and now has the responsibility of caring for my aging grandma with early Alzheimer's. So I think she feels envious of me. I almost moved home last summer, but I would be making myself miserable to make her happy. Charlotte is my home, so she needs to get used to it and accept that I'm happy here and so are the kids! I really wish they would just visit, but you can lead a horse to water but can't make him drink!

I'm watching *Golden Girls*. I could watch them all day! And anything supernatural involving ghost stories by ghost hunters, paranormal activity, a haunting. I love scary/spooky movies but not bloody/gory, violent movies. Like the *Saw* movies—not! But suspense/mystery I love. The scary movies that come out now are not scary, just very bloody and intensely violent. Don't like those!

Fell asleep . . .

5/22/10

So much for my summer job. Both fell through. First one was because I was not missing Jordan's graduation. Second one I didn't really want to do anyway. But I braided one of my Girl Scouts here last week and have another head scheduled in a week. It was supposed to be this past Wednesday. One of the ladies in the kids' watch at my gym saw my hair and wanted hers done, so I gave her my cell and home number and said to call me. So on that Monday when I dropped them off I was running late, so I was trying to sign them in and get to class, and she was asking what time should she come on Wednesday. We had already discussed it early in the morning, but I kind of just pointed to the clock and said we'll talk when my workout is done. When class was over, I grabbed the kids and we were out. Since she has both my numbers I figured she would call. I worked out on Tuesday but didn't see her. And Wednesday, no call or nothing! But I'm used to people doing that, so I was like whatever. So yesterday (Friday), when I get to the gym this chick has the nerve to say, "As you can see, my hair is looking the same!" What the hell? So I said you never called or came. And I don't have your number, you have mine! So she said, "Well, I asked you what time should I come and you were rushing to class." Duh! You see me rushing, so common damn sense would say just call me when I'm settled at home. So I politely remind her that I don't have your number. All you had to do was call me. So she is still interested, and the bottom line is I need money. So we were looking at the calendar and picked Friday, June 4 at 1:00 p.m. for me to give her a braid bob, and she mentions it was her birthday. I'm like, "Oh, mine is on the first," and she mentioned she would be going to Club Tempo that Sunday since it's old-school night and she likes the older crowd in line dancing/stepping. Then she said she was turning thirty-five! I thought she was like her early forties! She's only one year older than me! Wow! I guess you really are as old as you feel and act because most people I meet think I'm in my mid to late twenties. She acts old. Now don't get me wrong, I love old school.

Earth, Wind & Fire; Luther; Deniece Williams, too many to list. But I also love Keyshia Cole, 50 Cent, Lil Wayne, Usher, Beyonce, etc. So I'll be doing the little old ladies here hopefully on the fourth. LOL!

I joined the gym about two and a half months ago and started out with just hip-hop aerobics and a treadmill but wasn't really getting anything out of it. No toning or weight loss, so I stepped it up and started trying different classes with weights and more cardio. Too bad I love to snack! But my main goal is toning. I am content with my size, I don't like being jiggly, so I'm trying to get rid of the excess flab. I lost about one hundred pounds between 2003 and 2005 but wasn't exercising as I should, so I have a high body fat content. So now I'm just trying to convert the fat to muscle. I'm finally seeing results slowly, so it keeps me motivated to stick with it!

At my heaviest, I couldn't shop for jeans at Lane Bryant anymore and just wore skirts. Lane Bryant jeans stop at size 28, so I'm guessing I was about a 30/32. Now my top half is like 18/20 and my bottom half is like 20/22. Yes, I'm a pear-shaped! But all the pictures you have of me are a pretty accurate view of how I look. I just changed my hairstyle often. Braids are my favorite though, so usually it's braided half of the year. It took me a looong time to be happy with myself (the main reason for staying in bad relationships), and I've been heavy literally all of my life. I started getting chubby in first grade, and by fifth, I was 170 pounds; eighth, 220 pounds; twelfth, 290 pounds. When Jordan was born, 315 pounds. And when Justine was born, 360 pounds. I had maintained my weight loss up until this past year. I gained twenty pounds over the summer of 2009 to now, after being laid off and home all day doing nothing. So I said enough of the self-pitying bull crap. So I joined the gym.

I'm feeling great and my skin is even so clear now! I also struggled with acne since age twelve, and as an adult, I would break out every month during my cycle and would have dark spots. My skin is looking so much clearer now and few breakouts. Exercise really does transform you in and out. And once I really made up my mind to never go back to Quincy, I felt such a weight lifted!

And the possibility of us keeps me smiling. And longing! But if anything, you would be the greatest teacher, patience! As far as sexy, all day every day! And I will leave you with a PG thought, for now, no rated R yet. LOL. And that last letter when you said "I know what you need, are you going to let me give it to you?" Yes, my mind went straight to the gutter! So now I'm about to make us some lunch, then to the mailbox to see if I'm that lucky for letters two days in a row! I'll be waiting patiently . . .

Sincerely yours,
Janae James

PS: You're going to need to step it up and make those letters longer, LOL

May 24, 2010

Dear Bryan,

ROTFLMBO! Not sure if you keep up with the acronyms of text messages (rolling on the floor, laughing my butt off). But seriously, I know you don't have a ton of pictures of me but I thought you had a pretty good idea of how I look. I don't own a bikini, and I was trying to figure out what picture you were talking about. Then I remember the picture of the blue slide and I wrote on the back that I got on it. That woman looks <u>nothing</u> like me! She has skinny legs and is top-heavy and dark-skinned. I will give you the benefit of the doubt since it wasn't a close-up. I have thick legs and thighs, and much more in the hips and booty! So you're forgiven . . . for now! And I put a lot of pictures of the ship to share the experience. Maybe next time we'll be on it together.

I'm happy you like the braids because it's my favorite hairdo and the most versatile. I have four tattoos in all. The one on my chest was my very first. It's my name on top, a purple rose with four red hearts around it. Two years ago I added Que to the bottom, so I have to figure out how to alter that. But I don't sweat it for now. On my arm is the Gemini symbol with twin cherries in the middle and some scroll work. On my upper back is a capital J with scrollwork around it. And on my right foot I have a celestial sun. That one hurt like hell! And took forever to heal, and walking was a bit painful. I like one more on my lower back in a dragonfly design. Maybe you could help me design that one! You already know I love to write, so you don't have to worry about it. Stop laughing. My life is (was) a soap opera. Oh, I've got a ton to say! LOL.

I cut Jordan's hair mostly but very basic. I don't know how to line him up, and my clippers are basic. But I'd love to give you a shave! I don't really have to shave because I don't really have hair on my legs. A little around my ankles, but me and my mom got lucky I guess. She has no hair at all on her legs and I have very little. I figure if I leave it alone it won't grow longer!

I appreciate the faith you have in me about finding work. I'm trusting God, but I still worry. My unemployment benefit year is up in two weeks, so I do get nervous and it's a scary feeling, so I'm praying! I knew you would fuss at me about my hair. Everyone does and they say I'm so blessed to have long, thick hair. I will try to refrain from wigs, but in the wintertime, that's warm! LOL

Jordan took the retest today. He really ticked me off this weekend. He wanted to draw all weekend, and it was like pulling teeth to get him to study. He claims no one else is studying for the retest, and it's the weekend and he wants to relax and blah blah blah! I had to refrain from smacking him upside the head. He is so smart, but when it comes to the effort he wants to take the easy way out. Then poor Justine, her friend that lives behind us, they have two dogs, a pit bull, and a small breed. The pit is huge and scary looking, but she's really a big, overgrown teddy bear. Well, she ran outside last week and tragically was hit by a car. She ended up paralyzed and had to be put to sleep. Justine was devastated! She played over her friend's house for a while, and when she came home she kept saying she missed Sky. I gave her a hug and she just broke down. She cried for about twenty minutes. She loves animals so much! I get attached to animals just like her. I feel sorry when I see deer on the highway after being hit by cars, or when I hear about animals being mistreated I get so furious! Okay, new subject. Getting too depressing. LOL.

So 6'2", 230 lbs. Wow, sounds impressive and so tempting! Brooklyn told me you can bench press 300 lbs., so I was like ooh wee! I'm glad I'm below that. I can't wait to get more pics of you. I'm watching the *Golden Girls*, of course. I always right you after the kids are asleep and *Golden Girls* comes on at night. I'm going to make a cup of peppermint mocha coffee and call it a night with a sweet warm drink and sweet warm thoughts of you! Tomorrow is Girl Scout and Boy Scout meetings and more job hunting. So *buenas noches* for now and until the next letter . . .

Sincerely yours,
Janae

PS: What is that scent I'm smelling on the letter? It was a nice surprise!

May 27, 2010

Hi Bryan,

How are you? I'm pretty good, doing the usual job searching and preventing the kids from killing each other. Today was uneventful but some days they argue about nothing all day. I think back to when I and my brother were younger. We argued, but at Jordan and Justine's age, we overall got along great. As he got older he turned into the biggest, most conceited jerk! About his freshman year in '88 or '89, it started, and by junior/senior year he was definitely conceited. He looked exactly like a rapper from the early 90's and the females loved him. Plus, he ran track and was very fast. His girlfriend was gorgeous and a sweetheart. He went to the service and bought a fly ass car and it was really over then. You couldn't tell him he wasn't the shit! That car changed him. I resented him a lot as he got to high school. We were complete opposites, and my mom favored him heavily growing up and still to this day won't admit it. I was even jealous because he was mad popular too. I've basically just built a bridge over that, but it forces me to always try to be equal and fair with Jordan and Justine. Me and my brother are overall cool now, but he has a mean temper. He's the extreme Gemini, but I've always said May Geminis have the flip side way more than us June Geminis. For my birthday, I told the kids all I want is for them is to behave, not argue, and just be good. And that's the only gift I need. We'll probably go out to Golden Corral for dinner. On Tuesdays kids eat free, so we all can eat for less than $12! And their buffet is the bomb! (Fell asleep.)

5/28/10

Happy Friday even though it's evening. The kids are in my bed and we are watching *Madea's Family Reunion*. We love all Tyler Perry movies and plays. Handwriting a little shaky because they won't sit their butts still. LOL. (Fell asleep again, LOL.)

5/29/10

I was sleepy when the movie started, so I don't know why I thought I would stay up. I haven't been sleeping well these last few nights. When I filed my weekly unemployment I got the message that I had two more weeks of benefits. It was just a painful reminder that I've been out of work for almost twelve months! I've been working since I was thirteen! I did Mayor's Summer Youth for two years (my mom upped my age so I could start at thirteen instead of fourteen). Then I started as a cashier at Tops on Genesee Street in June of my freshman year, and stayed there all through high school. I wonder if you ever came through my line. I worked two jobs while at Buff State, Tops and the movies downtown, then Rite Aid on Bailey and the movies downtown. I was at the movies for three years, and that was literally the most fun job. We were all mad cool with each other, and free movies from 1995 to 1998! Then I went back to Tops and worked in the check cashing section, then was promoted to assistant customer service manager. I stayed there till Jordan was like six months old, then HSBC hired me. Stayed there almost five years before deciding to go back to school for my master's in education.

I feel like I wasted my bachelor's degree in biology, but I hope to teach middle school or high school science. I love science! My first year teaching two students from my class placed first and second place overall in the entire fourth grade annual science fair! So I know I would be the bomb science teacher! So bottom line, I have never been out of work for a year in my life and I'm used to always having something to do. But I just applied to Carmel Christian Academy yesterday and they have an opening for third, fourth, and fifth, so I got the transcript and résumé, cover letter. Then, since it's a Christian school, I had to type a personal faith statement about my journey from salvation to present. Then I hand delivered everything, and I'm really hoping they call me for an interview!

Then Jordan got in trouble at school and was suspended for Thursday and Friday. According to other students, he wished his teacher was dead and he wanted to shoot up the class! He admitted that he said he hated his teacher but denied the rest. I know he doesn't like her, so I know that there was some truth to the story. But I told him had he said that in high school or even middle school he could have been arrested! I'm so frustrated because I can't teach him to be a man, and their dad is 700 miles away yet he gives Que the ultimate respect. I know it's a man thing, but I constantly remind him that Mommy is the one who cares for him, cooks, cleans, clothes, nurtures, helps with homework, deals with the pre-adolescent hormones, etc. Yet I have to tell him more than once to pick up this or clean that or read a book, be nice to your sister, etc. But his behavior is perfect for Daddy. Honestly, it pisses me the hell off! I know he needs a man in his life, and this was another reason I figured try one more time with Que so that I could take that burden off me. But the stress of being with Quincy, it wasn't a worthwhile tradeoff.

I'm sorry this turned out to be a venting letter. I've just been in a funky mood and lack sleep. But I know this is just my storm and God will help me through it. Hopefully a letter from you today will put a smile on my face. Our mailman is so slow. The mail doesn't come in till like 3:00 p.m.! It's hot too, like ninety degrees. But I'd rather be hot than in the snow. I do like things like sledding and snow tubing, but I hate windchill. Charlotte does get cold though. Morning in the winter can be as low as twenty degrees but warm up to forty or fifty by afternoon. I wish I knew that before I gave away all my scarves and hats and gloves when I moved here. But hey, you live and learn.

So I got to spend two days at home with Jordan. We talked a lot. I always stress to him my love for him and my high expectations. He gets lazy when something requires effort, and I'm still trying to find ways to motivate him but in more intrinsic ways. I refuse to buy him stuff as an incentive, I want him to want to be better for himself.

Well, I guess I need to get some things done around the house. So please put a smile on my face so I can temporarily forget about my troubles like Calgon, take me away!

Thinking of you always,
Janae
xoxo

May 31, 2010

To the absolute sweetest man I've met,

I can't believe you made that card! That was the most thoughtful gift I have ever received! And it was so beautiful. Words can't express how special that card is to me. My birthday is usually the most uneventful day. The last party that was thrown for me was when I turned eight. And that was shared with my brother (his birthday is May 24). My family was never into gifts. I may have gotten $10 or $20 here and there, cards <u>sometimes</u>. So for you to put that much effort into making the card that intricate and beautiful, thank you, thank you, thank you!

You are very creative. That's a special gift. The kids thought the card was amazing. Not to put pressure on you, LOL, but Jordan's graduation is June 8 and Justine's birthday is August 14, and I bet they would love a card made by you. And no, it doesn't have to be that highly detailed like mine, so anything you make would be greatly appreciated. The envelope design was hot too! I actually like that for my last tattoo on my lower back, and incorporate the color lavender and Carolina blue into it somehow and draw it again.

The card and envelope definitely brightened my mood because I was in a bit of a funk last week. It's so nice to have today to just chill in the house. Since it's Memorial Day, everything is closed and the kids are home. It's been raining all day, so I've been cleaning and doing laundry. Yesterday I went to my cousin's jewelry party and to a get-together at my Sunday school teacher's house.

My Sunday school class is for single parents, and the teachers (now married) are always having something at their home. BBQs, parties, etc. But I never went and decided let's just go. Their home is amazing! The garage/guest house is literally another house, complete with a pool table, full kitchen, Wii, and built-in-wall sixty-inch flat screen. They have an inground pool, a fishing pond, and a stable with three horses. So everyone brought a dish (I made taco salad, the bomb!) and we had such a good time. It's so nice that they are always opening up their house to people. I had ribs, steak, huge shrimp, and a whole bunch of other stuff. I'm like, dang, all this time we could have been fellowshipping with everyone and having a great time. So if they do the Fourth of July, we are so there! The church we go to is a Southern Baptist and it's a mega church. Probably 10,000 members, but there are two campuses, so maybe more. It's like 65 percent white yet I feel totally comfortable there, and the kids actually like it, especially their Sunday school class. Jordan was baptized there, and they actually counseled him on what that means and why he's doing it so that he isn't just doing it just because.

Okay, my break is over. Another load of laundry to fold, and I need to braid Justine's hair for the week. Oh, I forgot. How about Jordan found not one, not two, but three 10k gold and diamond rings in like three days! One in the grocery store in the potato chip section, one on the sidewalk near our building, and one today out in the rain. His theory was that the heavy rain would wash the rig or whatever along the curb so he and Justine went out and he found it near the dumpster. I'm still in disbelief! So I know he's giving me one or two for my birthday and the third, I'll let him pawn. They are small and dainty, nothing over the top but he may get thirty dollars or so which is a small fortune when you're eleven!

So I'll say good day to you for now as I look forward to your next letter. And I hope all is well with you!

Yours truly,
Janae
Xoxoxoxoxoxo!

PS: What do those numbers on the bottom of the card represent, or were they just random? And is a paper rose ink the name of your tattoo designing business?

From the moment I received that birthday card (and honestly before that), I ate, slept, and breathed that man. Something about that card awakened feelings in me that was very unfamiliar. I've been in love before but this felt different to me. I had never seen anything handmade like that before, and my mind told me that so much effort and detail went into making it that I must be really special in his eyes. My birthday never meant anything to anyone. Thinking all the way back to my earliest childhood memories, I had two birthday parties that were shared with my brother. I wasn't showered with birthday gifts, not even a birthday cake or dinner. I didn't have cupcakes brought to my class or Chuck E. Cheese. June 1 was a regular day.

My class went on a field trip to a baseball game one year on my birthday, and I watched my classmates eat their bagged lunches packed from home. I didn't have one, so I sat alone, pretending to watch the game, hungry. One girl saw that I wasn't eating and must have felt sorry for me, and gave me a bag of chips from her lunch. Another year on my birthday our class was on a two-night camping trip and somehow the girl I chose to be my camp partner turned out to be mean and vicious toward me the whole time. We had been friends all school year, so when she asked to be my camp partner I was excited. I never knew why she switched up on me, but she made those two nights miserable for me!

My day revolved around writing letters, buying stamps, and waiting on the mailman. This man was only supposed to be my pen pal until he got out of prison. This didn't make any sense to me that I was feeling this way, but looking back, *now* it makes perfect sense. I shared absolutely everything about my life with him, and it's a dangerous thing to give someone a loaded gun. Then I shared my kids with him. When my son started to develop his own relationship with him and responded in a positive way, he had me. I yearned for my babies to have a loving and involved father, and I often felt guilty because I couldn't make things work with their father, nor could I make him do more, do better. Single motherhood sometimes used to really beat me up, and here was this man from a great distance giving me guidance that seemed to be working, so of course that strengthened the growing bond.

And I haven't even heard his voice yet.

June 1, 2010

Dearest Janae,

Happy birthday! I pray you enjoy your day and that nothing interrupts your happiness for the day as well as your future. Please forgive me for the birthday card. I had it made for you, and the reason for my apology is the guy that made it is young and has never experienced a woman; therefore, he put girl on the card instead of woman. I would have made him do it over, but I wanted you to have this card on your birthday so you would feel special 'cuz you are.

It was good to open up your first letter and read that you miss me. That means more to me than you will ever know. It also inspires me that you look for my letters the way I look for yours. For what I say in these letters is not for the moment but for later on in life. You may look back and say he showed and proved everything he said to me and some. I pray for this relationship every night that it will stand the test of time. Hopefully my words and wisdom will be the hugs and kisses that you truly deserve every single day that I'm not there to give them to you in person.

And to answer your own premature question, our future is not an *if.* Either you believe or you don't. There's no straddling the fence. But to the question at hand, after my reconnecting with my family, I will have no problem moving to North Carolina or wherever else you lead me, as long as I satisfy and stimulate you mentally, spiritually, and emotionally. I'm ready to make new memories and no time for games. As for lost time, that's exactly what it is, *lost.* Something that can't be found or retrieved ever again. And I know long-distance relationships don't last, so I would never be selfish enough to have one when I'm home. I'm happy you're being honest and open and speaking your mind. Please don't stop 'cuz I know you have crazy more, so keep it coming.

Yes, I enjoyed the picture. And yes, your babies look like their mother. And stop talking about your daughter like that 'cuz what you show her will make her the woman she will become.

That's real good news about the house. You definitely can save some money and experience home ownership. Just take it slow and go over all the particulars so you will gain and not lose. And stop saying *if* you find a job. You have to have faith that what you put your mind to you will achieve it.

The mailing system is terrible here, so just when you think I'm not writing you the letters are in the mail. It just takes like four days to reach you! I'm very happy to hear you're working out. It improves decision-making, as well as lengthens your life. That's good you will be able to keep the kids in good schools 'cuz they do not need to be going to schools that don't take teaching seriously 'cuz they will intentionally leave the kids down the wrong path of learning that has nothing to do with life.

And yes, the recession does suck big time. I feel it too.

That's crazy. I didn't know you could get stamps at the ATM what's next coffee?

I hope you stay on Jordan's reading 'cuz he definitely needs that. Are you buying him books to read? What about flash cards with paragraphs with meaning? I pray for you all without you asking. That's my duty. Also, congratulations on your award 'cuz I know you'll get it and a teaching job as well. But first you have to believe.

And to answer your question, I'm not settling ever in jail, I will never be comfortable in a surrounding such as this around oppressors. Also all these cats do all day is cut and stab each other, do drugs, borrow, beg, and steal! They moved me here close to Albany 'cuz it's their form of punishment, knowing I wanted to get closer to home. But it's just another stumbling block that I'll overcome. I give them two good years on parole my sentence will be over. And yes, I can transfer parole down South. Travel restrictions are only for a month or two, maybe less. I'm just guessing! I'll probably have to go to a halfway house for thirty days, but no house arrest! Well, I'm going to end this first letter right now since you cheated and kept stopping and starting. I pray Jordan's test went as planned. Until I hear from you again, sweet dreams.

Yours truly also,
Bryan
xoxoxo

June 2, 2010

Hello Sweeter,

I'm glad I made your day. Two letters on the same date were nothing. And I'm glad you are checking the mailbox 'cuz I wait every day for the guards who come by and pass out mail, and I'm crushed when he walks by and doesn't have anything from you for me! Once again, congratulations on your award. I'm sure you deserve it. Even when you're not recognized publicly, God sees all, so he counts when nothing else counts. I'm glad you're starting not to get upset about your past, but I'm counting on you to stick to your morals and principles.

I'm pleased that I'm not being compared to anyone else. I would never compare you to anyone 'cuz I'm sure you have qualities that can't be measured or put in a box! I also appreciate our relationship forming. And I wouldn't pressure you for sex, but what makes you so sure you wouldn't be pressing me for sex? And there's no such thing as being intimate too prematurely 'cuz if you set boundaries or stipulations on what is and what isn't there should never be a misconception. I was told this but I don't know how true it is, but they say women know within fifteen to twenty minutes of first contact with a man if they are going to be intimate or not. Is that true?

I'm glad you've talked to your children about what they witnessed between you and your ex. But what if you have a weak moment? 'Cuz the flesh is weak, as we both know. How would you handle it? And would you tell me? And I'm not taking a chance on you. All I'm taking is a leap of faith 'cuz I rather rely on faith than rely on chance. Faith has longevity, chance is fleeting. And yes, it will take great effort and plenty of work!

I have nothing against you publishing our letters 'cuz it would be fact and not fiction. And experience is still the greatest teacher, as long as you grow from it. And that's the key to our success, always being honest and open and optimistic. Even if it hurts, please always be truthful with me! And your letters might be a little longer but we are both equal in what we are striving for. And I don't know about you having the gift of gab. I just think you can stretch a sentence a long way! LOL. But we will see when there is no pen and paper and I'm standing in front of you, then I'll see how you flow! 'Cuz, being a Virgo, remember I hold the balance beam, my twin cherry, LOL. And I'm sure the postal service loves us. They could learn a few things if they partook in snooping.

I hope Jordan passed his retest, but you still could get flashcards and practice with him on the weekends, especially during the summer vacation, so he will never feel down on the subject. I agree that you should have not told your mother about the house. Envy runs through blood and water if you know what I mean! You have to come to grips with your mother not really wanting to see you grow past her as well as accomplishing things she never thought you would obtain. So when making progress, keep some things close to your chest until they blossom 'cuz you don't need nobody killing your drive or progress to happiness or self-fulfilled justice!

I like scary movies, but I like black drama movies that have a message and show people fighting adversity and poverty and winning, and putting other people over the hump so they can taste success. As you would, all my vision is like no other. I like creating paths that. Successful people don't like showing those lost, it deals with your spirit as well as character. Forgive me for being so deep on the last page but I'm hungry, and the day I get full is the day I stop growing! It seems like you're having a communication problem with people you're trying to solicit business with. Listen, miss, even though she had your number, you were supposed to make it your business to get these women's numbers and put them in a phone book. Never let pride get in the way of your prospering 'cuz you'll look back later and regret it. And remember, a little business is better than no business!

I'm glad you're toning up but please don't lose too much. I'm not into big, but I am into thick. And from the way you describe yourself I thank God for you, LOL. I'm blessed to keep you smiling 'cuz I haven't stopped smiling since you came into my life, and I'm not letting go for nothing. And I'm longing for us too, so you're not alone on that note! I'm not only a teacher of patience, I'm also a student. You never answered that question in my letter, so I'll ask you again. I know what you need, are you going to let me give it to you? And your mind wouldn't be in the gutter because you deserve love from the follicles on top of your head to the balls on the bottom of your feet, inside and out. And if I have my way, you will never be without because the body, mind, and spirit need constant nourishment!

Now I'll be waiting patiently for your response. Oh yeah, it should be another letter after this 'cuz it's my job to spoil you. So until then, I'll see you in my dreams . . . I hope I'm making these letters longer like you asked! Also, I'm still waiting for my pear-shaped pictures!

Sincerely yours,
Bryan Jarelle Edwards

June 2, 2010

Hey Baby Cakes,

I hope you have been having a good week so far. As you know, my birthday was yesterday and you and the kids were the only ones who made me cards. I received some calls and lots of shoutouts on Facebook. And surprise, surprise, no call or text from baby daddy. It used to hurt my feelings because I always would call him and make sure the kids called, made a card, etc. Until I realized he is who he is, and the important people in my life remember things that are special to me. Wow, I am officially in my mid-thirties! But I feel great and I'm working toward a better me, so as I get older I look at it as if I'm a fine bottle of wine, aging to perfection!

My cousin Nicole came over yesterday. That was a shock because she literally has not been to my house since we painted the living room and I bought my breakfast nook. She lives in northwest Charlotte and I'm in southeast Charlotte, so it's about twenty-five to thirty minutes. And when I move into the new house, we will be ten minutes apart. She's the only family I have down here (she moved here a year after me).

Bad news, Jordan did not pass the reading retest. I really feel like his teacher failed him because he has had B's in reading all year, and to fail means that her work was not properly aligned with the fifth-grade reading curriculum and was just too easy. I remember at the beginning of the school year at curriculum night when the teacher is basically explaining what will be covered. I was thinking this chick is such a scatterbrain! She was bouncing from topic to topic and seemed so confused! And Justine's last teacher told me that his teacher taught first grade last year. And when I told her Jordan had Mrs. Locker, she was like, no comment, so I already knew. I'm just glad there's one week of school left. I will be having Jordan reading and doing comprehension activities all summer, and he will have a fresh start in the fall. He's supposed to be in band next year playing the trombone, and I found out that the parent has to either buy or rent the instrument. And why is a trombone expensive as hell! We made a downgrade to clarinet, which is step one to saxophone. But I told him I'm not going broke to have him in there, and if he can't put forth the effort this summer to get better in reading. I'm so glad Justine had the best teacher! Ms. Harris is awesome and only a third-year teacher. Justine was so sad when her teacher was absent Friday and Tuesday.

Right now, my biggest concern is will I get another unemployment extension. My deposit today was only $53. My final week and they basically just stated if you are approved then you'll go back to your normal amount. So now my rent will be late because I was expecting $454. But nothing I can do. We have food in the refrigerator, so all I can do is keep applying for jobs in the meantime and trust God. I'm always working on my faith. I know I'm supposed to put my trust in him and he won't give me more than I can bear. Sometimes I'm a little impatient, but I'm trying because I know the perfect job is waiting for me! And possibly the perfect relationship . . .

The one thing I haven't asked you yet but I need to know is why exactly are you locked up? Brooklyn kind of gave me a very general explanation, but not detailed. My concern is that based on the nature of what you are locked up for, when you are released, are you free and clear? Or will you have to register as a sex offender? With my profession being teaching and the Girl Scouts and volunteering at the kids' school, I'm always around kids, and I know those who have to be registered have to keep a certain distance from children. I would be devastated if our developing relationship would have to be compromised, so I'm praying about that. I was telling Brooklyn that I feel like I like you more than I should, considering it's only been two months of communicating. But like she always says, time will tell, and just be open and honest. I also worry about do you like me because of a lack of options with you being in there. I don't compare you to my past relationships because so far you are exceeding my expectations, but I'm not used to a man being so considerate, and I appreciate it more than you know.

Well, my dear, it's bedtime for me. I will be glad when school is out and I can sleep in. Hopefully not for long, then I'll be ready for work. Or if I get an extension I won't have to worry about child care and can be home for the summer with the kids. So peace for now, and I'll be looking forward to your next letter!

Sincerely yours,
Janae

June 4, 2010

Dear Bryan,

Hi! I'm so sorry I was being a brat about the letters in holding out because I wasn't getting any fast enough. It was silly, I know. I have plenty of stamps, paper, and envelopes, so I will stop doing that. I didn't know that someone else made the card. It was still very sweet and thoughtful, and he has some serious skills! Don't worry about calling me "girl" in the card. I didn't take offense at all, and I know I'm all woman! I got two letters today after checking the mail all week, so I was very happy. I was on my way out to run errands and I really wanted to just sit there and read them, and it took a lot of restrain to wait until I got home so that I could take my time and savor your words. LOL, but I am serious!

I think you would really like North Carolina. And the best part would be having a road buddy to drive with to visit Buffalo and to help drive. Jordan is officially fired because he slept the whole way to Florida and back, and I had to pull over four times to stay awake! I told him he must have been having a growth spurt because he slept a lot on the cruise too. He can't wait to be sixteen and drive. But once, a year ago, I let him drive around a vacant parking lot with me in the passenger seat and he was on cloud nine. Couldn't tell that boy nothing, and he was pretty good!

As far as our future, yes, I do believe and I'm willing to take a leap of faith with you. I like you more and more each day, and the waiting will be hard but not impossible. Not hard because I'm worried about meeting anyone, but hard because I can't wait to see you and even hear your voice! Do you have a tenor voice or baritone? I've been told my voice sounds like I can sing really good, but I sound better in a chorus or choir. At one point I was in the choir my freshman year at Fredonia. I miss those days of living in a dorm. I'm hoping my kids want to experience dorm life, hopefully a black college.

And no, I don't tease Justine about being clumsy. I've learned to keep breakable things out of the way and remind her to just slow down. Many times she's just being quick and anxious. And I already told both the kids school is in session this summer and we will all have DEAR (drop everything and read) time daily because Jordan needs to build stamina. And Justine is a good reader but I want them to remain above average. I take them to the library occasionally and they check out books on their card, but Jordan tends to always get drawing books, playing books, Titanic books, etcetera, and never wants to read about these things. It's a constant struggle, and many times I just pick my battles with him because sometimes there are just more pressing issues than reading. Being a single parent is draining sometimes, but I love them too much to get defeated!

I hate to think about the atmosphere you are living in with all that going on. It's a shame about the drugs, but it's just like the borders of Mexico, South America, etc. If the drugs were not allowed in the country and not brought in the jail in the first place. But I'm glad you are a strong man mentally and physically, and I'm counting down the days right along with you. I remember when crack was first introduced to my family and the devastation it caused for so many years. I was too young to walk away, so going away to college was such a blessing. I just thank God that my family overcame! Sorry, I don't want to bring up negativity. I just want you to know about the background. I come from and overcame.

I'm sitting here watching—you guessed it, *Golden Girls*. So sad that Rue McClanahan (Blanche) just passed away. Now Rose is the only one left, and ironically she was the oldest! I'm sitting here sipping on a glass of wine getting ready to call it a night. Do you drink alcohol? I've never been a hard liquor drinker, strictly wine, wine coolers, mixed fruity drinks whenever I actually go out. Don't like the taste of beer much, and definitely don't like being drunk. The last time I was drunk I was like twenty, and I just don't like being out of control of my own body. And with the recession I pretty much drink J. Roget Spumante.

Tonight was the award ceremony for Girl Scouts to receive their bridging certificate for the next level. Five of my eleven girls will be Brownies next year and only three showed up! My so-called assistant, who for 90 percent of the year was trifling, called me at 6:00 asking what time did it start, even though it's in the girls' planners that I made and in the 223 emails I sent. I figured she would be late but she didn't even show up, and I hand-decorated shadow boxes and personalized each one for her not to come! She's moving back to her hometown, but her daughter is a sweetheart and I wanted her to have her gift. But her mom has an interview on Monday, so she will miss our last meeting on Tuesday. The other no-show is a new girl to the troop so she never had a uniform, so I didn't get her a shadow box. I got her a Daisy Scout necklace and Girl Scout socks so she wouldn't feel left out, just for them not to come either. But her mom's English is not the greatest, and maybe she got lost.

I like her mom a lot, and she stepped right up at the last two meetings to help with the activities, so I asked her last week to be one of the assistant leaders next year and she agreed. I pretty much did every job of the troop for the first year (cookie manager, financial manager, event planner, etc.), but with everything being a learn as I go. That was cool because I was more like how can I double gate if I don't know what's going on. But now that I know, I will be assigning jobs and I let the moms know you have to be involved in some way because I will not be doing it all. Since I was off work it worked out, but I plan on teaching in the fall, so I won't have all the extra time.

Me and my assistant at one point got into a heated argument on the phone and she hung up on me! If it's one thing I can't stand is to be hung up on. She felt like I was not including her in anything, and when I say I have tried to make her be involved from day one, which was October, so in February I was like screw it. But in March she finally got a clue when I started the parent helper rotation and the other moms started doing her job. Then she wanted to help. She was late to almost every meeting even though I pushed the time from 6:00 to 6:30 to accommodate her work schedule. But next year my troop will run like a well-oiled machine. Out of eleven girls ten are staying with my troop, and I received the Green Hornet Award, so I know I'm a good-ass leader! (Poppin' my collar, LOL.)

Well, I'm going to finish sipping my wine and call it a night and dream about you! I will be writing you another letter in the morning to make up for acting bratty! So, goodnight, and I'll continue this in the morning.

Dreaming of you . . .
Janae James

PS: I know you keep asking for pictures. I will take some soon, I promise! Jordan will have to be my photographer!

June 5, 2010

Good morning!

You would not believe what time it is! Barely 7:00 a.m., and I thought I would be sleeping in. I'm a morning person, and usually I'm up by 8:00 on the weekend but I kept hearing this noise. Jordan decided to get up and play with his remote control helicopter at 6:45! But on the weekday when I wake him up at 7:30 he's all tired . . . Go figure! I told him to turn that doggone thing off! But of course, once your sleep is interrupted it's hard to go back to sleep, and I promised you a letter in the morning.

Yes, I'm excited about the house, the kids having their own space again, and having our own backyard and a quiet street where they can ride their bikes. I can already picture myself on the patio at night listening to music and sipping my glass of wine, writing a letter to you, and eventually, you sitting with me!

Now, in one letter you were saying if sex happens too early in the relationship how things don't always go right, but in the last letter you said there is no such thing as being intimate too prematurely if you set boundaries. It depends on what your partner's intentions are because I've been sold the dream and made it very clear what I was looking for (not referring to Quincy), and was played in the end after being intimate too soon. Then another time I met a guy online and we were strictly platonic. He was an educator also and we emailed from time to time. Then graduated to phone, then decided let's meet. The conversations never got sexual, and he seemed genuinely interested in taking it slow and getting to know me. So we decided to hang out for the day and he was going to pick me up around 11:00 a.m. He called at 9:00 to say good morning, at about 10:00 a.m. to say he was about to shower and get dressed then walk his dog. At about 10:50 to say he was at the gas station about seven minutes away, and that was the last time I talked to him! I literally was watching the news to see if there was an accident because it made no sense to me. Then I realized I was just played! He texted me three weeks later saying I know you're pissed at me but you have to understand the circumstances. I figured he must be married and his wife must have called, and at the last minute had to change plans.

We had talked over the course of four to five months either online or on the phone, so in that situation I took it slow. And thank goodness we never met, but like I said if the other person is not being truthful, it doesn't matter what boundaries are set if they are deceitful. The other guy I met, we talked on the phone and met up in person very early on. And I was clear that I was done dating and wanted to focus on one relationship at a time, and he said that's what he wants also. And after being intimate he acted so amazed, like he couldn't believe a woman like me was single. And he said he wasn't going anywhere, and how into me he was. And blah blah blah because I didn't hear from him after that for six months! He called me up like two or three months ago like nothing happened, and said I told you I was trying to get my money right and my phone doesn't get service out here (he lives about ninety minutes south), like I was supposed to be on standby! He wanted to come see me, and I couldn't understand why. I said hell no! Had the nerve to say once we do it he will always be able to get with me. I told him he lost his damn mind, and that's the last time we talked.

So, Bryan, no, I'm not comparing you to any of these assholes I've encountered. But I have been sold the dream of happily ever after too many times to count, and I'm praying you are the one that will prove to me that there are real men out there who will love me from the follicles on my head to the soles of my feet! As Aaliyah says, "I really need somebody, tell me, are you that somebody?" and you have every right to question what would I do in a weak moment if me and Que were in a situation of possibly being intimate. I won't lie. Physically we always had a crazy connection, but I always attached emotion to it and it always got me nowhere. So in my mind I understand that going there with him will feel good for a moment but would be such a setback. I really have faith in what we are working through and do not want to jeopardize that. Every day I pray for strength to not go backward and to stand my ground because after knowing him for twelve years very little has changed. And for all I know, baby number thirteen is probably on the way. But enough about him. But to answer your question, yes, I would tell you. And no, I wouldn't expect you to forgive that. But at the same time, I've never been unfaithful, so I'm not really too concerned, and there are 700 miles that separate us.

Just got back from Zumba class at the gym. It was ninety degrees when we left the house at 11:00 a.m.! The kids are at the pool with my neighbor. She's white, so she likes to sunbathe. So I layered the kids in sunscreen and sent them off. I'd rather wait till later, plus I kind of have a headache. Her daughter and Justine are becoming best friends. And her mom and I are becoming cool. She was raised by a nanny and grew up eating chitlins! I was like, woah, 'cuz yes, I love chitlins, so don't hold that against me! LOL. So we kind of take turns swapping the girls, and when it's pool time Jordan tags along. My headache is from the heat, and I need to drink more. It's my body's way of reminding me I'm dehydrated because usually I try to avoid taking pain pills and look for a natural approach. It was a little hot in the class and I only had a Nutri-Grain bar for breakfast, and I knew better, so don't fuss at me. LOL. Now would be the perfect time to take a nap since Jordan busted up my sleep, but I'm totally energized now since working out.

Wow, I never heard that saying, "envy runs through blood and water." It's hard to accept the truth about that because when I look at my kids I want them to be ten times more successful than me. And if I don't get to visit every continent, I want them to send me pictures from their trip. And if I don't have any more kids (even though I would love one or two more), then I can't wait to love on my grandkids. So for my mom to envy me it's hard to comprehend, even though I know it's true. And I do talk too much! When good things seem like they are about to happen, I want to tell the world. And when they fall through, it's like damn! Got to tell everybody, never mind. I have learned to keep some things to myself or only tell Brooklyn, but it's something I'm working on. Like with you, I want to tell everyone I know about this great guy I've met! But I'm waiting until I can show everyone how cute we will probably look together! Knowing me, I won't be able to wait that long! LOL.

And no, I still have not braided that woman's hair. Honestly, I really dislike braiding! I love to make hair more beautiful with braids on myself, but I never liked doing other people's hair. It's like going to the dentist. You go because you have to. No one enjoys that hideous drill sound or them picking at your teeth. I braid because I have to as far as extra cash, but it's a long process and I get tired of looking at the person's head. So even though I could use the money, in the many years of braiding, women hate to drop money on braids because it's more all at once. But don't mind paying $50 every two weeks to get it washed and styled. And those are the chicks who constantly break appointments. Now, on the other hand, I've braided hair for one of my Daisies here a few weeks back. Her mom wants me to do her hair again this week coming, her two-year-old's hair, and her hair. So that's three heads in one week. So yes, my dear, I do go after customers. I just recognize which ones are worth it! That other chick at the gym had rescheduled for the third, and on like the first I asked her were we still on and she said something about working a double. She ain't serious. LOL.

Don't worry about me losing too much of anything! I really haven't lost any pounds because I haven't changed my diet, but I have toned some. Just trying to get rid of the jiggly! I'll never be thin, so you have no need for concern. And you keep saying you know what I need, am I going to let you give it to me? I'm really curious about what you plan to give me because I am more than willing to receive whatever it is. I'm not sure about the fifteen to twenty-minute rule of knowing if you will be intimate with a man. I definitely know I won't give that man the pot of gold right away, and I also knew from the first letter that you were a man that I would love to lose control with! So how do you plan to make me lose my breath?

Well, I'm going to brave the heat and walk to the mailbox and check on the kids at the pool. They've been gone like two hours but my headache is still lingering, so I'm going to just take an Aleve and find something to eat. Anything to take my mind off you for just a little bit. Not that it's a bad thing! But I'm scared of falling hard for you too fast. Is there such a thing as too fast? I wonder if you feel the same way? So until your next letter, take care of yourself and I'll be happily waiting for the next one!

Yours truly,
Janae

June 6, 2010

Dearest Janae,

Yes, I do keep up with acronyms of text messages even though I don't have a cell phone or pager. And I will apologize for getting you confused with that lady. That only goes to show that I need more pictures of you. My gut feeling told me that wasn't you 'cuz she wasn't thick below the waist. And yes, hopefully next cruise we will be on it together. I really like that idea! Why did I already know that one of the tattoos I was talking about was of your children's father? But I'm not tripping over that. When you feel you want to change it to a design, feel free, I don't want my name on your body, I want my name on your heart, mind, and spirit! The one you plan on getting on your lower back, I would love to be there 'cuz I have a couple more I need to get. I'm glad I don't have to worry about you writing, and I know we have plenty to say to each other as well as share, it's only the beginning and I'm playing for keeps the only way I know how. I would love for you to shave my head. I haven't been pampered in so long, I forgot how that feels!

Yes, I have faith in you finding work, but you still must stay aggressive and not let up, even when you feel you're not going to get it stopped by the places you put applications in and inquire. That will really show them that you're serious about your business! About Jordan, when explaining to him why he should try harder, continue to show him examples of why you stay on him as much. Also, some days on the weekend take him around town and show him examples of people who take the easy way out. Also buy books for him that encourage self-esteem as well. But don't let up. He needs you. I'm sorry to hear that Justine's friend's dog got killed. I hate animals being mistreated also so I'm with you on that. And yes, I am 230 pounds, 6'2". And it doesn't sound impressive, it's outstanding. And something don't have to be tempting when it's yours for the taking! I do bench press actually, 315 pounds. And as far as pictures, I'm trying my best to get some 'cuz it's so hard in here to get those things taken care of 'cuz they always cancel pictures. But I'm on it! I'm going to call it a night with warm thoughts of you, so *hasta luego* until the next letter.

Sincerely yours,
Bryan

PS: That scent is Sean John. Also, I know you're probably saying, damn, this letter is short, and you're right. I wanted to have something quick in your mailbox so that I could get started on the last letter you sent about your brother and Jordan getting in trouble.

June 6, 2010

Dear Bryan,

I hate to even write to you when I'm feeling this down, but my heart is so heavy. And right about now if I could just lock myself in my room and scream and throw stuff, I would! The day started off great. We got up early for church and had time to eat breakfast, and got to Sunday school on time. The lesson was right on target for what's going on in my life: can you trust God? So I left church feeling good and made lunch for the kids. Then I got a text message from my future landlord and ex coworker. She is missing two rings and wanted to know if the kids accidentally grabbed them or something. My heart sank and I prayed that the last two rings that Jordan found where not her rings. I knew the first ring was found in the grocery store since I witnessed that. Well, she sent me a description, and sure enough, the rings Jordan gave me for my birthday were her rings! Words can't describe the anger, shame, disappointment I'm feeling. Even after I asked him repeatedly he denied it and said he found them outside, until she came to the house and identified them and he finally admitted it. The fact that he went through such an elaborate story about finding the first then going out in the rain and finding the last one a few days later. He put that much effort into lying to my face! So I told her to press charges, and she was, like, am I sure. I told her yes because if he steals now with no serious consequence he'll do it again or graduate to more serious crimes. I just want to understand why he did it! Jordan knows my house was burglarized twice before he was born, and I told him how violated I felt. And this guy I was dating stole jewelry from me (luckily I got it back from the girlfriend—long story, different letter) and Jordan remembers that. So to know from my story how that feels and do it to someone else and possibly compromise our new rental situation is just too much to deal with.

Then on top of all this, I go online later to file my weekly unemployment and the message came back that my benefit year has ended so I won't get benefits this week. And I still have not paid June's rent, nor have the money to do so. So this whole day goes back to the Sunday school lesson—can I trust God? All I can do is pray because he will make a way out of no way. I just keep asking myself how did I get here and what did I do (am doing) wrong? I was actually going to write you a letter today anyway because I kind of feel like I should tell you the final straw, which really wasn't anything specific. It was more like you said, how it's insane to keep doing the same thing and expect different results.

A few years ago, before I moved to North Carolina, when Que was still with Wanda and I had recently ended things with Donald, we were talking and I had always told him I wanted a third child. So Que said if in X number of years if we both are still single he wouldn't mind giving me my third baby. I didn't take him very serious but kept it in the back of my mind. So after I moved and then he and Wanda so-called broke up, and prior to me spending the summer of '08 in Buffalo, we started getting close (long distance) and decided on his next visit we try to get pregnant. That was May '08. But when he came I was having second thoughts and told him with the distance maybe we should wait. So I spent $50 on Plan B, which is a pill that prevents fertilization in case birth control fails, so it's not an abortion pill. So fast forward to the disastrous summer in Buffalo and my disastrous second year teaching at Devonshire. Around fall of '09 we started talking on the phone a lot, like, literally all day long while he was at work since they were allowed to wear Bluetooth headsets at work. I went home to visit right after Christmas and had a few weak flesh moments and stirred up feelings again, especially about wanting more kids. After going back to North Carolina, we were talking about the baby thing again and I went back and forth so much, like, the kids would all have the same dad, I'm getting older, not meeting anyone. But then I was thinking why am I settling. I may still meet someone. If I don't have any more kids, it's not the end of the world since I have two beautiful children already. And in the summer of '08 didn't I pray for God to give me a sign if he was the one? And I found out he had a child on the way and was still with his ex!

But in the end, I ignored my brain and God's sign and we agreed on the next visit (end of January) we would officially try to get pregnant. In February I found out I was pregnant, and I was so happy to be having a baby but feeling doubtful about the situation. I didn't know if I could separate the two issues and would fall for him again or just keep it as a parenting relationship only. I felt like I deserved more. Why can't I have the baby and the man too??? But did I want him was also on my mind. Then in March I started spotting, then the spotting turned into a miscarriage. I was very sad but the sorrow turned into relief when I realized all of the heartache and grief that I would have put myself through having a third child and doing it alone! He's in Buffalo and I'm in Charlotte, and I would be a single mom of three, unemployed, and pissed at myself for thinking a third baby with Que was a good idea!

So he was thinking we should try again, then it hit me. This is insane! He is not going to change, so I basically told him it was all over! When he comes to Charlotte he needs to stay at a hotel, and when I go to Buffalo I won't be staying with him. I had asked him after the miscarriage if he saw a future with me and he said I don't know, so I told him if it wasn't clear by now after all these years that means it's 100 percent over and I'm not wasting time anymore. According to him it would be a nice thought but he can't say for sure, and I say anything you feel is worth the effort you work toward. So I finally understood after all these years all those sayings: "why buy the cow when you can get the milk for free"; "if nothing changes, nothing changes"; "people only do what you allow them to do." So I told him I'm done and I meant it, and I felt such a huge weight lifted off me! Having that miscarriage was really an eye-opener and God's way of <u>again</u> telling me not to compromise and settle for just being a baby mama. That yes, I can have the husband and another child and a man to be there for me 100 percent.

I don't know what you will think about me after this, but I want to be <u>open</u> and <u>honest</u>. And Brooklyn had given me your address many months before my first letter to you, but I didn't want to write you until I was sure I could let go of Que. Only a very small handful of people even know I had been pregnant by Que, of all people because I think I was ashamed. Like, how dumb can you be? My mom would have freaked! So if we can get past this, I'm sure we can conquer anything. But again, I want you to know exactly who you are dealing with. I've been hurt, but it's a learning process. And I wish there'd been more time since things officially ended with Que, but I can't change that. I would just continue earning your trust, and I need you to start opening up more to me. I feel like your letters answer my questions but I need more details about you. What are your favorite TV shows? Book? What games did you play as a child? How old were you with your first kiss? What girl broke your heart? Did you play sports in high school? Were you the class clown or jock? What do you like to cook? Favorite song, favorite actor, favorite holiday? Halloween is mine!

No, you don't have to answer all of these questions in one letter. I just want to know you on a deeper level. I'm a natural writer and very detailed in my writing, almost like a storyteller, and I don't expect you to be the exact same way. But those questions are just some ideas to get you started! Tomorrow, first thing in the morning, I'm going to Crisis Assistance Ministry to get help with the rent. A friend told me about them but you got to be in line early, like, 6:30 a.m., and it's getting late. I'm praying they can pay my rent because my mom is the last person I'm calling. But that's ammunition for her to tell me to move my broke ass home! LOL.

Again, I apologize for a letter of bad news, but if we were in person I'd be crying on your nice, muscular shoulder! I'm so mentally exhausted and I need some beauty rest, so I'll say goodnight for now. This should be your third letter in a week, lucky you!

Wishing I could be in your arms,
Janae James
xoxoxoxo

June 7, 2010

Hi Janae,

How are you? I'm pretty good, considering the last couple of letters I've received from you and the questions that finally came about. But before I get to that, I'm going to answer your letters in order, like I always do, as it's only fitting that I do that before I give you the realest shit I ever told anyone! I'm sorry to hear that the kids are bickering, but that's only unconditional love shown between the two that we all went through, so don't read into more than it is. And sometimes our first love is the wrong title 'cuz a lot of times it be our first infatuation. For one, you have to learn love and experience love to the fullest 'cuz faking an orgasm is not love. It's a feeling that passes every fleeting moment after the act, but can you transform that to everything in life with that not being the main focal point? Can you stimulate each other's intellect? But before I get too deep, it will take more letters than one to fully indulge on that subject 'cuz I know we have both been burnt a great deal of our life. That's why I feel I know you better than you think. It gets deeper later!

    That's good you have a long work history 'cuz you never struck me as a lazy person, and that's definitely a plus. And I'm pretty sure that work ethic will carry over to the kids 'cuz by them seeing Mommy making something out of nothing, that will give them the drive to be a success, as well as a motivator! I'm praying for you to get that teaching job 'cuz I see that's what you yearn to do and I see the fire in your writing when you expand on your favorite subjects.

    That's very shocking to hear about Jordan, especially the potential he has to do amazing things with his craft. And that's not a man thing 'cuz he gets his father the utmost respect. And this is just my opinion, but time may be telling a clue of what he wants to hear instead of telling him what's right and wrong. Maybe you have to try another approach with taking things away that he loves to partake in or do every day! Also, the last thing you want to do is try and compete with his father 'cuz that will cause destruction all around the board. And don't let Que's actions piss you off either 'cuz then he winds up causing you to think of compromising on things you said you were done with. And you're not venting to me, you're sharing with me and seeking advice on life dilemmas that I happen to be seasoned and well-versed on different experiences. So don't say you're sorry 'cuz I don't feel offended. Yes, God will bring you through, only if you believe and put in that work!

The next day

If I'm the absolute sweetest man you've met, you're my reflection 'cuz you're sweeter in ways that I pray God allows me to show you. I'm glad you enjoyed your card. I might not have made it but my ideas were put into the drawing, except the *girl* part, which I've explained. I'm glad I made your day eventful. As far as Jordan's graduation card, no problem. Just give me a second and that will be done, and Justine's too! And we'll have that tattoo made for you also.

And no, you are not overreacting when it comes to your cousin. You have to realize that everyone doesn't have gratitude in their system. It's a learned feeling that everyone can't or won't ever comprehend, no matter how hard one tries. Let me say this also. No matter what, just 'cuz you do the right thing and you have caring in your blood, never think or feel people are obligated to do something for you 'cuz you did something for them. Either they are going to 'cuz they want to or they're not, and that goes for family or friends! Remember a couple of letters ago I told you people see other people with potential and try and sabotage that person, or a set of people instead of uplifting them and backing them in their endeavors in life they hate, whether it be financially, emotionally, spiritually, or mentally. And hate is not racial. It comes in all shapes, colors, and sizes. And it's universal as well as local!

I'm happy to hear the good fortune that Jordan has come across. That's very unheard of to find all those rings consecutively, but not impossible. So maybe he'll get a little more than $30 for then. And the numbers at the end of the card is to make it authentic, I guess, and paper rose is his signature. But I am thinking about a tattoo designing business 'cuz I can draw a little when the feeling hits me, but not too often.

Night time

You were not being a brat about not writing and holding out on me. Sure, you have envelopes, stamps, etc., but when you write, I enjoy your literature 'cuz you paint a picture I drew before in some shape or fashion. And I'm glad you didn't take offense to the word *girl* on the card, and yes, you are all woman. I wouldn't have it any other way. Please don't refrain from reading my letters when you get them 'cuz they may help you make the right decision on any particular situation that presents itself at that moment. I tried to prolong reading your letters but it never works 'cuz as soon as I get them I can't wait to see the directions life has taken you on that time of day or week, and your experiences with what your kids have done scholastically—if it's such a word, LOL.

I'm glad you savor my words 'cuz they are serious and real 'cuz I hate fake! Yes, I would love North Carolina in many ways, and driving wouldn't be a problem. You have to remember, young boys grow in spurts, so him sleeping is healthy. When he doesn't sleep, then you should worry! It's good you're willing to take a leap of faith, and I'm liking you more and more also. I know waiting will be hard, but what in life isn't hard? Only thing easy in life is not working hard for what you want out of life. I'm not worried about you meeting anyone 'cuz everyone has choices and those choices most times shape your future. I can't wait to see you either, hug you, talk to you, look you in your eyes.

I'm a baritone. We'll see if you can sing 'cuz I'm going to put you on the spot! It's good that you don't tease Justine 'cuz that could mess her self-esteem up, which would lead to other issues. And school should be in session year-round. There is no limit to knowledge or teaching, and the only thing defeating about being a single parent is when you stop learning, so just keep leading and teaching in that order. For you to lead them, you have to be an outstanding teacher who leads by example.

The atmosphere here is 80 percent mental 20 percent immersion, meaning if you can't think, then you will become the environment—something I refuse to do. I know how to move in a room full of vultures, and yes, I'm a strong man and up-front. But some days are better than others, especially with you dealing with so many different attitudes and belief systems. And please stop saying you're sorry about bringing up certain things. How will I know you and about you if you don't bring up negative and positive? And I'm glad your family overcame it. Yes, I drink alcohol. I like white wines, daiquiris, and an occasional beer. I don't get drunk, I get nice. Tipsy at most, but always in control! I'm proud of you for your latest accomplishments you've made with your truth. And no one's going to put in the type of work you're doing without wanting accolades, without doing the groundwork. Success is a twenty-four-hour job that only has few employees!

Well, girlfriend, I'm not going to keep this letter away from its resting place so I may start on the letter you've been waiting on. I pray you do dream about me because I definitely dream about us. And don't worry about being a brat 'cuz that means more letters!

Dreaming of you also,
Bryan Edwards

PS: It's one in the morning, so I'm about to start that letter. Can't sleep. Hope you are! Also, I'll be waiting for those pictures you promised.

June 8, 2010

Hi Bryan,

I hope you are feeling in good spirits today. I'm sure my last letter put a damper on your mood, so no bad news in this one! Well, I went to crisis Ministries and they are giving me $400 toward my rent, which is great but I'm still short. I have three heads to braid, which should be $150, so I just have to come up with $150 more. I've been trying to get through to unemployment for two days, but the lines are always tied up. Going to food stamps in the morning and still applying for jobs. Today was Jordan's graduation and that was nice, then this evening was the last Girl Scout meeting at Space Cadets. Jordan of course, did not go since he's on punishment for the month. He seems to be doing better. He wrote a letter to Kathryn on his own to apologize to her. He wrote me another letter apologizing. And he's writing a letter to you! Justine is writing a letter to you! Obviously, they both see me writing a lot of letters to you and want to know more about who has captured my attention. And the mailbox runs. But Jordan has some questions, and I hope they are not offensive to you. He also is drawing you a picture, so I hope you enjoy both.

Fell asleep

Wow, this is officially the shortest letter I've written to you so far, but I've had so much to say in the last three. It's morning now and the kids just left for school, so now I'm off to Social Services, and as usual I bring copies of my résumé with me when I go places just in case! I'll be thinking of you the whole time I'm there to keep a smile on my face! I hope you like his picture. Jordan is very good with a ruler, and I can't wait until he takes mechanical drawing classes in high school. He whipped this picture up in no time, so he will be a beast when he's older! Okay, time for me to be out. I'll be looking for your next correspondence!

Sincerely yours,
Janae
xoxoxo

June 8, 2010

Hey Sweetness,

    Yes, I have had a great week this week so, far barring any disappointments. You say me and the kids are the only ones that mailed cards, are you sure you're not dissatisfied that someone that used to give cards or whatever didn't this year? And yes, you're in the mid-thirties but with you working out, yes, you will continue to look like a fine bottle of wine, thick in all the right places. Very sorry to hear Jordan didn't pass his exam. You should basically test his reading level yourself to see if he needs additional help that you don't know of. That's cool he wants to play an instrument. You should encourage that for the simple fact that he has to read music, so that will also help his reading and comprehension.

    Now, the question at hand. I'm locked up for rape in the first degree, and yes, I will have to register as an offender. And I don't have to keep a distance from children. That's for pedophiles and people that commit crimes against children (<u>not me</u>), and no relationship would ever be compromised. And before that would happen, I would man up and gracefully bow out. But that won't be the case, I pray. And I feel slighted that you would say that you liked me more than you should considering it's only been two months. Now we've moved to a phase of measuring emotions (equating, so to speak) with months? I'll tell you what I won't do, and that is put a cap or a time line on my emotions for you. I'll be open. I won't hold back unless you deem otherwise. And no, I don't like you 'cuz of a lack of options. For one, I'm not a charity case, nor do I care to be thought of as one. And I'll always have the option to want better, as well as choices. And my choice was to build a foundation with you that would blossom into something that can't be measured. Was I wrong? And are you sure I'm not being compared to your past relationships in some way? And of course I exceed your expectations 'cuz I know what it is to be shitted on, taken for granted, lied to, and betrayed. And you should be used to a man like me being considerate 'cuz I was grown from a different cloth and raised good. And through trial and error and my comprehension, was comprehended! Plus, I have a sister and daughters that I hold in high esteem. For me not to treat a woman like a queen would be a curse! And don't appreciate me being considerate. Instead, clutch it and embrace it

Now for the detailed account of why I'm in here. I was a drug dealer, a college student, a boyfriend/baby daddy with one foot in the church. I was in the street a lot, getting major money selling crack, partying, traveling to different cities, and going nowhere fast!

I went to a house party with two of my cousins that had came in town for the weekend. Crazy part was I didn't even want to go cuz I was trying to hit the mall first to buy something new for the party and after visiting family all day we ain't have time. So we showed up to the set and half the folks there was already pissy drunk but I peeped this chick Veronica that I wanted to holla at back in the day but I knew my mans Kevin had messed with her back then. But my man wasn't there so I was like whatever I'm shooting my shot! What I didn't know was Kev's boy Chris was at the party and saw me and shorty hugged up all night. We slid out early because she said her crib was five minutes away. Got back to her house and we smashed, then went right back to the party. What she didn't mention was that her and Kev had a kid together so they was on again off again (and at that time they was definitely ON. But I hadn't seen Kev in years. He went to the Air Force after high school and we wasn't tight like that for me to keep up with what he had going on.

So the nigga Chris told Kev that he saw me and his shorty dip and come back together like 30 minutes later. Kev showed up and pressed Veronica asking where the fuck she went and why was she with that nigga Jarelle and was going upside her head outside. But me and my cousins were already gone when he got there. So I'm back home in bed and my pager go off, it's Veronica. I call her and she talking about she ready for round two and want me to come throught. So you already know I was on it, so I got dressed and borrowed my grandfathers car and went to her house. I pull up and it's two cop cars out there with the lights on. I'm thinking oh shit what happened that fast. I get out the car and the one officer was like are you Bryan Edwards? I was still drunk from the party so I'm not as quick on my feet so I answered yes. Next thing you know them muthafuckers reading me my rights and handcuffing me talking about you're under arrest for the rape of Veronica Sampson! This bitch done told her man that I had a gun to her and forced her to her house and raped her! So I was arrested and sat in jail until the trial like seven months later.

Now, mind you, the medical report showed no signs of forcible intercourse—no tearing or nothing consisting of rape. So they tried to offer me four years if I plead. I went to trial and lost, and received twelve and a half to twenty-five years. My mother, sister, grandmother sat through the whole trial. When they were deliberating, they were asking me where I wanted to go eat 'cuz everyone knew I was innocent. Then they came back with guilty. I literally got fucked. Money gone, so-called people that love me also. Only people that stayed true were my sister, mother, and grandparents.

So there you have it. You're the only person outside my family that knows the real deal. And that there is the realest and truest shit I wrote so there will never be unanswered questions of what I'm in jail for!

Well, it's 3:30 a.m. And I hate to relive that, but honest and open is what our relationship stands on. So it's bedtime for me. May God continue to bless and keep you. And with this, I pray our relation continues to grow!

Yours truly,
Bryan Edwards

PS: I haven't done this much writing in one night since school!

June 9, 2010

Dearest Bryan,

I'm always amazed at how wonderful God is. And just when things seem like they can't get any worse, he makes everything alright! I just finished reading your short letter, so that was a nice thing to receive after all the negativity that's been going on. The enemy has been working overtime. That's why I'm so grateful that God is an on-time God. Well, after I wrote my last letter to you this morning I went to the food stamp office. I was in and out within forty-five minutes! Since I had gone to Crisis Ministry, they linked their files with Social Services, so my info was already there and clearly I have no income, so I was approved and will get my card and stamps within seven days. They're ass backward in the South, so you don't get your card right away and your benefits. So I will get $525, which is awesome! Then I just kept feeling like something wasn't right with unemployment, so I went in person to the Albemarle Road office instead of Monroe Road. Told the guy the situation, he punched in some numbers and told me I should be able to file tomorrow (Thursday) and the money should be there Friday. Just that simple! But the first guy on Monday was being lazy, I guess, and didn't want to figure out why my benefits stopped. But my benefit year doesn't end until June 19, so I should have gotten three more weeks. But I feel so much better and just thanking the Lord for working it all out! To answer my question from a few letters back, yes, I can trust God!

Right now I'm supposed to be braiding Monica's hair but as you see I'm writing you and watching *House Party*. Remember that? Love that movie, brings back early nineties fashion memories. So last night at Space Cadets with my Girl Scouts, Monica couldn't decide whether she wanted microbraids (done by me) or invisible braids, which I can't do so she would go to the shop. She kept going back and forth, and me trying to get my hustle on talked her into micros. Remember this was before going to unemployment, so I was really depending on her money. She was supposed to come at 1:00 p.m. today. I ran into her at the food stamp office (she's a social worker) and she says she changed her mind and wants the invisible braids! I was pissed because I would now have to come up with $230 instead of $150 more for rent! That's what I mean about people being serious. When you really want your hair done, you will get it done. But I gave my number to another woman at the food stamp office, so yes, I'm still trying to get them dollars! And I know I will find a teaching job. I haven't given up. And after the Lord just blessed me with a way to pay my rent, I don't doubt the Lord's ability.

As far as I know Monica is still bringing the girls over on Friday to get their hair done because they're going to Florida next week. And after seeing her daughter here two more Girl Scout parents want me to braid their girls' hair, but no appointments made so far, so we'll see. I like doing little girls' hair because I can get creative. Tonight I'll be going to Zumba since I didn't work out yesterday from all my errands. Tomorrow is my Pampered Chef party, so we'll see how many people coming. Four said yes, so they better not play me! And my cousin can't come but she said she will order online. I hate when people don't reply at all. At least they know you can't come. I invited eighteen but the hostess told me usually only 25 percent of invitees come. If I can make a little change on the side, that works. Okay, I'm about to get my workout clothes on and go to the gym. I'll finish when I get back.

Awesome workout tonight. My favorite part of Zumba is the Latin music. One of my goals this summer is to officially become bilingual and learn Spanish. I literally can read Spanish and speak it slowly, but you need to immerse yourself in it to be fluent. And I took Spanish from fifth grade to tenth grade, then freshman year in college. Charlotte has a large Hispanic population, so as far as getting a job, a lot of postings either require it or highly recommend it. So I'll be watching channel 65 and listening to La Raza 106.1.

Tomorrow I don't have anything planned for the day, and I hate to buy a lot of refreshments for just two or three people to come. I just sent emails and text reminders, so it will be interesting to see who comes. And last day of school finally. Jordan got the Shining Lion award this morning. He was so happy. Basically, a teacher can pick a student for various reasons to get the award, and the child gets to go on the school morning news and the principal reads the award and congratulates them. Justine received two this year, and Jordan just figured he'd never get one and he said he didn't care anyway. You know how kids do! So today he comes home and was, like, "I have good news." He was so proud, and I guess it showed him that his teacher doesn't hate him after all. It meant a lot to him, and his behavior has been great even though it's only been a few days since he was busted. Now I'm getting text messages from ladies saying they can't come. Idiots could have responded no to the email invite so I wouldn't be wasting my time! My cousin texted me that she has to go to court for an incident with her child getting in trouble at school. Kids don't realize the consequences of their actions! I used to feel so guilty because I blamed myself for not having a man in Jordan's life regularly and that was why he misbehaves, but she is married and her child still cuts up with two parents. I'm always trying to show Jordan positive things, and Justine. Like we'll drive around to the rich neighborhoods and I tell them that they can have a house like that with hard work. And I showed them the negative, like if you make bad choices or just a sub, mediocre one, then that's the life you live. Will be going to the library a lot this summer too. I love reading. I wish he had my desire to read. There's this book called *The Pact* about three young black men who promised to help each other get through college and medical school despite the obstacles, and in the end they all succeed it. It's an easy read that my neighbor let me borrow, so I'm going to have Jordan read it too.

As far as tattoos, I guess I can wait for you when I get it on my lower back. After all, I want you to be the designer! And I only added Que's name two years ago. It originally was just my name, and it's funny. I was going to add Quincy, but at the last minute I told the guy, "Never mind, just put 'Q'." It's getting easier and easier to put him out of my mind, especially the fact that he didn't even call to see if Jordan passed the retest! I'm over the stuff like calling on my birthday and anything to do with just me. But when he gets annoyed or mad with me the kids don't hear from him. I don't even know if he's mad with me, but when I first officially ended things we talked occasionally about nothing. But it doesn't bother me anymore. It is what it is.

Enough about him, I can't wait to shave your head! Honestly, I've never dated a bald guy. Fades, braids, low fro—no baldies. We will have a lot of firsts! And I will spoil you as much as you spoil me. I'm very detail oriented, and always try to do the little things just like you. For example, I dated this guy my freshman year and he had a little studio apartment and no pillows! So I sewed him a pillow by hand and skipped class for two days. The pillow was nice, I must say. And I put a puffy initial on it for his name, and this ungrateful MF said I should have put a different initial for his nickname. I know a man like you would have appreciated any letter I chose! Oh, and I'm a good (great) cook also, so we will get along great.

I'm getting sleepy now. I think it's like 10:30 or 11:00, so I'm going to call it a night. I'm annoyed because my box of envelopes got wet and they all sealed, so I got to get more. This morning (tomorrow) I actually have nothing scheduled, so I can get the kids on the bus and enjoy my last before summer vacation starts.

I know I said I need to go but it's almost like not wanting to hang up. I just keep writing. I want to hear your voice so bad. Brooklyn is not good at describing, LOL! Okay, for real getting very sleepy. I will be thinking of you. FYI, your name is already on my heart, mind, and spirit!

Yours truly,
Janae James

June 10, 2010

Hello Sweetheart,

I hope I have made up for skipping out on those letters to you. I think I have written you every day this week.

Well, the last day of school is finally done, and my Pampered Chef party is done also. It wasn't a huge success. Three guests came though I invited twenty total, and my cousin came after all. The food was really good. She basically cooked three pounds of ground turkey with fresh onions and garlic, then divided it into three portions: one for the turkey stroganoff and the other two for tacos and sloppy joes to be frozen. It's like a Tupperware party but with cooking and recipes. And I had three glasses of wine, so I'm really sleepy but I wanted to at least start this letter to you, then finish it tomorrow and mail it on Saturday.

Supposed to be braiding the two little girls' hair tomorrow. Wonder if she will cancel their hair! It was so hot today, like, in the nineties! So I walked to the mailbox, only to see the mailman still putting mail in. So I went back home in that dreadful humidity and sent the kids an hour later after they came home. I was like, "Aw man, no letter from my boo!" I don't know exactly what this feeling is, but all I know is I think about you <u>all the time</u>. I'm very much in like with you!

Fell asleep

6/11/10

Happy Friday! Wide awake at seven on the first day of summer vacation. But even when I used to go to the club and be out very late I could never sleep past nine or ten. I literally get headaches if I spend too much time sleeping. I hope you slept good and had a good dream! Do you snore? I don't, but sometimes I've been known to talk in my sleep, more like mumbling.

I'm wondering if Monica is still bringing her girls this morning. If I don't hear from her by nine then I'll be calling. I'm very annoyed at the people who didn't respond to my invite or even attempt to call! Very rude, and my one former coworker owes me since I have gone to two of her functions.

Oh, speaking of Monica, she just called, so her husband will be bringing the girls shortly. Justine is still asleep, but I know she will be thrilled to have company today. Jordan is handling his punishment pretty well, but yesterday his cousins were over and my company. And this apartment is so tiny, there really wasn't anywhere to send him, so he kind of got a break. But today he's back in the room, and the girls will be out in the living room with me. It's going to be harder for him now with school out and the temps in the nineties but can't go to the pool. I would love if you could write him once in a while from an encouraging male point of view. I haven't heard from Quincy in like three weeks, I guess he has an attitude because he asked were we coming for the summer and I said no. No gas money, and I just don't feel like spending twenty hours round trip in a hot ass car with no AC. He and my parents have literally been spoiled with me always driving up to bring the kids to them since I've made that drive about ten times! My parents have not been here ever, and Que has come a decent amount. But if they really want to see their kids/grandkids they know what to do!

So have you been working on my tattoo design? It's going to be hard waiting a year to get that one! In the meantime, imma get a dragonfly somewhere. I tried to get my tattoos and places that are not seen in the professional workplace but seen when I wear tank tops or lower cut shirts. Except the one on my foot is visible. I still remember the pain from that one! I don't know if I'll ever get it touched up unless you are there to hold my hand! Oh, my girls are here, so I'll end this letter for now and probably start a new one this evening. My unemployment is supposed to be on my card today, and I'm sure it will because God has been so amazing. Well, my dear Jarelle, I'll be chatting with you later!

Sincerely yours,
Janae

June 12, 2010

Good morning,

I hope you have been smiling more with all the letters I have been sending. My goal is to constantly keep your mind off your current location and keep it focused on our future. I've been up since a little before 7:00 a.m. on a Saturday. I've just accepted that comes with getting older! Waking up early is cool when I beat the kids though, since I get that quiet time to have a cup of tea or watch a little TV thinking about you. I baked chocolate chip cookies for my neighbor. She wants it for a friend of hers in the military overseas. She said her oven keeps burning baked goods, and asked how much I would charge. I told her to just buy the ingredients—sugar, brown sugar, flour, *butter*. She bought Blue Bonnet margarine, which to me is a no-no for baking. But I figured it would work.

Since I was up so early I baked them this morning and had made the dough last night. It was too mushy even after sitting all night in the fridge, so about three dozen came out pretty good but flatter than I like. The rest either burned a little or just didn't look pretty to me, and when I cook and bake presentation is important to me! It's going to be in the mid-nineties again, and I wasn't trying to have that oven on when it's too hot!

So I told the kids we can crumble up the bad ones with ice cream to make blizzards. They are playing cards right now, go fish, and Jordan just taught her speed. I play speed, tunk, rummy, and spades. Do you play? I never learned how to play poker, but I want to learn one day. While I was baking I came up with a great brainstorm. I live near tons of businesses and I'm going to pitch the idea to the managers for me to sell baked goods and sandwiches to the employees since I will have food stamps to buy a little extra food. And I make *pastelitos*, not sure if you've had those. It's like the Puerto Rican version of Jamaican beef patty, and the ones I've tasted in Charlotte can't touch mine! Do you remember Chat and Chews in Buffalo? Well, they've moved down here to Charlotte, but I haven't gone yet. My cousin went a few months ago. She said it was good. There are so many places I want to take you when you get out.

The mailman is getting on my nerves because he/she comes later and later! It'll be like 4:30, so I'll be hoping all day for a letter. But I'm not blaming you anymore, just keep them coming!

This weekend is the Taste of Charlotte and also the *Karate Kid* has come out. I really want to see it, and I'd like to go to the Taste of Charlotte but it's going to be so hot, then trying to find parking. My friend Diedra wants us to go on Sunday around five. She was a tutor at my school and was supposed to help me in math for the last thirty minutes of class. She will come on time but then go to the bathroom, talk on her phone, etc. She was laid off along with the rest of the tutors.

I had two interviews at Stonewall Jackson Detention Center to be a science teacher, and both went great. I thought I had the job! Weeks passed and they called for my references. I used Diedra since she saw me in the class daily and always agreed that Devonshire did me wrong. I also used Brooklyn, my mentor at Devonshire, who was also on my fourth-grade team and we were cool, and my cousin Nicole. They talked to Brooklyn and I know she gave me an awesome review. Nicole never got a call. My coworkers said they left her a voice mail and she returned the call but they never called back. And they spoke to Diedra. Of course she said she gave me an excellent review, but a week later I got the denial letter in the mail. Diedra seems to think my other coworker really did speak to them and badmouthed me just because she doesn't like her. But honestly, I really don't know, but I know you need excellent classroom management to work in a detention center. So I look at the situation as a blessing because God has the right job in mind for me, and that would have been a forty-minute commute and challenging.

I will never know if Diedra's reference cost me the job, but I have mixed feelings about it. We are both laid off, and she knows money is tight but always calls to see if I want to go out to breakfast or lunch. I always turn her down, but twice I let her pay since she was so persistent. I had to check her twice because she was rude to the clerk in Walmart and a waitress once for no reason. She did come to my Pampered Chef party, and at the party she made sure she asked if she could come over the next day because she needed help with her homework. That was another thing I had to put a stop to several months back. She would call and ask me general questions on her homework (she's in school for her PhD), and next thing you know I done did her homework. So I told her, "It's your degree! You do it." So she figured that an order equals homework help! But on the other hand, she has been very resourceful as far as unemployment questions, suggesting places to apply, always telling me to trust God when I'm feeling down.

Well, I'm going to finally get dressed and we're going to go to the thrift store, see if I can find Justine some summer dresses. She has grown so much this year. And I find good name-brand stuff there—Juicy Couture, Gap, Ralph Lauren, Talbot—but you just have to take your time and search. They both need shoes, so we'll probably go to the shoe store somewhere also. So hopefully I will have mail from you since I haven't had any in two whole days! Oh wait, not two, three! It will be four if I don't have anything today, then I'd have to wait all the way until Monday. Torture. So bye for now with sweet thoughts of you!

Janae

June 13, 2010

Good morning,

Right back at you. Before I go on this journey with you mentally, I pray I didn't scare you away with my last letter. If it appeared that I was edgy, it was 'cuz I don't like visiting that time in my life. I don't say woe is me, but why me? What did I do to deserve to be set up and treated like that? Was it the money? The position I possessed? The envy? To this day, after fifteen years, I still haven't received my answer. Don't get me wrong, I wasn't an angel but I never was a beast either. I would have gladly given up everything just not to be done dirty. But don't feel sorry for me please, now that you know the deal. I don't need charity, just love, loyalty, and prayer!

Moving along, when I said if sex happens early things don't go right, it's 'cuz sometimes it's done for the wrong reasons. On the other hand if you do it early then this should be the person you plan on doing it with on a regular basis! Now see, you said you would never compare me, but on the other note you're telling me you've been sold a dream and was played in the end for being intimate too soon. For one, I haven't met you face-to-face yet, so that doesn't pertain to me. Second, I don't sell dreams. I make dreams reality, to where you think I'm too good to be real, but I am. Another thing, Ms. Thang, I am too old for games, and people tend to cheat when they play games! I'm not used to losing in any aspect of life, and you shouldn't be either. And I only speak on what you've told me so far about your relationships in the past. You must learn from them and move on or you won't honestly let me give you what you need, and that's unconditional love, honesty, and loyalty—something you haven't had in a very long time and I feel you deserve it.

And I am a real man that was taught by good women—grandmother, mother, and aunts. Sure, I slipped in my younger years 'cuz I thought I knew everything and I didn't know shit, just the basics! To answer your question, yes, I am the one and the last one, but the ball is in your court. What you going to do, shoot or pass? I'm starting to really give you my all, please, please don't hurt me, Janae. And yes, I'm seven hundred miles away but that's only temporary, not permanent. So please don't let that be your excuse!

You have to eat more than a Nutri-Grain bar in this heat. You also are not drinking enough fluids, so please take care of yourself 'cuz you don't want a stroke. And yes, envy does run through blood 'cuz I have witnessed it firsthand and it's ugly. And we won't probably look good together, we will look great together. And I don't care who you tell 'cuz only you and I can make or break, not someone's opinion or remarks. And you should change your diet 'cuz you don't need a lot of the stuff you're eating anyway. And that's good you're toned, and please don't lose the hip. Because from what I see from the pictures (few) you sent me, they are shaped right, no complaints here. LOL.

And you say you're really curious about what I plan to give you. Well, I tell you this. I believe in giving my woman (wife) every possible love a woman cherishes so that she will never stray or be led astray. And you wouldn't be losing control, we would be controlling each other. And you'll lose your breath 'cuz I'll take my time making love to you from head to toe. Because every part of your body deserves love, I'll leave no skin untouched! And please don't take your mind off me 'cuz I haven't stopped thinking about you from day one. I'm hooked, line and sinker. You don't need to be scared to fall for me too fast 'cuz I'm yours already. I'm serious. I prayed for you, and God don't make mistakes. So please don't hope that 'cuz you deserve it—we deserve it! And no, there's no such thing as too fast. If you want it, go for it, don't play with it! And you don't have to wonder if I feel the same way. You have me, woman, without sex. LOL.

Well, I'm going to leave for now in order for me to get started on your last letter. Oh, well, that is a hell of a letter by the way. I had to sit down after I read it. You trying to push me away? Not going to happen.

So I'll end this with may you continue to think of me, and I'll be happily awaiting your next letter.

Yours 4 real!
Bryan

PS: Stay strong. I'm praying for you all!

June 13, 2010

Hi Ms. Short Letter,

I know you better not ever say anything about a short letter with the little letter you just sent me with Jordan's letter. And then you have the nerve to tell him that I don't write enough. That hurt. But you know me, I brushed my shoulder off and I got to writing cuz I don't ever want you to say I lack in any area when it has to do with us 'cuz I see someone else is counting on me too. And that's some special shit— 'cuz I love responsibility and love watering a seed and watching it grow!

So whose idea was it for a Justine to write me? 'Cuz that was real powerful. It touched a real soft spot in my heart 'cuz I would love for my daughters to write, but for some odd reason their mothers forget that we created them, not artificial insemination. But that's a whole other letter and time. And to let you know, I'm built for bad news, so don't worry. Whatever you throw my way, I can handle it. And I think you know that already, and that's what helps you grow also 'cuz you're starting to believe. You don't have to admit it, but I know I feel it. I'm glad to see God working in your favor like I told you he will. All you have to do is believe and keep the faith, and he's going to show you things come together that you thought wouldn't. But you have to do the ground work. Also, that doesn't mean you relax either. Stay on your grind, Mama, 'cuz you still have work to do. And I think it's so sexy to see a woman you dig handle her business and responsibility 'cuz she knows she's got someone rooting for her to win, ME!

And that's good you have some girls lined up to get their hair done. And don't concentrate on the ones that are shaky. Put your focus on those that appreciate your service. And don't be afraid to chase that dollar 'cuz you have kids to feed, and ain't no excuses or dealing with emotions when it comes to that! I'm glad you think about me when you're out and about. That means you're canceling your business and I'm along for the ride. And I always want to keep a smile on your face 'cuz I never want to see you cry or be miserable 'cuz you've had enough of that garbage. Yes, I like Jordan's picture. He has skills, but you must keep him focused on his behavior!

That's sad that the guy at the unemployment office was so lazy that he couldn't even get off his ass to punch some buttons. Those are the times I wish I was home 'cuz that's disrespectful. Playing with people's livelihood is not a good look. But don't wait until something good happens before you say I trust in God 'cuz you have to thank him for the bad times also. It builds character. And please don't get me wrong either. I never said you did that (I can see your lips moving now saying, "I didn't say that. What is he talking about? LOL).

I pray your Pampered Chef party goes as planned. But if it doesn't, don't fret. Just keep on moving. That's just a bump on the road. You must overcome and keep it moving. Remember, the same people that are on top, you will pass once you get to the top. But the only thing is when they are down, you don't kick dirt on them. You just teach them what goes around comes, and then you help them!

That will be a power move for you to learn Spanish 'cuz it's a great deal of work for those who are bilingual. Then you in turn encourage your kids to learn also because times are changing and you must multitask! That's beautiful that Jordan won an award. Maybe that will light a fire under him to get on the ball. He's just trying to find an identity right now, something all young boys go through at his age. So don't read too much into it. What's up with Justine? What's she saying about her mother's love interest? I know she has questions and is curious at the same time.

Their teachers never hated them. It's just as parents we want the best for our children, and when we feel they are not being taught to our expectations, we become somewhat alarmed over nothing (a hint, hint). And although he's only been good a couple of days, still encourage him to keep improving and that you're acknowledging his effort and output. Times are getting crazy where kids only duplicate what they see at home, on the street, movies, videos, and so on. That's why we have to pay more attention to them than when we were kids. That's awesome that you took them to the good and bad parts of town to show them the difference between hard work and being lazy! I've seen the story about those three black men that make it. I think they are doctors or lawyers if I can remember. That would be a good read for Jordan.

And what do you mean you guess you can wait for the tattoo on your lower back? If you want to get it before I get out, do you. I wouldn't be bothered by it. And as far as Que being on your chest, I would really love it if that was made into something else 'cuz I don't want to be kissing another man's name. Can you dig it! I'm not going to even touch on what you wrote about Que not calling 'cuz I addressed that on the letter before this. I'm just waiting on your response, so moving right along.

I can't wait until you're able to shave my head either. I think that's sexy also, as well as painting your woman's toenails. Are you ready for that? Question is, are you ready for me, period. And that's good you haven't dated a baldy. That means I'll be your first in many ways. Are you ready? And I will spoil you even if you don't spoil me. And yes, I'm very detailed with things. And there's no such thing as little, it's as big as your heart in mine, let's let it be!

And I will see how much of a good cook you are. Talk is cheap. The proof is in the pot, LOL! Yes, you must go get some envelopes 'cuz I just got some more. Now I have to go to the store and buy some more stamps. I know what you mean about not wanting to hang up 'cuz I don't want to stop a lot of times myself. I want to hear your voice also. Once you get on your feet moneywise maybe we can talk on the phone 'cuz it's very cheap, like, two or three dollars for like twenty minutes to half an hour a call. 'Cuz they had to lower the rates due to someone filing a lawsuit against them overcharging.

Well, I guess I'm outta here, being that I wrote more than you. Please know that I will be thinking of you also, and know that you had my heart from the first letter. And that's not a line or game. That's some real shit for you. You have my nose wide open!

Yours truly
Bryan Jarelle Edwards
Xoxoxoxo

June 13, 2010

Midnight

Sweetheart,

    I'm sorry about the things you're going through. I can't be there to bear the burden with you. Can you trust God? Because I do I talk to him every day and every night. He's the sole controller over everything, and you have to believe and have faith that he will pull you through. And about the money situation, you have to look at it as God testing you 'cuz he's not going to give you more than you can bear. So just hold on and pray.

    And please don't make no rash decisions. You've come too far to turn back now. Everything's going to work out. Remember, faith will move mountains. Also, don't sit at home pouting either. Get out there and make it happen. You're not a quitter, you're a go-getter. God also loves the person who strives to reach for the skies.

Now to the meat of this letter. I'm not trippin'. I wish you would have told me sooner. I could have handled it, but now that you have I'm still not going nowhere. If that was your best shot, you better change bullets 'cuz that didn't kill me nor will it. Just a little surprised. Are you or were you—or should I say competing with who could have the most babies by Que? And you say in 2009 you had a few flesh moments and stirred up feelings. A flesh moment, mind you, once in a while, not a few. So I'm going to move on. I'm going to ask this for the last time, are you tired of getting used, played, misled? Are you tired of losing? Or have you grown accustomed to these types of emotional feelings? These are questions, not accusations or assumptions. I just need a better understanding. I'm not going to lie and say I'm not scared 'cuz I am. 'Cuz I'm not just going to write you things that I think you want to hear. I'm giving you raw dog, me, no imitation, no movie, no stage play. I'm putting my heart into this, no games. So please be positive this is what you want.

Question, were you relieved that you had a miscarriage 'cuz you didn't have Que as your man? Or was it that you didn't want to have another child and be more attached to the person that you said after thirteen babies you can't do it no more? And when you say when he comes to Charlotte he needs to stay at a hotel, you sound like you're trying to convince me instead of believing what you say. Which is it? You don't sound stable on that note. 'Cuz he's been milking the shit out of you for crazy years, you know the definition for insanity? It's when you continue to do the same thing over and over and over again, thinking it's going to be a different outcome. Open and honest is great if you're trying to build a foundation that concrete, something that water or blood can't break. Are there going to be leaks early? And yes, we are going to get past this. And trust me, I know who I'm dealing with. By you being hurt so much, you allowed someone to continue to attack your self-esteem, thinking that was the norm. And when you seen it wasn't two beautiful children were made by you being mentally abused, you mistake it for love, when in all it was infatuation on what it could be if only . . . That's just my opinion. Please don't take offense to what I'm saying, but I'm not afraid to tell you what I feel!

Now, I'm going to tell you some things about me. My favorite TV shows, any black shows that do with family. *Good Times, Fred Sanford, Jefferson*—and yes, they still come on! Books, I like CIA, mob stories, Assata Shakur, Bible, Koran, and books on Africa. As a child I love football. I went to Sweet Home high school. I had a letter of intent to Ohio State, but the streets were calling and I answered the phone. I transferred to South Park and met my first older woman. She was a senior, I was a sophomore, and she did teach me some things. But that only lasted a year and a half. She left me for someone that she had a son with. Oh well! I can't really say she broke my heart 'cuz I know what it was heading for!

The first girl that broke my heart was a mulatto girl I had in seventh or eighth grade. She was all that and a bag of chips. We did everything together. That's when I had more white friends than black 'cuz I went to Black Rock Academy down Hertel by the waters. She started fucking with a white boy that was two years older than me that we used to drink at his apartment. She tried to hide it, but I found out halfway through eighth grade. It broke my heart. But to get back, I started dating the prettiest girl in the school. The other girl tried to come back but it was too late. I was ready for high school now!

I was a class clown and jock/nerd 'cuz I got good grades too! I played basketball, lacrosse, football, and I was nice too, LOL. I love seafood pastas and chicken wings. And I was raised on fish, definitely a favorite to cook. And I love to bake pound cake and cookies, brownies! My favorite songs, "Piece of My Love" by Guy and "Hey, Mister DJ" by R Kelly and the group he came out with first. Favorite actor, Morgan Freeman. Favorite holiday, Thanksgiving.

Well, that's another level you peeled back, so I pray you don't think I'm holding back. I just want to know if it's real or am I just stoking your curiosity. I can be a storyteller too, but I'd rather be a mind reader.

I hope you made it to Crisis Ministry on time, and let me know what happen when you can. Again, a question, are you mad that Que didn't call about the retests or that he didn't call at all? Just some questions to get you started on your next letter . . . No need to apologize for the bad news 'cuz we'll share both in due time and my shoulder is always yours. All you have to do is reach for me!

Wishing I could be in your arms also,
Bryan K. Edwards

June 14, 2010

Hi Bryan,

Happy Monday to you, it sure was happy for me! Last week was so trying and seven days later things completely turned around by the grace of God. And I got two letters from you, and long letters. I was like OMG! Very nice. I had an interview this afternoon at a summer camp for girls aged five to twelve that focuses on character development. It would be part-time, 6:30 a.m. to 10:30 a.m., so I could leave the kids home. And since I'm allowed $85 allowance with unemployment, it would be extra income to pay down some bills and get the AC fixed in my car! It was ninety-nine degrees today, which is a nightmare in a car with no air! The interview went great and she seemed very interested. And I love their philosophy about the whole program and it being run by two sisters. And it's only five minutes away. I should hear by Friday. It's really dependent on whether they get more girls enrolled so that they can hire two part-time, one full-time, or what. I'd love this job, so I'm trusting God. He knows what's best for me!

Okay, I didn't say I could sing! I said I sound better in a choir. Actually, I thought I had a pretty good voice until I worked in a suburban daycare with little brats! I lost my ability to hit a lot of notes from yelling and or talking loud because I didn't know how to deal with a class full of three- to four-year-olds at the time. I lost my voice a few times, and it's never been the same. To answer your question about the birthday card, no, I'm not disappointed about not receiving one specifically from someone. My parents one, maybe every two to three years. Que has maybe given me two in the twelve years I've known him, when he actually remembers. All I mean is that birthdays are very special to me yet mine is always forgotten or no big deal. My feelings be hurt but not at anyone specific, so I'm making it a point to make my kids' birthday special and my own.

I think you are taking what I said about my feelings for you out of context. I'm trying not to put a time frame on when certain feelings should develop, but it's hard not to. All I'm saying is I'm surprised that I like you so much and have not met you in person. This type of relationship is new for me, so I expected for us to be strictly penpals for the first several months, but I feel much more than that for you. Which is why the thought of building such a solid foundation with communication and growing so attached and to have that possibly taken away because of your conviction scares me. But if you have to register as a sex offender but it won't have any impact on your proximity to children, that would be great. But based on the shady way you were sentenced, you should fight having to register and I'd be willing to help.

I appreciate you sharing your story with me. Wow, it's unbelievable the way our justice system works and how people can do this wrong without a conscience. But it is what it is. And even though that's a crazy tough lesson learned, you're a better man because of it, and I am ready to reap the benefits of that! It was heartbreaking to read but the Lord works in mysterious ways. I'm sure you will be blessed for what you have endured and use your experience as a teaching tool. I don't mean to make it seem like I'm dating you as a charity case and we both have options. I guess I stopped believing in fairy tales and had accepted that I possibly won't get married or have more children. So I often view things as a pessimist because no one has proved me wrong yet. I haven't given up, I'm just trying not to hold anything back from you. And I know you're incomparable, but I've made some bad relationship choices and often feel like an idiot magnet, so I can't just change how I view things overnight. We just have to prove to each other that this relationship can stand the test of time! I understand your point about having sisters and daughters, so you know how you want them to be treated. I look at Que. He has a sister and eight girls yet still makes dumb choices.

You lived in Langfield? You may have met my mom. She worked in the rent office for almost fifteen years and was there when you were. The tenants loved her! She was good at her job. That's how I ended up there. I lived on Oakmont for a few years, Langfield Drive and Eggert Road before I relocated.

I went to the gym today and it was customer appreciation day, so they had vendors and four Carolina Panthers were there. The kids got their autographs. My unemployment was deposited right on time and my food stamp card came. I just thank God because he's always on time. If you weren't where you are I can almost guarantee we would have never met!

Well, I'm a little sleepy now watching—you guessed it, *Golden Girls*! You should be getting pictures around the same time as this letter. I'll be dreaming about you, waiting for your next letter!

Yours always,
Janae

June 16, 2010

Hey Luv,

You're getting better and better with the letters! Feels so good going to the mailbox. I'm having a good week so far. Kids are home all day and doing what they do best: play, argue, play, argue! My parents bought them a Wii and it came yesterday. Justine is also anxious to get a letter from you!

I know I need to improve my diet. It's been a struggle all my life 'cuz I'm an emotional eater. When I'm bored I eat—lonely, angry, frustrated, sad, I eat. It was a coping mechanism as a child, and sadly I have not conquered it yet. And with my life being parallel to a soap opera, I eat a lot of the wrong things. It's an ongoing battle that I will overcome one day. So in the meantime I'm trying to stay active. I get to the gym four to five days a week. I'm not toned yet, I'm working on it! I think I'm way too squishy, so I'm just trying to replace my very high body fat content with muscle. Hopefully by the time you get out I will have reached my goal!

Jordan, Jordan! That boy wants me to have gray hair. I'm in the process of trying to find a mentor for him. There are very few mentor programs for boys. They're all full, with waiting lists. And I will be making an appointment for him to meet with the youth pastor, the same one who baptized him. As for their dad, he doesn't call and talk to them, never really did. The only phone on at the moment is my cell phone. Unless I said to him "hold on, let me put the kids on the phone," they don't talk. He would say, "Tell my babies hi and I love them." He's never been good at communication, and honestly, the kids never just say, "Hey, I want to call Daddy." When we are/were on better terms he would literally all-day call while they were at school and talk to me. If my phone rang and it was him, the kids would just hand the phone to me and say, "It's Daddy," so I would always encourage them to speak to him, answer the phone, and they keep it brief and to the point.

I remember back in, I think, January I was having a hard time with Jordan and how he treated Justine as far as not hitting her back, remembering she is four and a half years younger, playing fair, etc. I told Que I needed him to talk to him. I said this on many occasions, and finally he had <u>one</u> conversation with him that lasted all of three to five minutes. So one day we're on the phone and I tell him about something Jordan did wrong. So Que says Jordan is so selfish and he don't know where he gets that from. So I, "I keep asking you to talk to him because I'm not getting through to him." This fool says, "I did talk to him!" I said, "You have to have more than one conversation!"

But as far as the kids respecting him, I realized that they don't respect him, they <u>fear</u> him. I think as far as whooping his kids he is way too hard on all of them. And even though my kids haven't been whooped in years, they're scared of the potential beat-down! Jordan has said I should whoop harder, then he thinks he will listen more. But I don't want them scared of me, I want their <u>respect</u>. Que pisses me off because he loves to take credit when they get A's and good stuff, and when they mess up he's always quick to say, "They don't get that from me," as if to say it must come from my side!

He actually called a few days ago, saying, "Hey, stranger, haven't heard from you, blah blah blah." So I said, "It's not like you called. And I'm not going to beg you to remember my birthday." So he's like, "Oh, that's right. I'm so sorry. Happy belated birthday." So he asked what's been going on and I give him a general rundown. I didn't tell him Jordan failed the retest, and he didn't ask! So he ended with, "Tell my babies I love them," and said he misses me and same old thing. Then later that day he asked for a sexy pic. We used to do a lot of sexting since we couldn't physically be there, but after my final straw I told him I would not send him any more. So I said, "no more of that, remember?" He replies, "Once in a while is okay!" I said no. It's not because it leads to the same thing, and I left it at that. A

And when I said a few weak-flesh moments in 2009, I was referring to my four-day visit, not spread throughout the year. After our summer of living together we spoke very little, which meant the kids didn't speak to him hardly ever. I went back to Charlotte in August 2008, and he planned a trip in February 2009 for Jordan's birthday and brought some ghetto hood chick, her three kids, and two of his other kids. They stayed in a hotel for those two days, which she paid for. You know how it goes with tax time. He also had the kids for three weeks in the summer because I drove down there in June 2009, so they split their time between my parents and him. He drove them back, and they stopped in Atlanta to visit his sister before Charlotte. He rode with the youngest baby's mom this time, and that's when I met that baby for the first time. They drove straight through that time since they slept in Georgia, but they stayed for maybe fifteen minutes. That was early July and we were civil, but that's all.

So around early October he starts calling me like every day while the kids are in school, and familiar feelings began stirring up. I was supposed to go home to Buffalo for a Halloween, then Thanksgiving—both canceled due to lack of money. So I made it back after Christmas. And that's when we hooked up. And in one of my last letters I explained how the whole pregnancy, etcetera, came about.

So to answer your question, *no*, I was not trying to be the baby mama with the most kids! When I say he has to stay in a hotel when he comes back to Charlotte, I'm not trying to convince you. He has a hard time driving alone for long stretches, so I was just saying on his next trip he can have one of his chicks get a hotel because I'm not letting him stay here. I could easily let him have the couch and I keep my bed, but I want his future visits to be all about spending time with the kids, not me. Even in February 2009 when he came with that girl, the kids said they would be in the room all day while the kids played. So there was no quality time spent. And his night if any of his kids are with him, that's not quality time. So he could be playing the PlayStation while they are doing whatever, but they are not interacting. What boy doesn't want his dad involved on a regular basis? When they made the Pinewood Derby car together back in December, Jordan loved it. I know he needs a positive man in his life.

About the miscarriage, before his visit that made me pregnant, I was having doubts then! I didn't know if I was limiting myself by settling on a baby with him if it would make me latch on to him even tighter and hope for a relationship. Or if I could just be pregnant without wanting more. I talked a lot with Brooklyn, and she kept saying it was two separate issues and that I could have a baby with him and not have a relationship. But I knew it eventually would make me want more. But I thought my biological clock was ticking and if I don't take this chance now I may never have a baby, so I was willing to go through the heartache for the sake of having a baby. There is a reason I want another baby so much, which I will stay for another letter because it's a long story. But when I miscarried my relief was that to me it was God's way of telling me to either wait and I will have another child with the right man or I already have two, and thankfully they are happy and healthy. Plus, the idea of going through a third pregnancy alone, doctor appointments alone, delivery alone.

Am I tired of the same lies, bullshit, deceit, abuse? Of course. And I wish I had had a good relationship at some point prior to this so that I could say I chose a good man at least one time, but I've never had that. I don't count my senior year of high school because my feelings for him were lukewarm at best. I've never had a faithful man, and it's embarrassing to me about the choices I've made about men. I feel like it's a direct reflection of my judgment. Like if I can't even get my personal relationships right, how can I succeed at other things? I don't always feel like that, but hate to admit that sometimes I do! I look at Brooklyn and Robert as inspiration. Sometimes I'm like, Robert just seems too good to be true! Your baby sis has a good man!

I will continue to be honest and open with you like you are with me. I'm falling hard for you and I'm so glad you only have one year left because I don't know how I would be able to take much longer than that! And I'm not trying to scare you off! But honestly, I figured after hearing about my crazy history with Que and my current struggles with Jordan that's a lot to swallow!

I'm about to get ready for Zumba class. I think I'll go a little early and do some treadmill. Did you enjoy the latest picture? That should be more than enough for now, and I hope they get it together soon so I can get some pictures!

Sincerely yours,
Janae

June 16, 2010

Good evening,

    Yes, I've been smiling with all the letters, and it does help keep my mind off my current location. But nothing will stop me from seeing, as well as thinking, about our future. And yes, getting older you tend to not sleep as much because you're busy trying to make your time count. And I feel I should come before tea and TV (LOL). That's just the order you put me in (reading your letter over) 'cuz after I thank God for waking me up, I think about how your day is starting. Are you happy? Are you sad? What's on your mind? And so on. Then I go about my day 'cuz it's a constant obstacle to maneuver around so many speed bumps and abandoned mind frames and attitudes.

    It's not fair that you're baking chocolate chip cookies and I can't eat none. And that was very nice of you to perform that gesture for your neighbor. I thought you said you can bake. You don't use margarine for big things. Let me find out lessons are in order (LOL). And you're eating a lot of sweets and I can't have none. That's not fair is it? I know how to play tonk, rummy. And spades is my all-time favorite. I used to play for money back in the day. Would you be the perfect partner or would you get us stuck? And what is speed? I never heard of that game before. No, I don't know how to play poker. I guess we can learn together.

    And that's a very good idea to pitch that business idea to the businesses, but what's even greater is having some of the things on hand so they will know how serious you are and they can stand for what you'll be selling. I'm with you all the way. When you're thinking, I'm thinking even more. I have heard of *pastelitos* but never had any, but would love to taste them. Yes, I remember Chat and Chews. That chopped burger got a lot of my money, and some! And I would be honored to follow you wherever you lead me. I know it would be worth my while.

Don't get mad at the mailman. Sometimes things are worth waiting on. It's about savoring it when it's received. Something like love. Will you savor mine or will you use it until you feel something appears better? 'Cuz illusions present themselves every day, and you deserve love 360° (meaning full circle). And I want to love you to the point where any man, past or present, will <u>look at you and know for a fact he has no chance, no matter what angle he tries to attempt. So he need not apply because I will overfill your every need and desire!</u>

I know Jordan is on punishment, but don't do so many fun things just for the sake of leaving him out of it 'cuz that will cause resentment, and that could be dangerous to a certain extent. So be careful, Ma!

And just your description of Diedra, I don't like her or her motives and if the kids see it, that should tell you a lot right there. Don't play with a snake and wonder why that snake bit you when you wasn't paying attention, cuz it only does what it was created to do- bite people and things. And I say you don't rely on people that will be good references, but outstanding references! That's your livelihood you're putting in people's hands. Remember I told you envy runs through blood and water, so please keep your blinders off and your microscope on so you can dissect the real shit from the fake shit.

And please forgive the profanity, but you got my heart excited again. Something I thought I would never allow again, considering what I've been through. So I state once again, please, please don't hurt me!

I'm going to touch on this and then I'm going to move on from her. If you think that Diedra was the reason that you didn't get the job and your gut tells you that, then nine times out of ten you're right. And for her to put it on someone you say speaks highly of you, then something's foul. So I hope you make the right decision 'cuz it will affect you if you don't. Remember, don't be around people just for the sake of being. Be around people that have things going for themselves that won't hesitate to see you succeed. Also, it's important to your livelihood!

Moving along, you're right, she definitely won't be at our wedding or at the wedding, period. And you're not scaring me off talking about marriage 'cuz that will make my life come full circle—something I will cherish and take seriously 'cuz I've been done playing games a long time ago! Games is the reason why I'm sitting behind bars now. The question is, are you through being put in game? Brooklyn would definitely be in the wedding, without a doubt! If your friend has someone that's serious about her and she's not willing to wait, she may regret it later on in life. 'Cuz God brings people into each other's lives at the craziest times in order for us to see if we are willing to take a chance on happiness or squander an opportunity that may never come again.

Something I must tell you also, I haven't properly mourned my mother's death yet. I've kind of put it on the side of the brain that they say we don't use! Actually, I'm scared 'cuz it's a lot of things I wanted to talk to her about that I didn't get a chance to. I also want to ask her—actually, I want to scream at her for leaving me before I could get out of this hellhole. But that will never happen, and that's one regret I'll have to live with!

It's not that bad. You're talking about two, three, or four days before you get a letter from me. Stop it, will you. Don't worry, I'm going to do my best right now to stack up on stamps, but you have to be patient because they haven't given me a job yet. I don't have money coming in like I used to. But don't worry, I'll make a way 'cuz I won't resort to hustling. Because that brings too many unwanted problems, and I don't want to do something to somebody over money. And if you haven't noticed, I wrote this whole letter in print 'cuz I'm practicing for when I write Jordan, also to show you I'm versatile in many areas of life.

Well, baby girl, I'm going to close this letter with thoughts of you. Hoping, praying that I made your day with my presence and words of wisdom, as well as understanding. Until I see you in another envelope, may your day be blessed with accomplishments and goals met!

Yours 4 real,
Bryan Jarelle Edwards

PS: Would love to see some pictures! And next time you talk to Brooklyn, tell her I love her and my nieces and nephews, as well as my brother Robert!

June 16, 2010

Hello Sweetness,

    Yes, you have made up for skipping out on the letters. And yes, you have written to me every day this week, but who's keeping count? Not me. I just love giving you food for thought 'cuz if you stay hungry you will never get enough of me!
    I'm sorry to hear your Chef party didn't go as planned, but the success of it is you still got through it. And the people that didn't show up lost out, not you. That just goes to let you know that people's word ain't shit and they can't be counted on, so you lose nothing. And it sounds delicious what was cooked. I wish I could have ate from your fingers and licked them clean! I would love to see you after three glasses of wine. I wonder if you would still be sleepy, or would you be excited? But I'm honored you stayed up to write me a letter 'cuz I haven't been able to sleep in order for you to have as many letters as you send me!
    And it's not that I don't write you right back 'cuz I do. It's just the mail moves slow from jail to you. You see, you get at least two letters every time you do get mail, and that makes my

day, knowing you have something from your boo! And I know you know what this feeling is. It's something you haven't been getting but you crave and deserve at the same time. And I think about you all the time also. That's why I need more pictures, so I can have you for every day of the week! I've very much been in like with you since day one. It's a gut instinct that never lies 'cuz it tells the truth.

And yes, it is summer vacation. And that's good you get up early 'cuz remember, the early bird always gets the worm. I get headaches also if I sleep too much, so we have some of the same things in common. And yes, I sleep good on some days. I also stay up late a lot, transferring things from my heart and spirit onto paper so I may enlighten your life and capture your heart. And imma snore if I'm really, really tired, but not on a regular. And that's good you talk (mumble) in your sleep 'cuz I'm a good listener. So you won't ever be able to keep anything from me!

If you do something from the heart, never feel that someone owes you something 'cuz you'll be disappointed more than satisfied. So your former coworker doesn't owe you, she just failed to live up to her word! And I'm glad you speak on trust 'cuz I'm very, very big on trust. 'Cuz once you betray trust, it's hard for the trust to be at a level it once was! I would be honored to write Jordan and encourage him from a male side. It's only right that I'm falling for his mother—a big part of something I desire and deserve! And I don't care about Que not calling, especially when his priorities are not being put before pleasure or leisure. I wouldn't ask when I could see my family. I would always make sure mine would have quality time, as well as food for thought. No matter how many kids I have, or where I would have to travel to make that circle complete, regardless if I'm with their mothers or not!

And as far as your parents go and if they want to see them, the same rules apply. There should never be an excuse when it comes to blood. That only means you refuse to acknowledge there is no concrete reason why you don't do what's right instead of what you think is reasonable in your eyes. When you're older, that don't always constitute you being wiser. Yes, sometimes you have to risk going too far to discover how far you can really go. And I believe you've gone overboard to accommodate them both and making it easier for them to see the kids, so now you must concentrate on what makes you happy as well as successful.

And yes, I've been thinking about what would complement your body 'cuz it has to be sentimental. You just don't want any tattoos. And I would love my name in it, but as long as my name is on your heart, mind, spirit, and your tongue, I'll be satisfied more than words can express! And I want to be the only one looking at your lower back and any other places that may require less clothing! And yes, I'll be there to hold your hand for any retouches. That's the only time I'll allow someone to make you frown from pain!

Well, my dear Janae, I must end here in order to start on the next letter I have lying on my chest. So I'll see you in the next envelope with love and food for thought!

Yours 4 real,
Bryan

June 17, 2010

Hi Jarelle

I hope you are enjoying my recent letters to you. Jordan got his letter today. I thank you so much for that! He was super excited and read it a few times. And I'm sorry about Jordan telling you that I said you don't write enough. That wasn't completely true. In the beginning I told him that your letters were shorter and your handwriting larger, so my letters were much longer. Plus, you were transitioning from Southport. So it was true at that time, so that is what Jordan based it on. I'm definitely not complaining now!

Yes, you stepped it up, and I'm a very happy lady because of it. But the things you said to Jordan (yes, I read it because I'm just nosy! LOL) were so genuine and sweet, and he was just like wow, in a good and bad way. He can't believe the stuff that goes on, and he appreciates the compliments. I did let him read it first before I did, and your letter had an immediate impact.

Earlier today we took a family photo at Walmart (you'll get these late June, early July) and they both had quarters for the stuffed animal vending machine. On the third try Jordan won the bumble bee from *Bee Movie*. Justine, of course, was sad, so he tried to help her on her turn and didn't win anything. So we go home. I made lunch, and that's when we get the mail. And yeah, a letter from you. Justine sees her friends out, so she gets her bike and she's out. Jordan stayed in and we read our letters. Then he's like, "I think I want to give Justine the bee." I was secretly hoping he would but didn't want to suggest it or make him so that she can handle disappointment better. She is sensitive and somewhat a crybaby, bless her heart! So he said he would put it on her bed. They have bunk beds and she's on top and has lots of stuffed animals. After seeing the mess on her bed, he said he was just going to make her bed. So he pulled everything off, made the bed, rearranged the stuffed animals, and made the bed, then put the bee on her pillow. Too cute!

And I don't plan to read the letters shared between he and you in the future without your permission or his. That's a relationship that I would like to develop and grow. You know their dad has never had a conversation with them like that. He doesn't lead by example at all. Like, he makes them wear seatbelts, which is correct, but he doesn't wear his. I told him he's not setting a good example, and he basically feels he's responsible for their safety but he's a grown man, and when they are eighteen they can make their own choice! I was like, are you serious? Yes, they make their own choice but it's based on what they see us do! And I only suggested that Jordan include a letter with the picture, and he was like, "Okay," and just got started. He can't wait to write you again! I asked Justine if she wants to write. She said no because all she will write is two letters: H and I. She hates writing, and it was a struggle getting her to write for her homework! So I told her it's fine as I'm laughing at H and I.

Speaking of hair, I have a mother and daughter scheduled for tomorrow (Friday) and Saturday, $80 each, so I just texted her to make sure she's coming at 8:00 a.m. and she replied right away yes. And another girl in my troop for next Thursday since she is going out of town for two weeks. That's $35. So yes, your woman gets her hustle on! I hate braiding but I hate my bills being late even more. But once I'm back in the classroom in August, I won't have to worry about braiding. Yes, I trust God and I thank him all the time!

And I think scent number three, which you didn't name, is my favorite so far. The smell eventually fades, so I've been smelling the letter all day. It means more for me to wait to get my lower back tattoo. I can wait! I can't afford a tattoo at the moment anyway, and I want to tone up more before getting any more. I doubt I will ever lose my hips, butt, and thighs! My concern is my stomach, upper arms, and actually my inner thighs, but I don't want to lose the booty! LOL. And I figured you would not want Que's name on my chest. Two letters is easy to cover up or alter. I'll do that before you get out. I would love it if you painted my toenails. That would be another first! I'm so ready to be spoiled. That would definitely be a first. And yes, I'm ready for you!

I'm watching *The Color Purple* as I'm writing. Sofia just got out of jail and now Celie just got her letter from Nettie, and she and Shug about to tear the house up looking for more letters. Wow, can we both relate? I know that feeling of waiting for the mail. Then when I get letters, I can't wait to read. And the kids be bugging me and trying to talk about something, like, really? You saw me doing nothing for the longest, and now I'm totally engrossed and they want to chitchat, LOL!

This movie is like twenty-five years old and I've seen it too many times to count, and it still makes me cry when the sisters separated, when Shug reunited with her dad, and when Celie meets her children. I would love to visit Africa someday. I have two cousins on my mom's side who have been there several times. Ain't it crazy how when they age

Danny Glover he looks exactly that way now? But Oprah and Whoopi look better now that they're older.

Oh yeah, you can't fuss about one short letter from me! Every letter I wrote you is long, so I get a short letter pass once in a while. Also if you spray the letter before you start writing, it will prevent the words from bleeding. See, I taught you something you didn't know. I was wondering would it be an issue if I put a little scent on your letter, or would that raise a red flag? I'm not really into perfumes because I have not found my signature scent. Like, my mom wore Chloe for years, then one Christmas my dad bought her Oscar de la Renta and she loved it and switched. My dad, when he actually wore any, it was Polo Man. For years my mom tried to get me into fragrance, but I could never be bothered. For the prom (I went alone!) she wanted me to wear perfume. Christmas parties and dress-up occasions. I do like body sprays since they're not as heavy, and when I find my signature scent I'll probably wear it every day.

Brooklyn told me that once she had tried to include a letter from your daughter in the envelope with hers and they sent it back, and said each sender needed their own envelope and that you could lose letter privileges. Is that still the case? I surely don't want to jeopardize that in any way! Maybe if I put Jordan's name on the envelope under mine so that we're both the sender. In the meantime, until you answer, I will let him send his next letter in a separate one.

I didn't realize calling would be that inexpensive. Maybe we could do a once-a-month call—something else to look forward to. I know your voice will just make me melt!

I'm getting a little sleepy now. Nothing else to report for now except you're forever in my thoughts, dreams, fantasies, and one day, my reality. So sweet dreams to you too. And yes, I pray for you, for me, for us every day!

Yours truly,
Janae James

PS: I can't stop smelling this letter! Definitely my favorite. OMG when I finally smell it on you . . .

June 18, 2010

Hello my sweet,

I am so tired. I mean TIRED! LOL. Today I braided a quite large head. And I cheated myself. I charged her $80, and when I saw how big her head was, that was a $9,400 job. We started at nine and finished at seven with a few short breaks. Most of the time I start at the back of the head while I sit, then I stand when I get to the middle and top. Well, this girl was my height, so I ended up standing the whole time. When I braid the little girls I sit on the couch and sit them on the floor on pillows, and I haven't done micros on anyone besides me in years. So nine and a half hours of standing. My feet ache and my fingers. Surprised I'm writing you, which is why I waited until now (10:00 p.m.). Then the girl is nineteen and said she only had two hours of sleep, so her head kept falling to the side as she was dozing. Then she let out like three or four silent bombs like I wouldn't smell it! Her mom canceled for tomorrow, which is fine with me. Two days in a row would be too much. I prefer the $35 little girl styles!

I have not heard about that part-time job yet. She said she would know by Friday what they need, so I called them and left a voice mail. They needed to have a certain number of girls enrolled to hire additional staff.

Fell asleep

My back is aching this morning. Ugh! (7:30 a.m.)

It's now 9:30 p.m. and I've had writing you a letter on my mind all day. Just running around doing this and that, now finally I can just chill. So this morning Justine comes in my room and asked what's for breakfast. Since they mostly fended for themselves yesterday with me braiding, I felt like I owed them. Until I caught a whiff of Neva's hutch and forgot that they were supposed to clean it out yesterday and didn't. So breakfast was put on hold while they shoveled out the bedding, scrubbed down the hutch. And of course kids never clean like Mom, so

I helped them to show how it's supposed to be. Then while the bottom pull-out tray was outside drying, Neva up and climbed inside and just stared down at the empty side like, "Where the hell is my food!" It was hilarious. I wish I could have snapped a picture. She is the cutest bunny ever! After we cleaned her hutch, I made scrambled eggs, sausage, and fresh blueberry pancakes. No berries for my picky girl of course. They had worked up that appetite!

Since this weekend is Juneteenth, I figured I would take the kids, and we have never rode the bus here in Charlotte. I called to get the bus schedule and map it out. Jordan didn't want to take the bus and was kind of scared because several months back a teen was shot at the bus stop. I convinced him it was an unfortunate random act, and we left. It was a beautiful thing rolling with AC, LOL! But then this woman gets on with two small boys, like two and three, and was really showing affection to the younger one, and the older one would be tapping her on the arm and she would brush him off. And I thought she was talking on a phone or someone else, but she was talking to the little boy! So the driver warned her to stop using profanity or she would be put off. Of course her dumb ass kept on, so the driver stopped and told her to bounce. The woman grabbed her stuff and kids, but the poor older one was crying, like, "Please no." It was hot outside and the younger one had the stroller. Then don't you know, her crazy ass started hitting the bus with the stroller and kicking at the door, cussing and screaming! So now I'm heated, 'cuz all I'm thinking is this poor baby lives with this! He's crying. Jordan is like, "Mom, be quiet please," because I was telling the driver to call the police so CPS can take these babies from her! We pulled off and the transit cops were at the next stop, so I hope they found her, which they said they would since they were on foot. And this incident didn't help my argument about how safe the bus is. But to top it off, on the way home, we get on the bus and the driver tells me that the kids need to pay adult fare if they don't have their student ID. Are you serious? A six- and eleven-year-old? And they threw those IDs away after the last day of school. So that was likely our last bus ride!

My Pampered Chef party sales were enough to get $15 off the item I wanted, so it was all good. We ate turkey stroganoff, and it was pretty good. I use mostly ground turkey in place of ground beef now. It's less salty. I also drink 1 percent milk even though most blacks I know still drink whole milk. Yuck!

You should have your pictures by now, and I hope you like them. I know you said you like thick but not big. I think I'm big, so I just wonder what is your definition of big? I wonder if you would have liked me at my heaviest. Que had said to me on at least a few occasions that he thinks I looked better when I was heavier, but I know that was an attack on my self-esteem to make me question whether I should have lost weight. My breasts got smaller. I went from a 44DD to a 38D or 40C, depending on the bra. He also claims I was more confident sexually before, which is contradictory, considering he hasn't stopped wanting it! I talked through the stuff I'm dealing with regarding him as a way of healing and reminding myself of what I don't need in my life, not to constantly bring it up to you. So if it bothers you, I'll refrain from bringing him up in letters.

Okay, Jordan did the cutest thing today when we were walking back to the bus stop. Justine was hot and tired of walking. She started lagging behind and whining. So Jordan stopped and carried her on his back! Mind you, it's like ninety-five degrees. We were all hot and tired, and Justine is not light. I told him that was so sweet and considerate. Literally since he read your letter I have seen a major change in his behavior and attitude. I'm loving the effect you have had on him. And if he continues to improve and you to form a special bond, that would be amazing. And I would not complain or pressure you anymore about keeping up with the amount of letters I write. It's wrong of me to assume you have nothing to do all day but write to me, and stamps are not cheap. I know the four-day lag actually has improved because of the date you write. I get them two to three days later. Since you're not working yet, I don't want to put pressure on you like that. I can really wait! You'll just have more to say when you do write. I will keep writing like I do because I want to keep your eyes on the prize and not deviate from that!

I love spades and I'm pretty good, but I guess you'll be the judge of that. You never played speed? It's fun and you have to think quick. Jordan recently taught Justine, so they enjoy it a lot.

Wow, it's 12:30 a.m. and I'm not sleepy. In between writing you I'm watching *Lockup* on MSNBC. I can't imagine what your day is like, so I try to picture what it will be like when you are out. Because the thought of you going through a lot of what goes on is heart wrenching.

Okay, I know you don't think I need baking lessons! LOL. Butter tastes much better than margarine when baking, but I can't wait to try your pound cake! Very few people make it great. And if you can, wow! You can read my mind because I had already decided I would bring samples of my food when I go to these car dealerships starting Monday. My famous butter cookies, *pastelitos*, and I'm thinking blueberry muffins. I wish so bad that I could send you the stuff I bake and cook.

I like the new handwriting, it's cute. If I had to write in cursive my letters to you would be cut by one-third, or maybe just one page, LOL. One last thing, I owe you a huge apology! You were beyond considerate in making sure my Mother's Day card and birthday card came, not only on time but early. And I let Father's Day completely slip my mind. You won't get this letter until probably Wednesday. Even though you can't physically do fatherly things in your situation, I know in your heart you are and will be a great dad, stepdad, grandad. So I'm wishing you a happy Father's Day (belated). And I feel like such a jerk because you put me first and I didn't do the same. I will make it up to you! Maybe.

So I will end this letter for now. We shall see what my kids do tomorrow to keep me laughing, smiling, or screaming and pulling my hair out, LOL!

Thinking of you always,
Janae
Xoxoxo

PS: I know I didn't answer everything in this letter, so I'll address Diedra in the next letter! And why I used her as a reference in the first place. And you don't <u>ever</u> have to worry about me hurting you. You have my heart, and I'm falling hard for you!

June 20, 2010

Heeey Bryan,

Happy Father's Day again to you. Actually, it's 12:40 a.m., so it's officially Monday. But Nicole just left like thirty minutes ago. It's way past my bedtime, but she came to pick up her Pampered Chef items and she had the boys with her. I was just thinking if it weren't for Nicole I wouldn't be writing this letter to you! Your mom was the coordinator for her wedding in 2001, and I met Brooklyn through Nicole. They used to work together, and I was a bridesmaid in that wedding on a very hot day in August. But we all looked good, and your mom did a great job. I still have my bouquet and glass that she had made for all of us. I met Brooklyn for the first time when we all went to the club one night at Sensationz, which may have been the Spaghetti Warehouse the last time you got in. I remember Brooklyn being very quiet and reserved. I later found out that was around the time she and her ex had broken up, and that weighs heavy on your heart.

We met a few other times, then at the wedding. When she moved to Rochester with Robert, we started emailing each other from work. We would send long-ass emails about some of everything! That's when we started getting close, and I sometimes would drive to Rochester to visit. One time she made me a big breakfast because I was going through it with Que. That was one thing I always appreciated about her. We all know I was wearing blinders when it came to him, but she never made me feel stupid or said, "Girl, wake the hell up!" Her famous line was always "Time will tell." Unlike Nicole, who would just come out and say, "Are you serious?"

Me and Nicole are both very vocal toward each other, and she did not like Que as far as how he treated me. So she would make smart comments sometimes. But she always said sincerely, "I love you and just want you to be happy." We've grown and matured a lot compared to years past, but we still have more to go. So, my dear Jarelle, we actually have to thank Nicole for bringing us together!

I'm so sleepy now, and I was dozing during the movie we were watching. But I wanted to at least start a new letter before going to sleep. So goodnight, and we shall continue tomorrow!

6/21/10

Good morning to you! Sorry but I made tea and watched a little TV before writing, LOL. Shame on me! And I had to straighten the kids out about arguing about the damn TV. It's always some type of issue between Nickelodeon, Disney, and Cartoon Network.

It was so hot outside again, upper nineties. I made the cookies and *pastelitos* this morning, and brought Justine along for the cuteness factor. Unfortunately, people just weren't interested. Some are leery about eating homemade food, some are cheap, some are broke, and some just said no. So I only made $3 after going to three places, and it was too hot to continue and I was annoyed! But I don't look at it as a loss. My kids love the cookies and *pastelitos*, so I threw them in the freezer. So now they can just grab one and reheat. I had made twenty *pastelitos* and, like, three and a half dozen cookies.

Your nieces and nephews love my butter cookies, especially Eddie! I sent Brooklyn and the kids cookies at Christmas around 2006, and he was, like, only two years old, and he recently asked for more. I couldn't believe he remembered! Then how about Patricia calls me today. She never responded to my invite or to the two text messages, then had the nerve to ask how it went. I told her it was fine, considering you never answered my invite. This chick said, "Girl, it was raining." I told her whatever because she never responded in the first place, so clearly she had no intention of coming. Diedra sent me a text saying she was nearby and wanted to get her stuff. She lives way on the other side of town, so it's not like she didn't know she would be in Matthews only a few minutes prior. I don't like people just popping up!

Now, as far as why I used her as a reference, I applied for the job in early September, and our relationship for the past year had been professional only. And she always said I did a good job with my students and was in my class for one and a half hours daily. So I thought she would be a good professional reference. We didn't start talking on the phone more or hanging out until after I applied, and then I was slowly seeing her personality type.

It was so hot I almost didn't want to go to the mailbox. But I did. No letter from you, but I got two on Saturday, so I wasn't expecting it. I know you write when you can, and my binder is filling up nicely!

Fell asleep

6/22/10

Hi, sweetheart. I've been online all morning on my job search and making follow-up calls. The kids are behaving quite well, and last night is water under the bridge. But less than for me. I need to be more consistent with discipline and being fair. I do admit I am more of a softie to Justine's tears. She's the only baby I've known to have tears as a newborn, and her cries definitely tug at my heart a little more. I will work on that because I don't want Jordan to ever think that there is favoritism involved. I had issues with my mom favoring Jordan heavily over Justine, so I tried to be equal with them.

We will probably go to the library today, it's so hot! Usually I would have adapted by now, so hopefully in another week because I hate sitting around. And I've been slacking with the gym. I only went two days last week and missed body pump yesterday, so I'm going tonight to Zumba and tomorrow body pump and Zumba. Thursday I'll be braiding one of my Daisies hair. Well, I'm going to pause here to get this letter in the mail since I haven't sent in a few days. I'll be thinking of you . . .

Janae

June 24, 2010

Dearest Bryan,

I haven't written to you in two whole days! Normally something is going on that I just have to tell you about, or some drama. But things have been pretty ordinary, which is a good thing. I applied for a new unemployment benefit year (my year officially ended on the nineteenth), and I got my approval letter yesterday. My benefits have been reduced by $22 a week, which may not seem significant, but it is a good thing because I qualify for food stamps. The only reason I got them this last time was because I had a lapse in unemployment and had zero income for two weeks. Before that I was over the limit by, like, $70 a month, which sucks! So I'm set for the summer financially, but I'm still on my daily hunt for a job and I have my heart set on three: a first-grade position at a charter school, academic advisor at a community college, and a customer service rep in some department at the same college. The academic advisor pays the most, but it's a multi-campus position, and the other two are the perfect location and good pay. The only downside to teaching is lesson plans! I absolutely can't stand writing weekly lesson plans. And there is no way around it as a teacher until you have taught the same grade for a few years. Then you can sweep them as needed. It's like being a student all over again. My first year teaching I would be up at, like, 1:00 and 2:00 a.m. on Sundays doing last-minute lesson plans because I am such a procrastinator. All my life I would do homework and study at the last minute, but still made merit and honor roll all the time. But the stress I put myself in was ridiculous! So for the first time, being in a customer service position is the most ideal. But incomewise, I would love to be an academic advisor and try something new and exciting, and finally be paid what I'm worth. I want to break into the $40,000 range and see what it's like to have a savings account with a balance!

Today I will be braiding Mia's hair, one of my Daisies. Her mom goes to my gym also, and her house is crazy! They have a guest bedroom completely furnished! That's one thing I love about living here. You see black people living well, with good jobs, and she don't dress her kids in all the crazy name brands. They wear ordinary clothes like Walmart. Same thing when I was student teaching in Williamsville. The kids wore basic clothes from Target, Walmart, Old Navy, and the sneakers were Payless, etc. But for spring break I swear 85 percent of that class were on cruises, Disney World, or some other place.

We (black folks) have such a bad habit of going broke trying to look good, making white folks rich wearing Nike, COOGI, Gucci, or whatever name brand on stuff that won't be in style in six to twelve months. But a vacation or any quality time with your family is a lifetime of memories. I haven't bought brand name sneakers for any of us in forever! Jordan's last pair of Nike was last summer. Thankfully he's into sneakers that look fly but he don't care too much about the name.

The school I worked at was basically a school with 95 percent kids on free lunch, but looking at their $100 sneakers, you would never know. One of my old coworkers called me up about braiding her two girls' hair, but she only wanted to pay $15 each and wanted me to come to her house! Way out near Nicole, like twenty-five to thirty minutes away! I told her she can bring the girls here. And if she wants $15 braids I could do larger $15 braids! She used to pay some college girl who came to her, so I'm like, "If you got someone willing to come to you and only take $30 for two heads, keep her!" I get $60 for doing Monica's girls and they look cute as heck. Plus the braids last like three weeks. You get what you pay for!

So I'm assuming by now you have gotten your care package. Sorry that I didn't include a letter. I was just so excited about being able to send it and surprise you by not telling you it was coming. Now there is a lot of junk food in there, so don't go getting chunky! LOL. I have enough body fat for both of us! I didn't know when in the near future I would be able to send you anything, so now was the best time. And I hope you are enjoying it. My homemade goodies are so much better, but you'll get to sample that soon enough. I'm not a coffee drinker at all, so when I saw all those varieties of Folgers I was like, huh? So next time, be a little bit specific. And with the tuna, I didn't know if you liked the different flavors, so I hope those were okay.

I haven't had mail from you all week but I'm not tripping! I miss hearing from you but I'm trying to be more patient and understanding until you start working again. But at the same time I can't respond to anything if you don't send, which gives me less to write about. So hopefully my oh so exciting days of job hunting and dealing with Jordan and Justine are sufficient.

They're doing pretty good. We are going to the library in a little while. It's been so damn hot outside, upper nineties and high humidity. Jordan started another letter to you, I think. I just gave him the envelope and stamp, and told him whenever he feels up to it. Justine doesn't like writing at all. So maybe she will draw a picture one day. She is very intimidated by the fact that Jordan draws so well, and I always tell her that everyone has a special gift and his happens to be drawing, and it's okay that she is not as good because she has gifts that he doesn't. I don't pressure her, so if you get anything, be grateful, LOL!

Well, hopefully I have a letter today. But if not, I can handle it. I know it's coming one day. I'm about to get dressed and go out into this sauna. Enjoy your treats and the pictures, and I'll be writing again very soon.

Sincerely yours,
Janae
Xoxoxo

PS: I hope <u>my</u> pictures will be coming soon. I can only look at these same pictures for so long!

June 24, 1010

Hey Luv,

    Happy Wednesday to you. First and foremost, you're an awesome woman. You caused a tear to fall from my eye. I never expected to get a package from you. And for them to call me the next day after getting pictures and a card was overwhelming. The only people that do those things are my grandparents and sister. I'm gone now, you got me. There's no more question marks for me. You said you were falling hard for me, well, girlfriend, I've fallen. My heart is in your hands to love, cherish, correct. And I ask for the last time, don't hurt it or betray it.

    Now to your letter at hand. Yes, you received two long letters, you deserve more, so I'm going to keep your mailbox busy. Just give me a second. And yes, God is good. And he's showing that through you and the blessing you constantly show me through your loyalty. Unless you show me different, I will never question your loyalty or your word.

    That would be a career boost to get the job at the camp. It sounds very inspirational and spiritual. I feel for you with no AC in the car. I wish there was something I could do 'cuz you should never be without air during summer! I wasn't shooting you down on your singing. I was just jabbing at you soft, LOL. I'm glad to hear you're not being disappointed about not receiving any cards because I will make sure you have every card you deserve and some. And God will bless me to take care of your every need, so please don't worry no more about not being sent anything!

    Now, about your feelings for me, I'm not nor will I ever take feelings toward me out of context. If you feel it's hard not to put a time frame when feelings should be developed, that's your opinion. I'm not faulting you in any way. I'm just asking questions so I know where your mind frame is, and help navigate our existence. They say the dumbest question is the question never asked! I wouldn't say you're so much surprised that you like me so much and you haven't seen me in person. It's just you're tired of losing and not being appreciated for the love you possess. You deserve to be showered with accolades and kind gestures instead of being shitted on and your self-esteem stepped on. I'm here to build both of us up as well, and love you the way you should be accustomed to! And what's crazy is I haven't even kissed you or held you yet, so imagine what will happen when we become as one!

And you deserve something new 'cuz the old has drained the vitamins and nutrients it takes to grow and blossom. It's something like a flower. If you don't water it and give it sunshine, it will die and not reach the potential it's set out to reach in the first place. And as we both know, we are so much more than pen pals 'cuz we have feelings in our writing as well as substance. We are striving to love each other while separated. Nothing will separate us from reaching destiny, not my conviction, not Que, no one. Through God, all things are possible. And I believe that wholeheartedly because my faith is tremendous and can't be broken.

And I won't be able to start registering until I'm free, so that will be one of the things God will see you through. And I welcome your help. And it's not just the justice system that's fucked up, it's the greed of other people also, especially those who claim to love you! I once had a motto when I was in the streets: "Show no love 'cuz love will get you killed." I no longer think that way 'cuz I love myself, which enables me to love others accordingly. And it's not a story I gave you, it was a tragedy and an assassination of character that can damage a weak mind. Fortunately, my faith and family carried me through! And the benefits you will reap 'cuz it's yours to have if your heart desires it.

And I don't believe in fairy tales, I believe in real 'cuz I hate fake! And don't accept nothing that's not good for you or your soul. And I want you to believe in marriage 'cuz I do, as well as children. 'Cuz I pray the Lord blesses me with a boy. But until then, I'm going to help you mold Jordan into a man! And you have to prove people wrong, not the other way around. 'Cuz you have to have a bullshit meter or detector 'cuz women possess the most game in the world. Therefore, no one should ever be able to put you in game!

And you can't hold anything back from me 'cuz your heart and loyalty won't allow you to! And you're not an idiot magnet, you've just been misled. And I'm not asking you to change your view overnight, but you do have to change your view and I'm going to help you do that. And we will prove to each other. We already have started by being open and honest. And you can't compare him to me. It doesn't and never will add up. He hurt you, shitted on you, left you for twelve to thirteen other women, only to try to do it over and over again. Something that's not even in my system.

Knowing what I know so far, I wouldn't have started this journey with you if I had any intention of doing to you what he has done to you. I want to love you, not hurt you. I know that will be a twenty-four-hour job 'cuz of what you've been through, but I'll keep my work boots on!

I've probably seen your mother but never said anything to her. I put that behind me 'cuz that was the worst move I made, moving to the projects! And why would you say if I wasn't where I am you can guarantee we would never meet? You can't say that. 'Cuz if you are close to my sister the way you say, I would have eventually met you. I can guarantee you this. You would have chosen me a lot quicker than staying with your baby daddy, and that's a fact!

Well, I'm going to start on your next letter, so let me go for now so I may return. Plus, I have to look at these sexy pictures. What do you mean? On one of the pictures you said "check on it." Girl, I've been checking on it since day one! And that picture of you going to church . . . Woman, I could eat you up. You look so sexy. If I was there you might not have made it to service!

Yours 4 real,
Bryan
Xoxoxo

PS: I'm working on your picture right now, don't worry. I got you! And just 'cuz you sent some more pictures, only two were current. I want more. I'm spoiled. And tell Jordan he got his letter, where's mine!

June 24, 2010

Hey Luv,

It's not that I'm getting better with letters, it's just that I can't stop writing you. It's like when you want something so bad that you'd do anything not to lose it. So therefore, as long as I have stamps, you will always have two letters at least in your mailbox. 'Cuz you make sure I always have, and I take equality seriously.

That was very sweet of your parents to buy the kids the Wii. They should really enjoy that. It also practices bonding and interacting. And you need to improve your diet and stop giving yourself titles and excuses. You have to cut out sweets, number one. It's all right here and there. You have to cut down that white bread. After six or seven you should be eating nothing heavy. Also, when you go through mood swings take a power walk. Incorporate big food in your life, a lot of fish is good, turkey wings, boneless chicken, and a lot of salad and vegetables, and plenty of water. Also, eat mixed nuts, peanuts, fruit for snacks. All this included with your workouts and you'll see plenty of results. And you're not going to overcome this one day. You're starting as soon as you read this letter. No more excuses, Mama. Either you want it or you don't. And I support you 'cuz I'm not going to allow you to continue to dwell on all the insecurities that have held you back from security, love of self, and confidence. I'm here, baby girl. I have your back and best interest at heart, so allow me to lead you and love you to the best of my ability until I can do it in person.

And you don't need no mentor for him, I got him. He will be mentored through my letters, so just be easy for a second until my way doesn't work, and then I'm all for you finding another mentor. And so what if his father doesn't call. Our teaching him can't stop and won't stop. It's his father's loss. If he doesn't want to enjoy as well as teach his son the basics, therefore I'll step up and teach him on paper until I can show him in person. So if he doesn't call, continue to do your part and God will do the rest. And remember, it's sad, but your kids aren't the only ones. Think about his other kids also. It's not fair, but it's reality for your ass.

And from what I hear, Jordan is not selfish. He's just growing and feeling his way out on how far he can get away with certain things before he's checked and stopped. And it's not good to be scared of your parents. Respect is number one, and know it's by example is key!

And as far as sexy pics go, those are done. He gets no more of those. I'm asking you and telling you at the same time. Take that as you feel it! Sexting over with, and I won't know if you stick to your word unless you tell me. And so far you haven't lied or showed me any snake tendencies, so I know you will handle that! And I know you're not trying to convince me, but I'm convinced he won't be sleeping on your couch no more either, so I'll leave that as is.

I'm not going to touch no more on the Que situation 'cuz I don't ever want him to be the basis of any of my letters. 'Cuz that only keeps his memory alive, and that's something I refuse to do. So from here on out, this is about our future and memories, not about what he did, what you used to do, and so on. So with that said peace to Que. And about that baby, I will do my best when the time is right to bless you with another beautiful, healthy baby that we will love and cherish and raise together! And now you do, you have a good man. You just have to secure that padlock around his heart and you got me, and I'm going to help you succeed at other things in life if you allow me to.

And sometimes I look at Robert and it does seem too real to be true, but he is and he's given no reason for me to think any otherwise 'cuz he has my blood in his hand. And before he ever turned left instead of staying right, I'll go pick him up and talk to him in a real quiet way that when I'm done he'll hear me loud and clear! To is my twin. And as long as I'm living, she will never be hurt by anyone. I won't allow it. And you will be put in that position also once I'm home 'cuz I will not allow anyone to hurt you or Justine, not even their father!

I'm glad I only have a year left too 'cuz I wouldn't ask you to wait any longer. It would be unfair to you and me! And it's too late to scare me off. I'm in now, so we stuck like glue until you break us apart and don't want it no more! And nothing is hard to swallow if you chew it 'cuz you have a choice to swallow or spit it out! And to answer your question, I will never have enough pictures of you, so please never say that you should be enough 'cuz we are just beginning. We need all we can get to build this house!

Well, I'm going to end this for now 'cuz it's 1:00 a.m. and I'm tired, and I must get up for breakfast and exercise. I just want to let you know I see you in my dreams. I see you when I'm walking the halls. I see you outside. I talked to your vision, I talked to your picture. Can you hear me? 'Cuz I feel your presence. Please take care, and I'll see you in the next letter. Tell the kids I said hello and I send my blessing!

Yours to have,
Bryan Jarelle Edwards

June 26, 2010

Missing you!

It's officially been seven days since my last letter I received from you. I understand if it's a monetary issue and I'm hoping that is the only reason. You know I've be watching *Lockup*, and knowing all the crazy stuff you have to endure, of course I'm concerned. Not worried yet, but dang, seven days! So on Monday, Bryan, I expect two or three letters!

I've spent the last three days braiding hair. Three little girls and micros on a grown lady, $190 so far, woohoo! I was supposed to be doing two more little girls tomorrow, so let me tell you why I'm not. The lady, Tracey, was a teacher at Devonshire, and Diedra told her that I braid hair. She has three daughters and wanted the older two's hair braided. She called me on Thursday and asked my price. I told her $20 to $35, depending on style, size, and if hair would be added. She tells me the college girl that usually does it only charged her $15 each and she can't afford my price. So I told her I could do both for $35 but the braids would be larger and a more basic style. She said okay. But then asked where I braid, at my house or hers. Duh! My house, and she lives like twenty-five to thirty minutes away. So we agree to Sunday afternoon.

Then she called me later that day and asked that I braid at her house after church, and she would pay me a little extra, $40. I reluctantly agreed because I can always use the money. But damn, braiding at someone else's house and coming straight from the church in my church clothes! So on Friday she calls me to say she referred another woman to me, who lives near her (which is great, more money), didn't tell the lady a price because the $15 was a special deal between me and her (whatever), but that if I slipped her a few extra dollars I can braid at her house. What! That annoyed the hell out of me, but she was speaking, then the lady butts in on the other line. This lady wanted her daughter's hair done that day since her birthday was Saturday. I told her I had two heads scheduled at 3:00 but she could bring her that morning or afternoon, since she called at like 8:45 a.m. She said her daughter was in day camp but wanted me to braid at her house. I told her no house calls. So bottom line, she could have picked her daughter up early to get her hair braided if she wanted it, and we couldn't work it out.

So Thursday I braided one of my Daisies. Yesterday, another Daisy and her little sister. And today, myself. So while I'm braiding today, Tracey texted me, asking can I come at 4:00 p.m. instead! Now, after church was a little better since church was at the halfway mark between our houses. So I replied that I'm willing to pick up the girls after service, bring them to my house to braid so I can change and braid in comfort, and she pick them up after. <u>Four hours later</u> she replies that her niece is going to come braid and she will use me next time. My thought was "good riddance." I ain't got time for bullshit.

Then at 9:30 tonight I have a voice mail from her. Her niece can't make it after all and she still needs me, and can she bring the girls between 3:30 and 4:00. Are you serious?? So now I'm like, fuck that! Cheap-ass people who want you to work all around their schedule. So I'm waiting until tomorrow and telling her, "Oh, when you canceled I put someone else in that slot." I don't even want her as a regular customer.

I spent eight and a half hours braiding today and I want a break! I'm sleepy as ever now, but at least wanted to start this letter and I will pick up tomorrow. Goodnight.

Sunday morning . . .

You were in my dream last night! I always go to bed thinking about you, but never had a dream with you in it. I had just sent the kids to the mailbox and Justine had an armful of letters and two really thick ones from you. Then here you come walking up on me and gave me such a strong hug. It felt so real and cozy. Then you picked me up and we both fell to the ground. I fell on top of you, then dammit, I woke up! I tried to fall back asleep and continue the dream but couldn't. I just wanted to write that while it was fresh in my head. Time to get the kids up and get ready for church. I'll continue this later . . .

Evening

I know I was talking junk earlier, but I kept thinking, "Is three hours of braiding going to kill me?" So yes, I ended up braiding the girls' hair today at four anyway. Those little girls had a head full of hair, and thick! But I did larger braids that took about an hour each, and it turned out cute! Their mom loved it and wants me to do their hair on a regular, like every few weeks. People complain, but when they see the final product . . . And she said I was fast, so $35 is cool for the work involved. I figured if I do a great job then she will feel foolish for doubting and trying to be cheap. And even if I don't do their hair again, I proved my point, and on my terms. I am not a traveling hairdresser! Will I keep doing their hair? We'll see.

Today was the ultimate in hot as hell! My car recorded 102 degrees for the temp outside. Since I had decided to braid Tracey's girls' hair, I took the kids' shoe shopping because it was just that time. Jordan is officially in men size 8. I wear 10 womens or eight and a half men, so I'm like, wow. What size shoe do you wear? I know a lot of women equate a man's shoe size to you know what. Even though I have found it's not always true!

Right now we are watching the BET Awards. What channels do you get to watch in there? I'm mad because I've been borrowing internet connection from someone in my building and either they moved or disconnected their service. How dare they? LOL. The tribute they did for Michael Jackson was good, and Chris Brown almost made me cry! Drake just performed, so Jordan was all into that. He loves Drake. I'm looking forward to the Lifetime Award for Prince. He is a musical genius! Played like seven instruments by age eight, and *Purple Rain* is one of my all-time favorite movies and soundtracks.

Okay, award show is over. Kids are in the bed and I'm up watching TV and writing. I have never had this much time pass without a letter from you, and it's just making me realize how much I like you and miss you. Ironically Que has been texting me almost every day. Just "good morning," which he used to do every morning. Except yesterday he also sent a message saying, "I still love you." I just replied with a :-), and of course he didn't say anything else. I'm sure he expected me to say something similar. And though I still have love for him, I'm definitely not in love with him. Not even referring to the lies and bullshit. Outside of the bedroom we just have very little in common. I'm talkative, and communication is super important. And he never expresses himself. I love holding hands and kissing and being passionate. He can't handle kissing for more than a few minutes before just wanting to jump in, and never displays public affection.

Moving on from that subject. I'm just hoping so bad that I have a letter from you tomorrow. It would totally make my day. Or evening, since my mail carrier gets later and later. It's on the way to the gym. We stop at the mailbox, I have a letter, then try to focus on my workout while wondering what you have written to me. After exercising, run to Walmart for something quick for dinner, more food for Neva, and some wine to sip on while I'm savoring your words at home. Hopefully that will be the case, or my next letter will have much attitude! LOL

Yours truly,
Janae

June 28, 2010

Hey Baby,

I was full of smiles this evening. Sure enough, on the way to the gym, checked the mailbox and I had two letters from you. Well, it's about darn time! LOL. So my semi-worrying was for nothing. And I had to work out and get some quick groceries while being so anxious to read your letters. Finally got home and settled on the couch to read. The scent on the envelope is my grandad's! Even Justine agreed it smells like Great-grandpa! So it's a nice scent but that's reserved for a grandad, LOL! The last letter is still my favorite so far. And what do you mean only two recent photos? Within one year is recent. I haven't changed except my hair. I thought those were pretty recent. And until I get some more pics, the ones you have will have to do for now. I really want some more of you! Are you allowed to take your shirt off for pics? I'm curious to know if you have the V to the valley! You know. the one just below the six-pack area. That is so hot! You already have a killer body, so maybe I don't need to see all of that . . . yet. There's a year left of waiting, and I don't want to get overly excited!

As you know, they never called about that summer camp. But it was dependent on enrollment numbers, and they were kind of short and couldn't afford more stuff. But I still love their philosophy, and maybe after my career is established it might be something I'll consider starting on my own one day in the future.

6/29/10

I've been sitting here rereading your words over and over. The fact that you are so committed to helping me raise Jordan just touches my heart. Everyone always has an opinion of what I should do, need to do, or stop doing with my kids, but no one ever offers to step in and help or give me a break. Never constructive criticism but always pointing a finger. And I can't teach Jordan how to be a man but I can teach him to be a great person. And with you helping me along the way, I know he's in great hands. I appreciate that so much! And Brooklyn did the sweetest thing ever for a Jordan a few months ago. He was a Cub Scout, and the Pinewood Derby was held in the end of January. When we went to Buffalo in December, Que and Jordan worked on his car, and that car was hot! Even if Jordan wasn't my child I would say his car was the best looking out of his Cub Scout pack.

But at the derby his car wasn't the fastest, so he didn't place in any of the races. But I was confident he would get the trophy for the coolest car. In his Cheektowaga pack, the boys voted for the coolest car by ballot. Each car had a number and the boys just picked their favorite, not knowing whose car was whose. This ass-backward pack! The leaders picked <u>their</u> four favorite cars and held them up one at a time, and the car with the loudest cheer won. You wouldn't believe the four they chose! The car that was shaped like a shark. And it happened to be a boy's whose father was one of the leaders! In the open-class division, where moms, siblings, and nine other scouts can race, the leader's wife and daughter placed first and second in the race. The whole thing was shady!

They gave out paper certificates in the end, and Jordan got one for fastest-looking car. And when they gave him the car back, the boys were like, "Whoa that car is awesome!" Jordan was so upset. He was fighting back tears because it was his last chance to participate in the derby. As a Boy Scout, they don't do the derby. And in the two years he was a Cub Scout back in New York, he didn't win, so he really wanted to get a trophy for anything! I told Brooklyn what happened and she felt bad for Jordan too. So maybe six weeks later we got a package in the mail from her. It's a trophy with a race car on top, and it's engraved "Jordan, Pinewood Derby 2010." It was the sweetest thing anyone has ever done for my child, and so thoughtful. That's why she is my girl and I love her like a sister! So the idea of her becoming my sister for real one day is awesome. I never had a sister, and always wanted one.

I have been quite lazy today, I hate to admit. I made summer schedules for the kids that officially started yesterday (Monday). I created a checklist for them with brushing teeth/washing face, make bed, thirty-minute silent reading, writing, math, reading comprehension, and free play mixed in between, as well as breakfast and lunch. I made it Monday through Friday, and had it laminated at Office Depot so they can use the dry erase marker to check off as they complete, and to give them structure. For the two weeks after school went out, it was just too hot to be outside. So they were just sitting around, and I said, "Oh no, this ain't going to work." I just finished grading their math, so they are done for the day and playing the Wii.

Jordan has been reading *Diary of a Wimpy Kid* and he likes it a lot! There are about six- or seven-chapter books in that series. And the font is larger and incorporates kind of sketch-type pictures, so it's an easy read. And the main character is, like, ten or eleven, so very relatable to him. Since he hates reading, this is huge that he likes these books! Justine is a very fluent reader, but I'm trying to get her to challenge herself with chapter books. For writing Justine works on her penmanship (she must be a genius or a future doctor because her handwriting sucks! LOL) and Jordan does journal reflections, book reports, or writes to you. He's enjoying the reflections, and I want him to start focusing on his feelings and choices. And he has finally written his second letter to you, and hopefully he has one coming from you.

Well, I'm going to stop this letter here so it can hopefully be postmarked today. Plus, I need to get up and out. I really worked out last night and my muscles are sore! So bye for now, sweetie, and we'll pick this up very shortly . . .

Yours truly,
Janae

June 29, 2010

Hey Luv,

I'm just sitting here in this cell listening to Xscape. I thought I would get to writing you a letter since I'm a couple behind. I know how you get if you don't have nothing in your mailbox!

Thank you for the package again. That was definitely needed at the time, but next time let me know when you are sending something and when 'cuz they changed their rules so much on what you can have and what you can't have. And I hate when I have to destroy things 'cuz that means the cops drink or eat the things that's not sent here! Oh yeah, I'm not mad you forgot about Father's Day. Won't be the first for me, so don't sweat it. You have a lot of things on your plate. But I will never forget any of your days.

I'm happy you got a chance to meet my mother. She was definitely one of a kind, and I wish she was still here 'cuz it's crazy things I would love to talk to her about. But I'll never get that chance ever again!

Moving on . . . you're soft 'cuz when kids do wrong you must stick to your guns and punish them accordingly. 'Cuz if you let up, then you will be sending out the wrong message that if they do something wrong Mommy will only punish us for a little while and then we are good. And sometimes it's good to look over the tears 'cuz that's a release that comes along with knowing you did something wrong and you have to own up to it! And you have to treat both equal 'cuz envy is not something you want among brother and sister. 'Cuz envy won't allow them to help each other in their time of need, and that can be a disaster!

That's all right they didn't want to buy none of your food, but that don't mean you stop there. 'Cuz if a person or people can go to the fast food joints, they can buy from you. Maybe you have to change your approach. And that's good Jeremiah loves them, but don't be giving my cookies away! You shouldn't be dealing with people that don't keep their word (Patricia). When you invite someone to do something and they give you lame excuses as to why they didn't come, then they are saying your time isn't as important as theirs. And I totally agree on people not just popping up unannounced. Their motives are not right and exact.

Sorry, so sloppy. I'm writing you lying down.

You're doing a lot of falling asleep. I hope I don't bore you to the point you get tired when it's time to write Jarelle! You can't be slacking on the gym either 'cuz when you do that your routine gets broken and you won't see the results you're looking for. And then you'll become discouraged, which leads to you giving up, and we don't quit. "Can't stop, won't stop" is the song I sing!

Well, being that I've written to all your questions in that letter, I'm going to do one of your numbers in and end this with stay strong, stay focused, stay sweet. I'll see you on the next line . . .

Hey, sweet lady. No, you haven't written me in two whole days. That's why the mailman keeps running right by me most of the week! I don't believe that everything is as ordinary as you say, something is happening in this sea of life). In different stages of love, growth, something is always happening. I hear two people got cut today pretty bad and I just shook it off like that's normal activity, and it's not! It's like I'm walking in the *Matrix* waiting for the phone to ring, but I keep running down the hall knocking on doors to escape back into reality.

I hope I didn't lose you with that. That wasn't my objective! That's good you're receiving your unemployment benefits and you're straight for the time being, but don't let up. Keep bugging the jobs that you interview for so they see you really want to work! Academic advisor suits you good, but remember, school's never out, so you must always put lesson plans together, not just for yourself but also your children because that will continue to sharpen your skills in the workforce. So when an opportunity presents itself, you will be prepared to fill that void and elevate your status and profession! And whatever one you do get, perform to the best of your ability and let your light shine.

I'm glad to see you're stepping your hair business up like I knew you would. One person will tell one person, and the next thing you know you, have a business. Did I tell you I can cut hair pretty good myself? I can even give women edge-ups also, so you never know what can happen when we get together and build. The same way you see those black people living down there is the exact way I plan on living. It's going to take hard work, but I'm prepared. I'm not into all the name-brand stuff either, but I do like to treat myself every now and then. But vacations I would take over materialistic any day 'cuz you're right, it's the experience that lasts longer.

Fifteen dollars a head is a disrespect due to the fact you couldn't get your hair done anywhere for $15 with wash, rinse, and the hairdo itself. Don't let no one play you short 'cuz you're worth more than that. Let that college girl keep doing her hair if she wants. And you're right, you get what you pay for, exactly! That would have been nice to get a letter in the package, and I did share 'cuz God is good and some people don't get anything from family and loved ones for whatever reason. Now, you're homemade goodies would be lovely, and I wouldn't share those with anyone.

The tuna was great. That's how I eat my tuna, out of a pouch. Also that sweet and tangy was the bomb. But next time I will be more specific on flavors, etc. You shouldn't ever trip about not getting any mail from me 'cuz you know it's coming eventually, but I don't want to just send you mail just to send. I like my letters to have substance, a message, something for your mind and heart, filled with a lot of love. And if I can't send you that, then I can't send you anything. 'Cuz it would be fake, and I hate fake. You should already know!

And there's plenty that you can write me about. You still haven't told me really why you want a baby so bad. What are your fantasies? What do you do when you get an itch? There's so many things you still have yet to tell me. So if you only have things to tell me about the kids, it's a blessing to share that with you, as well as helps guide them in the direction they are supposed to travel. Jordan can write me any time he wants, and you can best believe I will be real with him. And I don't mind if you read the letter only after he reads it first. And if he doesn't want you to read it, I will respect his wishes, okay?

Well, Ms. Lady, I will end this letter with great thoughts of you. Hope you are enjoying life and know that someone thinks very highly of you, ME!

Yours 4 real,
Jarelle

PS: I'm just waiting for them to call me. I've already purchased a picture ticket!

June 30, 2010

Hi Bryan,

How are you? I'm pretty good. Kind of bored because it's been raining all afternoon. I love the rain and thunderstorms. At my last apartment, I had a nice-sized patio, and I would sit out there in the rain and just take it all in. Jordan hates thunder and lightning because they flash flood and storm warnings on the TV a lot. At one point he was so scared and wanted to move back to New York, but now they both love it here. And five months of summer compared to five months of winter. We all prefer the summer.

Last night they both got on my last nerve, so I took the Wii for today and maybe tomorrow. Arguing back and forth and hitting. They were much better today. I sent them to the mailbox. And even though I tell you it's okay, I'll live, I can't stand not getting mail from you! Yes, I know it's coming, so I just say, "Okay, that means two tomorrow." I just read so fast that I zipped through your letters. I just checked out *Eclipse*, the third book in the *Twilight* series, and it's 629 pages. I can have it read in two days easily. I can get totally lost in a book and in your letters.

Evening...

I was feeling so conflicted today. My North Carolina teaching license officially expired today, and I knew this day was coming months ago. Yet I never even attempted to call the licensure department to see about getting it renewed. I can't really say why because part of me wants to teach so bad. But another part of me is just so unsure! So I decided enough is enough, let me get this over with and make the call. At first the lady just said as long as you submit your $55 fee and paperwork during your renewal cycle you are okay. But being a new teacher (less than three years' experience), I don't have a renewal cycle. It's 00/00/00, meaning my license is provisional. So I can't renew my license. I have to be hired by a school, and the school must request my license renewal. The good thing being I don't have to pay, but the bad thing is most schools/districts require a valid license to be hired. So I have to be hired by a school willing to accept my status as it is, which is possible. Just another hurdle to jump. Since I was laid off, there is nothing I could have done to prevent my license from expiring. When you are employed, the school takes the necessary steps to renew you as long as you take professional development courses.

7/1/10

I fell asleep with the TV on and the light. I hate that! I need silence and darkness to sleep soundly or I toss and turn all night. It's almost 11:00 p.m. now. I spent a good chunk of today reading *Eclipse*. At like 4:30 a.m., I had to use the bathroom and I was a little wired after that, so I read about twenty pages, then finally got sleepy again.

The day was mostly uneventful. I went to Walmart to return something. The bank, and unemployment again! After being on hold for thirty minutes they didn't give me the answer I needed. I received an approval for a new benefit year but got an error message after filing, so I went in person and the line was long! I was at the end and it was close to closing time, with one clerk at the counter, of course. But then some guy comes out the door to help me and called me first since I was at the end. Cool for me! He explained my problem, made the correction to my account, and said the funds should be there Monday or Tuesday. Just that simple. It frustrates the hell out of me that everyone in the unemployment office isn't on the same page! But anyway, came home, checked the mail, <u>nothing</u> from you again. Trying to be patient and understanding as I'm gritting my teeth! LOL. So then I started reading. I'm on, like, page 320 now. I was on page 30 at 4:30 a.m., so the book is holding my attention like I wish some letters from my boo work!

So I don't really have much to talk about at the moment since I think I've answered your last letter. I'm wondering how much junk food you've eaten so far! I've been making a conscious effort to try to eat healthier. I never had a problem eating and liking healthy food, vegetables, fruit, etc. Just the cravings for cookies and sweets that don't balance the good stuff. But with your support (sporadic as it may be), I am working on it.

And Jordan is anxious to receive your next letter as well. One thing I really want you to discuss with him is accepting responsibility for his actions. Literally 90 percent of the time it's never his fault. Justine always starts it, provokes him, or some other situation where he reacts because of what someone said or did. Drives me crazy! And apologizing. I have to remind him all the time, and then I get mad and say, "I don't want your apology if I've got to force it out of you." Then he will say, "I was about to until you said something." And I tell him, "I shouldn't have to wait. You should be very quickly saying sorry without my reminding." Oh, I'm getting a little sleepy now . . .

7/2/10

What a morning! Kids certainly know how to work your nerves sometimes. I guess Jordan woke up on the wrong side of the bed because he was fussing and nitpicking at every little thing Justine did. I was frustrated because I go in their bathroom and Legos, beads, Band-Aid wrappers, just stuff on the floor and counters. Tub needed to be cleaned, so I made them clean the mess and I cleaned the tub. Then I noticed there's no bar of soap in the sink. So I asked Jordan what is *he* washing his face with if there is no soap. He claims he did it in the shower. So I say, "No, I'm talking about each morning when you brush your teeth. And I asked you did you wash your face with soap and you say yes!" The dumb look on his face told me he's not watching his face and he's been lying. I tell them to remind me when they are low on tissue, soap, toothpaste, etcetera. And they use body washes in the shower and bar soap on their face. So I was annoyed by that because Jordan forgets deodorant and face washing way too much for his age and going to middle school in the fall. You don't want to be the funky kid! Plus, just respect for your own body!

Then later this morning the kids said they wanted a snack. So I told them no junk food like Honey Buns, get an apple, banana, plum, cheese and crackers, or something. Because lately they've been eating a lot of junk (my fault for buying it!) and I'm trying to make better choices for all of us. I didn't see what they got, and Jordan decided to just wait for lunch. When I started lunch, I noticed ice cream sandwiches were spilled out of the box in the freezer. I asked who had ice cream, and Jordan says, "Me, that was my snack." I went off on him because he clearly heard me say no junk. And normally he will sit on the couch and have a snack, but he stayed in the kitchen and ate it 'cuz he knew he was wrong. So I told him he gets no more ice cream since he wants to be sneaky.

It's stuff like that he does regularly like it's not that serious. That's outright defiance! So later I told him that was yet another opportunity to apologize that he didn't take and he should have because he was deliberately sneaky, knowing that they probably would have been able to have ice cream for dessert. It's so damn frustrating because it's little things but they build and build, and I saw such an immediate change in his behavior after your letter. But that's only one letter. And if you're serious about mentoring him, he needs reinforcements on a much more regular basis. I know he's not your responsibility (yet), and I pretty much stopped telling Que stuff as far as when the kids do something wrong. Because I used to all the time and would always play the "you want me to call Daddy?" card back when we were in New York. When it was time to move, I knew that was a mistake because I can call him all day but that would be useless 700 miles away. And I knew I had to get him under control myself. I've done pretty good because Jordan was a lot worse when we were about to move and when we first came. That's when I realized that consistency is key. So yes, I truly appreciate you offering to help me with molding him, but it can't be sporadic. If you need stamps, I will help you with that. What is the procedure for sending cash, calling cards, stamps, etc.? Once I'm situated financially, I wouldn't have a problem helping out here and there.

Ugh! I'm sitting here looking out my living room window and my trifling upstairs neighbor just walked by with his girlfriend. She works second shift and he be having female coming by riding in her car! She knocked on my door one day at like 10:30 p.m. I was in the bed watching TV and the kids were asleep. She asked me did I just knock on her door. I don't even know if she's on the second or third floor! I was like, huh? I said no, and she said she saw a black girl running from her door and thought it was me. Wow! She's Asian and he's black. So some chick probably ran when she realized the girl wasn't working. Drama! He be trying to kick it with other ladies here too. I'm either not his type or I've screw-faced him too many times! Lol.

This afternoon has been peaceful. The kids are outside riding their bikes, and the temperature is only in the eighties, so I had a quiet moment to finish this letter. Hopefully you have sent me something because you are like four to five letters backlogged!

Well, I'm going to get busy with whatever needs to be done around here, so I will be writing you soon!

Sincerely yours,
Janae

July 5, 2010

Hello My Sweet,

Consider yourself very lucky right now! Yes, I'm pouting because it's been so long since I received a letter from you. So I said I wouldn't write to you until you caught up somewhat. But I had to remind myself that you are not working, so funds are limited, which means no letters for me. But, dang, can you trade a Snickers for a stamp and hook me up?? LOL. I'm miserable! And I'm not trying to make you feel bad, but remember our relationship is open and honest, and I honestly feel like opening up a can of whoop ass on you!

I am just teasing. Because outside of missing you, I'm having ups and downs as usual, so I'll begin with some positive. I've been putting forth more effort into eating better. Since the holiday fell on a Sunday, most places were closed today but the gym was open, and I did go to body pump. Usually the Monday 5:30 class is very full, but there were maybe seven or eight of us. For dinner I had salmon, sweet potatoes, and corn. I have to drink more water, but I've increased it. I hadn't been to the gym since last Monday, so I've been seriously slacking!

It's been peaceful between the rugrats for the last two days. We went to Nicole's house for a barbecue for the fourth. She just bought a nice big grill, and Brooklyn came too with her for kids. We three used to barbecue all the time in Buffalo, so yesterday was actually fun. Then me and the kids went to see the fireworks closer to my side of town. The last time we went to a fireworks show, I think Justine was two or three. Well, I felt horrible because it scared her to death! She likes seeing them in the sky from a distance, but the booming sound up close was too much for her and she just cried, so I had to hold her in my lap. Next year, I told her, we'll use earplugs. But it was beautiful to see, and I already know I want fireworks at my (our) wedding reception. I'm sure Justine will have conquered that fear by then.

Now for the bad news. On Saturday the Curtises had another get-together at their house and we had such a good time. I made my taco salad again and they all loved it. The temperature was in the mid to upper eighties but it wasn't unbearable, and I didn't have to cook. On the way home there were lots of fireflies outside and it had cooled down to like seventy-three. We got home about ten and went to bed. I tossed and turned all night and just felt restless. Then in the morning Jordan burst through my bedroom door and said, "Mom, we were robbed!" The look on his face told me he was serious, and I swear my heart skipped a beat! Then he said he went to water his tomato plants in the window and saw our car window busted out. I was instantly relieved because I thought he meant that someone had been in our house while we were sleep! The idea that I could have slept through some burglars in my house with my babies would be more than I could bear. So I looked out the window, and sure enough, the driver's side window was shattered. And I'm pissed at myself because I left the damn GPS on the dashboard and usually I put it away at night. Plus, I just got it out of the pawn shop a week ago! Fifty bucks there. I paid 150 for the GPS just this March, and I didn't have glass coverage with my car insurance. Windshield, yes. Glass, no. And I thought I did.

So I went outside to check out the damage, and they only took the GPS. No stereo, CDs, twelve-disc CD changer in the trunk. Just the GPS that I so brilliantly left advertised in the damn window! My apartment was burglarized twice in Langfield. I had two purses stolen from me. And a man whom I mistakenly trusted stole jewelry right out of my house. So I'm grateful it was just a car break-in, but I'm so annoyed. I haven't heard anything about a job yet and I'm trying so hard to trust God, but discouraging thoughts keep popping in my head. Still waiting on unemployment. They owe me two weeks, and there was some error code on my account that I thought the guy in the unemployment office fixed on Thursday. And I couldn't call today, have to wait till tomorrow.

Jarelle, it's times like this when I wish so bad I could talk to you in person, even on the phone! I'm looking forward to the day we meet so bad. But for now I'm going to watch the rest of this *Lockup* marathon on MSNBC and hope that tomorrow there will be a letter (or two or three!) from you tomorrow. I will continue this letter tomorrow and hope to dream about you!

7/6/10

Good day to you! You've probably gotten a letter from me almost every day over the past two weeks or so. Wish I could say the same for myself. I spent one and a half hours in the unemployment line today. It was straight up torture and I'm hoping they fix the error code on my account because it's something I can't see on my end. They basically just told me to check in two to three days to see if the money is there. So the rent is late again, but we'll be moving in like six weeks, so I'm looking forward to paying less! Our plan was to go to the library afterward, and we pull up and it's closed! Due to damn budget cuts, it's only open four days a week, closed Tuesday, Thursday, and Sunday. So despairing. I was only going to Zumba class today but there is yoga at 5:30, then Zumba at 6:30, so I think I will do both.

It's 5:00 p.m. now and we went to the mailbox at 2:30, so there is a possibility that I have mail. You're probably saying, "Damn, how many times is she going to bring it up?" All I can say is it must be an indication of how I feel about you!

Well, time to burn some calories for me, and I know the kids will be happy getting to stay in the play area for two hours. So, sweetheart, I hope to hear from you soon!

Luv ya,
Janae
Xoxoxo

July 5, 2010

Missing you also,

I know it's been a while since you received a letter from your man, and you're right, it is a monetary issue. They still haven't given me a job yet, and the idle pay is only $3 every two weeks. That's what I go to the store with and I buy stamps with that. And I don't have nothing else to buy other things. I just had to buy you a picture 'cuz I want you to constantly be reminded of what you're waiting for and what will be yours if you be patient, keep it tight. I won't ask you 'cuz I never been one to ask a woman for money, not even my mama when she was living. But a $40 to $50 money order would set me straight, and you would never have to wait seven days to receive a letter! Because at this point these crackers are about to force me into a mode that I never wanted to resort to, and that's selling drugs just to survive.

I'm at a poverty level that I have never experienced in my thirty-nine years, and it's very stressful to the point I don't even want to come out of my cell. That, coupled with the high rate of racism that shows verbally and physically, I'm on edge right now. You're the bright spot in my life right now. Just 'cuz you don't get a letter from me for a couple of days, don't limit your pain from painting a rainbow on paper and letting it blow my way, even if you don't have questions to answer. I know you ain't run out of questions to ask either. What makes you cry? What makes you climb the walls with ecstasy? Do you have a temper? What's your favorite position when making love? I'm not asking you in a perverted way. I'm a lover, and I want to know how to love you completely. Would you fight for me or would you flee the first sign of misunderstanding? Just some questions to answer 'cuz I've been sitting here thinking about things. I have a lot more but you're not going to get it that easy. You have to be hungry 'cuz I'm starving. Are you? Or are you full?

I'm glad you're getting your hustle on 'cuz it shows you're listening, and also shows drive and your willingness to take care of home, and that's sexy to me. Just don't compromise for no one! When you lay down your rules and guidelines for appointments, they must be obeyed or they won't get services. No one should be able to dictate how you get that money when it's you doing the labor!

I'm pleased to hear that I'm in your dreams. I would love to be in every part of your body, your mind, your hair, your bloodstream, your ear, your heart, sight, womb, your sweat. That way, when you wake you won't have to worry about going back to sleep 'cuz I'll be there.

I wear a size 13, and yes, a lot of women equate shoe size with below the belt, so I'll even go this far. I'm not small and I'm not overly big, but I am the right size to satisfy all your needs and create waterfalls from the V in your body!

I watched the BET Awards, and my favorite part was Drake, Chris Brown, and Nikki. I'm thrilled to realize you really like me and miss me. I'm eager to the face of our life when I hear love 'cuz I'm yours unless you change direction!

Now, to the part of the letter I couldn't wait to get to. Woman, it's alright to tell me your ex texted you and what he said. But in my letter with he never expresses himself, something that you could care less for right now? Why are you telling me he can't or doesn't like kissing for more than three minutes before just wanting to jump in? Now why would you tell someone you like and miss something like that in any part of a letter? I don't want to think, let alone hear, about him doing anything to anybody I want to love. What about you? Are you having flashbacks? Are you missing what he used to do to you in the bedroom or wishing he still did? Let me know what's good. I'm a man with pride. And when I claim someone, I don't share. So in the future, do not tell me what he used to do to you in the bedroom 'cuz once I touch, caress, kiss, lick, taste, explore, it will never be a comparison. 'Cuz remember, what he did for you he's done to eight to ten others, baby mothers have received the same thing!

Well, I'm going to end this letter with something enjoyable. Here is your picture. It will be more to come when I get on my feet. It could have been better, but you caught me at the time of day that I just came from working out. So if I look like that now, imagine what I look like cleaned up!

Well, I hope I made your day today. I hope you read this letter good 'cuz it's serious for real. Tell the kids I said hello and I hope they are behaving themselves! Please know that I miss you, think about you, need you, want you!

Bryan Jarelle Edwards

P.S: Now I need some more pictures. It's summer, so send some summer pictures so I can see you as well as feel your presence!

July 7, 2010

Hi Jarelle,

I have a quiet moment for a while because the kids are at the pool with Tara and Courtney. It's over one hundred degrees outside, so I'm not even going to bake out there! We went to the library earlier, and the bank. My unemployment went through. Thank God. So I bought my money order for the rent and scheduled to get the window fixed tomorrow at 6:00 p.m. for $115. I found the guy on Craigslist and he was the best rate, and he will come to me to fix it. Safelite also comes to you but they charge an hourly rate, plus the glass, and it was too high.

No, you don't bore me to sleep. It's just that I write to you when the kids go to bed and I can write uninterrupted. And yes, I did get a letter from you yesterday. And I have to admit I was a little disappointed to only have one. Previously you said you wanted to spoil me with letters and make sure I always had something. But in that last letter you said you don't want to send me mail just to send me mail but to have substance, and if it doesn't, you can't send me anything. I understand if it's a financial reason as far as not having stamps, but considering we've barely scratched the surface of really knowing one another you should always have plenty to say, I would think. So if you want to decrease the amount of letters you send me in order to make the letters more meaty, I can handle that, I guess. I won't like it but I can adjust, especially when the new school year begins. I'm strongly thinking about going back to school for either an education specialist degree (EdS) or doctorate (EdD). I spoke to an admissions rep yesterday in detail.

Anyway, you wouldn't believe what I got in the mail last week! A letter from family court in New York with Quincy requesting to reduce his child support order! My order is only $20 a week for two kids, and the last payments I received was in January. Then I got a lump sum of $300 in May, nothing since. I was like, are you serious? The reason stated is unemployed and going to school. Now, I know you said you don't want him to be the basis of our letters, but he will come up in our conversation from time to time based on things going on in my life. Not because I'm trying to keep any memories alive, but just various things.

Now, back at the end of 2009 I did tell him it was a good idea to go back to school, and I knew he was quitting his job but I figured once he got in the swing of things as far as course load, etc., he would go back to work, Especially over the summer. He was with his employer for about five years, and he was very good at his job and they literally would hire him back in a heartbeat. And when I went back to school for my master's Jordan was five and Justine was one, and I still worked part-time and did school full-time, and cooked, cleaned, gave baths, did homework, and all the other stuff a determined person does for a goal. So hell no I'm not letting him reduce my support from nothing to nothing! Even sporadic payments is better than nothing at all!

One mother gets like $60 a week for one child. Another one with two kids gets, I think, $11 a week. So my court date is July 27 but I can do it via telephone. Honestly if I were financially stable I would be like, fuck it, and cancel the support order altogether. I can't make him financially help me with his kids or even call them! Yet he has time to still text me pics and dumb shit.

I'll leave it at that because I don't want you getting angry over nothing. You can trust me. I'm loyal to only you! Can you tell by how annoyed I am when I don't get letters? As far as why I want another baby, first of all, I always wanted a bigger family than what I grew up with, having only one brother. Another big part of it involves a mistake I made that I have to live with for the rest of my life. In January of 2001 I had an abortion, and the guilt of it haunts me still. The reason why I did it, you could have probably guessed: pressure from Que that we couldn't afford another baby (this was when there were only three to my knowledge). Then I made the mistake of telling my mom I was pregnant. She thought I was a complete idiot but ended up regretting what she said after I told her I wasn't keeping it, and tried to talk me out of it.

But the other big part of why I want a baby is sort of selfish on my part. I feel cheated out of the whole pregnancy experience. As I think I told you before, me and Que were not together when I got pregnant. The night before my graduation, I called him up for a booty call basically. When my dad found out I was pregnant, he was extremely disappointed and barely spoke to me the first five months of pregnancy. And since me and Que weren't together, he never came to doctor appointments or gave rubs on my feet or talked to my belly. We would go weeks without even talking. He had never even told his mother I was pregnant.

When I went into labor, my parents got to the hospital about 6:00 p.m. and the doctor told them it would be a while before delivery, so they left me! Seeing that Que wasn't there or anyone else! I had been calling him all evening with no answer. This was before cell phones were popular. At like 2:00 a.m., his mom answered and said he wasn't home. So I told her, "ut you tell him I'm in labor?" That's how she found out. At about 6:30 a.m. I was fully dilated. I called my parents, and my dad said, "Your mom is still sleeping," sounding half asleep himself. At 7:01 a.m., Jordan was born with no one there to help me, support me. I felt alone from conception to birth! Que finally showed up about 5:00 PM.

When I got pregnant with Justine, Que had moved to New Jersey before that to so-called go to school, and already had a baby on the way with a chick I had to see every Sunday at church. Living there wasn't working out at all, so after two months he came home straight to me, saying how much he loved me, and Justine was conceived sometime during that two-week reconciliation around Thanksgiving. Around Christmas time he decided he wanted to make it work with the pregnant chick (ironically, the one who gets $60 a week support). I was going to have an abortion because the emotional stress was just too much, but after doing that in 2001 I couldn't bear to do that again. When the girl found out that me and Que had been intimate (he was so-called feeling guilty but had not told her I was pregnant too), she called me up saying that she thought I was being disrespectful to her. And I told her he came back and came to me, and had me under the impression that it was over between them. And I never told her I was pregnant because he lied and told me he did and she told him to get out of her house.

So fast forward a little. Que tried to wear me down to make me have an abortion, even shed some tears and semi-threatened suicide. But I wouldn't do it, and he pretty much blamed me for things not working out with the other mother. Again, no doctor's appointments or any of that stuff that proud dads do. He did go with me for the ultrasound because I wanted Jordan to be there, and to have a child there you needed an adult present. So he came. And after I found out it was a girl, I was overjoyed! When it was done, I went straight to the bathroom since your bladder has to be full before. I came out and they were gone! I asked the nurse where did they go, and she didn't know. I sent him a text message, and he replied that he had to leave because he didn't want to act pissed off in front of me because he knew I was going to keep the baby then. It was shocking and hurtful.

I can almost hear you saying after all I've been through with him, why in the hell was I trying to still work it out and have a baby with him? But at that point I had decided I was done, and I tried to hit him where it hurt and took him to court for child support. But when he got served, he told me he hated my fucking guts because I was also suing for full custody. Closer to the court case date I was feeling guilty (don't ask me why), so at court I canceled the custody case. And when I was awarded $44 a week, stupid ask me asked the judge to reduce it to $20 because I didn't want to put a financial strain on him! I'm going to blame my stupidity on the pregnancy hormones! LOL. Shortly after, when he was making a little more money, the other baby was born, and she went straight to court. And that's why she gets the most. He had to take her to court for visitation and was awarded supervised visitation once a week, and now he doesn't see that child at all. But there you have it. He did come to the hospital for Justine's birth, and his pissy attitude literally melted away when she was born, and his attitude changed drastically. Not the promiscuous behavior and lies, but he matured more than previously. But I never got to experience either pregnancy with the love, nurture, and support that a mommy-to-be should receive, and I've always longed for it.

Whew! Reliving that was not fun, but it does help me as far as knowing why Quincy is not the man for me. And he never was, no matter how hard I tried to force it. I am going to end this letter here and return tomorrow to discuss my fantasies and what I do when I have an itch. At some point my mind is always thinking freaky, so I'm assuming you meant sexual fantasy and what I do when I'm feenin'. If I'm wrong, oops! By the time you reply I'll have written the letter, but I'm out of stamps as of now. And if I add a fourth page this may be a two stamper! Plus, it's time for Zumba, and I'm trying to keep at it.

So ta-ta for now, my dear Jarelle. And I'm looking forward to your next letter.

Your girl (woman!),

Janae

PS: Of course the kids came in while I was writing, and they just wouldn't stop asking me questions and talking! LOL. That's why I write in the bed!

July 8, 2010

My dearest Bryan,

You know, when I read your letter (6/29), even though I can't see your face or hear your voice, I could sense the tension in your words like you were fretting over something. Then I just got a letter today with the picture in it, and it confirmed that something was bothering you. But I'll start on a more positive note. OMG, I was so excited last night! I was watching the news at ten and they said something about CMS laying off hundreds of teachers, so why were there 260 open positions posted on the website? So I hurried up and went online to see what schools. CMS has over 130,000 students, so the district is huge. And I saw a fourth-grade position at Crown Point, Justine's school! I volunteered so much that most of the people there know me, so I was looking at it as the golden opportunity!

First thing this morning I typed up a nice cover letter and printed my résumé and went to the school. I already updated my employment application online, but the principal wasn't in, so I left my papers with the secretary, emailed him as a reminder. Then I followed up with a phone call this afternoon. I have a good chance of being called for an interview, so to be hired as a full-time teacher instead of a sub would be fantastic and such a blessing! I am officially getting the window fixed this evening, so I can stop putting a garbage bag to the missing glass every night. As far as the GPS, I can use my cell phone in the meantime until I'm more financially stable, or until the dumbass thief tries to pawn it and gets busted with stolen merchandise!

Jordan has anxiously been waiting on a reply from you, but I told him to try to be more patient than I have been! He was selected by his science teacher to help out the week of the nineteenth at Camp Invention, and the normal camp fee is $210 but he will be free as an assistant. And Justine can attend for $130 at a discount. Since I received food stamps again this month, I should be able to swing that cost for Justine to attend also. Last year they were at a Title I school and all three weeks of Camp Invention were free, with lunch and transportation included! So this will be a great opportunity for both of them, and give me four days of relaxation and a chance to pack and start getting rid of clothes and toys they don't need without the "I still play with that!" Or "I can still fit that!" LOL. Justine hates to get rid of clothes.

Jordan wrote you another letter and I haven't read either, but he wrote the last two after getting in trouble. And I told him he's not really telling the whole story, and writing from an angry point of view is not really fair to me, but I've respected his wish for me not to read it. They've been playing the Wii so much and it keeps them somewhat active since it's almost too hot to go out. When I went to Walmart around 2:00 p.m., it was 102 degrees. When I went to Zumba last night the teacher wasn't there, Sue was. Sue ain't no joke! Which is a good thing when you've been slacking, and my back was so wet. My face doesn't sweat a lot. I get shiny but my neck, back, under the breasts, yuck! That shower felt great afterward. The guys in the gym Is seem to look in on the Zumba classes!

On Saturday I will be braiding the girls hair again. This will be my third time braiding both, and the oldest fourth time. If I decide to braid regularly, I prefer the kids because of the creativity. I hate doing micros because that usually is eight or more hours. I was going to go to hair school back in 2001 and financial aid was approved, and on the first night of class I didn't have a babysitter. My parents just couldn't be bothered, and it was like pulling teeth to get my mom to keep him. And she always wanted me to be super specific about what I was doing, how long I would be. And she always claimed to have something to do at a certain time, meaning I had to get him early. I remember on my twenty-fifth birthday she agreed to keep Jordan overnight and keep him until, I think, 4:00 p.m. So I go out with my party-hard girl and have a ball. Got home like 4:00 a.m. and went to sleep. My mom calls at about 10:30 a.m., and I should not have answered it. She said she had some errands to run and a lot to do, and I had to pick Jordan up by noon. I said can't you take him with you? Of course you couldn't, and I cursed myself for answering the phone. So when she boohoos about missing them and wants me to come back to Buffalo, I'm like, really? I can't even count how many occasions I could have used help or a babysitter or just a break, but I guess she wanted to teach me a lesson about being a single mama.

See how I get way off topic!

So as far as hair, it was something I always did on the side, and at one point considered as a career. Me and Nicole were going to enroll together, but she ended up going later and got her license and works in the salon now. When I was supposed to go to hair school, me and Quincy were on bad terms and that usually meant we didn't talk, so he didn't get Jordan. And his mom works doubles, like, all the time.

Okay, let me address this now about me talking about Quincy. What I said and meant was totally mixed up. I was saying he didn't like kissing as a way of telling you that I didn't like that. If you remember, in one of my first letters I wrote to you how much I love to kiss, so it annoyed me that he didn't. And I'm hoping <u>you</u>, on the other hand, like to kiss for a long time, and not necessarily wanting to jump right into sex from just a few minutes of kissing. I hated that he wasn't very expressive because I want <u>you</u> to be the opposite and always express yourself to me verbally, physically. I hate that he wasn't big on foreplay, meaning, I'm telling <u>you</u> how much I enjoy foreplay and want you to be all about it. No, I'm not having flashbacks and wanting to be intimate with him! If I told you the truth that I faked 99.9 percent of the time having an orgasm, will that irritate you or make you laugh? I feel like I'm walking on eggshells and maybe I've shared too much, but you tell me. Don't hold back.

And part of my healing process is discussing some things about my ex! It wasn't the sex that made me put up with his bullshit for so many years. He took advantage of the fact that my self-esteem was low enough to tolerate it. And when I was feeling fat and ugly, he made me always feel like I was sex, and I fell for it. Now that I know I am so much more than that, I know I don't need him to validate me. And hell, I would love to have an orgasm during sex instead of faking It!

I'm sitting here willing to patiently wait over a year for you and you're still questioning me about him. Butt I almost can't blame you, but I've been honest 100 percent of the time! I'm sorry about bringing up stuff that you consider TMI, and I'll leave it at that.

Moving along! The first time I had an orgasm shocked the hell out of me! I've always enjoyed sex, but it was never mind-blowing and I was pretty good at faking it. But it was frustrating, so I went online and bought the Rabbit sex toy. I was convinced something was wrong with me. Nicole had told me about the Rabbit and how it was off the hook. So I got it home and tried it, and literally ninety seconds later I came and was like, what the hell! So <u>that's</u> what's supposed to happen during sex? I bought that when I was with Donald since he lived in Florida, to help me in between visits. So the Rabbit was my new best friend! But I noticed that the quick two minutes was now taking five, then I needed higher speed, then it was just taking too long! So I started watching porn, and that's more or less when I realized an orgasm is physical and mental, and my mind needs to be aroused also. I used to sneak and watch my parents videos when I was a teen too. Yes, I was freaky then but never acted on it! I was a prude. The only thing I can't stand about porn is when the guy cums all over the girl's face! That's just not cool.

So when I get an itch, I pop in a DVD and grab a toy and get busy! It doesn't replace the real thing, but I've gotten more satisfaction from my toys, ironically, than from a man.

Okay, it's now 6:15 and this damn guy has not called about my window yet. So I'll give him fifteen more minutes then call his ass. I want my window fixed! I'm also hungry too, and I have several issues I haven't answered for you yet, but I want to stuff you with as many letters as possible so you don't do anything stupid. Hopefully you'll get like three in the same day. So I'm about to eat, my dear, beef and broccoli (yum), and call this guy, and then pick up where we left off.

Sincerely yours,
Janae

July 8, 2010

Good evening

Okay, here's part two—actually, part three because I didn't mail the first letter yet. Like I said at the beginning of the last letter, I could feel your words on paper that you had a lot on your mind. That stabbing incident really bothered me, and I'm always worrying about you. When I get a letter it's like a confirmation that you are okay. I've become obsessed with watching *Lockup* because I don't like to ask you what goes on because I'm scared the answer will have me wanting to flip. But I still want a glimpse into how you spend your days.

I'm glad you got to see the BET Awards. Chris Brown almost had me in tears. And the next day a lot of news channels were trying to say he forgot the words, so just pretended to be emotional. It is! I know I've been putting pressure on you about letters, and you don't need that added stress right now. The last thing you need to be thinking about is regressing to hustling or violence. You're on a countdown and don't need anything to hinder that. I'm just being a brat, so ignore my whining about letters. On the other hand, I really want you to focus on Jordan so if I have to do without for a minute, I'll do that. When my finances get a little better, you already know I have no problem hooking you up.

But I also wondered what do you have as far as music? You said you were listening to Xscape. Do you have a CD player? I have two CD Walkmans collecting dust, and an MP3 player that holds, like, thirty songs. What non-food items are you allowed to have? Are there any books you are interested in reading? Do you need any personal hygiene items? Some things are very easy for me to get, but if you don't tell me I won't know. I wouldn't think any less of you if you asked. That's what I'm here for because when you are out, I know you'll make it up to me.

I was very happy to get a picture! And even in the picture you looked deep in thought, as if you've been feeling defeated. Please don't feel that way. You've come so far, further than any man I know given the same situation! I'm ready to talk to you now! What's the procedure for phone calls? Is it calling card or collect? And can you call cell phones or only landlines? You also need to send me an updated list of foods you want. Glad you liked the sweet and tangy tuna. I just bought some today to try out, and a hickory smoked flavor. I've had some financial hurdles lately, but God has been right on time and delivered me from each situation. So when he blesses me, I'm passing it on to you! I got the window fixed tonight, and it was a lesson to me that thieves will pounce on any given opportunity. And after all my issues with theft, I shouldn't have let my guard down. But my car runs and I still have so much to be thankful for!

So what are my fantasies? Nothing over the top really. I've always wanted to go on a romantic me and my man and stay wrapped up under each other the whole time. Making love in the rain or a swimming pool is another one, and making a video of us role playing and gradually unfolding into some off-the-hook sex! Like a nurse or school girl. I don't necessarily know what makes me climb the walls of ecstasy because it hasn't happened often. Back in my very early twenties I smoked a little weed, and that would get me so hot and bothered! It seemed to enhance all the nerves so sexually. Oral sex was never a big deal to me because you know who never really did it, and some attempts were mediocre. My best friend in Buffalo told me she felt the same way for years until her current dude did it right, and now she says it's the bomb! So I'm still waiting on that!

I don't really have a favorite position because I like to try a few during a sexual experience. And it depends on my partner's size. Positions that allow kissing are my favorite, but it's something about doggy style with my hair pulled slightly is such a turn-on! And I've always wanted to be held up against the wall with my legs wrapped around the waist, but I've never been with a man strong enough to hold me up—until now, so I'm looking forward to that! And I'm an equal giving partner, and try to please as much as being pleased.

Of course I would fight for you and for us. We have to endure a year of communication without touching, so why would I bail that easy? I don't really have a temper, but some things make my blood boil, like mistreatment of animals and children. I don't cry a whole lot anymore. I used to cry, mostly with situations involving Que, and I recently cried when I had to go to Crisis Ministry, when I got called in to the assistant principal's office about my negative observation. So basically when I felt that I had no control over my situation and felt helpless. I'm also a sucker for tears of joy, *Extreme Makeover home Edition*, weddings, a baby story on TLC when parents welcome a new baby, movies that involve reuniting loved ones. I think that answers your questions for now, keep them coming!

I will work on taking more pictures for you. My cell phone pics are sometimes a little dark. I got our family pics back. Honestly, I don't like them, but I would include those anyway. I guess I have to show you my good side and not so good side.

Well, it's after 11:00 p.m. and I am sleepy. I've got to make sure I buy stamps soon so you can have your three letters on Monday or Tuesday. Just remember what I said. As much as I love and crave your letters and whine about not getting them a lot, I will be fine! Try to get one out to Jordan for me, even if you have to include it with mine. I'm going to get some beauty rest, and I want to focus on our future. And don't get yourself in any trouble because our future depends on it. Stay positive and strong for me, and take good care of my body! And when I say "luv ya," it's somewhere between like and love because I'm way past liking you but I don't know if it's love. It feels good, though, either way. Can't wait to hear from you again. Luv ya!

Sincerely your girl,
Janae

July 11, 2010

Hey Babe,

Stop it with the "about darn time." You act like your man don't be writing you! You know if I have stamps your mailbox would be stopped, and you know it! And yes and no. I love when you worry a little bit 'cuz that means you cherish what we have going and not something to just pass the time. And I don't have no grandad cologne. You have to remember, other people write letters and I put stuff on their letters, and some scents may combined with other scents. And I'm glad you feel that way about the coffee 'cuz I hate to waste or throw away things got for me or I buy for other people. But next time, I'll just send a list and you can go from there. And it's not that I don't like surprises, but you have to be careful with these crackers 'cuz they are very hateful. Once again, I didn't know we was putting a time limit on pictures 'cuz I'm working on another one as we speak. So don't tell me those will have to do 'cuz then I'll think you don't want me to see you as much as I can. And that's not a good feeling, or something I want to accept. I don't know if you can take off your shirt, but I'll ask. Also, I don't have a V, but you wouldn't be disappointed either way! And what do you mean maybe you don't need to see it? It's yours to have, so that don't make sense to me. And you better be excited 'cuz I'm overly excited to see yours. It's meant to be loved, held, cherished, and to reproduce!

That's alright they don't call for the summer camp. Maybe that wasn't meant for you yet! They may have had many reasons why they didn't call or open, but if it's meant to be it will eventually happen! And why wouldn't I be committed to helping you raise your son? I keep telling you I'm not like other people you've had in your life. I can only show you and pray you cherish it and know what to do with it. And you don't have to worry about what everyone else thinks or says because you're not spending your life with them or trying to build something with them. And of course he'll be in great hands, yours and mine 'cuz we will do it together! And I'm not surprised at what Brooklyn did 'cuz we both have the same blood running through our veins and we were raised by incredible people that's God fearing and love unconditionally! About the fools that did that to Jordan, they will only make him a stronger person. And he'll realize that everyone in life won't always play fair, but he has to go right around the people to reach his goals. And he doesn't need a trophy to define his ability or worth, just real love and guidance from the people who show him real and not fake!

You should know this is not a perfect world, and people cheat more to get where they want to be. But in doing so they never can maintain or elevate 'cuz they didn't get there by honesty and hard work. And that's something we must constantly teach our children each and every day. Also, about doing the right thing every day even when wrong looks so tempting!

Stop it about Brooklyn being your sister one day, she already is your sister. But you will be even closer once I'm home 'cuz I'm not big on a lot of people. I like keeping my circle tight. I have trust issues with people, and I'm pretty sure by now you know why so, and we don't need in these people around! That's good you made a list for them 'cuz it's always good to lay a format in which you want them to feel a sense of accomplishment. Plus, it shows them it's a time for work and play!

Now, what do you mean you've been lazy? You have to be active 'cuz I'm an active person even on weekends. And when you're lazy, that's a good time to exercise. You don't always have to go to the gym and exercise. You could do sit-ups, free squats, jog in place, knee raises, more job hunting through the paper! And since you said Jordan hates reading, you should be encouraging him by showing him different books and creating a time out of the day where you are married to each other and talk about what you just read. Just some ideas I've been thinking about while I'm lying here 'cuz I don't stop thinking. I'm always thinking of ways to elevate. You are so lazy shouldn't be in your vocabulary!

I hate this pen. I've never written this sloppy in my life. I don't have a desk in the cell, so I'm writing on my leg. And when ideas come to me, I jump up and write them down 'cuz knowledge not shared is knowledge wasted!

And listen, Ma, you don't have to hope if Jordan is getting a letter from me. I told you I was in, so breathe easy and let me do what I was put on this Earth to do, and that's lead! So he's going to make better choices and open up. You just have to encourage him to be honest and not be afraid of showing his emotions or shedding a tear 'cuz whoever said men don't cry is a person that's not human!

Well, I'm going to stop this here so that I can get this letter out to you and Jordan. Tell him to read this slow and follow those rules 'cuz I will be hearing back from him and I want progress, no excuses! So see you later instead of bye, sweetie, and we will also pick this up very shortly!

Yours 4 real,
Jarelle

July 12, 2010

Hello Sunshine,

And I don't consider myself lucky. I consider myself blessed to have you. And another thing, from here on out, I will not have an excuse for not having more letters in your mailbox. I don't care what I have to do but I will bend over backward to make sure you do 'cuz you do so much for me just being in my corner. But that is why I know there is a true and loving God! I hate to hear that you're miserable, and I would accept you opening a can of whupass, not whoop, LOL! I know you having ups and downs, but that's what life is all about. I enjoy the highs and learn from lows. That's what shapes our character and allows us to explore different situations. I'm glad you're putting effort into eating better, but you must stay consistent. Because it will pay off in the end. And remember what I said in the last letter, the gym is at home also, so there should be no excuses whatsoever! And yes, water is the key 'cuz it forms muscles and flushes your body of all the stuff that's not supposed to be there. Fish and baked chicken are always good seven days a week. Also, you have to start eating salad at least two or three times a week, kids also!

That's good the kids have been on their game, but I'm sure once you've got the last letter (Jordan), I'm pretty sure that you'll love what I put down. 'Cuz I meant every word, and I expect him to follow those rules and regulations for the remainder of the year, no excuses!

I'm glad you were able to attend a barbecue 'cuz that's something I like to do year-round, especially shish kabobs, shrimp, and grilled fish also. And fireworks are my most fun thing to do (one of them), so I won't do them around Justine so she won't be scared of them! I would love to have fireworks at our wedding.

Now getting to this break-in, like I said before, I think your neighbor's boyfriend had something to do with that, or one of those girls that he was messing with did. 'Cuz I know you didn't have no one, male or female, in your house that you couldn't trust in the first place. It's a double-edged sword for me not being home 'cuz if I was, best believe I would have been at his doorstep feeling on his fucking head. That was a coward move. Also, what if the kids were home while it happened! And if it wasn't him, it was someone watching your movement and knew you would be gone for some time. So always pay attention to your surroundings when you're leaving the house. Also, did you tell anyone or talk to anyone the day of the barbecue and tell them where you was going?

I'm sorry that these things are happening, but God never gives us more than we can bear. And as long as all of you are safe, that's what counts the most. About the car, if they only took the GPS, that had to be someone close by 'cuz a real thief would have taken your whole dashboard (radio, CD). So keep your eyes open, woman, please. You also have to be more careful of what you leave out in the open. House, car, so on. That was a faggot move, whoever did that. You didn't tell me about someone stealing your jewelry. What bum was this? He needs his ass kicked real good! And please keep those discouraging thoughts away from you and don't stop trusting God 'cuz he will pull you through no matter what the storm. I'm a prime example! Your unemployment is just temporary. You're going to get a job before the summer is over. I truly believe it, so should you! And you will be able to talk to me now 'cuz I will put all the information and instructions you need to turn it on through your cell phone. I just hope you have the right phone. I'm also looking forward to the day we meet in person. I see you're stuck on that Lockup show. But trust me, it's a lot worse than what you see. Also, six people have died in the last couple of weeks. Three suicides and three so-called natural deaths. So the TV really don't show you the real stuff, just things that may seem interesting!

And yes, I have received a letter every day, damn near, and I'm overjoyed. 'Cuz you're the best and I love it, and you will be able to say the same this week and the following week. That's beautiful that you're moving in six weeks, especially after what happened with the house and car. I don't want nothing to happen to you all, and I'm constantly praying for your well-being.

That's crazy they closed the damn library due to budget cuts. This has really been a bad year consumer-wise, but like everything else, this too shall pass and everything will be back to normal for a change. And honestly, I don't get tired of you saying you hope you have mail 'cuz I don't ever want to hear you say you don't want any mail. And that's a very good indication of how you feel if you ask me.

Well, it's time for me to go burn some calories also in the yard, so I'll stop this letter for now, only to return to write another one when I come back from rec. I hope your day is blessed, sweetheart. And tell the kids I send my love!

Love you also,
Jarelle
Xoxoxo

July 12, 2010

Hi Janae,

How are you? You're pretty bored 'cuz it's raining. Well, imagine how I feel when it's raining sitting in a six by nine square, gate on it, sitting here wondering when will I hear your voice, get a hug, taste your lips, hold your hand, and look into your eyes. Excuse me, I just was in a moment. I've always been that way. When kids are very young, they are scared of thunder and lightning. As for me, I was kind of different. I made boats and let them float down the curb, and I played in the rain as well. And that's pretty good, five months of summer does sound like fun. But I like cold weather too. And I love snow!

I'm glad you are on the kids acting up 'cuz I wanted to talk to you. You must punish them equally. I know you spoiled the baby 'cuz she's the girl, something I would also do too. But you don't want to cause anything among brother and sister. Then when they get older they won't be there for each other. And that's a no-no! Evidently Jordan is feeling your choosing sides, so I have to ask you to don't make things so obvious when dealing out punishment, Ma!

I know you can't stand not getting mail from me, so I'm going to step my game up even further. ut I don't want to give you too much too fast 'cuz I don't want you zipping through my letters as you say. 'Cuz I don't read your letters fast, I savor them like wine and take my time 'cuz I don't ever want to stop reading. I guess you can call it being greedy when it comes to you and the love that's shown. You just don't know how much your letters keep me going, so I cherish every word you write. And I definitely don't take you for granted!

Now to you forgetting to renew your teaching. That's your livelihood! Your license, things like that should never be neglected! What if your phone rang the date of expiration and they were offering you a job but you had to have your license updated. You would be assed out! Come on, Ma. If we teach the kids to be responsible, we must also be the same in order to survive. Lazy is not an excuse, it's a feeling we must always overcome. Also, you have to come to grips with what you really want to do occupation wise. Either you want to teach or you don't want to teach. What are you going to do, baby girl 'cuz the clock is ticking!

So you're telling me if I want to watch TV late you can't sleep? Whoa! You need complete darkness and silence? What about music? That's something we will have to work on.

You and that unemployment office is going to make you go crazy. It seems like they can never get it right when it comes to you. Even more reason to get you a job you like, and soon.

Woman, I ate the package up within a week. And I worked very hard too, but I'm also going to eat better also so you're going to be surprised what I send you list wise when the opportunity presents itself again. Now, as far as you go, if you don't want it, then no matter how much I try and help you you're just not going to eat healthy, and it will cost you very dearly. It's all right to have sweets but not every day. And what do you mean "sporadic as it may be"? Listen, woman, you're always going to have my support. It may not be always when you want, but you're damn sure going to need it! About making Jordan apologize for things done, don't always make him do that 'cuz it won't be sincere. It would only be because you made him. Sometimes, just let him think about what he has done and allow him to mature, and eventually he will come around!

I've addressed damn near everything in your writing on July 2, definitely about cleaning and responsibilities as far as Jordan goes. And once again, don't tell me "if you're serious about mentoring him he needs reinforcements on a much regular basis." Woman, don't insult me like that ever again. Everything I speak is my word and my word is my bond, and I'd rather die before I break my bond! When I say I got Jordan, I got him! And if you are my responsibility just like I'm yours, why wouldn't Jordan and Justine be ours also? And that's good you stopped telling wrong stuff 'cuz if he was responsible he would have handled his business a long time ago! And yes, consistency is key, but you must not let everything he does get you excited. Sometimes just give him a look, don't say nothing. Try that sometimes instead of blowing up at an instant.

Now with stamps, you can't send them, so you have to send a money order with my name and number in an envelope just like you send my letters. When you get financially stable, then we'll see what happens. Until then, I will do whatever I have to do to keep the communication line busy. Also, the phone will become a part of our communication down the line also. I would be very careful of your trifling neighbor 'cuz I just received your last letter about someone breaking into your house. And I bet my last dollar that was him or someone affiliated with. 'Cuz his girl coming to your house and thinking you just knocked on her door sounds like bullshit to me, and then a couple weeks later your house gets broken into and your car vandalized. Something don't add up. And you shouldn't be worried if you're his type or not 'cuz you're taken already, aren't you?

And I'm not four to five letters behind 'cuz you write half a letter half a day, go to sleep, and then wake up and finish. That's cheating, LOL. Well, I'm going to close this one now so I can get on this last letter I received 'cuz I have some interesting questions and opinions about things going on right now. So sweetheart, I hope to hear from you soon!

Love you right back,
Bryan

July 12, 2010 (answering 7/7/10)

Hi Janae

I also have a quiet moment before I go to the yard, so I thought I would continue to write 'cuz you spend so much time making sure I have mail, so I'm definitely going to do the same! Glad to hear your unemployment went through so the rent is paid and the car window will be fixed. Handle your business, girl! Glad to hear I don't bore you to death. I also write you late at night also 'cuz it's more quiet. But I don't care if it's noisy, I'm still going to get it in! I'm sorry you only had one letter, but this week and next week should make up for everything. And I will spoil you. I was just going through a rough week when I said I'm not going to write you unless I have something of substance, and that was absolutely selfish on my part and will never say that ever again. And you will have what you need, all of me and some.

And I believe we have scratched the surface. This ain't day one for us. The beginning has already begun. We are only going to get better. And yes, I have plenty to say. I'll never run out of things to say, so once again, please forgive that statement. 'Cuz I myself don't believe in excuses. No, I won't decrease the amount of letters to make it more meaty. I will handle my business before the school year, during, and after! If going back to school is what you want to do, I support you 100 percent, but I believe you'll be working before the summer is out. New house, new job, new experiences! That's good you're talking to different people getting different ideas on courses. That way you will be totally prepared for whatever field you decide to take. Just make sure you enjoy it!

This Diedra I don't even know and already I don't like her. And if you have to lie about something you're doing in life, that means something is troubling her much deeper. So please be careful around her and keep every eye on her. Wow, family court, are you serious? Has it come to that? And what the hell is $20 for two kids? Are you serious? And so what if he's going to school, you still should be working. It's not fair to the other kids either. To me, that's some spiteful shit to me. And another thing. I understand now that it is a part of your healing to talk about certain situations that you went through with him. And I understand you're not trying to keep any memories alive, you're just simply telling me what's up! And I don't blame you for not reducing your support. If anything, it should be tripled and some! 'Cuz nothing from nothing leaves nothing. That's also crazy one baby mother gets $60 and you only get $20. That's past being unfair, that's a slap in the face. And for the court to allow it is even worse. That's good you don't have to travel all the way down to Buffalo. That would be a waste of money also. Now to this texting pics and dumb shit that you say you'll leave at that, that's not how we do, so please explain 'cuz I want to know everything and I'm not going to get angry! I know I can trust you, and you've already proven your trust factor and I know you're loyal to me only. And you had the best cosigner to your loyalty in the world, my sister. But I still want to know about pics and dumb shit as soon as you get this letter.

And yes, I can tell by the letters you send about your loyalty, and I'll never question it unless you give me a reason to, and which I pray never comes. Ma, you don't have to continue to pay for doing something you felt was the right thing at the time. And even though you were pressured, just think of what you know now compared to back then. You would have been more miserable and confused, all for the sake of a man. NO!

You know how I feel about your mother's treatment of you, so I won't speak about your mom out of respect for you. So if and when we are blessed to have another baby together, I give you my word that I will do my best and be there through everything and give you the experience that you never got a chance to feel, with the man of your baby standing right beside you step by step! And for your father to be disappointed about you getting pregnant instead of being happy is insane. What the hell type of parents did you have? How did you even meet Que? I mean, I can't believe you stayed with this cat through two babies, let alone one. And then to still go through with the shit he pulls now is even more crazier. So basically he played you from one girl to another. He was just having baby after baby and playing on your weakness and immaturity. 'Cuz to me, he never loved you. He only wanted something to control and have sex with. And just think if you wasn't a strong person today, where would your life have been? I mean, you're educated, a loving parent, and future wife of mine, and you're only going to elevate even more, your hand calls for it. But always remember, as much as given, much is required. So stop fighting for what you want. I know reliving all of that is enough to give you gray hair, but now I know some of the things you went through and still came out on top!

And yes, I was thinking freaky and sexual fantasies, so you hit it right on the head. But I won't get into that on this letter 'cuz I want to get this letter out so you will have multiple letters. And plus it's 2:00 a.m. and I'm tired. Please forgive me for ending so soon, but I promise to make the next one crazy longer. Please know that I love you for the simple fact that you're making my prayers and dreams a reality by coming into my life when I really needed you. 'Cuz I asked God all this time to send me an angel, and he sent me one at the end instead of the beginning! So may you sleep well, and tell the kids I send my love!

Love you for real,
Your man Jarelle

July 14, 2010

Hi Jarelle,

How have you been these past few days? I know I haven't written you in about three or four days, but I sent you three letters back to back and I was literally all talked out. And since I haven't received anything from you, I can't reply to any questions. You're probably thinking there is so much I can be telling you, but I've shared so much already that it's hard to randomly pick a topic. Usually you'll write about something, which will trigger a memory of something, or something may happen throughout my day that I can share with you. Honestly, I feel like you know way more about me than I know about you. Even though I appreciate the picture, with your money being that low I would have preferred you bought stamps instead to keep writing me and Jordan.

Brooklyn emailed me a few pics of you when we first started writing, so I had those printed up at a photo place, plus the first one you sent me. When I got this recent one it almost doesn't look like you because your face is so serious and weary. I know you had a lot of negativity going on around you, and I could tell your spirits were low, so that picture makes me kind of sad. So for my next picture, I want you to wait until your finances are better and you have received either a package from me or a bunch of letters. That way you will be smiling from the inside, which will radiate to the outside. I'm not going to send you pics of me if I have been having a bad week or bad hair day! LOL. You will have plenty of opportunities to see my bad side in person when you get out. Not that I really have a bad side, but it's difficult to be beautiful and sexy twenty-four hours a day, LOL.

I've been watching the Spanish channel mornings now, and they talk so fast! I'm definitely going to have to watch it every day to get used to this! At like 7:30 a.m., I was waking up and heard the Wii turn on, so I shouted, "Turn it off," because they have been slacking. Just getting up in the morning and completely ignoring their list of tasks. The first few things are brush teeth/wash face, make bed, eat breakfast, read for thirty minutes. Easy enough, right?

Well, Jordan is usually the first one up and he goes straight to the Wii, then eats, then plays either the Wii or Legos. On weekends I let them relax for the most part, but it's Wednesday! And yesterday, when I made him turn it off, then all of a sudden he thinks he woke up too early and wants to go back to sleep. But five minutes later he is playing Legos. Anything to get out of reading. He is so lazy and unmotivated! But he was loving that book and is on page 184. The book has 220 pages, and initially he would keep telling me funny parts of the book as he read. But now he complains that he feels like they have so much work to do over the summer. So I remind him that he *failed* the reading exam and needs to build up his fluency and stamina to read those longer, more boring passages like on the exam.

He does not have a comprehension problem because he passed the third and fourth reading exam easily and they are formatted exactly the same, just grade appropriate. He is just not self-motivated, and it drives me insane that he doesn't automatically want better for himself, knowing that he's failed and it's not going to get easier! So again if you want to mentor him, he needs reinforcements, more than one letter every few weeks. And yes, I know your financial situation, but if you want me to hold off on finding someone from here, I need more consistency from you. I'll send something very soon for you, and if you have to include a letter for him with every letter to me, then that's what needs to be done. Because every day he is anxious to check the mail and is disappointed when he has nothing, and I explained to him that you're still trying to get a job.

Now don't get me wrong. It's not every day that he gets like this, but it's happening more often. And I don't share anything of what goes on with the kids with their dad. He still will text me good morning most days and/or goodnight, but I literally can't remember the last time he physically spoke to either of them on the phone. And if I tell my parents anything negative that's just ammunition to tell me to move back home. I didn't even tell them about the car being broken into. See, even as I write, I just told Jordan fifteen minutes ago to get to his list and I heard him make breakfast, and now I hear him watching *Shrek*. Did not brush his teeth or make his bed or read. So now when I go out there and either smack his ass or yell at him, then he'll want to write you a letter about how unfair I treat him and let Justine get away with stuff. Well, she is still sleeping, and what he doesn't get is that he is the biggest role model to her. When she turns around and does dumb shit, it's usually what she saw him do!

Mid-morning

I had to straighten out Jordan, and he is either clueless or manipulative. I think 70 percent manipulative, 30 percent clueless. One thing I have gotten on him about in the past/present is about walking away while I'm talking. So I'm telling him what he is supposed to be doing. He was "reading" while watching *Shrek*, and when he reads he likes complete silence so he can concentrate, and turns the TV off. But now he claims the volume is low. So I told him that when I calmly tell him to follow his list, he doesn't. When I yell, he doesn't. So if I knock the hell out of him, is that what's necessary? So he shook his head no. So I asked him, "What do I have to do to get you to handle your business?" And he's sitting there like, "I don't know." So I said, "How about get your ass up and go brush your teeth?" This clown says, "What if I get up and walk away then you'll say I'm walking away while you're talking to me!" That's the manipulation! Trying to twist around what I tell him to his convenience. So I told him to get up and do what he's supposed to do. So as far as I'm concerned, this punishment is back on.

In the meantime Justine got up and asked what's for breakfast, so I told her to brush her teeth first, and she did with no argument. Now she's reading and Jordan is in the bed probably asleep. I know you said before that I'm too soft on them, and I can wholeheartedly admit that! When I was growing up I just did what I was told. I slipped up occasionally, and yes, I got whooped. But my last time being whooped I was seven! My punishments never lasted more than two days, ever. My parents caved in because overall I was a good kid, and so was my brother. Typically we got in trouble as a pair, so age ten was his last whooping.

This is the hard part of being a single parent. You truly need that balance of both parents because mothers are more nurturing while fathers are usually more black-and-white—right is right, wrong is wrong—so that it balances. Sometimes moms are too soft and the dads need to step in to be a little firm. Sometimes dads are too hard on kids. Any mom would step in and say, "Baby, that's a little too harsh." It's hard for me to flip-flop between nurturer and disciplinarian.

I don't want to have struggles with Jordan every few days about reading and being responsible. Because in between he is such a joy and funny, silly, crazy in a good way. But then he gets into a rut of just not wanting to do. Do I just let it ride or what?? I'm fed up, and it takes too much energy. So this is why I <u>need</u> your responses much quicker!

Moving on 'cuz I'm sick of this topic . . .

I've started packing up for our move. This time I was smart. I started their bedroom and sorted all the toys and clothes. Got rid of clothes they can't fit, and all toys are packed up. Justine has these Polly Pocket sets of little dolls with tons of accessories. Shoes the size of my pinky fingernail! So you can imagine how that was. There were about seven or eight pairs of shoes. Barbies and clothes, board games. It took me many hours, but it was worth it. Their room is always the most congested. And all that's needed to do is clothes, which can stay on the hangers and go right in the car. I'll be officially getting the keys to the house on Friday and moving their toys and kitchen stuff right away.

Next week is Camp Invention, so hopefully the responsible role Jordan has to play as an assistant will be a great character builder. His science teacher always speaks so highly of him and his potential. I just want him to show all adults that wonderful side of him. I'm sending Justine also, so I will have four days of aaahh!

It's about 11:45 now and I have to run a few errands. Jordan is funny. He just asked me can he make lunch, and I told him as soon as he reads for thirty minutes. So now he's sitting on the couch looking simple. Justine read and did her math, but there are huge bees near the patio so she's mad because she can't get to her bike. Jordan has been awake for, like, four hours and only managed to brush his teeth and eat breakfast. So since he's wasted the morning, he will just be hungry until he makes the right decision. It's idiotic! Oh well, let me get going. Hopefully you will have written and he will have a letter of motivation because nothing I've said has made a difference lately.

Hopefully you are in good spirits, and I'm hoping you found a job. My search continues, but my eyes and heart are set on Crown Point, God willing! So take care, and I look forward to your next letter.

Sincerely yours,
Janae

Later on that day . . .

Wow, my child is stubborn! At 11:45, as you recall, Jordan asked for lunch and I told him thirty minutes of reading first. At 12:15 he asked, and I told him if he had read at 11:45 he would be eating now. Justine came in at about 1:00 p.m. to eat, so she had peanut butter and jelly, Beefaroni, and grapes. And Jordan said, "I want to eat too." I said you know what you got to do. Then I had errands to run, and I knew if I let him stay home he would eat. So I brought them both with me. As we passed the rent office we saw the mail truck, so he got the mail and was literally jumping for joy because he had mail from you! Talk about perfect timing. So he read as I drove. We made four stops and got home at 3:00. He hadn't eaten since, like, 8:00 a.m., but that's nowhere near starving. But he decided it was finally time to read at 3:10. Earlier he had even tried to say he can eat now and read when he's done. I said, boy, please! He just wanted to see how far I would let it go on, and we would have gone all night! He also wrote those spelling words thirty times, and I was cracking up that you told him he had spelling errors because the teacher in me is constantly correcting your spelling but I never tell you that. But it's whether, not *wether*! LOL

And I never said my grandad's cologne was an old-man scent! I'm not putting a limit on pictures. I'm just not always in a picture-taking mood. And I have to take them on my phone then send them to my email, then email them to Ritzpix, then pick them up at a later date. But most importantly, I need to be in the mood so you can <u>really</u> smile! When I say I don't need to see <u>too</u> much of you, I mean just that! There's a whole year before I can see it in person to touch, caress, etc. So I'm not going to tease myself and have to wait that long. Now, one–two months before your release, that's a different story! I definitely want to see more because it will almost be tangible.

I read with the kids all the time and let them see me reading 600+ page books. Because if you can read one page, you can read 1,000. I used to check out two of the same book so that me and Jordan could read alternate pages, and we have quiet time so we can all read. A lot of our thoughts are often the same, except doing sit-ups and free squats!

Maybe we can do it together when you get out. That's why I joined the gym because I do not do stuff like that on my own. I need a cheering section, sad to say, but true. Just being real!

You know I love and appreciate the advice you give me and encouragement. And you answer questions, but I'm still not hearing enough about <u>you</u>. Tell me about your favorite Saturday morning cartoon, your first family vacation out of town. Did you and your siblings get in trouble together, or was it a solo thing? Are you and your brother close? I think he's neck and neck with the kids' dad as far as offspring! LOL. I asked Brooklyn was it okay to bring up your dad, and she said you don't deal with him but I could ask you. So what happened between you and him? You ever foresee a reconciliation? Have you been taking classes/courses while locked up toward a degree or certification?

My favorite cartoons are the original *Scooby-Doo* and *Tom and Jerry*. I used to love the *Smurfs*, *Thundercats*. Honestly, I was a cartoon junkie and couch potato. Last summer my apartment complex had a pool party with a DJ and they had a name-that-tune TV theme song contest. I blew the competition away and got seven out of ten right. So this big black hater chick go on to say, "You just have too much time on your hands!" I told her those were shows I watched as a child, not an adult, and left it at that. Dumbass hater! LOL.

I just had to send Jordan to handle this fifth grade girl that keeps being mean to Justine. She had her two Barbies outside, so this white girl, who is too old to be hanging with second-graders anyway, comes with her dolls and tells Justine her dolls are ugly. Justine comes home crying, so I first had to tell her to stop being a pushover and defend herself and let the girl know it don't matter what she thinks about her dolls. But since the girl is older, I sent Jordan to quietly observe and put the girl in her place. So Justine went back out with her two dolls and her Hannah Montana doll that switches from Hannah to Miley—it's off the hook. And I told her don't dare let anyone play with it. I was bullied in fourth grade by the new girl and I never told anyone or stood up for myself. I just remember always being intimidated, and I see myself in Justine. So I'm trying to get her to stand up for herself now so that people see she's not a pushover.

Well, I guess I should make an attempt to cook something for dinner. I don't really want anything, but I know they will come in starving. And doggone it, I went to the store and forgot to buy syrup. I'm watching *Extreme Makeover* now. What are your favorite TV shows to watch right now? You are about five or six letters behind it seems because when you're responding I'm like, what is he talking about?? Then I think back like, oh yeah, now I remember! You know you can always be writing me even though you may not have the stamps. Just your replies can be written and ready while it's fresh in your mind after reading my letter. Okay, let me get dinner prepared for my babies. Have you thought about the first meal you want me to prepare for you?

So I'll be chatting with you later, my dear Jarelle, and waiting for your replies. And Jordan let me read some of his letters, so I'm respecting his privacy and the bond forming between the two of you! The scent on this letter is Victoria's Secret Amber Romance. It smells slightly different on paper, but what do you think?

Yours truly,
Janae
Xoxo

July 15, 2010

My dearest Janae

You're starting to know me too well 'cuz I was very pissed that day of the picture. They wouldn't let me change my clothes to look more presentable. Correction, I don't fret over nothing I just may be a little annoyed or pissed is more like it! You have twenty-year-old white boys working here telling you to tuck your shirt in, get in line, shut up, and so on, knowing damn well if we were out in the real world they would never say one word to me.

Moving along, I'm so happy that you are finally about to embark on another teaching job. And to be at the same school where Justine is at is a blessing in itself. For people to know you are ready, and being familiar with you can't hurt at all. Now you have to stay on them and show them you really want that job 'cuz you know there's a whole lot of other people trying for the same position! But I believe in you, woman, and God has our back. So do you. Also apply for the other openings as well 'cuz you don't want to put all your eggs in one basket.

I'm glad you're getting the window fixed today, so by the time you get this letter it should be done already. Hopefully you found out who did it or have a good idea. I don't know yet what they took, but whoever did it had to be closed by also. I hope you wasn't sound asleep when they did 'cuz that's not a good look, especially with children in the house.

Hopefully by now Jordan has gotten his letter and abiding by the rules and guidelines I set forth for him to follow with no excuses! And yes, I pray he's more patient than you. But if not, it's something we all will manage to get through no matter what. Communication is a must! Also, tell him congratulations on being picked by his science teacher at Camp Invention. Also, it's a blessing that you don't have to pay for both of them 'cuz without that discount . . . word! So what will you be doing for those four days of relaxation? Don't get in no trouble, woman! LOL. That's good you can start downsizing stuff so you don't have to move so much junk with you, and there are needy people that probably could use some of those clothes they can't fit! We already figured out that Jordan was writing from an angry point of view, so I know he was trying to flip things. But you have to remember what I said about dividing the punishments evenly to keep down envy! And if he asked you not to read it, well I don't know what to say about that. I guess I have to respect it also!

You know I had to skip a whole paragraph to the bottom of the first page where you say the guys in the gym always seem to look in on the Zumba class. Oh, that's great, as long as they are looking at the other women around you 'cuz you're spoken for, my dear. Don't let nobody steal <u>my heart!</u> I'm glad to see you're still hustling with doing hair also. Oh, that's good 'cuz it gives you time to think and ponder on things while using your hands. And I guess it's easier to deal with the kids rather than the grown folks. That is so crazy about you not being able to go to hair school because of a lack of babysitters. As much as you've gone through, it's a wonder you don't have gray hair. I'll tell you one thing now, I'm not really looking forward to meeting your parents after all you have told me about how they treated you and the kids. I just don't know. And for her to always say she misses the kids, she don't even come to see them. Love is just not buying games and sending stuff, it's about going to see those people you say you love 'cuz we are not going to live forever. And that's what I regret about not still having my mother living 'cuz I will never be able to tell her I love her no more. Sure, I'll talk to her spirit, but it's not the same as being in person!

I do notice you do get off topic a lot, but I'm not mad at you. I love to hear you release things that hurt you so they won't ever hurt you again. It's a process that we will get through together. Wait until you move into the house. I bet your mother comes down there just to be nosy and envious. But if she do or don't, that shouldn't limit your progress or accomplishments or goals. Like I always say, it's their loss, not yours. This Nicole seems to be very popular in your life. She's family or a girlfriend? And has she ever thought about purchasing a salon? Just keep in mind that's a good investment to think about, also 'cuz I have plans to retire early to enjoy the fruits of labor. Although I have much labor in store, it will be successful to the fullest extent!

Speaking of cereal, what is your favorite? Mine is Honeycombs and Captain Crunch Peanut Butter Balls, Crunch

Berries also. And I don't put a lot of milk in my bowl 'cuz I can't stand soggy cereal! I totally understand once again about why you talk about Quincy. And it wasn't mixed up, I just read into it totally wrong. And as far as kissing for a long time, I don't mind at all. And of course, I don't want to jump right in us for the simple fact that I would hope we could please each other before just jumping right in. Also, there will be times where we can't resist but to jump right in 'cuz when I love, I love for real, in any shape or form. There's never really a script unless we create one!

And I have no problem expressing myself to you verbally, physically, or mentally. And to tell you the truth, you don't have to want me to be all about it 'cuz I am 'bout it, 'bout it. That's just something, or I should say, one of those things I look forward to among other things. That's crazy that you faked 99.9 percent of orgasms. And no, it wouldn't or isn't irritating to me 'cuz I wasn't your man. And to be very blunt with you, I will make you cum one way or another. It won't be no faking with me, and you can bet the house and farm on that. Imma look at you, probably got moist just by me saying that. And no, you're not walking on eggshells with me. And the day you feel like you've shared too much is the date our house gets torn down! Yes, I told you to don't hold back 'cuz if you do, how can we grow as one? The vital information you hold back from me may keep me from reading the potential level you need me to be at. I don't hold nothing from you 'cuz I know what you've been through!

Let me give you a little something, can't NO man make you feel sexy if you yourself don't already know you're sexy. Sexy is not just facial and body, it's the things you do that are sexy, like paying your bills, hustling on the side to put extra money away, keeping the house clean, making sure the kids grow and are respectful, making sure you go hard for your man every day, and expect him to do the same and check his ass if he don't go hard! That's sexy to me. And you must have a pure heart 'cuz without that I don't care how big your ass and titties are, you're not sexy! And yes, you are patiently waiting for me. But one thing I won't stop doing is questioning you about anything 'cuz if I'm yours and you're mine, the dumbest question is a question never asked! And I appreciate you've been 100 percent honest with me 'cuz that's what I've been with you. Also, I've always enjoyed sex also, but it's going to be like my first time all over again. Will you be gentle with me? Will you teach me some things? I'm telling you right now, please do not fake nothing with me. And I don't mind using toys with you to help you reach the top, but one thing for sure, you're not sticking anything in my butt. And when I say toys, I don't mean no big-ass dildos and shit like that 'cuz I'm good downstairs on that note. But there are toys for couples. I love porn, especially with my lady, but I don't need porn for me to perform my duties to my woman.

My mom had Playboy channel way back, and I used to sneak in her room to watch it. So you're not by yourself with that at all. And yeah, I'm not with cuming all over anyone's face, but you, on the other hand, do what you wish. I'll be there to please you, that's my goal! And your toys won't ever give you more pleasure than I can, trust me on that. What other issues you haven't answered for me yet, I'm eager to know. And I won't do anything stupid. You've just given me a reason to love trouble free!

So I'll end this here so I can start on my last letter. So how you like going to the mailbox and finding me in there, yum!

Your man 4 life,
Jarelle

July 15, 2010

Hello my dear Jarelle,

 See this is exactly why I am so frustrated! I'm feeling like everything I say is completely taken out of context or I'm not fully explaining myself, or you are not thoroughly listening, on top of the lag in between responses (not faulting you, just saying). Then me trying to clarify. I partly feel that I should apologize for the letters you've received in the past two weeks because honestly, I was in a pissy mood at the world, including you. I'm in no way trying to compare our situations because there is no comparison, but I'm in a financial, social, mental place I've never been in and it's eating away at my spirit. And I feel like I always have to compromise my happiness and be understanding about why everyone else's issue has to take precedence over mine. And I should be grateful because I still have X, Y, and Z, and I could be like so and so who doesn't have that! Everyone seems to think I'm doing <u>something</u> wrong because if I was truly this and that then there's no way I'd be in my situation. And I'd be working and my kids would be better behaved, and I wouldn't be struggling with my weight. And I'm sorry, but life is not that black and white, and I can only keep trying until I get it right if ever!

 Okay, I'm really sorry, but if I could, I'd send that to every person I know or some people could just take a glimpse into my mind. I feel like I have no one who understands me or that I can talk to. I'm not trying to put the pressure on you. I know the circumstances, but when I'm stressed about something I don't have someone I can instantly run to or call up. I've let it build up inside because everyone has their own problems, or they are judgmental or just not available. I regret writing all this already because I don't even know where all this is coming from. And please don't respond to this part. It's just my need to vent some. Moving right along . . .

 I just got your letter dated 7/12. And yes, you are four to five letters behind because you're replying to stuff I wrote almost two weeks ago. But it's <u>okay because</u> I know it's coming. First of all, I read and reread and reread every letter you write me! Of course, the first time I zip right through it anxiously, but later in the evening I sit back and savor your words.

And obviously you are not reading through clearly because there was <u>no way</u> that I could renew my teaching license! Yes, I was very negligent, but the bottom line is for a <u>provisional license</u> to be renewed, you have to be working during that time and your school submits your observation reports, etc. To convert the license to a five-year permanent one. You are right, someone could have called me for a job, but it would be up to that school to request my renewal. I do want to teach, and honestly, I don't have the desire to go back to school for anything. I just want to be a teacher.

Do you really think I'm not <u>trying</u> to find work?? If I'm willing to relocate to Colorado or Utah or something there are teacher jobs in this country, but I'm trying to give the kids a stable home, and they have been to three different schools since we moved here. I dread even moving to this new house next month, but they need their own space. And I'm praying it's the right move to make, even though it limits my geographic options as far as where I can take a job and be able to take the kids to school, instead of them going to a ghetto, low-performing school.

Charlotte is huge! Eighteenth largest city in the country. I'll be living in the northwest and the kids going to school in the southeast—more east—so I'm trying to make it all work. And my mom still tells me to send my résumé out to Buffalo. Am I wrong for not wanting to move back?? I'm trying to listen to and trust God, but I'm still learning <u>how</u> to do that. I don't know where I'm meant to be, but it seems like he's laying the foundation for me to stay in Charlotte!

Yes, I need silence to sleep. So you could stay up for a little while with the TV on, but after a while I would have to turn it off. Music is cool to fall asleep to, but I set the sleep button so that it's <u>off</u> after sixty minutes. Silence and darkness! LOL, not sure how that will work. And I've been fat since the age of six, and food has been my reliable best friend all my life. So even though I know I have your support, I can't change overnight. And I really hate when people say either you want it or don't because it's never that easy! It's been a constant struggle all my life, and caused me a serious amount of pain from fourth grade to eighth grade. Sometimes I feel like I have too much baggage for you and you shouldn't even be bothered! You even said you like thick and you're not into too big, and I've told you I'm <u>big</u> and you've seen my pictures. Can you honestly tell me that if you had never been locked up I would have been someone you would have considered? Lately I feel like somewhat a disappointment to you, and I know that sounds silly. I really did not want this letter to be so great and unpleasant!

No, I don't make Jordan apologize for every little thing. My issue with him is that he never apologizes and he usually doesn't understand why he should. Now I feel like I've given you an image of a monster of a child because there has been so much negativity I've shared with you. I don't tell you every little thing he does. I just give you examples so you can see what I'm talkin' about. I guess I need to start sharing more positive things he does. I'm just literally <u>scared to death</u> of him going down the wrong path because middle school shapes so much of who he will become and who he lets influence him. And the responsibility, bottom line, will fall on me. Ten years from now no one will say if Que would have been around or if his grandparents visited more, or if Jarelle had written more. It will be what JANAE should have done more or less of! Oh wow, time for yoga. We'll have to pick this up later this evening . . .

Aaaah, I really needed that. Yoga is a good stress reliever, and I was running late and frustrated because the kids were taking forever to bring their bikes in. And I was about to say forget it, but I said let me shake off this funky attitude that's smothering me. Even though a lot of what I said is what I'm feeling, I don't want to unleash all of it at once. As far as letters, I expect two to three letters per week, or more if you want! But I want your thoughts and words on my mind every day, and one letter a week won't help me. I'm greedy too. And if you expect me to keep you full from letters, it's only fair that you do the same. And where did I say my <u>house</u> got broken into?? I said my car window was busted out and the GPS stolen. That chick came to my door a while ago, not recently, so her dude may be involved or may not be. But I'll be moving very soon and much more cautious. And I could care less about him maybe or maybe not liking me! Stop taking everything I say out of context! Did I say, "Dang, I don't know why he ain't kicking it to me?" Or, "I wish his cheating ass was sweating me!" Really, Jarelle? I don't know why you keep questioning my loyalty to you. I have guys trying to get with me on a regular—young, old, handsome, ugly. But I have zero interest in them, and I'm willing to bottle up my sexual frustrations to save it for you!

No, I didn't punish Jordan after all. I mean being put back on punishment. He was obviously testing the waters, and today he did what he was supposed to do with reading without the drama. And I don't nitpick on or want to nitpick on every little thing he does. I suppose that he discovered I wasn't going to waver. Thirty minutes of reading—consistency! I finally got him to go to bed. He literally gave me about twenty goodnight kisses! Since he's older and not as affectionate, I have to get them when I can. When he was seven I was no longer allowed to give him hugs and kisses at the bus stop (fell asleep).

7/16

FYI, I don't break a letter apart into more than one letter if I leave out or fall asleep. Whatever ends up in the envelope, I count as <u>one letter</u>, silly. And you can't debate that I send you more. But as you said before, who's counting? ME! It's kind of like the saying, "As long as I owe you, you'll never be broke!" So I'll never be broke, I guess.

Today was awesome because I bought Justine a bed and mattress for $45! An adorable white metal frame daybed in excellent condition. My budget was going to be $150, and now Jordan can keep the bunk beds. I had been checking Craigslist for the past two weeks for a bed for her! We got the key to the house today and did the walk-through, but they were still loading the truck. So tomorrow afternoon I can officially go through the house and take it all in. I just pray that everything works out with a job so that this move is all worth it. A five-star preschool called me today that I sent my résumé to in May to see if I was still interested. Since it's a daycare it's much lower pay, but I told them I was interested. So they are supposed to call next week to possibly set up an interview. It's right down the street from Crown Point, which is also a plus.

Oh, I finally tasted that tuna in a pouch, the hickory flavor. OMG, it is so good! I made a sandwich wrap out of it yesterday, then had it on crackers later on. I'm wondering when you are going to send me the updated list of what you want or need. I should have continued this letter earlier. My eyes are so heavy!

7/17

Yes, I fell asleep, I was so sleepy. When me and Justine drove to Rock Hill, South Carolina, to get the bed it was in the mid-nineties. And on the way back we had the mattress and bottom frame on the roof of the car with bungee cords, so I was driving at 45 mph most of the ride back. And we went straight to the new house, so when we got there I was literally soaked with sweat. Eighty percent of my shirt was visibly wet! Luckily my pants were black, so it wasn't obvious to anyone that I felt like I peed on myself. And even though I had eaten breakfast and drank a lot of water before we left, we were gone almost three hours and I ended up with a heat headache and dehydrated. I just didn't think that much time had passed, and I had a juice pouch for a Justine but nothing for myself, so that was a lesson learned. Then severe thunderstorms rolled in between 4:00 and 6:00 p.m., and I was glad we left early to get the bed! But the rain was relaxing, and I should have taken a nap right then. You should be used to me falling asleep writing you anyway.

This morning I'm getting the oil changed at church. The single-parent ministry does car care/clothes closet once a month, where able men change the oil on the ladies' cars, families bring in clothes and do a clothes exchange, and the ladies bring in a dish for the men to have lunch afterward. I cleaned out the kids' closets and drawers right on time. I saved the good jean skirts and shorts for Jasy and Nene because at the last clothes closet this African lady, who was not even a member of the church, literally took <u>all</u> the clothes I brought in before anyone had a chance to go through them, in addition to filling about six garbage bags full of clothes in multiple sizes! They said she does that every clothes closet, so I was like damn, I could have saved the really good stuff for Brooklyn. And why hasn't anyone put a stop to this greedy lady yet?? He must be selling the stuff somewhere, <u>and</u> she has a decent job at the bank, so he is going on!

    Well, anyway, it's time for me to roll out and get the oil changed. Jordan is awake but Justine is still asleep. As far as page 1 of this letter, don't take it personal at all. I just needed to vent and I had a lot on my mind. But one thing I want to stress to you, <u>relax</u> and stop taking everything I mention about the opposite sex out of context!

Sincerely yours,
Janae

July 17, 2010

Hey Jarelle,

    You're catching up! LOL. Just got your letter this afternoon and it made me smile. I appreciate the apology, but I bet you'll probably want to rescind it when you read the letter I sent you prior to this! I'll be glad when we're on the same page. And I'm glad we both just went through a rut of feeling like shit, but you sound a lot better and I feel a lot better, so I pray everything goes uphill for us from this point on. That last letter I was just letting stuff pour out, and at first I was going to rip it up and start all over. But that would be the exact opposite of open and honest.

    I guess tomorrow or in the next few days I'll be going to Home Depot to buy toilet seats for the house. I don't know what they thought, but the master bathroom has one of those cushion toilet seats but the damn thing is torn. And that's something they should have changed that I'm deducting the price of from my first month's rent. Then I have to take pictures throughout the house because I learned my lesson after my previous apartment sent me a bill for $558 for bullshit charges. Only the carpet I accepted full responsibility for, since the rabbit dug quite a few holes in. But that heffa was making up charges and trying to charge me for dirty walls, $200, when number one, they have to paint any time a new tenant moves in. And number two, it was the entrance wall where the kids made the wall dirty kicking their shoes off, and hands dirty after being outside. I cleaned that apartment completely but didn't bother with walls since I knew they would paint. So I was like, are you serious?? It wasn't even one full wall!

I've packed five more boxes today, and Kathryn left two night tables and a TV stand that we can borrow. Lawn mower and leaf blower also, and water hose, so Jordan is excited about cutting the grass and Justine about the leaf blower. I mostly can't wait to put together her new bed. It's so girly and just right for her. I need a new bed and mattress. I've had this mattress for over ten years, and I like my bed but I want a nice, modern upgrade.

Yeah, I was only getting $20 a week, and like I said, I haven't got anything since early May when I was shocked to get $300. That was right after the cruise and I know he had just got back his student loan money, so I guess he decided to pay some down. If he wasn't such an idiot and so selfish, I could definitely sympathize with his situation. I saw his pay stubs. And of course he had to pay child support, but in addition he has to pay the medical cost of the delivery of the kids whose mothers were receiving Medicaid while pregnant. I received Medicaid when I had Jordan but was getting insurance from my job when Justine was born, lucky for him. So after all the deductions he was literally bringing home $125 a week, and $500 a month is not hardly enough to support yourself. And of course he was denied food stamps. But he kept doing the same dumb shit. And after the grief he put me through when I was pregnant with Justine, he still had three more kids <u>after</u> her. So I did understand his desire to go back to school and thought it was the best idea to try to dig himself out of the hole, but to expect the moms to carry 100 percent of the financial burden of caring for these kids and give him his space for the next three years so he can focus on school! And with this crazy economy, ain't no guarantee he will be making good money.

But I've actually been considering canceling the entire support order. I mean, it's not like he calls the kids. And even during our reconciliation we talked on the phone all day every day, and for the most part it was all about us, not including the kids. And I have to accept some calls for that, but I always encouraged the kids to call him up. And sometimes they would play pool online. And his visit in January wasn't all about me. It was the father-daughter dance for Girl Scouts and the Pinewood Derby weekend. Unfortunately we had an ice and snow storm, and you already know if they get a dusting of snow in the South everything is shut down! So the dance was moved to March and the derby was held the following Monday, so he missed both! My thoughts were why should I force you to take care of your responsibilities and call your kids because the kids will see for themselves. The last time they talked to him, they called on his birthday in May. I guess he was busy because he said he would call them back. And when he did, they were asleep. Two months ago! And his nonexistent $20 per week is not making any difference right now to my financial situation. So I have until July 27 to decide what I will do.

So now you want to know about the texting and you won't get angry, huh? Yeah right! LOL. Basically you know he had stopped calling for a while. I had been spending a few days organizing my CDs and DVDs and remembered that Que had all my rap CDs from the summer of '08. I brought them to Buffalo with me to let him listen to them, not keep, but at the end of that summer I couldn't get out of that house fast enough, so I wasn't thinking about it then. And Nicole was supposed to go to Buffalo like mid-June, so I figured she could bring the CDs back with her, along with some new DVDs since his friend has the absolute best quality DVDs and there were some movies I wanted. So I texted him in early June to let him know to gather them up. He replied that the CDs had been with him all this time and that they are his by common law. WTF! So I said, "No, you've had them one year and I want them back." So he called.

You probably remember when I told you he called after, like, three weeks of silence. So we talked about nothing for a few minutes, then my battery died on the phone. He texted me later saying, "I guess your battery died," and I replied, "Yeah, and it's raining like crazy with thunder." So he was like, "Do you like that?" Duh, he already knows I love thunderstorms, so I said, "Yeah, but Justine is not liking it at all." That's when he sent dumb text number one, saying it would be nice to get a nice cleavage pic with the thunderstorm in the background. I was polite and said, "No more of that, remember?" He replied, "Once in a while is not bad." So I replied, "Yes, it is 'cuz it always leads to the same thing." From that day he started texting good morning to me. Sometimes I replied with a simple good morning, sometimes I don't send anything. On one time when I did reply, he sent back, "I still love you." I didn't reply back to that one because this has been our dysfunctional relationship for so many years and I wasn't getting reeled in.

So he called maybe two days later and we talked about nothing, and he said, "Tell my babies hi and I love them." I didn't say nothing because he should have been asking to speak to them himself. Later that day he sent me a picture text of him standing in front of his van. He had on sunglasses. And I replied to that, "I don't recall ever seeing you in sunglasses." He replied, "You like?" And I'm thinking, does it matter? So I replied it's a nice look, and left it at that. I get a few more good mornings and/or goodnights. Then on the Fourth of July he sent me a pic of fireworks and "good morning." That was the morning of my car break-in, so I replied, "Maybe for you but it's fucked up for me," and gave him a quick rundown of what happened. He replied, "Wow," with a sad face, asked if I had glass coverage. Which made me more mad because I didn't. So I replied no. No more replies from him till the next morning. He said, "Good morning, when are you getting the window fixed?" I said I have no idea. He asked how much is it, and I told him every place I called was closed since most places we're closed the Monday after.

Later that morning my phone beeped and it was on the table. So Jordan said, "Mom, you got a message," so I told him to bring me the phone. I opened a pic text of his damn penis with the message, "Something to brighten your day!" Money to fix my damn window would have made my day! I was glad Jordan didn't open my message! So he called later asking if I liked the picture. I answered by saying I was glad Jordan didn't see it since he had my phone, and ignored the question at hand. I know right now you are angry and probably saying why didn't I say more or cuss him out or <u>something</u>! Because it's not worth the effort. And it doesn't mean I'm wavering in any way about ever getting back with him. That door is <u>closed</u>!

So anyway, he sends a few more good mornings and one day asked what we're going to do that day. I told him I was braiding in the morning and no other plans, and he replied, "Oh." I had been replying good morning back but as of that past Monday I just stopped because I'm really like, what's the point?? So since I stopped, he has also stopped. And you know I thought he was asking about the window because he was going to help me get it fixed. He never mentioned it again, even though that day he called I told him I had no idea when I would have the extra money to replace the window.

So, my dear, that's what I mean about the dumb shit that ain't worth mentioning as far as texting. I just don't look deep into its meaning because I already know it's his way of trying to keep himself fresh in my mind. He was always on my mind but totally not in that way. I constantly remind myself of the emotional abuse I've been through for twelve years and think about how liberating it is to know I won't ever have to go through that again! So as much as you asked me to please not hurt you, I'm <u>asking</u> and <u>demanding</u> the same from you since I'm willing to say no to all the clowns out here who want a shot at your girl, and wait twelve more months to make things work with you!

I tried the sweet and spicy tuna today, and hickory smoked is still my favorite so far. We went over to the new house around 1:00 p.m. (that you didn't even know is Sunday, 7/18, and I fell asleep like two pages ago, LOL). I put the bed together with the kids' help, and actually both toilet seats are torn but mine is torn much more. And again, something they should have handled prior. I cleaned all the countertops and wiped the inside of the fridge and freezer. Overall they left the house pretty good but they had two big dogs, so Jordan's allergies were bothering him after a while, meaning there is a lot of leftover pet dander and hair. I didn't bring the vacuum cleaner yet, but the kids were so proud to be unpacking stuff for their own rooms! The stove is a glass-top stove, which I've never cooked on before. And the oven needs cleaning as well.

I took pics all over so that there is no confusion or misunderstanding. I'm going to find some movers on Craigslist in about two to three weeks when I'm ready to move our big stuff. I got two guys to move me for $120 before because it's hard times for a lot of people and people are hungry. When we moved to these apartments in Matthews it was literally me and Jordan, no other help!

I may be doing a road trip to Atlanta the week after next to visit Brooklyn during her birthday. Hopefully I will have a job lined up very soon, so nothing is set yet as far as visiting her. Camp Invention begins tomorrow and I'll be going to see the third *Twilight* movie, *Eclipse*, one day minus the kids! A pedicure would be fantastic, so we'll see.

Well, Bryan, this letter and the last were super long and it's almost 8:00 p.m. and I'm hungry. So I'm going to pause our conversation here, and we'll pick this up tomorrow. *Quiero mucho*, baby!

Yours truly, truly yours,
Janae

July 18, 2010 (answering 7/8)

Good afternoon Janae,

Before I get started, I was just reading over letters from a month ago from you and you mentioned this is all new to you and you've never had a relationship with someone in prison. And I wanted to reply to you that love may not always come in the form that everyone else thinks you should have.

Sometimes we go through life thinking the unexpected is not normal living. When in fact, when you don't expect things, reality seems to always give you what you need in life.

I hope I didn't lose you or bore you. It's just that I think a lot more about our relationship from day one, and the progress is mind-blowing due to the subject matter we've discussed, dealing with our past highs and lows, family, our goals, our fantasies, wants, needs, and so on. So I don't want you to think I'm not really reading these letters fully and going back and rereading them over and over.

Getting to your letter, I did and always do have things on my mind constantly. The constant maneuvering I have to do in this place is draining. Your love for me keeps me sane and energizes me every day, knowing I truly have a purpose to get home to besides family, and that's starting my own family. And just like I'm confirming to let you know I'm alright, vice versa! I want you to know that every day is a constant obstacle, from waking up, back to the cell, and so on. And in between all that there's programs to take if you need them or your assigned job if you're lucky to receive one. I constantly think about you and family! About Chris Brown, society always loves to fill you up in order to tear you down when you make a mistake. They don't know the full facts of what happened. You're not putting distress on me about letters. Stress is when I don't get any from you, wondering if I've lost your interest in me and what we can become! I'm not going to regress to frivolous behavior. And you're right, I'm on a countdown, but we are both brats.

I will focus on you and Jordan so you would not do without, ever. As far as music goes, I have a Walkman flash radio with a few tapes. And once my finances get right, I have to buy some more headphones. As far as non-food items, books, personal hygiene items. I either have to buy them at the store or order them myself. When I get to a medium-security prison, which will be in about three to five months, then you will be able to send me those types of things! I'll let you know when that time comes, but I never want to take away from you or the kids! And that's without a doubt, I will make it up to you when I get out, and some.

Oh, it's just a blessing to have you in my life! And yes, in that picture it does say a lot of things. And defeated at times is an understatement, but our future looks brighter every day 'cuz you really give me a sense of purpose considering the situation. And I'm ready to talk to you now, so that's why I sent you the information in the last letter 'cuz <u>I need to hear your voice yesterday.</u> So if it don't work on cell phones, then landline it will have to be. And at the end of this letter, I will send you an updated food list and the tuna will definitely be on that list! And I'm blessed that God has blessed you in order for you to pass it on to me! And yes, you can never let your guard down 'cuz the devil works overtime. And yes, we both have so much to be thankful for that God allowed people in our lives to bring us together!

Your fantasies are similar to mine 'cuz I definitely want to go on a romantic getaway and just cuddle, among other things a couple does to unwind. Swimming pool action and the rain is a must. I've never done it and would love to try! Yes, the video and role-playing is a definite must, just so long as you don't get mad and sell it to the highest bidder, LOL! I'm sorry that you haven't had someone that make you climb the walls. We will have to work on that! Now, I'm going to be honest with you like always. Here and there I do smoke a joint and lie back and listen to some music. And that shit does enhance all the nerve cells sexually, so I'm not against that. But that's <u>the only natural drug I indulge in</u>! Oral sex I'm good at, not that I've had many recipients, only two, so pump your brakes 'cuz I know you were going to be like, "Good to who?" But that's something we will explore when the time comes, and it will come literally!

My favorite position is missionary so I can look into your eyes as well as have full view of your body, and definitely doggystyle. To see that ass you possess will be like Christmas,

LOL! And I definitely can manage to hold you on the wall. That's why I pump these weights harder every day. I'm glad to hear you are an equal giving partner. That's very important. And that's pleasing to hear you would fight for me and us 'cuz I'm fighting every day for you and us to get home.

I have somewhat of a temper when I'm lied to or when I'm put in a situation that may harm me or my family and loved ones. I also don't like people that harm children or senior citizens! I'm not afraid to cry either, especially over some movies and tears of joy. Also, *Extreme Makeover* is a must! I'm glad that you will take more pictures. Thank you for sharing the family pictures with me. That was very deep for me! Yes, you do have to show me your good and not-so-good side. You see, I started off with my not-so-good side!

Well, Ms. Lady, it's 12:00 midnight Monday, so I'm going to end this letter so I may get some beauty sleep myself. And I will focus on our future, and I won't get in any trouble that will dampen our future. You have my word. I'll stay positive and strong for you also, but you must continue to take care of my body also, and that means eating right and plenty of rest! And I'm not confused when I say I love you 'cuz your spirit allows me to love you and I was passed gone when you wrote that letter to the parole board! It's no pressure 'cuz I know you'll be in love with me shortly 'cuz God never lied to me! Can't wait to hear from you again!

Sealed with my love to you, your man,
Bryan

July 19, 2010

Following your letter right back,

    I hope you're happy now 'cuz as soon as I received your letter here I am writing you right back since you said I'm like four or five letters behind. But you must have not been checking your mailbox 'cuz I swear I'm caught up and answered all your letters.

    Jordan is just feeling himself, but you must stay consistent when you lay the law down. Mean it and don't keep repeating yourself. Once you told him, that's it. Then start taking away things he likes and let him earn them back. But I'm glad he saw the mail truck 'cuz I didn't want him to think I was selling him a dream. I never want to be put in that category. I'm glad to hear that he wrote those words that he misspelled, but I want him to show you those rules I told him to put on his wall that he must obey each and every day. And let him know I'm waiting on my letter now. And if I misspell something, it's due to me rushing to get something in the mail or me being disturbed by things around me while I'm writing you. But I'm human also, and I wouldn't be mad at you if you told me I spelled some words wrong. It's not that serious!

    I am understanding about the pictures, I guess. But me, I'm going to show all sides to me no matter what I go through. That's why I put that first picture. But if you have to be in the mood, I respect that for now, LOL! And I'm going to smile regardless 'cuz I know what I have and my aim is to keep you interested in me for life, not just for the moment, woman! And you don't know what God has in store for us. He may bring us closer to each other where you can touch, caress, and so on. I might move closer to home and you may visit while I'm closer, you never know. You always have to think outside the line 'cuz tangible can always happen at the drop of a hat!

That's good you read with the kids all the time, but it must be a time when they will come ask you if they can read to you, initiate the quiet time, then you know it's on! And what do you mean our thoughts are the same but sit-ups and free squats are something you won't do unless you're at the gym? Sounds like a cop-out to me, and you don't strike me as a woman that cops out. Anything worth having is worth working for. You said yourself you wanted to tighten up. That means working out at home when you have free time on your hands. At the same time, I'm not making a workout video. But extra work never killed no one. If you cheer for yourself, it doesn't matter if you have a cheering section or not. The main thing is you made the effort by yourself. And of course, I will help you when I get home. But what about now?

Now, my favorite cartoons were *Hong Kong Phooey*, also *Space Ghost*. Last but not least, *Ren and Stimpy*! My first family vacation was when we went to Disney World in Florida, where my brother drowned in the hotel pool and some white man came out of nowhere and jumped in the pool, clothes and shoes on, and brought my brother out of the deep end, performed CPR, and brought him back to life!

My brother was the one who really got in trouble the most. It really hit the fan. While we were catering a reception at our church, my brother stole the car and was gone for a whole day. His father found him and brought him back to the house. That's when my grandparents kicked him out of the house and he went to live with his father. I went and visited him over there, but it just wasn't the same. I was in seventh grade at the time, and we was always close at the time. But our relationship got strained when he went away to the army and then came home and got this chick pregnant with my first niece.

At the time I was going to South Park High School, so I started going out with this girl. She was a senior and I was a sophomore. She so happened to be friends with his baby mother, and they lived around the corner from each other. Well, my brother went back to do one more year. While he was gone, my ex-girl threw a little get-together with food, drinks, weed, and invited some people over, including the baby mother. Well, the baby mother decided to fuck someone I know at the party, and I told her she was dead wrong. Well don't you know, she told my brother that we had sex and my brother believed her and thinks his son by her is mine.

After that, our relationship has never been the same. Also, he's always been jealous of me because I was the spoiled one out of the boys. He got mad 'cuz my grandparents gave me my first car and sent me to basketball camps, and so on. I was the one that never got in trouble, and he couldn't stand that. And he, to this day, still chooses his friends over family. Out of fifteen years, he's only been to see me twice, and just in April sent me $20 after fifteen years. Also, he still tries to sell me dreams over the phone about what he's going to send me, knowing he's lying. So I really don't have words for him, to answer your question if we get along fairly. And that's just fine with me 'cuz before you put water over blood, I'll never treat you like blood. That's why me and Brooklyn are so close 'cuz I would never let anything happen to her no matter who you are! And it's sad that he has all those kids 'cuz he don't take care of them the way he could. So yes, he and your ex are neck and neck.

As far as me and my father, motherfuck that faggot. He never did anything for me. I saw him once when I was in fifth grade about to go into the hospital to get my appendix removed, and I didn't see him no more. And no, I don't see any reconciliation in the future. I have nothing against you asking my twin nothing, but give me the benefit of the doubt and ask me. That's what trust is about, that you can trust me enough to ask me anything and I will tell you the truth. I have nothing to hide from you. But it's a process from being in the life of hustling. Sometimes if you don't ask me I'm not quick to tell you, and that is something I'm truly working on, so please help me!

My favorite TV shows to watch right now are *Big Brother*, *CSI*, *TNT*, *TBS* shows. That's about it 'cuz the rest is sports or writing your four or five catch-up letters! Now you see how I'm listening to you. I hope you're doing the same for me!

Well, miss, they just called recreation, so I'm going to end, little mama. So now I'm waiting for your replies, and tell Jordan I'm waiting his also!

Love you,
Jarelle
PS: That Victoria's Secret smells tasty. That's the one!

July 21, 2010

Hi Jarelle,

Happy Wednesday to you. I'm sitting here watching *Dr. Phil* and the kids are at camp. I just finished reading your 7/15 letter for like the fourth time. By the time you get this letter hopefully you won't be too annoyed with me because it will probably be like a week of getting no letters from me. My reasoning is basically to let you catch up on my previous letters so that you're not replying to any emotion I was feeling several days back, or the fact that sometimes I get in a zone of writing and forget what I've said. And when you answer I'm trying to recall what I even said. It's not to punish you, and this is not me still complaining about not getting mail. I just want our conversations to match and us to be on the same page so I already know I'm forgiven. So now to start answering your first letter.

Of course I'm staying on top of the prospective job at Crown Point. The only problem is the principal is at an out-of-town training, so

I've not talked to him since our conversation almost two weeks ago. And yes, I've applied to other schools as well. But when I check on the status for each position, there are more than three hundred other people applying for each job! To say the competition is fierce is beyond an understatement, and it truly becomes all about who you know and networking and God! I don't want to be forced into an occupation outside of teaching just for the sake of having a job, but in ten weeks my unemployment extension will end again. I appreciate your confidence that I will be working by the end of the summer!

Jordan did the assignment but he hasn't been doing that list of fifteen things he is supposed to do daily. No major behavior issues. And between camp and playing outside, they both have been playing hard. But I told him to transfer the list to a chart so I'll mention it once. But that's between you and him.

Today I plan to go to the 1:20 show of *Eclipse* alone. I worked at the movies for three years, so going to the movies alone was always cool to me. I was going to call Nicole but she may be working. She is my cousin by marriage. Her mom married my uncle on my dad's side when she was like eight and I was like seven. They had a son together, my blood cousin, and she has a middle brother also not blood related. They've since divorced, but me and Nicole have a unique bond because our parents both made very poor choices as we were growing up. She was working at JCPenney Salon but recently started at a salon, and it seems to be working out great. As far as gray hair, I've always been surprised that I don't have it yet. And thank God because the women on my mom's side gray very early! But the crazy thing, I have like five gray pubic hairs! I yanked one out and decided, never mind, I'll let it grow 'cuz ouch! Speaking of pubic hair, do you like au natural, shaving, or combination? And are you circumcised? I also hate soggy cereal! Too funny. Froot Loops is one of my favorites, but I love cereal, so I have many.

Speaking of my parents, I'm going to write two separate letters going in detail about each. I can almost guarantee you'd really like my father. He was extremely disappointed about me being pregnant, but I think it was a daddy thing and the fact that he thought I was a virgin! Really!

I was like twenty-one! You and my mom is hard to say. She's almost a completely different person from decade to decade, and I think she's nearing a mental breakdown. But like I said, that would be two separate letters on my parents.

About sex, just because I like kissing doesn't mean that for every sexual experience I want a full kissing, foreplay, etc. before intercourse. Variety is important, and there's nothing wrong with a quickie! My biggest issue with Que was how routine the experience seemed to be, almost like I could put a stopwatch to each thing. Not going into detail, but I'm looking forward to experiences with you. But <u>please</u> do not make it your mission to make me have an orgasm! You'd be surprised to know that up to 70 percent of women don't have orgasms during intercourse, and it's nothing the man can do about it. It's about the woman, not what the man is doing or not doing. A lot of it is mental. I just don't want it to become a situation where hours later you are still waiting for me to come. Because it may or may not happen, but if I feel pressured, how can I focus on the enjoyment of it? I think that's why I figured faking was easier, but I promise I won't fake with you.

I'm not into dildos really, and I'm not into anal anything! You're asking <u>me</u> will I be gentle with <u>you</u>?? I was wondering the exact opposite! It's been a hell of a lot longer time for you than me! Will <u>you</u> be gentle with <u>me</u>? LOL! The toy thing is something I've mainly done alone, so doing it as a couple will be kind of new. I went to an adult store a few months back and one of my Girl Scout parents was there. She looked embarrassed, and my thought was we're both single parents and some satisfaction did not come from our kids, so do you!

And to clear things up, <u>yes, I know</u> I'm sexy. It just was something that I wasn't sure of at one point, but I am! As always we are being open and honest. Quincy actually called me yesterday but the kids were at camp. He said he misses us, and the funny thing he said was if I don't find a job by the time my unemployment ends, how soon after that do I plan to move back to Buffalo? And my mom, I swear, is praying that I don't find a job so I can move back. And live where? Back in BMHA or my parents? Or with him and his mom? Seriously! I told him then

I'll work in some braiding salon, which I truly don't want to do! LOL. So I'm still praying for God's favor to put me exactly where I need to be.

I'm about to pack a few things to take to the house and get ready for the movies. Until our words meet again . . .

Luv ya, papi!
Janae

July 21, 2010 (evening)

Hey Sweetie,

It was awesome! Definitely my favorite of the three *Twilight* movies so far. It definitely did the book justice because you know usually the book is way better. Like *Waiting to Exhale*! That was the biggest disappointment! The book was absolutely fabulous and the movie was mediocre at best.

Tomorrow is my last child-free day. Today was so freaking hot outside my back, thighs, under my bra, armpits, just sweating like crazy against them damn leather seats in that car. It registered 100 according to my car's external temperature. I didn't get a letter from you yesterday or today and I was totally fine, so I'm getting better! I will be getting my PO box tomorrow and you will have to start sending mail there. My new physical address will be 344 Touch Me Not Lane. Isn't that too funny? This heat is taking a toll on my body. I sweat underneath my breast. And since I wear underwires, I've started chafing and now I have an ugly rash. It's not severe by any means, just two-toned, and I'm glad you don't have to see it! Trying not to scratch is difficult. Actually, that's wrong. It's more like a heat rash, not as bad as chafing. I'm sleepy. This week of getting up early for camp is kicking my butt. I'll continue in the morning.

7/22

Last day of getting up early for camp, finally. I didn't take advantage of this break from the kids as much as I should have. The movie was nice, but I spent the rest of the time packing and unloading. But it's cool. I'm so used to having my kids 24/7 that getting a break almost feels unnatural. Plus, this past school year with no job has been the ultimate break in a good and bad way.

At the school, the parents got to see what the kids have been doing all week. And Ms. Lester (science teacher) told me Mr. Walker (principal) is back! Of course he was gone, but now at least I know he's back in town. I'll get right on that tomorrow.

I had to change clothes after running my errands this morning from sweating. Ugh! I was in Family Dollar and saw the cutest basketball lamp for Jordan. I told the clerk not to put it in the bag so that I could hold it and it won't break. So my clumsy ass drops the doggone lamp and it shatters! And that was the last lamp. But he was nice enough to call up other stores, and finally found one near the new house.

After I picked up the kids I checked the mail and had two more letters. Such a great feeling! The kids went straight outside so I could read in peace, but Justine came back, like, two minutes later and said it was too hot. Then of course she wanted to tell me about this and that, and I was thinking, oh man! Lol. But as I was reading, I think one of your letters was lost in the mail! I never got anything from you about how we can start phone calls, and you said it was sent in the last letter. Now I'm wondering have any of mine never been received or if any others of yours been lost before I got them. So I still need to know how we can begin phone calls. I bet hearing your voice will make me turn to mush!

But I kept thinking there was stuff I talked about or asked you about and you never replied, so maybe that letter will surface. But if not, I don't remember everything from that letter, and I'm sure the conversation will come up again. And at the same time I'm thinking, man, what did you write to me and I'm missing your words, wondering how you were feeling. And feeling a little guilty because I was fussing about not getting letters when you sent me something that's lost. Oh well, now I'm sleepy, so I'll continue in the morning.

7/23

Another hot, hot, hot day. High, in the upper nineties, but the heat index says it will feel like 105–110! We haven't left the house yet, and I wanted to take some more stuff to the new house. It's now 6:00 p.m. I started cleaning and cooking dinner. The kids went swimming, and now Jordan is back on the computer and Justine went back out. I'm making barbecue wings in the oven and waiting for my friend Kimberly to come over. I'm braiding her daughter's hair, no charge. We both are in the same situation—single mom, two kids, no child support, no job, college degree. When I was in a bind she <u>gave</u> me $100 in food stamps, and she has no hairstyling skills, LOL. So I told her anytime. When I move she will be about seven minutes from me, Nicole will be ten, Rhonda will be almost thirty since she's in Gastonia, into the furthest almost forty minutes.

While I'm sitting here with a quiet moment, let me get two questions in your last letter. I didn't think you would be moved again. That would make visits to New York so much more worthwhile. Would we actually be able to touch in a medium security? Or a kiss?

I know there is more I can do regarding my personal goal of toning and healthier living. The one thing is that I do love healthy foods, just have to work on my cravings.

I recall the song for *Hong Kong Phooey* but not *Space Ghost*. I liked *Ren and Stimpy* also, and now I actually watch *SpongeBob* even when the kids aren't home. But the original *Scooby-Doo* is my favorite, and I couldn't stand Scrappy!

I am in shock at how much you have endured in your life. To witness your brother drown! It has told me about your brother, and it's a shame he's in his forties and still behaving like a teenager. I thought you've been in twelve years, not fifteen! I bet it's mind-blowing to you just watching on TV how technology has changed, but when you experience it in person . . . ! Like my cell phone. I have a Palm Pixi, which has a touchscreen and keyboard combo.

And the movies. I have a large collection. *Friday* is one of my ultimate favorites, and *Money Talks* as far as comedies. You only have a Walkman and a few tapes, that won't do! So am I allowed to send you my MP3 or CD player? Are you only allowed a certain number of packages each year? But if I send you one now, I can't send any more for 2010? That would suck because I want to send you more, then your birthday in September I want to send you something too.

I have a landline phone, so when we start talking on the phone it should be okay.

I can't wait until October to decorate my front yard for Halloween, my ultimate favorite holiday! I'm going to have a party on Beggar's Night at the house, then take the kids out for Halloween night. We've never been home on Halloween night, so I never know if we get trick or treaters. Ironically, my due date was 10/31 and my first concern then was who would take the kids out on Halloween night? Silly, right?

Their dad called me again yesterday, two days in a row. It's funny how I knew his every move but fell for it time and time again. And he's been texting me good morning again. This is literally how I got caught up all over again back in October. We hadn't talked for a long while since he brought the kids back to Charlotte in July 2009. Then he called one day and we were on the phone all day then he was calling all day everyday and feeling stirred back up. Except this time is different because I have a good reason not to regress. It's gotten me absolutely nowhere, and my heart belongs to someone else: you!

I find myself thinking about you all the time! You don't have to worry about me losing interest! So what are some of your fantasies that I didn't mention? And why would I trip on how many partners you've had or what you did with them? They are the past, I am the present and future! I Love missionary as well because it's easier to kiss, gaze into each other's eyes. And your hands can grip beneath my hips far deeper . . . I better stop! It's going to be some serious lovemaking! I like to ride also, and I can't wait to be up against the wall.

Last week we were at Nicole's house having girl talk, and she said her coworker is frustrated because her husband has an extremely small penis. The size of her pinky, no exaggeration! But he was great at oral sex and so good to her, she married him. And he often straps on a dick. But she hates it now and they haven't had sex since December! I stopped seeing a man because of a small penis before, and I thought I was very shallow for it. But I realized intercourse is very important to me, and I'd be lying to myself staying in that relationship. I wonder if all those pills they sell to increase a man's size works. I can't imagine doing it doggy style and it keeps slipping out! Frustration is not even close to describing that! I have ass for days, so are you really ready for it? LOL. I'm glad we won't have that problem!

7/24

I was going to finish last night but I was sleepy. I want to make sure this gets out in the morning mail so that you have it by Tuesday, and the fact that you haven't had mail in a week from me. I made breakfast for us (eggs, bacon, waffles), and we're watching *Extreme Makeover* as I write before we head over to the house so I can hang up pictures and photos. And last but not least, I'm enclosing this money order for you and I hope it helps out. I don't want you to have any added stress so that you can take care of my body and soul. Until our words meet again, stay strong, be blessed!

Luv ya!
Janae

PS: This scent is Mary Kay's Embrace Romance. Hope you like it!

July 22, 2010

Ms. Lady,

How are you doing? I hope fine 'cuz Janae is bugging right now. 'Cuz you said I take everything you say completely out of context, and that is far from the truth! And you're explaining yourself clearly. It's just sometimes my opinions may be too strong for you or you need to relax more! And my comprehension level is beyond graduate school! You say there is a lag between responses, I don't run the mail system. Just like today, it's the twenty-second, but I received a letter today that said the fifteenth and yesterday, fourteenth. So you tell me about the lag. I tried to tell you it takes them damn near four days for my mail to get to you and I'm thinking vice versa!

There's no need to apologize for the letters you've written me in a bad mood 'cuz you'll probably get your share from me too before I get out. 'Cuz I'm sure I'll be in some bad moods days to come. So just like I'm understanding, please be the same on my days! Although I feel we are going through the same things, but I feel you shouldn't have to compromise your happiness. Nobody runs Janae but Janae. You have things to be grateful for but you're not content, and my opinion is you don't have a job and it's eating at your core 'cuz you're used to working. And it seems things are moving at a snail's pace, and it's frustrating. And just like everyone's input, everyone has one just like they have assholes, so what. When you continue to listen to that bullshit, then you start consuming that garbage in your mental!

If the same people are so interested in saying things, why aren't they helping you in your situation? Your weight is not a problem to me, so get that out your head. But I'll touch that later in this letter! Why do you always say you're not trying to put pressure on me? Listen, I'm 100 percent man and I've dealt with pressure, even at childbirth trying to get out my momma's crack. So until I tell you I can't handle it, please don't assume or speculate. When you're stressed, you're supposed to pray and thank God for the good and the bad. That's what faith is. And always having someone to call or run to doesn't always equate to your problems being solved. In fact, it may increase them instead of decrease them!

And you say don't respond to this, why not? You say you want someone to talk to, so let it out, speak your mind so I know what I'm dealing with. Don't hold back. And I am reading your letters. I may have misread that part about your license, but it ain't that serious for you to call yourself correcting me, and to ask me do I really think you're not trying to find work. Are you serious? I think you need to take a few steps back and come again. You know damn well I know you're busting your ass looking for work, so that was a waste of ink! Listen, miss, by all means give the kids what they need—stable house, solid school. I'm all for that. And you know it's the right move to a house 'cuz it's something you've been wanting since adulthood. So stop second-guessing yourself and look forward instead of backward!

You have to live with the decisions you make, not the ones who are telling you what you're doing and not doing right. Live, baby girl, do you. Everything else will fall into place, you'll see! Don't look for Jordan to apologize all the time 'cuz then he'll start doing it only to appease you and it won't be heartfelt. Let him do it on his own. And if he doesn't do it, move on. Say your peace and leave it at that. I know you haven't given me an image of a monster, just a little boy who is smelling his self at an early age. And compiled with your frustration with life itself, you're giving too much on what he's not saying sorry for instead of just checking him and moving on. And he's not going to go down the wrong path. Speaking it into existence 'cuz what you put out into the universe comes back.

Yes, school influences to a certain extent but not entirely, but as long as you do your part 100 percent, you will not be blamed for nothing 'cuz you know the truth! Now, if you want two to three letters a week you got that, I have no problem with that. I'm going to feed you like you feed me.

And I could have sworn you said Jordan came in your room and said you were burglarized while you were asleep, another misread on my part. And you read too much into the situation with your neighbor's boyfriend. I see you get real fly out the mouth real quickly over some dumb shit that doesn't make or break us. And I'm not questioning your loyalty. I don't care if the president is trying to get at you, I got locked jaw, so that don't move me. That's exactly where your sexual frustrations will be, in a bottle, until I pop that top. And as far as you breaking a letter in parts, that was a joke that you literally took out of context. Talking about calling the kettle black! LOL. No, you'll never be broke dealing with me. You can take that to the bank 'cuz I chase money but the money never runs!

Congratulations on getting a call back for an interview. I pray you get something 'cuz you deserve it. I'm also happy you're getting stuff accomplished as far as the house goes. Make sure you take pictures of it once you get it done! I'm glad you finally tasted the tuna 'cuz that is definitely a must-have. As you said, I'll have the updated list by the time you get this letter!

Well, I finally have some good news today. I finally got a job I wanted in the soap factory. I make soap, box it, and get it ready for shipping. I also make germicidal soap, hand wash, wax for the floor. We make these things for hospitals, schools, businesses, and so on. I get paid $17 every two weeks, so give me a week or two and I'll start buying my stamps so that I can keep you full, LOL!

That's crazy that a lady that works in a bank goes by the churches taking clothes she knows she's not going to give to needy people but to sell. It's foul, God don't like ugly, and she will get hers for doing shit like that. Then again, it might be an inside job.

Well, I'm going to end this right here. I'm not going to take your first page of that letter too seriously or personal, but I did answer back to it just the same. Venting is good, and I have a big back, so I can handle it! I don't take everything you say about the opposite sex out of context, I just put in place.

Sincerely yours,
Jarelle

PS: Jordan's letter will be included with this.

July 24, 2010

Hi Janae,

    How have you been these past couple of days? I know you haven't written me the last two days, but I understand you're all talked out for now. But by the time you get this letter you should have gotten three to four letters from me. I pray by now you are learning more about me as the letters continue. Please be patient with me 'cuz I'm usually a private person considering all I've been through from the street until now. I've seen that firsthand, as well as many other things.
    I've never really taken the time to comprehend what drugs were doing to people and families. I used to literally find people that were doing drugs and couldn't provide for their selves. Something a lot of people didn't know, including family, I used to do a lot for senior citizens around the neighborhood, like clear their yards for free and take them plates of food from somewhere. I called myself giving back, but I still feel I have much more to do for the damage I've done for some drugs.

Don't worry about me buying pictures instead of stamps. Nothing is going to keep me from writing you and Jordan! And where did you put those pictures you got printed up of me? Are they around the house, in your room, the car? And I apologize about the picture you received of me. I know I look weary and serious, but I go through a lot in twenty-four hours than a person goes through in a couple of hours! I don't mean to make you sad, but finances has nothing to do with me sending you a picture that makes you smile. But I can't wait until all these good things you're talking about have reached me! 'Cuz you definitely make me smile, and it radiates from the inside out. And I couldn't be more happier to have you in my life. And that's crazy to say that you're not going to send me pics if you're having a bad week or hair day. I want to feel all of you—bad day, good day, when you're down as well as up! You're not going to always have good days, neither am I. That's why I'm glad you saw that picture 'cuz you'll have an idea how I look when I'm serious and weary. You said you wanted to know me. I'm sure I'll see many sides of you when I get out. Until then, I'll take what I can get!

I watch the Spanish station too, but only certain things, game shows, the weather, and their version of *Survivor*. I'm pretty sure the kids will settle down once they are in their new house and have more room and privacy to do their own things. With Jordan, he's at an age where he likes to play mind games. So in order to combat it you have to sometimes act like you don't even acknowledge what he's doing. But later on pull him up and explain to him the do's and don'ts of the type of things he's doing. Another thing, don't always yell at every single thing he does. Sometimes just ignore it and just give him a look and see what happens next. And when it comes to reading, just ask him did he read today. And if he says no, just look at him and move on. Don't yell, just look! Eventually he'll get the picture. And 'cuz he's gotten used to you yelling all the time, do the opposite for a minute and see his reaction. But don't let it get out of hand! He's self-motivated, just not in the things he should be. He's still young, so he doesn't really know what's good for him totally.

And all this is just my opinion. I'm in no way, shape, or form telling you that you're doing wrong. Or if something goes wrong it's your fault, and so on, just to clear that up. Firsthand, I'm simply saying try a different angle! Please stop telling me he needs more than one letter 'cuz I know what he needs. I was once a young boy. Also telling me if I want you to hold off on finding someone here you need more consistency from me, what the hell is that supposed to mean? Please explain 'cuz I don't want to read too much into anything, remember! And I understand he checks the mailbox. One thing he will learn is patience 'cuz I learned at an early age. But now that I have a job he can get two letters a week, but he must wait 'cuz I have to earn the money. But I can add a letter in with yours until then.

Children might be manipulative, but you're the parent. Try this when he walks away next time you're talking to him. Follow his ass and just look at him. If he's supposed to be reading and he's watching TV, go and cut the TV off. See, you have to put your foot down 'cuz you're Mom and Dad right now. And when you say something, there is no other option other than what you say to do! That's another thing, you don't whoop him 'cuz it seems to me you're soft, too soft! I got my butt whooped and that set me straight for a long while. And yes, you need a balance of both parents, but I know a lot of single parents that are holding it down. And they definitely whoop that ass if you get out of hand! A long time ago I used to let it ride only to check it later, so sometimes you do let things right to a certain extent, nothing serious.

Well, I'm glad you're starting to sort through different things for the house and throwing things away that were not needed. Who are you getting to help you move? And be careful when you pick your crew 'cuz it's some weirdos out there!

That Camp Invention coming up shortly, have you figured out what you are going to do with your free time? Well, sweetness, I don't want to end this but I start work tomorrow and I must get some rest and get ready 'cuz I have a feeling they're going to work me like a slave. So please think about me today and tomorrow 'cuz I think about you yesterday, today, and tomorrow. Tell the kids I said hello, and tell Jordan I said no excuses!

Yours truly, truly yours,
Jarelle

July 24, 2010

Hey Baby,

I knew I had it coming. And didn't I tell your hard-headed self not to reply to my venting? LOL. So thank you for putting me in my place because yes, my alter ego was tripping. You got yourself a Gemini, so it goes with the territory. But I see you won't let me act up. That's kind of sexy too at the same time. But as you can tell, this job thing has me bugging the hell out. And you're right, I just have to praise God through it all and everything will be all right.

I am so, so happy for you that you got a job! And it sounds pretty cool to be making soap and stuff. I made Pac-Man soap in third grade. I thought that was the coolest thing.

Jordan was happy to get a letter. And to clear things up for him, that last letter you got from him, he wrote it ages ago and had it sitting in his binder. I told him to mail it, and so he actually has not replied to your last letter. But I bet he'll get right on it. And this morning he finally finished that chart of fifteen things he's supposed to do every day. You know he's been so busy this week as a volunteer at Camp Invention and with his friends afterward.

I just mailed a long letter to you this morning and I still have so much to say. Well, in that letter we were about to go to the house and take some more things. We left at almost noon and it was ninety-three degrees. We get there and a damn hive of yellow jackets has formed above the front door, in the alcove! When I was there on Wednesday I noticed, like, three or four wasps going in and out of a slightly higher hole, so I texted Kathryn to let her know. And there were only a few and they weren't trying to come in the door, so I figured no big deal. So how about we pull up to the driveway and slightly below where the wasps were there are like thirty yellow jackets! All clustered up, making a new home!

One thing you will learn about me, spiders don't phase me, snakes don't phase me, then there are roaches! Enough said. So we couldn't go in the front door, and luckily I have the patio door key so we were able to get in. I texted Kathryn right away to let her know that she will have to get it exterminated before we move in. This chick replies that the nest wasn't there when they left (on 7/16), and for me to try spraying it. I wanted to ask her what she on, crack or heroin! So I said no, I would not be taking any chances getting stung or not getting all of them.

So she said for me to get some quotes on the bee removal then forward her the bill, and she'll deduct it from my security deposit. Hell no! I had to remind her that the purpose of a security deposit is, in case we cause some damage to the home, it will be covered, and the remaining will be forwarded to me when I move. Then I said I didn't bring the bees with me! So I said I'll call some places for a price and we can either deduct it from my first month's rent or if she can send me money for payment. I guess people really think they can run game or she's just clueless.

She said to hold off on calling because her mom has a friend in Monroe about an hour out who owns a landscaping and extermination company, and they will call him to get a cheap price. And if she tries anything dumb, technically our lease doesn't begin until August 1. So regardless, they need to make sure the house is safe. And I don't care if that's six months from now. It's her house, and I'll be damned if I get stung or the kids. And I ain't paying for a shit!

Then she texted me, like, an hour later. Her husband's friend is going to come on Monday or Tuesday and try to spray and remove the hive himself. He gone get his ass stung the hell up if they try to be cheap! LOL. But they better hope that works because I will not pay any rent until it's safe for us.

So I didn't get much done over there because I was aggravated by her stupidity and the fact that it was so freaking hot. I had to turn the AC off on Wednesday, so the house was hot. I turned the AC on but it was taking forever to cool off, so I didn't feel like hanging up pictures. But I took down the blinds and curtains in the living room and hung my own drapes. Their dogs had tore up the blinds to where it looks tacky, and there was dog hair on the curtains like crazy. When we left and got in the car, it was stifling hot! The outside temp hit 102, so the heat index must have been 110 to 115. And we all got booty sweat when we got out, looking like we peed on ourselves! LOL. The AC in the car is my next step to get fixed, and I think Meineke just advertised a free AC check, so I can at least see what the problem is. One place told me it was the control module and the part alone is like $300, but I think it's just a leak, so we will see soon.

Man, you got really aggravated about me talking about a lag with the mail, I see! That's exactly why I waited a few days to send anything. I'm getting your mail like two days after you send it, which is great. But like I said in the last letter, I think one of your letters was lost in the mail. And I admit I have written and had a letter sitting in my purse for days, but I don't do that often because you can't respond if I don't mail it. And now you reply to all my letters except the super long one I mailed this morning, so we're on about the same page.

I admit I was a little nervous to open this last one you sent (7/22) because I knew you were going to chew me out! LOL. I'm so out of that right now. Overall I feel good, but would feel much better working. I left a message for Mr. Walker on Friday and sent him an email. I didn't hear back from the Goddard School, that daycare that was supposed to call me this week for an interview. They were looking to fill a 7:00

to 3:00 p.m. shift, which would have been a real struggle since Jordan's school is 8:30 to 3:30 and Justine's school is 9:15 to 3:30. So I would not have had a way to get them to school. I didn't tell them that, but I was sure thinking it! Plus, daycares pay very little. Lead teachers make about $10 per hour and they want you to have a degree. Assistants usually make minimum wage and do just as much as a lead.

And I know that you know I'm trying. I was just going through the motions and not being fair about how uplifting you've been to me. I know that you know how it feels getting mail, and you have kept me full all week. Four letters this week feels great, so scratch what I said about two to three letters a week. You're a working man now, and I want to hear from you as much as possible! And again, Jarelle, I am so happy for you because working helps the time pass. And once we're both working, before you know it, your time will be up and you will be out! In the meantime though, is there any chance of you being transferred to North Carolina? Doesn't hurt to ask. But if you are moved close to Buffalo, then I believe I will be coming to see my boo!

So I guess I'm seeing more. You just have a sense of humor, but sometimes it's hard to understand the tone on paper, which will make our conversations so nice! But fly out of the mouth? Yes, I was being a smartass! LOL. I have a great sense of humor usually but sometimes slow with the comebacks when ribbed on. I will relax more and not take you so serious. Brooklyn did tell me you were a joking person.

7/25

I fell asleep with one of your pictures on my pillow. I was watching *Lockup Raw* and all I can say is I can't wait for you to be transferred to a medium or minimum security prison. It really speaks volumes about your character, strength, family support, and faith that you've come this far and still have your sanity.

We went to church and it was eighty-six degrees at 9:00 a.m., so by the time noon rolled around it was ninety-nine again. We've been exceeding the normal high for two weeks. Last summer was perfect, and summer '08 was spent in Buffalo. But when we moved here in August

2007 it was 105 for that first week straight, and none of us were ready for that. Then coming from Langfield I was scared to use the AC since I never had to pay for electric, but after a week I said forget that!

When we came, our furniture was a few days behind us, so we slept on air mattresses. Around 3:00 a.m. I was lying awake in the middle of the night and saw a big black mass on the ceiling. Didn't think nothing of it until it started moving! A water bug! Just a cute name for a big, oversized black roach! It freaked me the hell out, and they are so hard to kill. In the first apartment, those water bugs came in often and I had to get it sprayed many times. Have not had any problems in my current place or the ones I lived in last year.

I really liked Heatherwood Trace, and it was three bedrooms. But when I got laid off I knew I had to downsize, but my first thought was to run back to Buffalo. I know my parents and Que were disappointed that I changed my mind and decided to stick it out in Charlotte at the last minute. I had Que enroll Justine in school too, but I was trying to make everyone else happy. It's a lot less stressful when I'm only trying to make four people happy—the kids, me, and you!

The kids are at the pool, but with the high temp it's like taking a bath outside. I think it's time to take my braids out. I'm missing my hair now and my head be hot. We are still trying to go see Two next week, maybe Wednesday through Friday or something. So if the braids are coming out I need to start today. Hopefully I will have made up my mind before I go to bed, or I can take out the first few rows and give myself a retouch.

Well, it's time for me to get dinner started. And I would complain about your letter only being two full pages when mine are so much longer, LOL. But since you were fussing at me, two pages was plenty! And when you receive the letter just prior to this, I already know I was forgiven. But like you said, there's nothing wrong with venting once in a while. I'm really anxious for your next letter to see how we can begin our phone journey! Until then, take care. Stay strong and always in my thoughts.

Janae

PS: This scent is Moonlight Path by Bath & Body.

July 25, 2010

My dear Jarelle,

Do you realize I have been writing and thinking about you all day? I finished a letter to you earlier and here I am, starting another. It's very late, almost midnight. I needed a few things from Walmart so I waited till 9:00 to go. And don't you know, it was still in the upper eighties even that late. Well, I've decided it's *adios* time for the braids, so I'll start that in the morning. And I was trying to decide do I want to share with you about my mom, dad, or begin with the darker side of growing up with a crack epidemic in my home. But I'm so sleepy now, so I will sleep on that decision. But I've had this on my heart all day. I think I've officially fallen in love with you, but how do I know when it's love or just something new and exciting? So I want you, in an upcoming letter, to explain to me how do you know it's love with me. In the meantime, I'm literally about to fall asleep writing, so until the sun rises. Goodnight, baby!

7/26

It's about 11:00 p.m. and I can't believe I've refrained from writing all day. I talked to Brooklyn this morning to wish her a happy birthday, and sad to say, we won't be driving to Atlanta this week after all. I mean, just as bad it is with everything going on in both our lives. So that gives me more time to take the braids out. And I've decided it's time to see about getting that AC in the car fixed.

7/27

Dang it, I'm so sorry. I fell asleep again! And I was watching *Selling New York* on HGTV and missed half of it. But at least I have a funny story to tell you. As you may remember, this morning was my family court hearing by phone for child support. I had to call at 10:00 a.m. So when I was connected the magistrate asked, "Are you employed?" I thought she was talking to me, so I said no. I was laid off in June 2009. She said, "No, ma'am, I was talking to him," and he said he quit his job in December to attend school full-time. And that woman pretty much ripped him apart, and it took all I had not to burst out laughing on the phone! Her bottom line was that he <u>voluntarily</u> quit his job to go to school when he has twelve kids (seven support orders) with a baby mama fantasy. The youngest baby's mom has not taken him to court because, obviously, he still hittin' that. And how dare he think he can just stop taking care of his responsibilities!

He kept arguing that all of his money from his job went to support, so she said, "Get two jobs!" Then he was saying after support and bills he doesn't have money to eat. And she said, "Your twelve kids have to eat!" And she said tons of people work two jobs and go to school, so she dismissed all of his petitions for reduction, and I literally didn't have to say a word! I immediately had to call Brooklyn and tell her. And he actually texted me, saying, "See the rude shit I have to put up with." He still thinks he is the victim. Can you believe it? Then he called me while I was on the phone with Brooklyn, so I didn't answer. Then he texted me, "Are you busy?" So I just replied, "I'm on the phone. I'll call you later."

I don't want to hear his pity party, and that's all it is. Because, initially, I was very supportive of him going back to school and temporarily not working, even though I didn't think he should have just quit his job. I was trying to show him then that I had his back, and of course at that time we were planning to have a baby and I selfishly was thinking of our future with Jordan and Justine, not of the well-being of the ten other kids. And I really do care for and love them all. But when I realized how stupid the whole scenario was and how I was being played and how selfish he is, and that <u>I can do so much better without him in my life</u>, how crazy is it for him to just take four years off of being somewhat responsible. Because that's all $20 a week is, some help, nowhere near adequate. So it would be interested to hear what he has to say about how unfair the system is to him!

I'm so glad the temperature is cooling down a bit. It's 1:00 p.m. and in the mid-eighties instead of low hundreds! We went to the $0.75

Monday movies to see *Marmaduke*. It's $1 on Tuesday and $2.25 the rest of the week. When *Eclipse* comes to the cheap movies and *Karate Kid*, we'll be going to see those.

Talked to Kathryn yesterday and supposedly the bees are gone. Their friend went over and sprayed, so we will go later today to see and take care of some miscellaneous stuff if the bees are gone!

I went ahead and applied to Stonewall Jackson again, the Department of Juvenile Justice. That was where I interviewed for the science teacher position that I thought may have been sabotaged. But Nicole told me that her friend that originally referred me said that they really liked me but they just wanted someone certified to teach science. I was on their website and they are hiring a teacher's assistant and the salary range is 27K to 36K. And I applied for youth counselor, which has continuous postings because it's always a critical need.

As far as child care for the kids, I will be able to change Jordan's bus stops to Justine's school and enroll both of them in the after-school program (ASEP), which is before school and/or after school care. It starts at 7:00 a.m. and ends at 6:00 p.m. So as long as I get them to Crown Point at seven, I could literally work anywhere. So I won't be limited to only working in Matthews or Southeast Charlotte. And the money I save on rent can pay for ASEP. Hopefully I would only need mornings, which is cheaper than afternoons. Still waiting on Mr. Walker at Crown Point, but I've done everything to express my interest. So at this point the ball is in his court. You know, I'm just remembering I started this letter with the intent of telling you about my parents or the drugs, and as usual got way off topic!

I would have to say overall, up until the start of fourth grade, literally the first week of school, everything up to that point was great! I was smart in school. Had my two best friends, Hope and Angela. I was chubby but no one seemed to think anything of it. I had the friends on my street, Colorado Avenue, and we all got along. My parents had always smoked weed—my mom once in a while and my dad almost daily. I remember going to the corner store to buy E-Z Wider papers, and the album cover they would use to separate the seeds, LOL. When I was in third grade they experimented with the powder form of coke and it was no big deal. I guess, closer to the end of third grade was when my parents started using crack. When fourth grade started, Hope went to a separate class, and me and Angela we're in class together. And at Waterfront fourth, fifth, and sixth grades were placed in one large intermediate group, so some classes were independent and some in groups.

Angela decided she wasn't my friend anymore, and hung out with the more popular girls. We were both chubby in third grade, but over the summer she lost weight and I gained weight. For the first time I wasn't chubby anymore and graduated to fat, and my parents started coming home from work and going straight to the bedroom to get high. So I watched TV and ate. The teasing in school increased, so I ate.

I stopped doing homework, and Mrs. Summers saved my life. It was a simple lie I told. I said I did my homework. She saw I didn't, and marched me straight to the office. She had to see there was a bigger issue somewhere because what teacher is going to personally walk a child to the office for lying about doing their homework? They called my mom at work and I was crying! She came in for a conference because I really wasn't doing any schoolwork. And I got stuck doing three weeks' worth of homework and classwork that night, so I was locked in my room for like five hours! I thank Mrs. Summers to this day for saving me academically, and it should have been a wake-up call for my parents to pay attention to their child.

Fifth grade was the same with teasing, and you can imagine gym and swim classes were torture. It sucks always being picked last by four teams! But my mom put me in Girl Scouts, and that was such a wonderful time, meeting every Thursday from 7:30 to 9:00 p.m. We had to pay the $0.50 dues staggered, eventually getting to the point where they didn't have my dues money, and she just stopped taking me. With more and more money going to drugs, I had fewer school clothes and was getting fatter.

Sixth grade things got worse. They got into check writing, and they would buy VCRs and other quick-sell electronics and sold them to this white man. I was letting my hygiene go and would wear the same panties for up to two weeks and wasn't showering. Something a parent should notice, but a teacher did. And CPS was called, which shook my mom up! So we went to the mall and they bought me two outfits, and I started taking baths more often, but not daily. The panties thing actually started in fourth grade, so I'm surprised no one noticed sooner!

The check writing continued, and I would always ask, "Can you write checks for some clothes?" Never did. Lucky for my brother, he could still fit his clothes. He was very handsome and well-liked and athletic. Then the worst happened. My mom was arrested and spent thirty days at the holding center. She was gone for Mother's Day and my birthday. That was such a lonely, dark time, and having to lie to everyone about where she was. In the meantime, my dad got a settlement from a car accident that happened months earlier. He got the money like two days after the arrest and smoked it all with random people in and out of the house. He had the money to bail her out but chose to get high.

Seventh and eighth grade were the worst as far as teasing at school goes, and I hated school. Things at home were the same. And while most kids look forward to payday, I hated payday because it meant they would be locked away in the room. We couldn't keep TVs or VCRs or things of value. My bike was gone, watch, Nintendo gone, then dodging phone calls. My dad would miss so much work, drug dealers looking for their money! One night our car was set on fire! It was burned bad on the inside but the outside was okay, and I had to ride in that damn car to my eighth grade graduation!

Shelby was my best friend beginning in seventh grade, and I ate dinner at her house 90 percent of the time <u>and</u> ate dinner at home. And I was with her at her house all the time. So I survived elementary school, and thank God high school wasn't about all that teasing! Maybe because it was Hutch Tech and kids were more focused academically. And I worked Mayor's Summer Youth the summer after eighth grade, so all that money went to school clothes! At the end of freshman year I was hired at Tops as a cashier and stayed there all through high school. For the first time I had cute clothes, jewelry. And by never having money to get my hair done I learned how to do it myself.

So my parents still got high even though they seemed to be trying to stop. Almost two to three months would pass, then a relapse. But with work and school, I stayed busy. And I would go to Shelby's house on my off days. She got pregnant at fourteen, and my parents were scared to death I would be too, but guys weren't into me like that. One day my dad was gone and I laid it all out to my mom about everything I knew about the drugs. She was so shocked that she stopped, then and never did it again!

My dad didn't officially stop until probably my sophomore year of college. During my elementary days he was good at doing radios and alarms in cars. And a lot of times that's how he paid his debt to dealers. Now they built a garage at the house and that's the family business, along with remote parts, TVs, anything electrical. It was truly by the grace of God that they were able to stop doing crack because I'm sure you've seen the devastating effects of crack. I always salute my mom for being able to stop just because of me, but the addiction hit my dad way harder than her.

So that's another journey that I went through as a child and teen, but I overcame. It's also one of the reasons I want to work with children because I can relate to almost anything they have gone through. It's also one reason why I spoil the kids and it's hard being tough on them because I never want them to experience the things I went through.

Well, here's another long letter. And it's now 3:00 p.m. and I haven't even left the house or gotten much accomplished outside of writing you and making lunch. I hope I can get this in today's mail, but if not, you will get it soon. Brooklyn says hello 'cuz I'm on the phone with her now! Until our words meet again…

Love,
Janae

July 26, 2010

Hey Janae,

 And no, I'm not catching up. I caught up! Surprising, huh? Glad I continue to make you smile. es, I wanted to resend my apology when I read that letter, but then that would be selfish 'cuz you're allowed to vent. You're human and going through a lot on your own, and I'm just trying to comfort you the best way I can until I can do it in person. And I am a lot better because I don't have to do this by myself anymore! And everything will go uphill for us 'cuz we already know what the bottom feels like. I'm glad you didn't rip it up 'cuz that wouldn't have allowed me to see you upset and feel your emotions!

 That's good you're still getting stuff for the house together. You sound excited. Are you? They probably thought since they were leaving they didn't have to replace the seats. It was up to the new homeowner! Yes, that's a good idea to take pictures of the house 'cuz people are dirty where they will charge you for a shit you didn't mess but said you did! And yes, they do paint walls when tenants move out.

 So since Kathryn left two night tables, a TV stand, lawn mower, leaf blower, what else do you have to get as far as inside the house? You say Jordan is excited about the lawn mower, but how long will that last before you have to tell him to go cut the grass? And yes, I do hope you get a new bed, something that's bouncy 'cuz we are both going to need something with a lot of cushion and sturdy springs 'cuz we have a lot of work to do in the future, wouldn't you say!

 I'm not mad at him texting you as I already know you're mine. If he wants to see your tatas, tell him to go into his memory bank and pull a picture. I'm not going to tell you what to do about him texting so much when he's really not doing for the kids, so I'll leave the decision to you. But please don't encourage him thinking he got a shot at getting back in your heart 'cuz it's not enough room in your heart for me and your ex!

Well, I'm writing as I'm reading your letter, and that's it for the texting. All that showing his dick on a phone and you telling him your business is a wrap. DEAD it right now! If it's about the kids, cool. If not dead it. Unfuckingbelievable, are you kidding me! And why didn't you cuss his ass out? You know what? I'm going to move on.

You thought he was going to help fix the window? Be fucking serious. Your business, if any, is OFF LIMITS! You don't mention that type of shit to me. I care not to hear it. Just handle your business the right way and stop with all the chitchat! I know it's going to take me some time to get him out your mind completely, but I'm up for the task. I'm going to have to buy some extra stamps 'cuz it seems you need way more letters 'cuz you got too much texting free time on your hands! And I'm not going to hurt you, woman. I'm not in the hurting business. And them clowns out there you talkin' about wanting a shot at my woman have a better chance at the lottery 'cuz I'm yours, you're mine. What really separates me from them is they just want pussy. I want a family and someone to love until I'm old and totally gray!

As far as that tuna goes, sweet and spicy is the shit, but I like what you like. I'm glad you got a chance to put the bed together. That's good overall they left the house in good condition. What does Jordan use for his allergies? That's nice a glass-top stove. I can see you now cooking in front of it with me behind you asking what's for dinner while I'm nibbling on your ear! Make sure you take pictures of the house so I can see how you hook it up. Once again, be careful on who you pick to move. You make sure you do background checks real good 'cuz I do not want to come home and have to put in some work. I just want to chill and live out our plans and raise some kids.

That will be real nice of you to go see Brooklyn. I can't wait to take that trip with you to see my nieces and nephews and shoot some pool with Robert. Do you shoot pool? What about strip clubs, do you go to them with your man, or would you? I should ask you 'cuz I believe I am your man by now? Tell Brooklyn I love her more than life. And make sure you give her a kiss for me!

Well, my wife-to-be, I'm going to end this so I can start on this next letter I just got from you with a money order. Woman, what did I do to deserve you? And you smell good too. Put you in some gravy and eat you up, literally! So our spirits meet again, hasta luego, mamacita.

Always yours, yours truly,
Jarelle

July 27, 2010

Que pasa, mama?

Happy Wednesday with love and kisses. I thought I would follow your lead and continue with this phone call 'cuz I couldn't hang up. I want you to hear my voice and only my voice!

First and foremost, I want to thank you for sending me a little change to work with. I will definitely be buying some stamps immediately and a few things. Although I didn't get no letter from you in a while, you smell delicious. It smells like you're right here with me. I'm talking to your picture right now, can you hear me? And don't worry about forgetting what you said in previous letters 'cuz if it's meant to be you will remember what you said eventually.

And I'm glad you're not complaining about you not getting mail 'cuz when you do, all you have to do is walk to the mailbox and it should be something in there from me! And yes, you're forgiven, and we are finally on the same page. And it feels right 'cuz you're definitely handling your business, Ma! glad to hear you're staying on top of your job hunt 'cuz that will put you where you need to be. So what there are 300 other people? You're the one that deserves it. And I constantly pray about it every day and night. There is no competition 'cuz God, who is in control, has your back, so do I. So we good! And if you do have to take an outside job until the one you want comes along, so be it. You got bills and a new house, so you have to do what it do. And it's not just confidence I have, I believe in you for real. You make me a believer, so it's hard not to.

So Jordan hasn't been doing the list, huh! Don't worry, I have another letter following this one for him. Trust me, I'm on my job, no days off! It's good to hear no behavior issues. And yes, tell him I said to transfer that list to a chart, not now but right now! I hope you enjoy your movie. Make sure you don't pick up no fans, LOL. That's cool you and Nicole are close to where you are. She sounds like someone I'll enjoy meeting.

I can feel your pain about the crack. What I'm about to tell you stays between me and you. If I hear Brooklyn got wind of this, our relationship is over. Word is bond! I don't know if Brookly never told you about her favorite teacher Ms. Donovan when she was in sixth grade. But toward the end of the school year her teacher started missing mad days of work and was getting disciplinary action write-ups. What she didn't know was that Ms. Donovan ended up strung out on dope- and she was one of my best customers. I know she would hate me forever if she knew that information because she eventually lost her teaching job and Brooklyn couldn't figure out why her teacher changed so much. She was her second grade teacher, then when Brooklyn got to sixth grade her teacher had moved up to teach middle school so she was so happy to have her again. Then she was so heartbroken when she watched her teacher transform into a stranger.

I'm going to say this one more time, I'm sharing things with you that I've shared with no other woman, so take that to your grave. I don't know what it is, but you got me saying things to you that I locked away. But like we said, open and honest for us! That's good she works. Maybe we could all open a salon/barbershop 'cuz I definitely want to own some property rentals or whatever. Speaking of gray hairs, I have a couple in my goatee. But that's awesome you have gray pubic hairs. Does that mean it's seasoned? LOL. Oh! And to answer your question, I like it shaved but not bald, enough where I can see your clitoris. And yes, I'm circumcised, with a nice helmet. Well, I'm glad to hear you think I'll like your father. That's great because I believe I can handle your mother just great because I was raised by women!

That's good to hear kissing doesn't always mean full kissing for every sexual experience. Variety is definitely important. And you're right 'cuz a quickie can be done anywhere, anytime! My mission is not to make you have an orgasm, my mission is to give you experiences you'll keep coming back for and won't give you room to stray! And you don't have to give me a blueprint on orgasms 'cuz I'm well advanced on that course but never scared to learn how to please you completely. And it won't be a time where I pressure you to come 'cuz I want you to enjoy it and savor it, cherish it. And I don't want nobody else to have it. Are you ready for that job? There is no retirement, but full benefits!

And I won't allow you to fake it with me. I'll go for a walk before I allow you to do that. I don't like dildos either. Now with anal sex, I've never done that before, but seems to be very popular on DVDs and porn magazines. But that's a whole 'nother story in itself 'cuz <u>I definitely don't want nothing in my butt at all</u>. I'm going to tell you now, I will be semi gentle with you for the first round 'cuz it's been a while and it will probably be quick, not two minute quick, but to get me out of the dirt. But the second round will be oh so good! I will use toys with you sometimes 'cuz I want to pleasure you completely. I'm not a selfish lover. And I want to show you pleasure with hot oil rubs, massages. Some days I might just want to taste it. We will probably go to the adult store also just to keep things fresh and exciting. And that lady shouldn't be embarrassed. You can't put pleasure in a box. It's free and constantly evolving!

And yes, you are sexy. The things you do, the things you say, just your being is sexy! Only way you're moving to Buffalo is if we decide, no one else. You don't have to lie to him 'cuz it's none of his damn business. And I wish you would stop discussing your movements with him. That just gives him a false sense of being back together. So please stop!

Until our minds, hearts, and souls meet again, I love you,
Bryan

PS: That Mary Kay scent is you. Also, Jordan's letter will be included with the next one.

July 28, 2010

Hi Jarelle,

Ugh! Me and my so-called trying to get us synced up with our letters. I've been waiting all week, but of course you hadn't received anything from me, so nothing to reply to! But if my timing is right, I should have a letter tomorrow. And if not, I'm not tripping, just missing my man! Technically it's Thursday since it's after midnight. And thank goodness it rained yesterday because the temperature cooled down and it only hit ninety-two. Crazy ninety-two seems mild!

We went over to the new house and the bees are gone so far. There were a lot of dead ones on the ground and some of the honeycomb, so I hope he got it all. I'm liking it more and more, and Jordan can't wait to cut the grass. We're going to officially move the furniture on Tuesday evening, and it looks like we'll be driving to Buffalo on Thursday. Nicole was going from Thursday to Sunday, and Rhonda was going that day, so I really wasn't into it. But with all of us driving, even though we'll be in our own vehicles, I was thinking it may be cool—except the AC! But my dad told me to get it fixed tomorrow and call him and he'll pay it by phone! And my mom is going to have my grandmother (she has Alzheimer's). The cool thing is Nicole's friend Evelyn is supposed to ride on the way with Nicole, and her friend Evelyn will ride back with her, meaning Stacey can ride back with me and help with driving and gas. We should have it worked out for sure tomorrow, I guess.

I'm about to go to sleep, you know how I do. So, my dear, I'll continue in the morning. Sending you hugs and kisses!

7/29

Aaaahh! That's exactly how the car felt when I left Firestone. My AC is fixed, but here's the crazy thing: the problem was not the control module like this one place told me in May 2008. He said the part alone was $300 new, plus labor, so it never got fixed. Today they couldn't find any leaks, no issues with the compressor. It appears to just be empty, so they charged it and put the dye in just in case they miss something. So if it stays cold for two weeks then there was no leak! But they said there was definitely nothing wrong with the control module. Ain't that some shit?? Ripping people off for no reason. And it cost me $153 with tax, so I could have taken care of that two years ago! But thank God my dad paid because back-to-school clothes, supplies, moving, etc. will all be coming up shortly.

And of course my parents are so happy they can see the kids, and I guess I'm happy to be going because. Once school starts I plan on working somewhere, so taking time off at a new job is not going to work, and I really don't think we'd be going any time before spring break. Hopefully by then you will have transferred close to Buffalo (or Charlotte!) so that the long drive will be like a breeze.

I told Que we were coming, so now he can't wait to see us. We are staying at my mother's house, and you already know you can trust me. Hopefully he will gather up some or most of the kids so they can see their siblings. I really want all of their phone numbers so that I don't have to depend on him to keep the kids in contact, but a lot of the mothers don't care much for me because even though he was a lousy boyfriend, he's put me on almost a pedestal to a lot of them so there's resentment. Plus, there is no telling what kind of relations have been had regarding me, and some are just ghetto and immature. The bottom line is keeping the children in touch with each other in a healthy way, regardless of the he-said-she-said.

I remember when Jordan was a baby Que asked me to do his daughter's hair. I was like, sure, whatever, and he dropped her off and went to work. So while I'm doing her hair she asked if she could call her mom and I said okay. After a few moments on the phone she asked to speak to me and was pissed that I was doing her hair because she told him specifically that she did not want me doing her daughter's hair and that he was supposed to take her to the salon. I basically told her if I knew that I wouldn't have done it out of respect. Plus, I wasn't getting paid! I knew her wounds were fresh because as you recall Que's mother didn't know about Jordan till I was in labor, so you know the first baby mom, and only one at that time, only recently found out! So when he came to get her I asked him and he said yeah, she told him that, but her reasoning was petty. I told him he was wrong for putting me in that position, and regardless if it was petty, that's how she felt. Moving on!

I will be doing the girls' hair on Friday and Saturday, and I've planned a skating day for my Girl Scouts on Saturday afternoon. I sent the email, like, a week after July 4 about skating on the thirty-first, thinking if they couldn't come they would email me so that if needed to I could change the date. One parent emailed me out of ten girls and said yes, so I just sent another email two days ago. Four parents replied saying they can't come! It pisses me the hell off because I always give advance notice, and if most of the girls can't be there, I could always change the date so that most of them can come! And I still have no answer from, like, three parents, and I sent text messages telling them to please check their email. They all know how I do communication and 100 percent agree that email was the best method because I'm not making ten phone calls! I'm just hoping that both do come, plus siblings will make ten or more, so we can get the group rate. And I invited Tara and Courtney too. And I plan to skate! LOL. I love roller skating anyway, but I wish I could skate backward—never learned.

The kids are at the pool, and when I checked the mail at 3:30 they weren't done, so I'm going to go now since its 4:30 and I've got to run to the pharmacy to get Jordan's inhaler. I better have a letter or I will be pouting in the rest of this letter!

6:00 p.m.

I AM PISSED! All that freon has gone out already, meaning there is most definitely a leak. For it to leak out in literally four hours means a huge leak, so right now I am back at Firestone, sweating through my dress because it's ninety-eight degrees right now. The leak may be internal in the condenser, but since they close at seven and the only technician still at work that does ACs is in the middle of a brake job, I just have to wait. Bottom line, they won't be able to fix it tonight. But at least I will know where the leak is when I go back first thing in the morning.

But on the bright side, I had a letter waiting in my box. And no bills! So that was pretty cool. That will help me fill up this letter by responding to you.

I'm sure if drug dealers really stopped and thought about what happens when the drugs leave their hands, those with a heart and conscience would probably not do it. But the addict made the choice to start in the first place. I don't hold any grudges about that particular era in my life because the high individual is literally a stranger, it's not the person you love. But when they come down from that high, that's what determines their true self and if they are strong enough to stop. Thank God both my parents overcame!

Okay, stop whining about the pics. You know I got you! And you have way more of me than I of you. I keep the pics in my binder with all the letters you've written me. Since Two emailed them to me she scanned them. When I printed them off they were not the best quality, but I look at them each time I write you and every night.

I know I yell too much at both of them, and I know they don't like it and how ineffective yelling is (it didn't work in the classroom either LOL). And I know a big part of it is my frustration at my situation in general. Why do you think Jordan doesn't get whooped?? You can ask him. He definitely gets whooped, but lately I've not given him a good one. But I'm sure he could stand to get whooped more frequently, but dang, tartar, I'm not that soft! LOL. When I was saying he needed more than one letter a week, I think you had only sent him one or two letters and you've sent him more, so again, that was then, I'm not complaining anymore, and now that you're working I know you will hook us both up. Justine would like a letter also! I can't promise she will write you back but she did mention it. She will take a little longer to warm up to you because she still sees her dad as part of our family. But I'm very comforting to her when I explain that Daddy loves them but he's not a part of our family the way we were portraying, which was another reason I had to put an end to that dysfunctional shit.

Camp Invention was July 19 through 22 and they had a good time. Justine had a ton of inventions made from recycled everything and I had to let her know you keep one thing, the rest gets recycled all over again!

You don't ever have to put in a letter to please think about you. You should be exhausted every day from running in my mind! Yeah, I know that's an old one but so true. I wake up thinking about you. When I cook, I'm wondering if you will like it. When I'm lying in the bed I'm wondering how you will feel next to me, how you smell, taste, if you would be mad that my dress is showing a little too much cleavage right now in the auto shop! The one guy in the lobby is actually asleep, so no one is staring at your goodies!

And I'm sure Que is excited for the wrong reason about us coming, and you have nothing to worry about. And I will be open and honest with you about any attempts made. I'm starving now, and of course didn't make dinner 'cuz I was so focused on getting here for this AC problem. Rather than waste stamps, you can include Jordan's letters in with mine. I don't read them unless he says okay. And you really got on his case in that last one, which is good. He constantly is in competition with Justine and it drives me crazy. Household chores and things he doesn't care to do he wants to split 50/50, but when it comes to sitting in the front in the car, portion sizes for food, allowance, or anything that would benefit him, <u>then</u> he wants the Big Brother title! Like the other night, putting up groceries this clown leaves out frozen stuff and said he put away half and the rest is Justine's. He constantly needs to be reminded that as the "male of the house" he should have more responsibilities. And again, I don't yell at every little thing, and I do all of the things you've suggested, giving him the look, turning the TV off, taking away privileges. He just needs male reinforcement. He wants a man living with us so bad! With the guys I've dated and brought home, he latched on so quick. And I literally only have introduced a few, but unfortunately they turned out to be assholes. So he's really depending on you, Jarelle.

That poem "If You Come Across an Angel" was absolutely beautiful! If that's how you view me, all I can say is wow. I don't know if I'm that worthy. That's a high standard to uphold! But I'm on the job, and that's just how I'm feeling about you!

It's now 7:00 p.m. and I'm still here. I was thinking of bringing the kids, but Justine came with me this morning and was there for two hours, so I figured she wouldn't want to wait twice. But they're probably acting like they're starving! LOL. But there's ravioli, grapes, hotdogs, plenty of quick food for them to eat.

Speaking of food, I've bought some of the things on your list but the Chips Ahoy with Reese's is in those resealable packages, so I got you the Keebler version, which is similar. For peanut butter, do you like the smooth or crunchy or the honey kind? If I find honey and crunchy combined that would be my favorite. Do you like plain cashews or honey roasted? The Cheez-Its have a new spicy version and there is parmesan, white cheddar. Which do you prefer or not like? If you only get one package, I want to make sure you like everything 100 percent. Almond Joy? Yuck! Guess that's the first thing we don't have in common, LOL. And the Hostess Brownie Bites, Aldi brand is just as good, Mr. Name Brand! Just teasing you.

But all this talk about food is not helping since I'm hungry. They just gave me an update, still don't see the leak! What the hell! This is driving me crazy! So I'm going to end this letter here, and I better see some more depth and length coming from you with the letters. Oh, I just had a freaky thought—more depth and length! This is going to be a long year! But it will be worth it! Until our words meet again, love you!

Sincerely yours,
Janae

July 29, 2010 (answering 7/21)

Hey Chocolate

I'm glad to hear you enjoyed your movie. And you're right, sometimes the book is more interesting than the movie but sometimes there are exceptions. Waiting to Exhale to me was male bashing. I didn't really dig it, although Whitney looked clean and off drugs (temporarily). I would love to see how you look wet 'cuz you're always sweating and all that heat. Do you like water fights? 'Cuz I'm very good at starting them. And I love showers. I can stay in the shower a long! Now you're telling me you're getting a PO box and I should write you at that address. What's the science behind that? Why won't I be able to write you at your house? Your new physical address (344 Touch Me Not Lane), is that your attempt at humor? 'Cuz it's cute. How about your new phone number, 1-800-why-I-smile-have-you-seen-my-boyfriend?

Do you put baby powder on your chest before you sweat? It keeps you very cool. Also, for your heat rash try some hydrocortisone ointment or cream. It works wonders. That's what I used and continue to use 'cuz I get heat rashes during summer on my inner thighs. Well, I'm sorry you didn't spend your free days resting, but you know work must be done. In order to have order, you must organize as well as strategize. I wish I could be there to take the brunt of the load off your shoulders, but it's only going to make you stronger. And continue to appreciate the way God is continuing to bless you and guide your steps and keep you safe and sound. Yes, you're used to having the kids 24/7, but Mommy needs a break also. It's not unnatural, it's needed so you're able to get your thoughts and perspective in tune. All work and no play makes you miserable. That's why I look forward to Mommy and Daddy day as well as family night, movie night. I also would like to hear the kids' thoughts throughout the week when I'm home, that way they will always feel comfortable with discussing life's issues instead of keeping stuff bottled up inside where it'll stunt their growth, thinking they can't relate to grownups. That's good Mr. Walker is back now. Stay on his ass so maybe he can do what needs to be done to give us a job! And let me know what he says so we can put our heads together and form our next phase of action to gain employment!

 Let me find out you have butter fingers, LOL! How the hell you dropped the only lamp in the store. Granted, you found another store to purchase the same one, but wow. How you going to hold on to me if you have butter fingers, LOL! And while he called for stores, what, was he trying to do get brownie points from you? Watch out, woman, you know these cats are thirsty for what's all mine! And of course you checked the mail and there I was again and again What a feeling. If you could only see the smile on my face when the cop stops by the cell to drop mail off to me. You just don't understand the feeling that runs through my heart and soul. It's like getting a love shot when you're sick. It's hard to explain. Just keep handling your business, Ma, 'cuz you are the truth! Justine has a little woman's intuition. That's why she's around when you're reading. She knows Mommy is happy again, and she's probably curious and wondering why, and happy at the same time. Remember, I told you kids are real receptive to what's going on around them.

Now, about that letter you were supposed to receive. They returned it back to sender 'cuz I didn't put the apartment number on it. But you should get it around the same time you receive this. I truly apologize. It was a small mistake. I never want to leave you without some brain food and medicine for your heart! And hearing you will definitely make my year. And when you hear me, you might have to take a shower afterward, LOL, and smile at the same time!

Yes, that letter that was lost will certainly answer your other letters and some, so hold tight 'cuz I got you covered. And like I said if I didn't answer anything and if it's meant to be it will come up again. Pretty sure also that I was feeling good and cherishing and thanking you for being in my life! And you should feel guilty fussing about not getting letters when I did send you some but they sent one back.

That's good you do free work for other single mothers, but you can stop saying you're single or putting yourself in that category because you're very, very taken. You have a man, boyfriend, companion, better half, future spouse, your boo, and so on. That's good you'll be close by all your friends. That's important, especially Brooklyn, the one I cherish the most. Plus, she can keep an eye on you and keep my shit tight, LOL!

Yes. sooner or later I will be moved closer, maybe at the end of this year. And if and when that happens, I expect to be holding you and kissing you in someone's visiting room. And it will be a lot more lenient as well. And yes, we will be able to touch one another in many places, but I don't want to send you home too hot and bothered. That would be unfair!

I'm very pleased to hear you say there's more you can do to tone up, and healthier living and loving healthy foods is a must. Your cravings will soon go away. But even if they don't, I still need you, want you, crave you, and have to have you!

And yes, I have endured a lot in my life. That's what makes me strong and knowledgeable in a lot of issues, in situations dealing with life, family, relationships, and hardships. As for my brother, I love him but I'll never trust one word that comes out of his mouth, nor will we ever be hanging out brothers. Yes, it's definitely mind-blowing how far technology has come, but trust your man stay up on things, so I know a little bit! You'll have to give me a quick course on how to work the computer. I'm a fast learner, so you only have to do it in a day and I'll bet I'll be working it the next day. That's good you have a lot of movies 'cuz if I'm not at work I'll be under you, on top of you, on the side, in the back of you. Wherever you let me be, that's where I'll be.

Oh, my bad, I got off track. Those cell phones are amazing. All the things you can do on them and with them. I'll definitely have to have one! *Friday* will always be my favorite for me also. And yes, I have a Walkman and a few tapes. I'll probably get a couple more tapes once I get to a medium. But no, you can't send me your MP3 or CD player. I wish, but not in this jail or any other. Yes, here I'm only allowed two packages because this jail is called a TV jail, meaning whoever can afford it has one in their cell (yes, I have one). So you're only allowed two twenty-pound packages a year from home but you can order thirty-five pounds of food from an outside vendor every month. That's why everyone uses their two packages from home and then have whoever send money to them and they order from different places. Once I get to a medium then I will be able to get thirty-five pounds from home each month, plus clothes, sneakers, boots, cosmetics, under shirts, and so on. When my birthday comes close, I'll find someone who don't get packages and get it sent in their name. I'll just give them a snack or two!

That's good you have a landline 'cuz you're going to need it. And yes, we will be all right once the phone gets on! Halloween is my favorite also. I like dressing up and taking the kids trick-or-treating and going to parties. Well, that's not good he called you again. And it's not funny how you go for it time and time again. It's sad to be taken advantage of and not know it, but that's over now! And you already know how I feel about that texting shit. You don't need to literally be thinking about how you got caught up back in October. That's over. You definitely have many good reasons not to regress: me and then some more me. And your heart is mine and the rest of your physical as well!

I find myself thinking about you all the time also. I'm glad to hear your feelings grow daily 'cuz I'm trusting you faster than I've trusted any woman—and that's a first. I would love to go to a strip club with you. It's one of my fantasies, to make love in the ocean, video tape us making love—I've never done that. My ultimate is to have a wife that loves me unconditionally, and be able to look in each other's eyes and know that I'd rather die than forsake that love or bond we share. Are you that woman though? Are you ready for that type of commitment? 'Cuz I am! Yes, you are the present and the future, more so that I talked to my grandfather tonight and I broke down and told him about us. That's how serious I am about you!

Yes, missionary is definitely my position 'cuz I will be looking in your eyes, kiss you, and I'll definitely be grabbing your thighs for deeper penetration. And please don't stop. Don't be afraid to express yourself to me. I'm yours, you're mine! It will be very serious lovemaking. Good to know you love to ride, 'cuz I'm going to give you something to ride. And I'm getting my squat game together now so I can put you all over the wall.

That's sad about Nicole's coworker, but you can rest assured I don't have a small penis nor big. I'm a size that would definitely get the job done and big enough to not ever slip out during doggy style. And as far as you haven't asked for days, I was built for an ass like yours. And it's not am I really ready for it, are you really ready for me to have it!

And you're damn right we will never have that problem once again. Thank you for the money order. And yes, it will help me out. And I don't want you to have any added stress either. And you better take care of my heart and all my ass! Until our love collides, stay mine, stay blessed, and be about your business!

I LOVE YOU, WOMAN, 4 REAL
Jarelle

PS: Embrace Romance got to have it. Also, Jordan's letter is enclosed in here!

July 30, 2010

Dear Jarelle

    Happy Friday to you! I hope you are in good spirits and doing good with the new job. I spent the morning—all damn morning—at Firestone getting the AC officially fixed. There really was no leak. I needed a condenser, and the price, $430! I just felt that was too much for my dad and he had already spent $153. But the $430 was $195 for labor and $210 for the actual part was taxes. Since I had already paid for the performance check and recharging, they didn't charge me for recharging it a second time, which was yesterday evening and he had to keep adding dye searching for that leak. But that's when they discovered it was the condenser. They had to charge it a third time once it was repaired, so all together that was almost $600. And I'm thinking if I had gotten the control module and spent all that money for a make-believe problem all the while still having a separate problem.

    So at first my dad said he could cover $200 if I could do the rest. I figured the car is paid in full and I really can't let this AC problem go on for a fourth summer, so I said okay. Then they called me last night and said don't worry about the rest, they will take care of it. So now that AC is blowing like a freezer, way cooler than it was yesterday when me and Justine first left the place! I feel like the technician should have caught that because the air was cool only. And since I hadn't had air in four years, cool was feeling great, but it was nowhere near where it should have been on full blast. But bottom line, thank God it's fixed for real! So if I get food stamps this month, on the eighth I totally got to hook up my parents.

I've gotten more packing done, so moving the big stuff next week will be a breeze. And when we get back from Buffalo I will paint the living room walls back to white and clean up. I will have my key until the sixteenth so we can still use the pool. Honestly, they never check for pool passes, so we can go swimming whenever. Right now I'm waiting for Nia and Nyree to get here. I'm doing the younger one, Nyree, today, and Nia is here in the morning. So far only three of my Girl Scouts are going skating tomorrow. Another parent emailed me saying they can't go today. She could have sent that damn email two weeks ago! So two parents have not replied, and to me that's a no. So with the siblings going we only have six kids going. If all three parents, Kate, and Tara brings Courtney, then we have the group rate. But if not, oh well. I'm going to have fun regardless and whoever joins us. The kids are at the pool now, and yesterday I went to check on them. They are totally fearless in the water! Justine ran and did a flip/cannonball and I was like, wow! She only started swimming in the deep end on the Fourth of July at the Curtis' house. I'm glad because unfortunately inner-city/minority kids are so much more likely to drown because they never learn to swim compared to white kids.

I hope I have mail from you today! Even though I just got mail yesterday, it's always such a great feeling. Justine just came in from the pool and said the mailman was only on the first panel. There are six total, and mine is number four, so we have a little while. But once the girls get here I can't just be like, "Hold on, I need to read my man's letter!" LOL. I'm watching this commercial for Carowinds. Oh, the new roller coaster, the Intimidator, is the largest in the southeast. I love amusement parks and rides, and I'm an adrenaline junkie when it comes to rides.

Just came back from the mailbox and taking Justine back to the pool. No mail, and Monica is running late. I don't care, but there is a water balloon fight scheduled for 5:30, and if she comes on time I would be done by then. And I had planned on doing Nyree's hair so that Nia could play with Justine, but their mom said her husband is taking Nyree to the doctor. So I'm doing Nia's hair but I don't want her to miss the water balloon fight. I can't punish my child for them running late. I'm sure it won't last longer than thirty minutes, so they can still play together. I told my kids to come home at 5:00, then I'll let them go to the water balloon fight and come back. Nia is the oldest but the most wiggly and talkative and whiny, and having no one talk to me actually makes my job braiding easier. Her mom is stuck on those black beads though. I love beads and I do patterns, various shades, rainbows, but she only likes the black beads. It's her choice though, but last time she let me use clear on one and white on the other, so she's easing into variety slowly.

While I was getting the AC fixed I finished this book called *Derelict* about this guy in prison, and I thought based on the back cover summary that it would be good and you could possibly relate. It turned out to be a disappointment, and the last few chapters really sucked. The ending left me like, okay, what happened next? So whenever you are allowed to have books I can send it to you, but please know that there is no comparison between you and the main character!

I feel like I have idiots coming at me from all directions. I've got to tell you about this guy named Frank. When I was teaching, there were outside-vendor tutors that came two days a week, and my classroom was one of the rooms they used. Since there was always work to do, I stayed after a lot. He was one of the tutors in my room, and his girlfriend that he lives with has a fourth-grader at my school. He was always polite and very good with the kids. And as far as looks, he was average.

So one day I get an email on Myspace saying something like, "You look good, but I love checking you out in person." I didn't recognize his photo, but then realized who he was. At the time I didn't know he had a girlfriend, but I suspected he was with someone. So I was like "thank you," and he asked if we could see each other outside of work. I asked him if he had a girlfriend. He said yes. So what's up with me and you! I told him I can't be a homewrecker, especially with a child involved. In the meantime we saw each other two days a week at school and maintained our professional relationship. But his eyes said it all: he wanted me bad.

When school let out in June and I was laid off, I was feeling all types of ways and ended up moving to our current apartment. He found me online again in the fall and kept saying how good he could make me feel, what he wanted to do to me, and on and on! Even though I was saying no, I was leaning to yes. I was stressed and sexually backed up. My biggest issue was that he had a live-in girlfriend. Then I started thinking, hey, it's all about me. I'm a grown-ass woman and have needs, and the kids are going to be in school. So we set up a date for him to come over in the morning. But all night I kept thinking how would I feel if it was my man? It <u>was</u> my man because every relationship I had I was cheated on. If I was the other woman, how can I look at myself? So in the morning I texted him never mind, I just can't stoop to that level. It's not who I am, even though our prior phone conversations had me so horny and ready. I didn't want to be a homewrecker.

He would text me once in a while or email and I basically don't reply. Oh, I forgot. When we first met he was doing this business thing, like a pyramid-type business, and I was never interested. But he convinced me to have a business meeting at a donut shop. But traffic made him late, and I gave him fifteen minutes and bounced, so I never heard his proposal. Fast forward to this past Wednesday, I get a text from him saying, "HI, hope all is well," and am I still in Charlotte. Several months, almost a year has passed since I talked to him. So I replied, "I am great, still in Charlotte." He brings up the business thing and how there's a conference call he wants to invite me to. So after literally begging, I figured, okay, it's only twenty minutes and I'm not obligated to anything.

That evening I listened to the call and already knew I didn't want to be bothered. So he called afterward, hyping the company and selling me the good points. So I'm like, sure, whatever, and he said he'd follow up after I finished moving and was back from Buffalo. But he kept it all professional. Until the texting began, which is the new way a man cheats. He will be sitting with his girl while texting these chicks on the side. So he texted me that he'd love to see me in person. So I'm thinking, I just spent twenty-five minutes on a dumb conference call and another thirty on the phone with him, so he owes me. I say I'm moving next week and could really use the extra help. This fool said, "You paying?" I said <u>no,</u> it's strictly voluntary, and if you can't it's all good. He asked was my man going to be there. I said no, he's in New York. Then the <u>real</u> reason he texted me started coming out. He asked me was I still thick and juicy like he liked. And I asked, "Are you still living with your girl?" But then he was getting way too personal and said he knows I want him to bust that ass and lick that pussy! I put a stop to it right then 'cuz where did I give him the green light to get all vulgar? And we ain't and never will be on that level!

So I haven't heard from him since. And if I do, I'll let him know not to contact me again for nothing. Don't need your help moving, not interested in your business, and definitely don't want you! I can't believe how close I came to letting him get with me last year!

7/31

Hey, baby, just finished braiding Nyree's hair and she was so fidgety! Found out she just had an albuterol treatment for asthma, which has that effect on some kids. About to quickly eat and head out to skating.

Thinking of you always, love ya!
Janae

July 31, 2010

Good evening Jarelle,

Today was just a busy day! I'm tired too. Well, as you know, I started off doing Nyree's hair and my normally "sit still and quiet as a mouse" client was a fidgety chatterbox because of the medication she had to take, and it made my job much harder and it took longer. She didn't get here until ten and they left at about 12:45. I hadn't eaten, so I hurried up and fixed myself something to eat. And we were out the door at 1:15 to get to the skating rink. Even though there were only three of us and our kids, it was the parents who I liked the most, Leslie and Monica, and I braid their daughter's heads. We had a lot of fun but I didn't realize their girls don't know how to skate! Justine had roller blades and she was out! But came back periodically to help the girls. One of my girls' brother skated, so he and Jordan hung out. We stayed till about 4:30. Came home and packed up some stuff, and at 6:00 we went to the house.

It started raining, of course, so we hurried up and unloaded. I really don't need to buy anything for the new house but I have lots of wants. I want to do new shower curtains, rugs and towels for the kids bathroom. Since Jordan now has two beds, we need a new comforter. We need another TV because they share a nineteen-inch now. Oh, I have a nineteen-inch in my room, and the flat screen in the living room. But I want to give them the nineteen-inch TVs and get a flat screen for my room. The dining area has a nice cherry wood—no more mahogany—breakfast nook that I want to buy cushions for because sitting on hardwood is not comfortable (unless it's your hardwood!). So I have lots of wants for the house, but until I get my first paycheck from work we are good.

So after unloading we went to Northlake Mall and I took the kids to Build-A-Bear. They've been wanting one forever, and Justine made one for her birthday last year. Both of them turned out really cute, and Jordan named his Jarelle! Justine named hers Little Heart. So we came home about 8:30, ate dinner, and now they are probably asleep while I'm writing and reading your letter.

I knew you would be mad about that texting! And like I said, you got me. I'm yours, and I won't disrespect you like that. So if you're telling me to kill the texting, it's done. I did always tell him everything going on in my life. And you're right, it does give him that indication that he still has a way in. So I will save all of my conversations for you! So where are the pictures of me and yourself? Do you share a cell. And if yes, are you cool with your roommate? Do you show me off or are you more like "you ain't looking at my woman!" I must say though if the thought of Que texting me makes you write me even more, that makes my day, LOL.

Yeah, Jordan is allergic to peanuts, cashews, pistachios, dog dander, cat hair, tree pollen, and has asthma! He can be around dogs and play with them but must wash his hands often. The tree pollen just makes him sneeze, and he gets itchy, swollen eyes in the spring. It is not enough to affect his diet, and he takes Advair twice a day for asthma. But he's been careless with that lately, which means he needs the albuterol way more often, so I just got on him about that. Cigarette smoke and cats and dogs trigger the wheezing, which makes trips to Buffalo harder on him. My dad smokes and they have a dog. Que's mother has two cats, and in my dad's side of the family everyone smokes cigarettes. How I managed to stay smoke free is a miracle!

When we were in Buffalo in December we spent half the time with my parents and half the time with Quincy. I hate it there because who has a basement yet keep the cat litter box in the bathroom? Now his mom is always at work, so between Quincy, his brother Wayne, or his cousin you would think one of these grown-ass men who should be on their own could change that stinking, nasty litter box and not wait for her to get off work to do it! Taking a shower smelling cat shit, I said never again!

We will be moving big stuff Monday evening. I'm renting a U-Haul and Nicole and her husband and Kimberly are helping. Last time it was only me and Justin, and we worked our asses off! But Nicole had just had a baby two weeks earlier, and I had only met Kimberly a few weeks prior. And all the buster-ass dudes trying to holler at me probably would have helped in exchange for some ass! I wish I could see Brooklyn this week. I miss my girl, but we talk almost daily. School for her kids starts, I think, on the sixteenth or maybe Labor Day weekend.

I shoot pool but I'm not the best. You'll have to stand behind me and guide me. I've never been to a strip club with a man. I've seen male strippers and love the turn on, but never did a woman's club. I honestly think woman on woman is sexy, but not sure I'd like it for me personally. In porn I've watched girls with girls, but I could never get turned on seeing two dudes! LOL. So the strip club will be another first for me to do with you. And I'm super excited about the $0.96 phone calls! As soon as I turn the internet on at the new house and switch the house phone over, it's on! You just don't know how amazing that would be for me, for us! And it will pass the time so much more, and with more letters on top of that.

Wow, it's 12:30 a.m., and if I plan to wake for church and not be tired I better push pause and continue tomorrow, or I should say, later today. So goodnight, my love, until later!

8/1

I'm back! We didn't make it to church today. I woke up at like 8:40, which is so late for me. And the kids got up around 10:00 or 10:30. I changed my mind about my hair and decided to rebraid the first few rows to make it fresh. With moving tomorrow and packing, I just didn't see having time. It looks good though and brand new! I'm definitely getting excited about the move and still amazed at the idea of renting for only $450. The house right next door, which is an identical model, is renting for $875, which is really overpriced and should be more like $700 or $750. Either way, got me a great deal.

We went to Nicole's house around six and stayed until, like, ten. Rhonda wants to still go to Buffalo, and her ex-husband is being such a hater! They recently reconciled and he sold her the dream over many phone calls, but now that he's back he's a total asshole and she has realized he's no good still. And he hates her being around positive people like me and Nicole. He doesn't want her to drive to New York, and is trying to say the car won't make it. But he's driven to Atlanta and Alabama. Nicole thinks he will leave out Wednesday and make her miss out by staying out, so we told her to have all their stuff packed, go to Nicole's house, and just spend the night because he is shady as hell!

So Nicole waxed Rhonda's eyebrows and did her hair, so we are going to Buffalo to cut up and get loose! Our friend Stacey is having dinner at her house for us with some more friends on Thursday and Friday happy hour. I'm excited now because my visits are always so boring or were centered so much on Que. So to go and hang with the girls and just let loose now, I can't wait! But I will be good and not do too much flirting! LOL.

And I called that phone number for phone calls and it's landline only, so I have to get the internet on at the new house so I can plug in my phone and get ready for our calls. I plan to talk to you on Wednesday, so I don't know if you just call or what. And if I mail this letter first thing in the morning you should have this Wednesday. My home phone number is 704-563-4566, and I don't know the times you would call. I hope late afternoons, like 3:00 to 4:00 p.m., or after 9:00 p.m. We shall see. Or in the mornings. Since it's the day before hitting the road, I'll be very busy. So if you can call during those times, it would be best.

And what is awesome about gray pubic hairs? LOL, I'm glad you've been snipped and no foreskin! I'm not so sure about anal. Looks like it would hurt! I think about times when I've been constipated, wishing the turd would come out, so the idea of shoving it back in . . . ! LOL. Guess only time will tell if we go there. I already know the first time won't be your best performance. We have a lifetime of pleasing to do with each other, so it's all good!

Well, I'm going to get some sleep now because it's official with packing the rest and moving tomorrow. Going to sleep with tender thoughts of you and dreaming of our first everything!

Love always,
Janae

PS: This fourth and final scent I own is Body by Victoria!

August 1, 2010

Hey Love,

    Yes, you did have it coming. And yes, you did tell me not to reply to your venting, but I'm a real one. And if I don't put you in your place, then you won't respect me. 'Cuz when I'm out of pocket I expect you to check me also. That's what real couples do. And yes, I have a Gemini but you got yourself a Virgo. But no, I won't let you act out to a certain extent 'cuz like I told you before, there will be days where you might want to vent. But I will tell you enough is enough!

    I'm glad you think it's sexy, but what's more sexy is you acknowledging strength in your man! Make-up sex would be off the chain, but I don't plan on fighting at all 'cuz we have so much to learn and love each other about that. It will balance itself out. Don't let that job hunting bug you out 'cuz anything you don't control controls you. So you will eventually get a job. Just keep putting in that work and everything will fall into place. Yeah, my job is pretty interesting. At first I was packaging the soap, now I'm running the machines. You know your boy got skills!

    Speaking of Jordan, I just wrote him in the last letter I wrote you, and don't be letting him slip on writing me 'cuz I start writing as soon as I get his. So tell him to stay on his job, NO EXCUSES! And I'm glad he finally finished his chart. But it's more to it than that. I want you to make sure he's on his job at all times, and please tell him that if he's acting up I want to tell him to man up! And I hope he enjoyed Camp Invention and learned something as well. But now that it's over, I expect him to be reading even more, getting himself ready for this upcoming school year 'cuz it won't be no failing test when you could have been practicing and studying!

    You have to be careful when dealing with the bees and insects. I'm just like you, I never had roaches when growing up and I can't stand them or houses that have them. As far as the lady acting up, you always have to remember, when people are doing others a favor they tend to forget that they once needed a favor to get to a higher position, and it's quite evident that she's forgotten. But you must look past things like that 'cuz it's only going to make you stronger to get the things you deserve so that you won't have to depend on others to clean up the mistakes they created on their behalf! And be careful about the so-called friend that she has coming over. Don't be letting him in the house and all that, alright! That's good you started turning the house into a home, hanging drapes and things. That's good, and I know it's a big accomplishment to even be experiencing your own house. Now that's some sexy shit!

Yes, I got really angry about you talking about the lag in mail 'cuz I was doing everything I could to get stamps without doing anything illegal. 'Cuz one thing I don't do is borrow or beg for nothing. And I'm so used to having that sometimes reality punches me in the face and lets me know that some days I won't have. And I have to be able to take the good the same way. Bad comes around, and that's something I won't get used to but I have to endure while I'm in this place. And when you're asking for mail that I know I sent already then you're saying all this other stuff, I felt it was time for me to check you on it.

One of those letters I remailed 'cuz I made a mistake and didn't put the apartment number on it, and I know you can't respond to it if I don't put all the information on it. But, baby, I'm human too. And we'll always be on the same page. And when we are not, then we have to put that work in together to get back on track! I'm glad you were a little nervous to open that last letter. That means you're beginning to feel my vibe a little better 'cuz you knew I was going to chew you out. I think—rather, I know you would have been disappointed if I didn't check you. 'Cuz you don't want no soft man or husband! And you will feel much better working, you just have to believe!

Did you call that Mr. Walker back or any other of the jobs you applied for? Everything is going to work out with the kids being close to school and everything, just keep praying. Yes, I know you're trying, and please don't stop either. You take one step, God will do the rest! I won't stop being uplifting to you. I have your back and your front. I'm going to make you great—not good, but great. And together, ain't no limit to the goal set forth to accomplish. But faith will always be needed 'cuz without it we are doomed!

And just because I'm working you're still going to get plenty of mail from me. And it doesn't just pass time but, woman, I'm striving to capture your heart and be your everything. This is not a game to me. I want you and need you all in the same breath. I'm tired of getting beat up by love or so-called love, and damn sure know you are. So this is more than time passing until I get out. This is my life I'm pledging to you, so I'm asking you for the last time, please don't ever hurt me 'cuz I'm giving you my all. That's why I go so hard every day to be the man you need and cherish!

No, there is no way I can transfer to North Carolina, but I will be able to transfer my parole down South once I'm released. And when and if I get transferred to Buffalo, you're right, I know I'll see my baby. So I'm praying about it too, and I hope you are too! And yes, you are seeing more, and I do have a great sense of humor and you will eventually understand the tone on paper. 'Cuz I strive to make my understanding understood when needed. And our phone conversations will be better than nice, it will be elevating! Yes, fly out the mouth, that's what I said. And you were being a smartass, but as you can, see your man can handle his. But I'm nice on comebacks. And please do relax 'cuz you'll know when I'm serious and when I'm playing.

That's heartwarming to know that you slept with my picture 'cuz I have your picture on the side of my TV, so every day and night I watch TV I watch you! I myself can't wait to be moved to a medium prison either. I can't wait to hold you. I need that like I need freedom. I need to hear from your mouth that in person or the phone that we are going to be all right. And me having my sanity, I give God the praise first and then my family. My strength I get from my grandparents and sister. My character I get from the things my mother taught me. And you. I needed you at the beginning. I even asked God, but I feel he thought I wasn't ready so he gave you me at the end through my sister, my twin. That's why I'm not taking you for granted, and I cherish your every being. Oh, you came into my life for a reason, and that's to be loved and guided. And I will do everything the power of a man possesses to make that a reality!

I'm glad you didn't run back to Buffalo when times got rough. That shows character and drive, something I look for in a woman. 'Cuz someday I will expect you to push me 'cuz I'm damn sure going to push you too. Great! Yes, it is a lot less stressful making only four people happy, and I'm honored to be one of those people. I was going to surprise you but I'm going to tell you. I'm going to take another picture in a couple of days! I hope you got to go see my twin. Make sure you give everyone a kiss and a big hug, except Robert. Just give him a handshake, LOL.

Stop complaining about two pages 'cuz you know I give you more long letters than short! And I wasn't fussing, just making things clear, LOL. Yes, you are always forgiven in my world as long as it's something forgivable. And our journey already began when you and I were blessed to be introduced.

Well, Ms. Lady, I will end only to begin again. Until then, stay blessed. Stay strong, stay sexy, and be about your business, for you are always in my thoughts and my heart.

Love you for real,
Jarelle

PS: Next time you sign your name it better be something next to it instead of just Janae. What's up with that? I know you not slipping, LOL, a little!

August 4, 2010

Hi,

OMG! I've been running nonstop since Monday morning. I haven't been able to write you, so you will have, like, three or four days' lag. But what I'm most sorry about is I didn't set up the phone so that you could call me, and in my last letter that you should receive today I promised to have that done. So I hope you can forgive me! This would be the shortest letter ever since it's 8:30 p.m., clothes still in the dryer at the old house, had a very unexpected last-minute interview today at 4:00, which threw my day off whack but it went great! Still have to pack so we can hit the road in the morning. Officially moved all the big stuff Monday evening. Kids still need dinner.

I received two letters from you on Monday and didn't even get to read them until 11:30 that night! Spent Tuesday evening applying for a ton of teacher jobs, but since I was borrowing internet signal from a neighbor it kept cutting off, so I was doing that past midnight. So I just wanted to let you know you've been in my thoughts all day, every day, just trying to catch my breath. If I'm not too tired tonight I'll write you again, but at least you know you're on my mind! Luv ya!

Janae

PS: I'm three letters behind now. How did that happen? LOL.

August 5, 2010 (answering 7/25/10)

My dear Janae,

Yes, I do realize I and you have been writing and thinking about each other all day every day, which is a good thing. 'Cuz with our thoughts the things we can create and conquer are limitless! Now, with your thoughts and pocket will the heart follow?

So you took your braids out. Are you putting them back in or are you letting your hair breathe? I'm glad that you're sharing things about your parents such as drug abuse and other things of that nature. But before I get to that topic, I want to tackle another topic!

Now, you say that you think you're officially falling in love with me but how do you know when it's love or just something new and exciting? Well, first and foremost, loving someone new is always exciting due to the fact that, that person has never hurt you, lied to you, cheated on you, took advantage of you, never attacked your self-esteem. Love also allows me to share things with you that I wouldn't share with any woman no matter who she is! And I don't want you to think you'll fall in love with me. I want you to know for a fact that I'm the one you're going to give your everything to that no man or woman can divide, conquer, or destroy. I'm convinced already that I love you. The last and only step left is to make it official 'cuz I feel there's nothing else out there for me and I'm not going to play Russian roulette with my penis! I'm at the age where games for me have been over a long time ago! It took a woman of your status to love me when I'm down, so I know you will love me when I'm up for all the right reasons. So I pray I answered your question to the fullest of my ability. Now the ball is in your court!

You're falling asleep a lot. Question, do you sleep a lot when you're pregnant or are you cranky and uptight? Just a thought! I'm just sitting here looking at your picture you took on your way to church. You look real sexy in that lime green skirt and top, and that ass is poking out, smiling too. I'm going to enjoy massaging that with flavored oil and baby oil, wow! LOL

I'm glad you keep constant contact with my twin. Next time you talk to her tell her the pen game is slipping and my mailbox is getting empty, and that's not a good thing. Well, you fell asleep again. I hope you get all that sleep out before I get home 'cuz you're going to need your strength and flexibility 'cuz damn near twenty years and you're going to need it! Well, that's very interesting that you received the ruling you did on your court call, but I knew that already. 'Cuz no judge in America is going to allow you to quit your job literally to go to school when you have twelve to fifteen kids. That don't add up. And then you're going to argue with the judge. Hell no! Yes, I can believe he's acting like the victim 'cuz that's what constantly kept you under his spell for so long, and he deemed that adequate a lot more than he didn't. And you shouldn't be interested in hearing anything he has to say 'cuz he's not talking about being a father or upping his child support. No, he's constantly scheming on the way to get back in your heart as well as between your legs 'cuz to me he feels that's where he can control you.

Remember the text. Honestly, what was your initial reaction when you received it? And be honest, 'cause I'm confident I have you so I can accept your answer! I'm glad to hear that Kathryn's friend finally took take care of the bee situation. It was long overdue. You applied for Stonewall Jackson again, that's good. Now you have to constantly stay on these peoples asses, showing them you not only want it but you need it. And don't just make them like you, make them feel like they need you, 'cause they may like a lot of people, you know? Now I hope I answered the things in your letter the way you thought I would. I always want to be eye to eye with you so we will always have a better understanding of the things we came from as toward the things we will accomplish if we stay true. That's beautiful you want to work with kids, 'cause I see myself working with juvenile kids also, being a drug counselor. 'Cause who better to understand drug addicts than an ex-drug dealer and witness to drug abuse!

But one thing I must say, you can still spoil the kids and all. But when it's time to get tough you must, 'cause they will know Mom loves us and wants the best for us. So it's a balance you must keep and implement on a daily basis! They will never experience what we went through.

Well, my dear, I have to end this for now in order to get up for work and start on your two letters I just received today! Until our words meet again, may you stay blessed and about your business. Stay up, love!

Love you,
Jarelle

August 6, 2010

What's up Janae

We are synced up with our letters. Some days I get your letters two days after you've written them, next time I get them four days later. Take for instance, yesterday was the fifth and I got your letter dated 7/28! And like you told me, you don't have to have a letter from me to write me 'cause you should have plenty to talk to me about. And yes, it seems your timing is a little off, 'cause every time you complain about no mail it be in your mailbox. So I'm not going to trip off that.

And I miss you also. It's good to hear that the bees and nest are gone, but still be careful when entering the house! You're going to move furniture Tuesday, but when are you moving in? You're driving to Buffalo, what's the occasion? Seems contradicting to me, 'cause Nicole's going prompted you to go? What happened to "come and see you"! You eased that trip on me out of nowhere, and the timing is crazy. But if you think it's "cool" as you say, enjoy yourself. I'm glad the kids are excited. It should be interesting for them. Don't count on someone riding back with you, 'cause someone always backs out at the last minute.

If I'm not mistaken, I told you to be careful about going to any service station, 'cause they always tell you something else is wrong than what you went to get service for, especially as a woman, they don't care about nothing but that dollar. Trust me. I've been there before and it's not fun. I went to get an oil change and next thing you know they did something to my brakes and they didn't work when I left. That was nice of your dad to pay for the service. I know that must have felt good considering what your past was like! I'm not real enthused about you going to Buffalo, but this is where our trust and loyalty kick in at. I'm happy the kids will see their grandparents and their great-grandmother. And as far as telling Que you were coming, that's not your job anymore to tell him when you're coming and going. That will be great if all the kids can be around each other, but will their mothers let that happen? The way you say it, they don't like you, and I'm pretty sure Que had a lot to do with that! I'm sure he's telling you he puts you on a pedestal but to them he's probably saying different things. It's like playing the middle against the end, an old trick I learned in fifth grade! Bottom line, don't be disappointed if it doesn't pan out the way you wanted to!

That's nice to her you're throwing a skating party for your Girl Scouts. Can you skate? 'Cause I would love to see that. I'm a great skater, so that's something we can do together, as well as bowling! You know how these people are nowadays with emails and texting. They want you to call them, constantly hold their hand all the way up to the event, only for them to cancel or say they didn't get the message or memo about the event!

Baby, always continue to do things for the kids, 'cause these parents are always neglecting activities for these kids to do until they start getting in trouble, pregnant, or whatever, then it's too late! See, you had a letter in your mailbox waiting for you after the service station. How about that? You're right, I don't put 100 percent blame on myself for people getting high. It's their choice. Also, even if I didn't sell it they would have sought out someone else. It's good that you don't hold grudges about that particular era in your life, which shows me growth and character on your part. And I'm happy for you that your parents stopped also, I know that was such a relief!

Baby, I don't whine. Is it such a crime to ask your woman for pictures 'cause you can't get enough of seeing her and the things she possesses? :) I'm working on you having just as many pictures of me that I will have of you, trust me! I'm sorry you don't have any quality pictures of me that Two sent you, but I promise, the next letter you will have a picture of me so you can add to your collection. Also, I can be the last person you see when you go to bed!

Yes, your situation in general is only temporary. And yes, you will yell too much to a certain extent, but that's what mothers do. If after the jewelry you should have given him a whooping but you didn't, and that's what was needed. I know you say you didn't 'cuz it would have seemed like child abuse, but I'm pretty sure you wouldn't have gone overboard with the punishment! But you must keep a strong hold on him so he won't get out of pocket by thinking he can get away with things not allowed! And you are soft 'cuz you can't parallel what you went through as a child with how you raised them 'cuz you haven't subjected them to drug abuse or teasing. So you have to be firm but fair and doling out punishment when it's needed!

And my letters to him have increased, so you definitely can't complain about that anymore 'cuz I'm at my job. And he doesn't want me to be soft 'cuz he won't respect it if I was to be! And just 'cuz I'm working won't interfere with my teaching him what's right and what's not allowed! As soon as possible I will write Justine. I have no problem with that, and even if she doesn't write back it's still a blessing to communicate and grow together! It's not about her warming up to me 'cuz I'll never be able to take her father's place, but I will fill that void by helping you raise her on every level! I'm glad you don't get them confused about him not being with you but still loving them at the same time, even though he damn sure doesn't show it. And you're right, that was some dysfunctional shit and some!

I don't ever want to be exhausted from being in your mind. And I ain't running. I want to stay planted in your mind, heart, soul, spirit, and your body! I wake up thinking about you also, as well as fall asleep after praying for you and your elevation above all things that trouble you and stand in your way as obstacles! If you can cook, I'll definitely eat it. If you can't, then I'll show you how! I also was wondering how you would feel next to me, how you smell, taste. But about me being mad about you showing too much cleavage in the repair shop, not at all 'cuz you said your mind and loyalty is all I want. And knowing what is being seen is all mine, why be mad? Insecurities don't run through my veins. I'm very confident and secure. And I know you will check a nigga if he get out of pocket staring at my goodies! I'm not worried about Que being excited about you coming for the wrong reason. And you can't help but to be open and honest with me about any attempt 'cuz you don't want to lose this blessing God has sent your way. But the ball is in your court. You can't allow yourself to be swayed or put in an awkward position where you feel weak, but I feel you're strong beyond your belief and you will check that shit at the door! See what I said? I knew someone would renege on the trip, but you make adjustments as they come.

I'm not wasting stamps when I write Jordan's letters I separate them to give him a sense of responsibility. And you shouldn't read them unless he gives you the go-ahead. It's my duty to get on him 'cuz I will not lie to him or lead him astray I'm striving to make him a responsible young man but in stages. You never give a baby a steak, you chew it up first and spoon-feed him!

Don't worry about the competition. That will pass. It's called sibling rivalry. We all went through it! And he will have a man living with him, your man, me! I'm depending on him as much as he's depending on me. I've been taught right, so it's mandatory I lead right. And yes, I view you as an angel. Why wouldn't I? A real man puts his woman on a pedestal. And never say you're not worthy. Every black woman is worthy until their actions speak otherwise. And you will uphold it 'cuz I won't stand for anything less. If you know better, you always strive to be better. And it's not just a job, it's an adventure! And I'm glad you're feeling the same way about me.

That's cool you got Keebler. I sent you some more cutouts to choose from the Crystal Light, should be in the little packets like I sent you. Remember, peanut butter cookies, not the jar of peanut butter! The cashews can be either or whatever you like! Parmesan would be cool on the Cheez-Its.

I will like everything you send no matter what you send. It's just a blessing to have something that's sent with love! Almond Joy was just something different, not a must-have! Anything is just fine with me! Yes, you will see more depth and length in due time and on paper. I stay with freaky thoughts, so you're not alone! And no, it's not going to be a long year. Just stay true and keep your grass cut low so you can see the snakes, 'cuz they're everywhere! Yes, your patience will be well rewarded, trust! Until our words meet again, I love you, woman.

Always your love,
Bryan Jarelle Edwards

August 6, 2010 (answering 7/30/10)

Dear Janae,

    Yes, I'm in good spirits and doing good at my new job. They are working me like a slave, being that I know a lot more than some of the guys that's been down there way longer than me! I'm glad to hear that you finally got the AC fixed even though that price is outrageous. Once again, that was nice of your dad to chip in and help his baby girl out. I know that pleased him more than you probably can imagine! You're blessed you didn't go through without having it checked two or three times, or your bill would have been outrageous!

    Now you can sit back and let your hair blow in the AC as much as you want. Just make sure you get checks on it every now and then so you won't have to be without anymore! That's right, thank God 'cuz once again he provided for you when all else failed. That's why I feel I don't give him enough praise for bringing me so far, keeping me safe, healthy, and having something to look forward to! That will be nice for you to send food stamps to them, that's awesome.

    You say you've gotten more packing done, what day are you moving in and why don't I have the address yet? And why am I writing a PO box that you have yet to give me? I still can't believe you're still going to Buffalo. I'm not going to lie to you, I'm kind of nervous, something I normally don't feel being in the place I'm in. And it's not that I don't trust, it's far from that. It's just you're going around someone you've known for years and had two children with, and the silly games I know niggas pull when they feel their game is superior! But you have my undivided trust just. Please hurry up and come home! That's good you're still doing hair in between all you have to do. That's right, handle your business, girlfriend. I'm very proud of you if no one else has told you this (better not have, LOL)! And that's all right if only two or three come to the skating party, as long as you enjoy yourself as well as your kids, that's all that counts.

That's good Justine knows how to swim 'cuz they just had something on CNN about inner-city kids and the rate of drownings due to the fact that a lot of our kids are not taught how to swim like the white kids are. Do you know how to swim? 'Cuz I can't wait to get in a pool with you and show you the breaststroke and backstroke!

I hope you have mail from me today too 'cuz I've definitely been pumping them out left and right. And you're right, it is such a great feeling to send and receive mail and read great things. And you're right, you can't just stop and say, "Hello, I need to read my man's mail," or can you? I didn't know you like roller coasters 'cuz I'm an adrenaline junkie too. I still want to skydive and bungee jump. What about you? Are you game? I'm sorry you went to the mailbox and didn't find anything, but I bet there will be something in there when you check it again. Wow, you have water balloon fights too? That's awesome. I can't wait to get home. It's so many things I miss about summer and being around family, and that special someone to share it with. I hope you took some pictures on your trip to Buffalo! About that book *Derelict*, what was it about? 'Cuz you mentioned it but never told me anything about it. I can relate to anything as long as it's dealing with knowledge, wisdom, and understanding. And if it was such a disappointment, why? Did you check and see if it had a part two? And why do you say please know that there is no comparison between me and the main character?

You do have idiots coming at you, huh? But are you enticing them in any way 'cuz you're not an ugly woman and you're thick in all the right places. And considering you had a revealing shirt on at the repair shop, you think niggas ain't going to crack at you every chance they get? And for you to even give a thought to fucking with someone who has a girlfriend 'cuz you was once in that position and you was without for a while is a lame excuse, and definitely not a power move. 'Cuz when the dust clears the girlfriend's hurt, he thinks he has someone he can do and say anything to, and you are using yourself for all the wrong reasons for a nut! And if you are stressed, join a book club, find a hobby, or something, but don't go left. 'Cuz to keep going left you're bound to hit a brick wall!

But I'm glad you canceled at the last minute, but it shouldn't have come that close. 'Cuz you're grown-ass woman, make grown-ass decisions and think that the daughters they have and raised will do the same thing once they reach that level of maturity! And that business thing was only game and he was putting you in game. I've seen that scenario plenty times in my life to see it through!

And your first mistake is accepting another text (you and these texts). Second mistake, you didn't tell him you had a man and you don't think he would like you conversating about anything other than school business, and you wouldn't disrespect him by doing so. It's none of his business if you're still in Charlotte! And why does this man know you're moving and going to Buffalo? And why on earth would you ask a man that you were considering to have sex with help you move to an address he's not supposed to know about and I don't even have yet?

I'm going to take it back a couple lines to something you said, "I figured, okay, it's only twenty minutes, and I'm not OBLIGATED TO ANYTHING." So why give him a second? 'Cuz you give a nigga an inch he'll try a mile. Same thing I tell you about your ex. Leading them on rings trouble 'cuz they feel they can say and do anything! You gave him the green light by not keeping it professional and drawing the line and sticking to your morals and principles, you know, THAT GROWN WOMAN SHIT!

I'm going to end this letter here. This will be the shortest letter I ever wrote. You just don't know the power you possess over my love already. Therefore, I must go exhale 'cuz I let myself be moved by nonsense. And I have to understand I'm not out there with you yet, so I can't stop the bullshit that comes your way on a daily. All I ask is please make wise decisions. Your safety and heart and the kids are my only concern, and I don't want nothing or no man to come between us. Love you!

Bryan Jarelle Edwards

August 7, 2010 (answering 7/31/10)

Hello Janae,

    Faith has a limit only if you allow the devil to dwell in you or around you. Love has no boundary as long as you create new paths to make the love stronger that it can withstand any negative force or energy! Hope has no end as long as that hope is not built on or guide by false pretenses.
    Hope by now you're back and enjoyed yourself in Buffalo. I know you have plenty to tell me, so I'm all ears! That was nice of Leslie and Monica to keep their word and show up at the skating party! I'm pretty sure you have lots of thoughts on how you want to hook the house up. Just take your time and everything will come together in no time. I know for sure I have to have a flat-screen TV in the bedroom 'cuz that's one place I spent a lot of time in even when I was free. I do a lot of strategizing in the bedroom. And yes, you definitely need cushions for the nook 'cuz we don't need no hemorrhoids, LOL! Unless it is my hardwood, and you have built-in cushions I prefer. I'm happy that a bear was created with my name involved. Tell Jordan thank you. Also, let him know that when the bear's cubs act up and get in trouble you know what happens, right?

Why is it that when the topic of texting comes up you say I got you. You're mine and you won't disrespect me, right? Then you write and say if you're telling you kill the texting it's done, yet the letter before this one you talking about some Frank cat with the same thing, texting and talking on the phone and asking him to help you move to a new address, which once again, I don't even have. And it would have happened if he didn't open his mouth and turn you off. So what's really good, Janae? Am I a joke? Am I chasing an illusion? 'Cuz I put my feelings into this for real faster than I'm used to. That's why I wrote that short-ass letter before this one 'cuz I got cut up and had to take a step back! The same inkling you give your ex you was giving this cat Frank by listening to some bullshit business idea and then asking him to help you move. I mean if I'm reading too much into this, forgive me. I'm not into sharing mine. And when I love, I love for real. And every decision I'm making here I know it's not just for me, it's for all of us. Are you seeing that same vision?

The pictures of you in my cell are on the TV, two of them are. So every time I watch TV I watch you! No, I don't share a cell with anyone. First of all, I'm too big. Second, I don't trust none of these dudes but maybe two or three people!

I'm more like, "You ain't lookin' at my woman." I'll show you off when I'm in the picture with you or you're visiting me before I come home! I'm going to write you more anyway. What you indulge in against my wishes has no bearing on my obligation to keep you focused. It just makes me question why would you say something like that. If he texts you and you constantly answer and it's not about the kids, what is this, high school?

I'm glad to actually know everything Jordan is allergic to. That way I won't cook or feed him nothing he's not supposed to have or be around. That's good he can be around dogs 'cuz I definitely want a dog or two. How do you feel about that? I don't care how many cats your ex's mother has. I know you're going to here and there talk about him to get it out of your system, but I don't need to hear about his brothers and so on!

That's nice Nicole, Melvin, and Kimberly are helping. I wish I could be there for you 'cuz I like moving and organizing things and decorating. Does it have a basement? Well, it looks like you won't be having no buster-ass dudes helping you seeing that, that ass is mine. I wish you could have seen Brooklyn this week. Tell her to get on her pen game. She's slipping, LOL. That's nice of you to babysit Michael. What, you getting some practice? LOL! You shoot pool but not the best, I can go for that. And I will have no problem standing behind you and guide it—I mean guiding you. :-)

I'm sure you've liked male strippers, but I won't be going to see that. To hear you say you think women on women is sexy is very surprising, but you're not sure you would like it personally. I'm going to leave that alone and visit that another day! I like to see porn with two girls also, but I will never see or watch or entertain no homosexual activities, so we don't have to even talk about that.! But I'm glad it will be a lot of firsts together. With the strip club thing it will also boost our sexual cravings, being the fact that just 'cuz we go to one doesn't mean I have to have a stripper dance for me when my woman is sitting next to me, and they have private booths!

I'm pleased to hear you're excited about the $0.96 calls while you're switching everything over. It should take about two to three days to put this phone number on the list and send it to my counselor and she'll put it in effect. So by the time you get this letter I should have called you about two times! Yes, that would be amazing for us. And it will pass the time much quicker. And yes, with more letters. That must mean your letters to me will increase, huh?

This is where you said goodnight but you didn't make it to church huh Ms. lady! LOL. What's up with the half braided hair? That's something new or what? Yes, that is a blessing on the rent you're paying for that house. Did you sign any type of contract stipulating that the rent will stay the same no matter what? And while you're cutting up and getting loose, remember your man is in a cell probably going nuts until he hears from his boo, knowing that she's back home safely and about to go to work and come home and talk on the phone to the one that makes her heart beat faster! And I know you will be good. You ain't trying to lose this and I'm not trying to lose you to nothing or no one if I can help it. I know you planned on talking to me Wednesday but it would be more like Tuesday of next week.

I can call you late afternoons, not three or four, more like five or six all the way up to ten and then it's over. But it will be up to 11 p.m. in the minimum on the weekends here. I'll be calling you in the morning or afternoon or at night, whatever fits you! And please don't say you'll be busy 'cuz if I'm not at work I will never be too busy for you!

And what is awesome about gray pubic hairs is I never saw any in my life and never heard anyone talk about them. And I don't know what you mean about snipped and no foreskin. I ain't had nothing cut or a snip, so I'll pass! Now anal, I guess only time will tell if we go there. To think about it, my first time will be all that and a bag of chips. I'm a patient lover, not a speed demon! And yes, we will have a lifetime to please one another!

Well, I'm going to go to sleep now for I have work in the morning and it's 1:30 a.m. So welcome home, hope you're happy to have mail in your box. Now I'm going to sleep with tender thoughts of you and also dreaming of our first everything also.

Love Always,
Jarelle

August 7, 2010

Dear Jarelle,

I've missed writing you sooo much! And I have to apologize for not being able to write sooner. I know you are wondering where the hell I am. I'm in Buffalo right now, and of course, being in my parents house, they don't have lined paper to write on. So the good thing is that this letter will be nice and long since I type much faster than I write. Also, since I'll put this in the mailbox before I hit the road on Monday, you should receive this on Tuesday. I have three letters here from you that I tried to thoroughly read before I left Charlotte and literally sped through them, so I will respond to those when I get home. In the meantime, let me tell you about my trip:

Thursday: Since me, Rhonda, and Nicole were all driving our own vehicles, we were going to meet at Nicole's house at 5:00 a.m. so we could hit the road. I was a little late! LOL. But after we had a circle of prayer we were off. Nicole was in the front, then Rhonda, then me. They had GPS but I've made that drive over ten times, so I didn't need it. Nicole started speeding on and off and kept getting way ahead of us. When we were in Pennsylvania on the 79N, Nicole was so far ahead of us we couldn't see her. But she called periodically to check in, but then said her GPS directed her to the 76E. I said to stay on the 79N and it takes you to the 90. She figured the GPS was giving her a shortcut, so she went from being fifteen minutes ahead of us to forty-five minutes behind us because it took her in a circle back to where she came from! I told Jordan to text her and say that's what you get for leaving us. I was annoyed because she was the one who wanted to travel as a group. We could have left at our own times and I could have slept longer, but it was cool. We got to Buffalo around 4:30 and my mom had taken my grandmother back to a nursing facility for, like, the fourth time. As you recall, she has Alzheimer's, and my mom puts her there because it's getting so difficult to care for her. But then she feels guilty and takes her out weeks Later. So I made dinner right away, beef stroganoff, so that when she came home it was done and one less thing for her to do. Got the kids fed, then me, Rhonda, and Nicole went to Stacey's house (mutual friend but mainly Nicole's friend) for a potluck and drinks. I had four glasses of sangria and a glass of Moscato, so I had a good time! Even after that I still woke up at like 8:30 a.m.

Friday: Everyone started waking up around 9:00, so I make breakfast—eggs, bacon, and pancakes. My mom was like, "I'll get that," but she put so much on herself, and goes nonstop but doesn't really accomplish anything because of the stress she puts on herself. So I planned on cooking as much as possible while here. So I made breakfast and our plan was to go to Beaver Island to the beach around 2:00 p.m. I told Que earlier in the week to see if he could gather his clan so that Jordan and Justine could see their siblings, and everyone was actually able to come. I tried to get my parents to come but they didn't want to intrude on a family day. So I said it's not a family event, it's all about the kids, but they stayed behind. When I came around 12:00 with three of the kids, I asked him what we would be doing about food and drinks, and he said just bottled water. I said, "Are you serious? You know they're going to want snacks," and he said he wasn't bringing anything. No, I'm not the type to have stuff for my kids and not anyone else, so I bought a box of juices, pretzels, chips, and Rice Krispies Treats, and wipes for their hands. Like, less than $10. And them kids tore those snacks up! His little funky water bottles, maybe three were drunk. Not that kids don't need water, but it's a fun day, so let them splurge a little. Afterward he bought a sheet pizza and wings, and I was like, aaahhh, a real pizza! LOL.

Now, his mom's house is tiny, and the living room is mad cluttered and the one little couch seats two people. So the kids were allowed to have fun since they ain't been together with all of them really since Justine was a baby, before the last three were born! So they were excited and someones pizza ended up on the floor. Que goes berserk, saying, "Y'ALL SIT THE FUCK DOWN SOMEWHERE AND STOP ACTING SO FUCKING WILD, AND ACT LIKE Y'ALL GOT SOME DAMN SENSE AND BLAH BLAH BLAH!" I was like, "Are you serious? It's two seats. Where they supposed to sit? And it's not that serious!"

Anyway, I got a lot of pics of their brothers and sisters, but the little baby's mother came literally right when we got back, so the final group pic she wasn't in. While we were at the beach. He had his cell phone in a Ziploc bag, and he was standing ankle and knee-deep in the water texting through the bag. I was like, who does that? Really, can't you just leave the phone on the chairs?? Dumbass! But around 5:00 he was like, "Let's wrap this up," and it was getting breezy, so I was like, cool. Then as we're all packing up it started raining! Most of them were already wet, but the rain is colder. So his four-year-old was moving in slow motion, putting her clothes on and shivering, and he's yelling for them to hurry up. So he grabs my cooler and starts walking while the kids are scrambling to get their stuff to keep up. So I yelled, "HOLD IT!" They looked and I said there are still shoes here and towels and stuff. They were so busy trying not to piss him off that they were forgetting stuff, then he'll be yelling at them for leaving stuff.

So when we got to the house and the youngest baby's mom showed up not even five minutes later, I'm thinking like, "Damn, she the reason you was rushing the kids to hurry up?" But the bottom line, all the kids got to see each other as a group for the first time, and it was really cute. And Que didn't try anything with me, so I didn't have to check him at all. He wasn't even funny acting, so I was like, cool. But I did text him later, letting him know his reaction to the spilled pizza was totally over the top unnecessary. And of course he didn't answer that. Maybe if I included a nipple shot with the message he would have responded! LOL. Yes, that was a bad joke. You know I'm all about you!

We left the house around 6:00 p.m. and came to my mom's house, stayed for a little while, and then me and Jordan went to Shelby's house. We got some more Moscato and talked for hours! Basically four months of catching up. The last time we talked I had just had the miscarriage, so there was a lot to talk about. We left there around 11:30, and Jordan was still up. So I was on the couch, Jordan was on the other couch, and my mom was standing, talking to us. Next thing I know *thunk*, she's on the floor, passed out. Lying straight on her back, eyes just open, but she fainted! I yelled for my dad and we got her up, and she kept saying she was fine and she was just talkin'. But this is the stuff that's been going on. She is so stressed about everything, and literally goes days without eating and drinking! Her siblings are out of state, and my aunt that's in Buffalo gets my grandmother like two weekends a month but the burden always has fallen on my mom. My grandfather passed in May 2008, so she's still healing from that, missing me and the kids, my grandmother's Alzheimer's, everything. So needless to say, I didn't get much sleep last night.

Saturday: We had cereal for breakfast and my mom actually made herself a small bowl. I'm glad that Jordan witnessed the same thing because that may trigger my mom to take better care of herself, being that her grandson saw the effects of his grandmother not taking care of herself. Today we went to the flea market on Walden Avenue. My dad gave the kids $10 each, so they were in their glory, buying this and that! I picked up Shelby and her daughter to tag along with us. I'm so sleepy right now, so I'm going to save this document and finish typing *mañana*!

Sunday: Good morning. So, continuing with yesterday, I love going to the flea market. I bought a cute baseball cap for me that said "sexy" for those days when I don't feel like doing my hair, and a cute cookie jar and some Avon products. Exciting, right? Then I ran a few errands for my mom and was supposed to link up with my girl Lonette at 7:00 but she never called me back, so I actually just chilled while the kids played the Xbox. Nicole called saying they were going out again! I didn't feel like it, but since I didn't go to happy hour after the beach I figured I might as well go have fun. Then she called and said she was driving back in the morning instead of Monday because Evelyn, the girl who rode up with her, has to work and didn't want to call in sick. So me and Rhonda are leaving tomorrow.

  This morning I went to Steve's Meat Market to get my Buffalo necessities—Sahlen's hotdogs, chicken nuggets, pizza logs, Camelia sausages—to put in the cooler. Then I came back and made breakfast again. Even just two days of us all making my mom eat, she was looking better already because she would literally go days and only eat a bite or two of food. The main thing now is for her to leave my grandmother where she is and not beat herself up over the need to put her in a facility that can better care for her. I hope I don't have to ever make that decision one day, but I know Alzheimer's is serious and my mom is not able to care for her. Later today I'll be going out to Riverside to see my other grandmother. That's my father's side of the family, and just about all of my cousins live out there in Schaefer Village. All of my cousins also live out there, and I think it keeps my grandmother active. When I compare my grandmothers, even though they are the same age they are so different as far as abilities with old age. Staying active keeps you younger. Both of my grandfathers have already passed, and Que's father passed two years ago, so my father is my kids' last living grandfather.

Justine is playing the Wii right now and Jordan is upstairs on the Xbox, so I have a little quiet moment. I'm going to be busy as hell writing you back to respond to your recent letters. I left Thursday at 5:00 a.m., so the mail on Thursday, Friday, and Saturday likely had one or two letters from you, plus the three in my purse that I quickly read before hitting the road. And I still have to turn the internet on at my house so I can hook the phone back up so you can start calling.

As far as the interview I had on Wednesday, I feel like it went great. I never heard back from Mr. Walker either! I called him and emailed him, and it seems like his mind is made up already, which is disappointing. But in this case I don't think no news is good news. I have been in his face all year inquiring about working there, so it is what it is. Just means I have to continue putting my energy elsewhere looking for work. You know what's so crazy is that Que kept texting me that he's so excited that we were coming. I didn't hear from him at all Saturday though, and this morning he texted me asking what were we doing today, and I said we'd be going to see my grandma and had no other plans. He hasn't asked to get them or come by or anything, so I'm like, yeah, you were really missing them, huh? I think he was looking for a sign from me that we were going to get busy, and when I didn't even give him a second glance the exciting part of us coming to town probably fizzled away! So if he comes to get them, great. If not, we're leaving in the morning. It's about noon right now and the kids are quiet, so I might as well go ahead and answer these three letters in my purse now while I'm in the typing mood!

The first letter was the lost one, and we pretty much touched on that already. You know that my house was broken into and what I had said was that Jordan came in my room that morning and said, "Mom, we were robbed," and my initial thought was, "Oh my God, someone was in my house while we were asleep!" But then he said our window in the car is smashed, and that was when I realized he meant the car was broken into. And I definitely believe it was someone in my building because the way we park you don't see the front of my car unless you are specifically looking. And no, I don't tell people my every move, I don't even talk to most people in my building except a quick hello as we pass each other.

Moving along to letter number two, dated 7/29. Yes, I love water fights, balloons, hoses, super soakers. I'm not one of those black girls who are scared to get their hair wet! Unless I'm fresh from the salon, of course. I do put baby powder on my chest, but I think it was the underwire from my bra combined with the friction or whatever, but the rash is gone. The skin is still darker though, so I hope it gradually fades back to normal. Yes, Touch Me Not is the real street name! Cute, isn't it? The reason you have to write to a PO box is because Kathryn cannot have anyone renting the house but she is moving back to New York, so she can't change her address. So I'll be sending her mail every two weeks. But I think in your case it would be okay to use the home address. But just in case, once I get the PO box use that. And once you get this letter you hopefully can call me and I'll have the PO box number. In the meantime, do not send any more mail to Matthews, send it to 344 Touch Me Not Lane.

Now, to answer your 8/1 letter, that's good you're working the machine now, moving on up! The guy that took care of the bees didn't come in the house, he doesn't have a key. And I saw honeycomb on the ground, so it looks like he got it all out! I'm so glad the mail lag/infrequent letters, etc. issue is done and resolved, so you can stop whining. Do I need to give you a bib and pacifier? But now the shoe will be on the other foot because I've been thrown all off track with coming to Buffalo! But I write fast, so you'll be hooked up in no time!

I didn't think you could be transferred to North Carolina, but hey, it never hurts to ask. I'm glad I didn't move back to Buffalo also. I've been ready to go home already. It's so boring here! Plus, I miss my bed and haven't got to really enjoy our new house yet. I hope Neva is being a good girl. That doggone rabbit chews just to be chewing, but I closed off all the doors. And the living room floor is hardwood, and she doesn't like to walk on hard floors, so she won't go there. But the molding at the bottom of walls she chews on, so I'm praying she is still nervous and stayed in her hutch!

I'm so mad I didn't bring any picture of you with me because I miss looking at it too. I can't wait to get the next picture you're sending me. Well, my dear, I have a few things to do this afternoon to get ready for the drive back tomorrow, so I got to be going. Know that you are in my thoughts and heart. And until our words meet again, take care, stay blessed!

Love ya!

PS

So what did you mean about adding something to my name when I signed? Were you meaning something like this, Janae Edwards. Hmmm, that looks kinda hot!

8/11/2010 (answering 8/5)

Hi Jarelle,

Yes, I'm officially home and in the new house. We moved all the big stuff Monday, the second, so of course we slept in the new house. All that's left are some small things, cleaning, and painting the walls back white. I have four letters to answer since I got three today, but before I get to those let me tell you about that doggone drive home!

Nicole had to leave on Sunday, so it was going to be Rhonda and her three boys in her car, and me, the kids, and Stacey in my car. I told Stacey I was leaving around 9:00 or 10:00 a.m. and would call in the morning to let her know when to be ready. I called her at 8:00 a.m. and told her I would be there by 9:45. Then I said, never mind, I plan to arrive at 9:30 on the dot and wanted to be on the highway by 10:00. She said okay and that she wanted to get a sandwich from some store and hoped they were open. So I get the kids up, we eat, and take everything out to the car—my cooler loaded with goodies! The trunk is so full, so I was thinking hopefully Stacey didn't over pack since she said she would stay only about a week. We arrived at her house at 9:32, and I had already caught Rhonda and she was going to meet me there. I be thinking she would just come out. She poked her head out and said, "I thought you would call first." I said, "No, I figured since I said I would be here at 9:30 that was sufficient." This chick says, "Well, usually people call first. I still need, like, twenty minutes." I'm thinking, shit, here we go! But I hadn't gassed up yet or checked the air pressure, so I said, "Cool, I'll go to the gas station, get some snacks, then you should be ready."

So we get to the gas station, fill up, but the air pump is sucking my air out instead of putting it in! So, bordering pissed, I drive to another and Rhonda's friend Yvette calls me and said Rhonda left a bag in the bathroom but Rhonda doesn't have a phone for Yvette to tell her. So I called Stacey to tell her that when Rhonda comes to let her know. And since Yvette lives near the 90, it's cool. But Stacey was like, "If Rhonda comes and we are not here, what will she think? And I can't leave to go to the store yet." What the fuck, this chick ain't left yet??? So I tell her to wait till Rhonda comes, and my pissedoffness is just growing! Then Rhonda calls me, and I'm like, "What phone are you on?" Her mom bought her a prepaid phone and she never mentioned it! So she called Stacey to tell her to go to the store, and she said she already talked to Yvette and had the bag. So I'm thinking, great, we can roll when Stacey comes back!

Me and Rhonda wait outside at Stacey's house and she takes forever, like fifteen minutes we wait. She bought a sub and some damn hair weave! Then her bags. A huge suitcase that had to fit between the kids in the back. Another suitcase full of shoes that went in Rhonda's car, another bag of pants because she said she didn't know how the weather would be even though I told her it's been upper nineties for over a month! We finally start driving and she's like, "Oh shit, oh shit." So I immediately beep Rhonda to pull over and stop. She forgot to leave her daughter's social security card, so we turn back around and she's apologizing and I don't want to hear it! Her daughter was actually walking up the street, so she gave it to her and then we hit the road. At fuckin 11:00 a.m.! Ninety minutes after the fact!

Driving is going fine. I had never discussed gas money with her, and I wasn't going to say, "No, you can't ride," if she said beforehand that she couldn't. But at the rest stop, before I could ask her, she said she was living off social services and couldn't offer cash but would use her food stamp card to buy road food and pay the tolls. So I was fine with that, even though the cash would be better. On the road she was a Facebook junkie, on her BlackBerry updating her page all day! But I wasn't tired and I was good. We stopped in Pennsylvania, then drove, then stopped in West Virginia, about three hours from Charlotte. This time it was my fault that our stop lasted longer because I got the kids hot food at the gas station. So Rhonda's oldest son came in and said his mom wanted to know what was going on. So I said we are coming.

Mind you, we were there almost fifteen minutes and Stacey stayed in the car the whole time. I started the car and she offered to drive. I said, "Nah, I'm good." And Jordan was like, "Mom, you always say you want help driving." So I said okay. So we switched. She looked at my drink and said, "Maybe I should get a Pepsi." Are you kidding me, fifteen minutes later? So I just took her money and bought the fountain drink. And I know Rhonda was pissed, like, what the hell! She started driving but she's driving like an old lady, fifty in a seventy-mile zone! I told her she can speed up, but on S-curves she's doing almost eighty and making the wheel vibrate. And she said she's not used to the highways. And Rhonda basically left us, which I didn't blame her at all. I held out for about thirty minutes and said, "I can't take it, pull over." So she was apologizing and saying she wasn't used to it. With me back at the wheel we were out, but I hate driving in the dark because I can't see as good and I am always worried about hitting an animal.

Now Stacey was supposed to stay with Nicole, so we called her and this heffa is in Mount Holly, about thirty minutes from her house, with her friend Evelyn. So we told her we were about forty-five minutes away. We finally arrived at my house about 11:00 p.m. Rhonda unloads Stacey's stuff and drives home. Stacey calls Nicole to pick her up, and this heffa tells her they're watching a movie and she'll be here when it goes off. I told her to ask how long, and she answered she doesn't know. So I'm yelling, "How long has it been on? Is it in the beginning, middle, what?" So Stacey hands me the phone, and since my pissedoffness meter was off the chart at this point, she probably shouldn't have given me the phone! So I'm yelling at Nicole that she should know how long the movie is or how long it's been on, and I really don't remember what else. Nicole said, "Who you think you talkin' to?" And I said, "You." So of course she said, "Well, since you want to yell, I'll just call when my movie goes off," and hung up!

My whole thing was how the hell you know you have company coming into town and you not home, and you can't even estimate how long the movie will be? And I'm sure her thing was why was I talking to her like she was my child! I definitely took my frustration out on the wrong person, but Nicole should have been home because I was so sick of being with Stacey and I wanted to go to bed! So of course she didn't call until almost 1:00 a.m., and I dropped Stacey off so I could finally get my TV that was left in her truck when I moved last week and I was out! I had to wait until today to talk to Nicole, and it was her and Melvin's anniversary today also. She said she understood why I was frustrated because I was tired, and she hung up because I was yelling, so it's squashed. But all I know is I can handle the damn highway myself until we roll together! So I hope you drive as well as me, LOL.

So back to the letter you wrote me. I love sleep, and I sleep more when I'm pregnant, mainly the first trimester. And I'm a happy-go-lucky glowing type of pregnant woman, but sometimes emotional, never cranky or uptight. I really would have preferred to see Brooklyn in Atlanta instead of driving to Buffalo, but she asked could I come another time. So maybe Labor Day weekend. You seriously asking me what was my reaction to Quincy's picture text! If you are confident you have me, you sure always keep doubting me. I've told you everything and then you say you don't want to know. But, baby, please believe nothing about the picture excited me, okay? Your picture excites me! My reaction, honestly, was yuck! Moving along! No, I have not heard from Mr. Walker and I had given up, but after reading your letter I think he owes me either an interview or a reason why not. So I called again yesterday and left a message, and today I went there but he was out until tomorrow. So I will go tomorrow. I've still been applying to other places in the meantime, and I sent a follow-up email from my interview last week.

Now, to answer or reply to the topic of love. I know how I feel about you. And I really do believe it's love, but it scares me to totally let go and embrace it. You are everything that I've ever wanted in a man, and it almost seems like a fairy tale. But the thing that scares me is what will happen when you get out. I know how hard it is to find a job with two college degrees, so finding a job with a felony will be so much more challenging and almost impossible. And my other fear is the fact that you have to register as a sex offender and my career path with children and parents. I remember when I first brought it up you said if it impacted my career or relationship you would man up and gracefully bow out. After all the feelings and love and time invested, the idea that I could lose it all scares me. All I or we can do is pray and trust in God that we were meant to be. But after so many disappointments in life, I almost expect things not to work out. And I'm working hard to get rid of that negativity because God has gotten us through so much!

And I set up the phone number and put money on it. The internet is still not on but my home phone calls are forwarded to my cell, so that should work because the home phone is a landline. I can't wait until I hear your voice!

Love you, Jarelle!

Janae

8/12/2010 (answering 8/6 letters!)

Hey Baby,

I see I need to really put your mind at ease so you can relax. First of all, I actually think it's kinda cute that you were nervous about me going to Buffalo! And you're right, I had no intention of making that drive, and when Nicole mentioned she was going and Rhonda was going I still said no because I just wasn't up for the drive. But the idea of all of us driving together sounded fun (I know you've read my typed letter, so you know how that went!), and I told my parents that they were driving up and I was only considering it. But I told them probably not because the car would be too hot, so my dad was like, "I thought you've been got that fixed," so he said he would take care of it. Then there was the issue of where to sleep and my mom said she would send Grandma to my aunt's house. Then I was thinking pizza, wings, Wegmans subs, so I decided okay because I don't see any other time I will be driving again before spring break if even then. I'm glad I went because after witnessing my mom faint, we've been on her. And Jordan calls every day and asks her what she ate, and she emailed him what she eats. And he calls my dad to make sure. Jordan is her soft spot, so him seeing that made something click. And I hope she gains five or ten pounds because she got too small. I reconnected with Shelby again, so the visit was worth it, and the kids got to see eleven out of twelve siblings. And Que didn't try anything. And when he realized I was staying with my parents the whole time, he understood—for now because I know he won't give up that easy. But moving on.

Jarelle, I knew that Frank had no real intention of helping me move. As far as listening to the conference call, I really was curious since he bugged me about it before. And I wasn't purposely enticing him. And yes, I did tell him I had a man! When he asked was my man helping me move, I said, no, he's in New York. The reason he asked me originally if was I in Charlotte still was because I told him last summer that I was moving back to Buffalo. When we did the conference call and his sponsor did the follow-up call after work on the three-way, she was asking when did I want to speak again. And that's when I said I was moving and going to Buffalo, and I wasn't sure if I wanted to be bothered and that I needed time to think it over. I never gave him my new address either! I just told him the area, and it was more of a confirmation for me that he was full of shit because he wasn't trying to help me move. Baby, I'm sorry for letting it go that far, but I really didn't think it was that serious and he doesn't have a chance in hell at getting with me. Now I see my man is quite the overprotective one! So I will try to be less naive and not lead any men on. I don't try to flirt or entice, or purposely swish when I walk. How about dingy T-shirts and sweats until you get out? Yeah right! LOL. I will tell these clowns to back the hell up from now on, okay? And you don't have to rub it In about me almost letting Frank come over last year. I knew it was wrong, and I was newly laid off and depressed. But I didn't go there with him because I know what it's like to be cheated on, the other woman, etc. And I'll never compromise myself in that way ever again. And why should I? I have you!

Yes, the AC is blowing good and strong! And no, I didn't just go to any backyard repair shop. My dad told me to go someplace where I can get a full warranty, and I've been dealing with Firestone for years and the bill was high as hell! But it was a necessary repair. It was 100 degrees yesterday and today. I was on the phone with my dad every step of the repair so he could okay everything. And as far as my hair, I unbraided the first few rows then rebraided them so they would be fresh and tight. Not leaving them loose, no, that's not a new style! I love amusement park rides and have always wanted to skydive, but not bungee jump. Weird, right, that I'll jump out of a plane but not bungee jump! I do know how to swim and skate, but I wish I could skate backward. I've actually planned a water balloon fight for Justine's party this Saturday. I can't believe my baby is turning seven! I also bought a slip and slide and a blow-up pool. Jordan cut the grass, which literally had grown into a forest! They found a frog, so they rescued him and took it to the woods. I rigged up the front grass and tomorrow we'll rake the back.

Derelict sounded like a good book. It's published by 50 Cent's company, G-Unit Books or something. It's about this guy doing seven years for money fraud and he was set up by a dude that got large as hell in the right business while he was on lockdown. He had two girlfriends/baby mamas that lived together and shared him as their dude. And there is the prison psychologist he keeps making an appointment with, and eventually they have sex and she falls for him hard. So for the first three-quarters of the book he seems focused on getting out and doing right, but toward the end he gets cocky as hell and dogs the psychologist just for head, knowing that she's in love. Talking to the baby mamas like they're his kids. And when he finally gets out, his boy convinces him to forget about his kids and girlfriends and get revenge on the rapper dude, and it abruptly ends. I was liking the guy in the beginning because he was focused on living right, but in the end he let his friend convince him to do wrong, so he's weak-minded. Not sure if there is a part two or if I would even read it!

I'm surprised to hear you say I shouldn't have told Que we were coming to Buffalo. I know he's not handling his business as a dad, but why would I not give the kids an opportunity to see him? What I'm trying to do is get all the baby moms' numbers so that the kids can call each other without having to go through him. How do siblings not have each other's phone numbers? Because he still wants to go back and forth and don't want them talking and spreading his business or busting him out! He will soon see that a soldier usually falls on his own sword.

OMG I'm so sleepy! It's got to be after midnight and I still have to answer your 8/7 letter. I was hoping you would call tonight and the call forwarding should work. And yes, I know I still got to get some pictures to you. Don't worry, baby, as soon as I'm done at the old apartment and get Justine's party done I'll take care of that. Please know my love for you grows every day and I ain't going nowhere! I will continue tomorrow, my dear Jarelle!

Love you,
Janae Edwards

8/13/2010 (answering 8/7)

My worrywart Jarelle,

I'm supposed to be asleep but I keep reading this letter. And you have me at a loss for words because I thought I addressed this in the letter I finished thirty minutes ago. But the issue is clearly weighing heavy on your mind. Number one, Frank is a dead issue. Nothing was going to go on between us. I gave you my new address. And I see now that I'm a little too open with you, so I will just avoid any conversation dealing with the opposite sex. You say you want me to paint a picture for you of my days, and I guess I am just naive or maybe you have possessive tendencies, or I'm just not being sensitive to your feelings. But bottom line: <u>I love you</u> and I'm willing to wait for you, which means telling niggas <u>no</u> left and right. And I just wonder why you still question my feelings for you! You're asking me are you a joke or am I making you chase an illusion?? Yes, you are reading too much into this, and that really hurt my feelings. You're making me feel like the biggest idiot. And I guess I just talk too much and you don't need to know about every encounter of my day. As far as texting with Que, I told him we were coming in town and you're saying I should have kept my mouth shut? When I was talking about his mom and the cats and the grown-ass men not cleaning up, I was just making conversation. What the hell, Jarelle! Please stop reading so much into absolutely nothing! What do I need to do or say to convince you that I'm in this with you 100 percent? And I turn down phone numbers every day with you in mind? I need to get off this subject before the tears fall again!

Jordan and Justine painted at the old apartment today. We have to paint the accent walls back to white, and luckily that latex paint rubs off in water because they had paint all over. I ordered Justine's birthday cake today, Hello Kitty, and bought the cups, plates, balloons, etc. Jordan left a note on my nightstand to tell the Tooth Fairy to come. He wants to be grown, that kid! His tooth came out at a rest stop on the road, and Justine put hers yesterday in the car. I was always afraid to pull mine!

Fell asleep…

It's now 8:00 a.m. on Friday, the thirteenth! Oh, LOL. I thought I was watching Diedra's ten-year-old son Isaiah this morning and she never called. Jordan was excited to be having company too, so I don't know what that's all about. But yes, I'm enjoying the house more and more. We have to rake and sweep the back today in preparation for Justine's party tomorrow. And I'll be sure to take plenty of pictures. I barely took any in Buffalo except of all the kids at the beach. And I got a cute one of Justine and Remy (see, my parents' dog is half mini Doberman, so he's little) in their sleep. I definitely want dogs, two or three. Got to have a cute small one and a big playful one.

This house doesn't have a basement but does have an attic with the stairs that pull down from the ceiling. Creepy! Reminds me of the scene in *The Exorcist*!

Being in the baby room at Sunday school every other week changing diapers is plenty of experience. I just hope my eggs are not shriveling up! My periods are so much lighter than they used to be. Hope your sperm are good swimmers!

I haven't been to see male strippers in, like, two years, and before that it had been about six or seven years. I definitely don't like seeing men on men either, and you don't have to keep bringing it up or bringing up that you don't want anything in your butt. I get it! I'm not sure about going into a private booth at a strip club. Do they thoroughly clean them between guests? Because I don't want anyone else's juices on my body!

I feel so bad that you only got one letter from me the week of 8/9–8, but at least it was a long one and I mailed it before we hit the road. So this week coming up you will have lots. I'm still waiting for the phone to ring and you being on the other line. And I did sign an official lease with Kathryn, so my lease goes up until 7/31/2011, and we agreed to see how the first year goes before making it longer. I can't wait to buy my own house, but I want something bigger than this.

I'm sure you were happy to know I didn't even get loose and cut up either. Slightly tipsy at best. And hanging at Stacey's house and Shelby's house is hardly cutting up! LOL, of course you haven't seen gray pubic hairs! You were still in your twenties when you went in. So unless you were creeping with little old ladies, you shouldn't have seen any gray hairs down there. Snip and no foreskin refers to an uncircumcised penis, and even though it's the natural way a male is born, it looks ugly! What do you be thinking that I'm talking about? I can be freaky but I'm not a super freak! LOL.

The kids have just woken up. I've been hearing that rooster calling all morning. I'm so hungry and thirsty all of a sudden. My plan now that Isaiah isn't here is to head over to the old apartment early to get stuff done. It really did not seem like a lot to do, but getting back from the road so late on Monday threw me off on Tuesday. I actually called human resources at CMS to see what the deal is regarding being hired. Bottom line, it will be virtually impossible for me to be hired again because I was on an action plan, which is like performance probation, since my classroom observations were all ranked below standard. So I'm almost blacklisted from any CMS school, and they told me that they send the principals a list of <u>highly qualified</u> teachers to interview. So Mr. Walker will not be calling me. Maybe he just didn't want to be the one to tell me. That damn Devonshire has permanently tainted my reputation as a teacher! So I have to try with Union County schools, that's where I had that interview right before I left for Buffalo. I have applied to like ten or fifteen jobs there, and I interviewed with three of their schools this past school year but wasn't hired. This has passed the frustration level. Something has got to give. I refuse to continue trying to get unemployment extension. And honestly, I don't have any desire to go back to school at this time. All I can do is trust in God and pray!

Well, my dear, I'm going to make me a bagel with cream cheese and get some grapefruit, make the kids get some cereal, and we're going to get it done at the other apartment. Put your mind to rest about all that nonsense and just trust me when I say you got me!

Love you!
Janae

8/14/2010

Good evening Jarelle,

What a busy and exhausting day. My baby girl turned seven. Still amazed it's been seven years. I planned her party for 3:00 to 6:00 p.m., and I swear the time flew by and next thing you know it was already 3:00. Now I remember why I started doing Chuck E. Cheese and other not-at-my-house parties. Two hundred fifty water balloons, the pool, and a slip-and-slide with twelve kids was very interesting! But the main thing was Justine had so much fun, as well as the other kids. The crazy part was how long it took to fill those balloons and how fast they went through them, and why was I the initial target? LOL. But it was like ninety-three degrees, so I didn't mind at all. We had four pizzas from Walmart, $5 each, cake, ice cream, and chips. I didn't go overboard spending. But I wish I had enough money to buy loot bags and a piñata but it all went well. One of my Girl Scouts, Amanda, lost her earring in the pool, and ten minutes later Nia stepped on it (I didn't cut her). So even though that hurt, I was glad we found the earring!

I'm sitting here listening to Pretty Wings on the radio. I could listen to that song all day. Justine loves it too, so when we're in the car and it comes on I'm sure Jordan be like, dang! All day long when my cell phone would ring I was hoping it's you. Then this evening I was telling Nicole that I was waiting for you to call the house phone, and she said I thought your phone was off. I told her until I turn the internet on I'm having the calls forwarded to myself. So she dialed my home number and gave me the phone, and how about it stated the number is disconnected! So I went online (still borrowing a signal, LOL) to Vonage and checked my call history, and my last call received was May 24. All the damn time I've been paying the bill but the calls weren't coming in. Because of that brief time when I was supposed to do that work from home job and had to get another landline phone through AT&T, it affected something up with the Vonage signal, so I never knew. And I've been sitting waiting to finally hear your voice, and I don't even know how many times you have called. And you won't get this letter until probably Wednesday, so all I can do in the meantime is hope that you will try to call one of these days, hopefully tomorrow (Sunday) because I need to hear my baby's voice! I got it all straightened up with Vonage and they gave me a credit to my account. Jarelle, I need you to feel my vibe and know to call me!

Tomorrow we'll be going to clean the other apartment. The walls have been painted, and most of my clothes are folded and out of there. I want to be done, and I'm so tired now. After a good breakfast I better have energy. Talk about being sleepy! I'm about to totally fall asleep and dream of you. I'll pick this up later tomorrow. Know that I'll have you on my mind! Luv ya.

Sunday…

Good morning, baby. Well, it's 8:45. This is a late wake-up for me but I slept good. I forgot to buy milk yesterday, which means I'm forced to cook breakfast instead of making them eat cereal. Ugh! But then again there are waffles in there, so maybe not. I love having a side-by-side refrigerator because I can fit so much more in it, especially the freezer. When we first moved to North Carolina I had a chest-style deep freezer, but money was so tight and my two-bedroom apartment was too small to put it anywhere, so I sold it within the first month.

I've bought and sold so much on Craigslist. I love that site! The kids' bunk beds with mattresses, $150; Justine's daybed with mattress, $45; TVs; GPS (the first one I had, I sold it there). And every time they outgrew clothes I would put an ad up. I got a full encyclopedia set on there too, the 1983 World Book. I kept that in my classroom because so many of my students barely could do a Google search, let alone use reference books. And yes, technology is great, but when you don't even know how to look up information alphabetically that's a problem. I've been holding out literally till the last minute about taking all my teaching materials out of my storage closet on the patio in the old apartment. My hope was that I would have a teaching job by now and could just transfer it all to the car, then straight to the school. But I have to turn the keys in on Monday, so I have to take it with me back to the new house. I wish I knew what God has in store for me as far as a job because another school year is beginning on the twenty-fifth. Teachers report on the eighteenth, this coming Wednesday. There is still a possibility that Wingate Elementary will call, but my only issue will be getting the kids to ASEP early in the morning. I'd actually have to be at school by 6:45 and ASEP opens at 7:00 a.m., and the school is thirty minutes from Crown Point. Still waiting on Stonewall Jackson, CPCC, and other Union County schools. I just have to trust that He have it all worked out!

Justine has $24 now, so I know she can't wait to go spend it. Justine blows through money like it's water, but he did give her a dollar for her birthday. I have to remind my parents that they owe Justine a gift. Jordan being older, he emails them pictures of stuff he wants for his birthday (February 17) and they order it online. The gift they got him last time literally took six weeks to ship and they thought it was lost in the mail, so they sent him $50 in the mail and he bought a Super NERF gun that left him with $0. Then the remote control helicopter came in the mail and we were like, huh! But my mom's going to tell me the Wii was for both of them for Christmas, which is great, but she's trying to count it as Justine's birthday gift too, so hell no, it doesn't work that way!

Just like a few weeks ago somebody came by their house selling a brand-new boy's bike and she said they were going to get it for Jordan for his birthday because it was too good a deal to pass up. So I told her no, he has a bike and his birthday is several months away while Justine's birthday is coming up. So she wants to try to count the Wii as part of her gift. I don't think so! So I will be letting Justine go online and pick something out and they better order it.

It's not even about the dollar amount because she likes simple girly things. It's just that this happens every year, and they say it's because Jordan always calls or emails them to remind them and Justine is much less aggressive when it comes to birthday gifts. But fair is fair, so they just have to come out of their pockets again. But that's what I mean when I say my mom favors Jordan. Because I told her when the helicopter arrived that late he was in school and didn't even know, so I said we can put it up till Christmas. And they were like, "Nah, go ahead and give it to him." Don't you know, he broke it not even three weeks later! I don't even get him expensive stuff anymore. They got him a PSP. The screen ended up getting an internal crack, which could have been fixed, and I told him, "Use your money to fix it." But he bought the NERF gun. Then he literally took the PSP apart and it's destroyed, so I told him he'll never get a Nintendo Dsi from me when he deliberately messed up the PSP.

Oh yes, speaking of birthdays, that punk-ass dad of theirs did not call yesterday! This is a first, and thankfully Justine had so much fun she didn't notice, but what the hell! But I got a text from him (calm down, I know what you're thinking!) that he must have sent to his contact list asking to please support him, selling fuckin raffle tickets for his football team for $5 each, and he has to sell them by next Saturday. Number one, as much as he complains about never having time to so-called spend with the kids because of working (see, the so-called reason he had to quit his job), he totally make sure he is at every football practice, game, or event, and barely gets play time anyway! That summer of 2008 we went to all the home games and I was looking like, "Okay, why are you on the team?" LOL. And he told me, like, two months ago that his mom had ordered football jerseys with his name and number for Justine and the rest of the girls. I never heard anything else about that, and I thought he was waiting till her birthday to get it. Glad I never told her about it.

But yeah, that some shit to not call your child on her birthday, no excuses! That's why I will be so glad when you come home, especially if you get out before or on her birthday. She thought you were getting out yesterday and was excited, but I had to explain to her that will be when she turns eight! They need a regular father figure in their lives, and I'll bet they will be wanting to call you Daddy. I know I will. Especially in the bed, or the kitchen, or living room, we're outside in the rain!

Again, I'm wishing you will try calling again today. I can't imagine what you're thinking when the number said disconnected. I'm glad Nicole told me that because she had been calling and thought I'd turned that phone off. So, Jarelle, please, please call! LOL.

I'm about to find something to eat and get washed and dressed so we can head over to the apartment and get it done. Remember I love you and always think about us! And I'm just about done with your package, so you'll be getting that soon!

Love you!
Janae

It wasn't too late to walk away at this point in our developing relationship. So why didn't I? In these letters, I'm telling this man that everything is flowing so smoothly and I don't feel any insecurities, and I'm straight lying. I didn't like how the mention of Quincy sent him into a frenzy. But I needed to talk it out to release these years of pain that I've been holding on to. I didn't like how the mention of a random nobody like Frank had him questioning things I say and do. I haven't given a single thought to being with any other man, yet I'm having to explain why I think and say what I do. I wanted him to want me and trust me.

And I'm trying not to overshare my life. Every time I say too much I receive a letter in the mail questioning my loyalty or taking what I say out of context. This man kept asking me to paint a picture of my day but seemed intimidated by the bold streaks of color I used. You want me to water it down but then tell me don't, you like the portrait I'm making for you. I'm very confused and frustrated, yet intrigued. I tried to excuse it away as the environment he's in had him tense, in a fight or flight mode 24/7. I'm a carefree spirit in many aspects of my life and he was making me feel anxious, but I convinced myself that once he was released he could relax and let his guard down.

The lag in communication was frustrating. We would be talking about a situation, and somehow what I wrote would be taken out of context and needed to be explained, again! The mail delays would drag a situation out. And I'd be thinking all is well, we have moved past that, just for it to come up in the next letter. The questioning always felt like an interrogation, and I needed to prove beyond a shadow of doubt that I was loyal. I changed my mind and decided to take a last-minute trip to Buffalo and had to explain in a dozen paragraphs why. My street name was a funny and quirky name, yet I had to explain that instead of just having him trust in me. I don't know why I didn't just say "fuck this" and walk away. I believe with everything in me that I genuinely loved him before we even heard each other's voice, and I wanted to fight for true love. This was just the enemy trying to break apart what God was putting together . . .

8/15/2010

Hi Jarelle,

Almost done with the old apartment. I had the kids cleaning the dirty parts of the walls and painting the molding at the bottom of the walls, where my bad little furball Neva was chewing. Never heard of a bunny that likes paint! She's lucky that she is so damn cute! That's my Nae Nae. Tomorrow I turn the keys in, and I just have a little left over to do. But, man, all my teaching supplies in the storage closet. Ugh!

I've been in agony this evening too. Nicole held a candlelight vigil for the shooting victims in Buffalo this evening at her house. We didn't make it because by the time we left the apartment and came home and cooked it was almost 9:00. So sad now five dead out of the eight shot. Senseless. But I was texting Brooklyn and told her about the phone situation and about that idiot Frank situation, and she agreed I never should have asked him to move even though I wasn't serious. Then she said you may end up thinking I'm playing games, and that hurt because that's the last thing I want you thinking. This has been weighing so heavy on my heart this evening because I can't just talk to you now and clear it up, and you probably won't read this until Wednesday. I hate to say it, but I actually think the reason why I always feel the need to share every encounter I have with the opposite sex is to keep you interested in me. I don't mean to even put you near the same category as Que, but my theory was if he knew how desirable I was to other men it would make him want me more and not want me to go with some other guy. But that never really got much reaction from him. So when I see you get so angry it's almost confusing to me because my intention was never to make you mad or jealous, just keep you interested in me. Honestly, I worry about when you do get out, looking all good and all eyes will be on you. And what if you lose interest? My insecurities have been getting the best of me lately. You just don't know how often I daydream about our future, but it often feels too good to be true and I feel like you might get bored with me. I know it sounds silly, but you just don't know the effect you are having on me!

I made spaghetti for dinner. It was so good. And yes, I can cook and well! I hung up almost all of my clothes and organized them by categories. And my goodness, I didn't know I had that many clothes, damn! I have two closets in the master bedroom and both are full! But I promise I will make room for your stuff when that time comes. Just got off the phone with Brooklyn. She said you got three letters from her and answered all of them in one letter. You know that's cheating! We were on the phone for like an hour. I know she's glad to have a break from everyone now that school is in. I remember the summer when the kids spent three weeks in Buffalo. That first week I was like, hell yeah! No kids, freedom! But after about ten days I wanted my babies back! They go back to school in less than ten days. This summer really flew by. Can you believe we've been writing each other for five months almost? I guess this last year will really go faster than I thought, especially when we finally get to talk on the phone.

It rained almost all day yesterday, and I'm so glad it didn't start raining on Saturday until the evening so Justine's party went smoothly. Still no call from their dad, but how about his punk-ass texted me good morning at, like, 6:00 a.m. But you can't remember your daughter's birthday! I ain't responding to that shit. Frank requested me as a friend on Facebook, so I clicked ignore. Then he sent an email on Facebook (you can email someone even if they're not on your friends list) saying he broke his phone and lost my number and can I give it to him, and I did consider the business proposition again and give it some serious thought. So I replied that my communication with him is officially over because my man ain't having it and don't contact me anymore, business or personal! Frank or any other person is not worth the risk of pissing you off or losing you!

Well, it's now 11:00 a.m. and I only just ate. Called the rent office and scheduled my move-out inspection for 4:00 p.m., so that will give me time to finish up and finally be done! Then I can get back to the gym. I managed to get only one day in last week. But with Buffalo and moving and the week before that, well, let's just say slacking time is about to be over. Now that it's a new week, hopefully you will try calling again even though it said disconnected. I will have my phone glued to my hip! I'm going to pause for now so I can get moving with all the stuff to do, and I will be writing you again very soon! Sending you all my love.

Loving you more every day,
Janae

8/17/2010

Good morning my dear Jarelle,

I'm feeling great because I finally finished getting everything out of that apartment and turned the keys in! Still need to do the move-out inspection though because the maintenance guy was behind schedule. And even though they said I don't need to be present, I plan to be. I got screwed at my last apartment, so not this time! So I'll be doing that at noon. I'm trying to get this letter out to you before the mail comes. The mail truck actually comes much earlier at the house, usually around 11:00 or 11:30 a.m. So you know I'm happy about that. I thought I would have mail from you at the new house by now, but I think the damn post office is holding my stuff, trying to verify that I live here. I called the post office where I opened the PO box and it's still pending, and they said they still have not got the verification from the Oakdale office near the new house. Of course this just could not be a simple process! So in the meantime I have to give my credit card companies and everyone else my new address.

I need to go to Aldi this morning to get the necessities—milk, bread, butter, cheese. Oh, some fruit. Then I have to go to the post office anyway to send Brooklyn the clothes for the girls, send your package off, and my card to my mother. Then I have to go to Family Dollar or Walmart to buy a new broom and other cleaning-type stuff for the house. We've been only using the one bathroom because of the torn cushion toilet seats. I had bought a new cushion seat but then decided I like the hard seat because it's more sanitary and easier to keep clean. So I took that back. All my teaching stuff has taken over the living room, so I can't wait to get all that organized. One thing I love is the shower head in my bathroom. It's one of those multi-pulse detachable ones. How about yesterday when I was at the apartment cleaning I told the kids to take showers. They both used my bathroom! I can't wait to get cable and a TV in my room. In the meantime, I hooked up the converter boxes in the kids' rooms so they can get the basic channels.

Wow, it's already 10:00 a.m., so I'm going to pause this letter and pick up after the move-out inspection. Hopefully I won't be complaining and will not have any crazy fees. I took pictures when I moved in, so the only thing I should have to pay for is the light cover in the kids' room that Jordan broke, and possibly the carpet in their room where Neva chewed. I was hot gluing the pieces on, which blended in less than okay. I thought it would look more natural, but oh well. I'm keeping my fingers crossed, LOL!

Later on . . .

Well, the inspection went well. Funny thing is they didn't mark down for the carpet like I thought or the light. I was marked for the blinds to the patio door because there were many bends in it, and the carpet in the living room had a bump in it from moving furniture. He said each would be like $20, so I signed and was out! Then I went to the post office to mail the stuff off (your package will be tomorrow, hopefully), and I asked the guy about my PO box. He was surprised I didn't have it yet. He told me to hold on, and came back with keys to my box! The last clerk, I guess, had me in the "suspicious" pile or something, but this was a middle-aged black man and he was nice about the whole thing. When I called this morning the lady was kind of rude on the phone. One thing you will see when you come down here, they are ass backward in the South! Efficiency and common sense are very low!

So I went to the store and got two hard toilet seats. Can I tell you how much I hate toilets or the idea of being on the floor with my face so close to unscrew those damn cushion seats? But I like them so much better, and those cushion seats were small. Me and my big booty weren't working at all. Even the kids said they were small.

When I left this morning the mail had already came and nothing from you, and still no phone call either. You just don't realize how much I'm missing you! The last reply I've got from you was probably that very short one-page letter I sent just before I left. That typed letter was very long and had the new address, so I really hope I have mail tomorrow.

And I didn't make it to the gym today, but tomorrow most definitely. And I bet you'll finally call when I'm at the gym sweating it up!

I still can't believe school is a week from tomorrow. I think I have to take Justine to the doctor tomorrow. She's broken out in some type of rash. Yesterday I noticed she had bumps on her cheeks that almost look like small pimples, but they didn't itch her and no fever. So I washed her face and figured let's see how it looks today And this morning the white head part of the bumps are gone, so they look like mosquito bites, but still not itching. So if there is no change in the morning, I'll call Dr. Breach. If it were just a few I'd let it go, but there are several on each cheek.

I mailed the application for another position at Stonewall. I wish they took faxes or emails. Then I called the principal, Peter Brown, and ended up getting his doggone voice mail. I want to talk to him, so I'll give him till midafternoon to call me before I call again.

Baby, I am so sleepy! I started going through all my crates, boxes, and containers from my classroom. It was very unorganized, so I'm grouping them by subject. Okay, I feel my handwriting getting very sloppy as I'm dozing, so I will finish this in the morning. I love you, Jarelle! Goodnight, baby!

Good morning again! I slept pretty well last night, and I hope you did also. I think you should have received the letters I've mailed to you by today, so you should be aware of the phone situation and be able to call me tonight. All I can do is try to patiently wait even though I've been bugging out since Saturday when I realized the phone was off. I called Shelby yesterday and she said, "Guess who got back together," which shocked the hell out of me! Her oldest son's father, Victor, who last I had heard move to Louisiana years ago. I had mixed feelings about it since they were only around fourteen when they met but now we're all in our thirties . . . sooo we'll see!

I'm so glad I have a man who has a plan despite the obstacles he will face! Since you can cut here, are you able to get a license to do hair while you're in there? Or what about the tattoo thing, do you need a license for that? Even though I cook really well, I can't wait to be able to share that duty with you. I'm still looking at these closets wondering where your stuff will fit, LOL! We will need a dresser or something because I don't have one. With so many shelves in the closet, I have a spot for everything. This house is perfect for now but we will need a four-bedroom house after a while.

Well, it's already 10:30, so I need to get this in the mail before the mailman comes. Can't wait to see if I have mail from you. It's been a whole week! But if I get a call tonight it will be worth the wait! In the meantime, be blessed, stay focused, and know that my love for you is real!

Love ya!
Janae

8/20/2010

Where are you Jarelle???

Okay, I am officially bugging the hell out! And I don't know where to point the finger at, even though I'm sure it's the damn post office. The last letter I received from you is dated August 7, and it's been nine days since I got mail from you. I don't know if the post office sent the mail back to you undeliverable, and that would mean you're thinking I gave you the wrong address. Or did you write the address wrong? I still can check my mailbox in Matthews, so I know you haven't sent any there. Or did that incident with texting Frank chase you off to the point where you just decided you'd rather not be bothered with me? Or did you get angry and do something stupid and get put in the hole? Or did you get hurt by someone and are unable to write me? Or did my past five letters not get to you somehow so you're not even aware of the worry going through my mind?

I was at least expecting a phone call by now because I got that mess straightened out with Vonage, so my phone number does work! Again, the number is 704-563-4566. And I finally got the PO box. Doggone idiots were just holding my application for no good reason. Even though I prefer to get mail at the house and if I have to go through all this hassle, then send it to my PO box. The address is PO box 690 743 Mint Hill, NC, 28227-0743.

Nothing else has really been on my mind the past nine days that I haven't already addressed in one of the five letters already sent to you, so if you get this and don't have the five previous, then we have a problem. I already know money is not the issue, so all I hope is that the idiots at the post office sent my mail back in error and that you can get it right back out to me.

In the meantime, I've been applying for more jobs as usual, and I'm about to take a shower and then make some follow-up calls for these applications. Then maybe hang up some more pictures and finally put the canopy up on my bed. Anything to make my mind stop assuming the worst.

So, Jarelle, hopefully this will be the last "stressed out" letter you get from me, and I hope my stress doesn't cause you to feel the same way. I'll be praying for you, for me, for us!

Love always,
Janae James

8/21/2010

Hey Ms. Lady,

It's been a while since I wrote you a letter and didn't get a response, so I'm back at it again. But one thing I must know, why you put me on punishment so fast? Meaning, I talk to you finally on the phone Friday and Saturday, and you tell me to call you back so you can finish the other little girl's hair. And when I call back I get voice mail all night. Then I get up

Saturday afternoon and call you and get voice mail again. What's up with that? You spoil me then take away the spoils?

Regardless, it was a blessing to hear your voice. I got kind of tongue-tied at first. I don't think you caught it, but I recovered. It was a lot of things I wanted to say, but I felt the time wasn't right 'cuz people were around and in your face! I wanted to ask you a question: why me? What is it that makes me feel worthy of you? Why are you so interested in me? Is it need, want, both, or none of the above? Just some questions I was thinking about that I didn't get a chance to ask you.

Once again, I hope your mother feels better. Oh, did you ever find out what was the cause of her falling out? Well, you already know this going to be a short kite to see what's up with this mail shortage. One last question, you was very short on encountering your ex! You mean to tell me he texted all these messages, even one of his jump off, and even asked to see your tatas, an you mean to tell me he didn't try nothing or even discuss trying something when you went to Buffalo? That's unbelievable. Are we that locked in or is it you don't care to repeat things discussed between you and him? Because the way you describe your encounter with him and getting all the kids was like too plain, but I guess it is what it is!

I tell you one thing, I'm blessed to have you as mine. And I will cherish you when no one will not. Thats not my obligation but my duty. Well, love, I'm going to cut this short so it may start its journey down south!

Love ya,
Jarelle Edwards

P.S: I hope I don't get voice mail no more. That's a tease!

8/22/2010

Dearest Jarelle,

What can I say? Hearing your voice for the first time has literally had me on cloud nine all weekend. I have anxiously been waiting for two weeks and I was totally bugging out, wondering why I wasn't getting letters and then finding out the phone was disconnected. But, damn, it was worth the wait! Your voice is so velvety and deep and sexy all at once. Now I feel like I can't get enough! I already know you won't be calling until Monday evening, and I'm wide awake in anticipation. It's been this way all weekend. Now to figure out where the hell are our missing letters! Do you have someone that's straight up hating on you right now in the mail room? Because the letter from Buffalo was the first missing one from me and you should have got it before I officially applied for the PO box. I'm not going to get into too much with this letter just in case our mail situation is not resolved yet. I can't wait to send you your package and some more pictures.

As bad as I was wanting you to call, I was praying that you would not call on Thursday! After our conversation about my Sunday school lesson, I feel like I have to come clean about why. I'm hoping when you call tomorrow that I have the courage to tell you because I didn't do anything wrong. And in the end what I had to prove to myself was that I'm really over Que and committed to you and I did! My main thing was I didn't want to tell the kids to keep it a secret. That Que came and visited overnight and have you find out because one of them slipped. And the foundation that our relationship stands on is being open and honest. I was really scared that I wasn't going to be strong enough to resist temptation of the flesh, and I definitely didn't want the situation to turn into a straight-up struggling match with me either caving in to avoid a potentially violent situation or me getting loud and crazy, which would have scared the kids awake and seeing Mommy being attacked. So I just stayed calm and firm, and said it ain't happening no more. And he finally got the point. And my other thing was I didn't want him thinking he was being turned down just because I have a new man. I wanted him to know that I'm saying no because it's <u>over</u> for good because I said so and I know he's no good for me. Jarelle, you just don't know how empowering it was to stand my ground, and that incident confirmed for me how much I'm loving you!

But after I realized that the last letter you received from me was that short one-page letter saying I was going to Buffalo and you literally didn't hear from me again, all I imagined was you finally calling me on Thursday and hearing Que in the background. You would have been beyond pissed, and probably would have dismissed any explanation I tried to give. And Brooklyn said you would probably think I was playing games, so I decided I just wasn't going to tell you that he unexpectedly popped up. But that would be dishonest if I made the kids lie, and the bottom line is that they got to spend an unexpected day with their father.

I was glad I had a leaders' meeting with Girl Scouts so that it could truly be all about them spending time together. And the fact that he left at 7:00 a.m. and then you called me the same day, that was God! If you had called one day earlier I could have lost you! I'm so glad you decided to try calling me one more time. I just love hearing your voice! I'm already looking forward to tomorrow night.

Good morning! Guess I was more tired than I thought because I fell asleep almost instantly. I'm going to wake up the kiddos because we have a busy morning. I want to go to Hickory Grove School to talk to the principal about this pre-K parent school advocate position. I applied and sent her my résumé, and I'm just going to show up this morning and hope to speak to her. Then Jordan's open house is this morning at 10:00 a.m., then braiding Nia's and Nyree's hair at 11:30, so I have to get straight home for that. I'm going to pause this letter here so I can get busy, and hopefully this would be in your hands on Wednesday or Thursday. In the meantime, I will be anxiously awaiting your call tonight!

Love you, baby,
Janae

8/22/2010

Girlfriend,

    Just got off the phone with you and I'm kind of depressed 'cuz it's never enough time to really express myself the way I like. So this is where our letters will come into play big time. I love how our conversations flow so fluently. Getting back to the conversation, I do not want you to lie to your mother about where I am, due to the fact that you only get one time to make a first impression. And although I want your parents' blessing on our relationship, it's not a necessity because we are the sole players in this thing called love to falling in love. So other people's opinion won't make us or break us, especially if our bond is strong, which it seems to be so far. I'm extra excited that your friends know about me and you discuss me with them. I discuss you with my grandfather and the other guy in here. My boy in here was clowning me that night I got off the phone after talking to your voice mail. He said she has her other man over, and I popped him upside his head playfully. But otherwise I'm kind of selfish when it comes to you, so I really don't discuss you with these cats in here 'cuz my temper wouldn't allow me to!

    You mentioned something about having an open house, what is that? Are you talkin' about the kids' school or something else? As soon as this mail starts flowing again I will take another picture and send one. I have to send to one to Brooklyn 'cuz she's been asking for the longest, and when she asks for things I do my damndest to accommodate her wish.

    Well, baby girl. I'm going to end this little kite for now so I may get this out in the mail and see what happens. But know that you're in my every thought, and I pray your day is consumed with thoughts of us and what's to come!

Love you,
Jarelle

8/23/2010

Good evening Mr. Edwards,

    This is literally my last sheet of notebook paper! I'm going to have to rob Jordan's school supply stash, LOL. Again, it was so great hearing your voice. And finally you got your letters, so I'm hoping mine will be at the old mailbox. They move tenants pretty quick, so I have to check, like, tomorrow to see if I have a nice thick stack of letters! The radio is playing Michael Jackson's "The Lady in My Life." I love, love, love that song! I'm so glad you are in my life. Just the fact that you are so positive and strong and determined is so damn sexy and admirable. Jordan likes you a lot, and I know Justine will too. Our conversation about Quincy's pop-up visit went better than I thought it would. I really thought your initial reaction would be kind of like going off. But I want to know what was up with that chuckling laugh? Was that your way of hiding the fact that you were really pissed? I won't dwell on it since it's the past now, but I still want to know.

    I have not heard from Kimberly and I'm supposed to be braiding her daughter Mahogany's hair first thing in the morning. It's already 11:30 p.m. and I told her to come early, like 8:00 or 9:00 a.m. I plan to get this letter in the mail tomorrow, and if there are no issues with mail at my house, then of course I want you writing me at home instead of the post office. Now I'm thinking the jail must have been holding up outgoing mail. Oh damn! I just remembered, the letter you'll get before this one had a torn envelope and I sure meant to tape it first. But I told Jordan to grab the mail off the couch and put it in the mailbox. So when you see the torn envelope, that was me! Even though I'm sure the CO read a decent amount of mail. Well, my dear, I'm getting sleepy as heck, so I'll continue this in the morning. Love you.

    Good morning, my dear, I'm wide awake at 7:00 a.m., but watch, tomorrow I'll be struggling to wake up. First day of school tomorrow and I know the kids will be excited. Plus my interview after I drop them off. I feel so encouraged after talking to you last night, like that job is already mine. I really hope my start date is after Labor Day so that I can go see Brooklyn and we can take a bunch of pictures.

I just went in Jordan's room to get some more paper. He was wide awake, and they both will probably be very wide-eyed in the morning. I wish their buses came at the same time in the morning. Jordan's comes at 8:00, and Justine's at 8:33, but once I enroll them in ASEP at least they will be getting dropped off together in the morning. I'm hoping the hours for this job are over by 3:00 p.m. because Stonewall Jackson is in Concord, which will be a forty-minute drive from there to the bus stop. The afternoon bus is only ten to fifteen minutes' drop-off difference, but ASEP in the afternoons will cost $60 per week each, and before that school is $50 for both. That's why I hope I get off early enough to pick them up because $170 per week will be insane. But I really believe the hours will be like school-day hours and I will be able to pick them up.

I'm so excited myself because I've been out of work for fourteen months now and just ready to be grown again. One thing I've always wanted to be able to do is go to the hair salon every two weeks, but I learned to do my own hair more out of necessity. And I'm good (nah, great!), but I want to pamper myself more, and maybe a pedicure once in a while. In between writing this letter I was hanging the curtains in the kitchen window finally. Justine straight up was not going in the kitchen at night because she was scared someone would be in the backyard. I don't blame her! LOL. The curtains are a little too long, so I'm going to hang them later.

Okay, why did Diedra call me, like, three times yesterday while I was braiding Nia's hair? So I finally answered and she asked could Isaiah come over today while she did drill. Now that you got my past four to five letters, you remember she asked me, like, two weeks ago but never showed up. When I asked her what happened she said she ended up having to leave much earlier and didn't want to wake me. A text would have been nice, right? But anyway she was supposed to be here at 7:30 and now its 8:52 and again I have not heard from her. And I was on the phone with her last night when you called, so I told her gotta go, bye! That girl is something else. And Nicole is losing her mind, ready for Stacey to get out her house. She's riding back to Buffalo with Rhonda on Friday. Why Rhonda is waiting until Friday to get her daughter is beyond me. School starts tomorrow, so her daughter will miss the first week. And being in high school, I just think that's bad.

Kimberly is supposed to be bringing her daughter this morning to get her hair done. I told her come at 8:00 or 9:00 because Tuesday is reserved for my baby to get her hair done and open house is at 3:00, plus any last-minute school shopping, etcetera. So when she had to cancel for Sunday, I said I could squeeze her in this morning because I got stuff to do. It's now 9:06 and I haven't talked to her since Saturday. I think she's going to get pushed until the weekend. I bet she would say she overslept, but if I'm doing you a favor you should be up and ready. So when Justine gets up, I will be taking her braids out and washing her hair and hooking her up.

Damn, why is she still asleep? She must be growing because she's been sleeping late for a few days now. I usually block out two hours for braiding each girl, so if she comes at 8:00 she could be done by 10:00 or by 11:00, and I would be out doing my errands by noon. Because I'm not going to have her up late tonight braiding. She likes to take lots of breaks in between, and I let her when we don't have anywhere to go. And once open house is done, I'll grab my mail from the old apartment and the PO box, hoping I have lots of letters from my boo! Then I'll have some nice letters to cuddle with after we talk on the phone tonight.

Now, Kimberly is going to have to wait. I already know she will call and say they just woke up, and they will likely have to eat and get washed and dressed. And by then it will be 10:00 or 10:30 before they come, so it's a wrap. I'm about to wake up my Sleeping Beauty so we can be ready to do what we got to do. I still prefer all the shopping areas in Matthews, so if I can get her braids out and hair washed by noon-ish then we can go back to Burlington to take one of Jordan's shirts back and get him a few more things. Walmart for school supplies, and any other place, get to Crown Point right at 3:00 and meet her teacher, then be back home by 4:00 p.m.-ish and do her hair and chill so that we are all rested for the first day of school and interview.

Okay, it's now 9:30, so I'm going to pause for now so I can get this in the mailbox because the mail comes so early here, which is great!

No more waiting until 4:00 p.m. to get mail from you! And I haven't eaten yet either. So throughout my running around today know that you will always be in my thoughts and heart. I'll chat with you soon, Papi. Love you!

Love Janae
xoxoxo

8/23/2010

Hey Sweetness,

    Just getting off the phone with you, and I just got done writing Jordan his letter, so now I'm writing yours. Don't laugh at me, but I think I sent one of those letters to your house but put Mint Field, NC instead of Charlotte. So you will probably get the one I sent to the PO box but not the second one. So when they send it back, I will send it right back out!

    Congratulations on your third interview with the detention center. Remember what I said about your business and get your foot in the door and on that position. Please know I'm rooting and praying for you 'cuz I don't know any more deserving person or qualified on that note! My trust meter is on the last right now. Even though you told me a couple days later, you still get the ultimate cool points for telling me about your ex showing up unexpected, and then then being confident enough to where you shunned his advances, not just for me but for us. And I commend you for being strong and loyal and telling me the truth. For that, I love you even more!

    I want you to open your Bible when you get a chance and turn to the twenty-third Psalm, which I have tattooed on my right chest. Now I want you to read this every time you get discouraged and think you can't let go, and embrace our love. I want you to read it when you think our fairy tale will come to an end once I get out. And nothing is impossible with God on our side. He will provide. I believe that 110 percent 'cuz he hasn't let me down yet! My registering will not affect your progress in fulfilling your career goals, and you will not lose me unless you stop loving me! Never expect for things to not work because they won't if you apply that to your thinking. What you put out to the universe will return the same. I just want you to keep loving me and allow me to love you, and our love will most definitely grow. We have some God-fearing people rooting for us!

And to answer your question, you're not too open with me. I enjoy your openness and any conversation dealing with life, period. And I don't have possessive tendencies, I'm just hungry for a true love. And I'm not questioning your feelings for me, I feel them in the air. I hear the confidence in your voice and in your letters. Trust me, I feel it completely. I'm sorry for hurting your feelings. My intention is to never hurt any part of your existence! You're not an idiot, and you don't talk too much. I enjoy your voice! I never want you to cry tears of pain 'cuz I don't bring pain, I bring joy and satisfaction. And yes, there's a guarantee on that! And yes, my sperm are good swimmers, so you need not worry one bit. It will happen if you want it to!

Glad to hear that you enjoyed yourself and didn't get loose, as you put it. But if you would have, you know who you represent, US. My penis is just fine, thank you. Nothing was snipped and all that other stuff. It has a helmet on the tip and it doesn't shrink back up into skin, so that should answer your question. I don't need you to be a superfreak, freaky is just fine for now until I'm home!

And FUCK MR. WALKER with his punk ass!

Well, my dear, I hate to end this letter But if I don't get some sleep for work this morning I will probably get in a little trouble, something you know I don't need. Please know that your mother is in my prayers as well as you and the kids. I'm really honored that Justine wants to write me. I will do my best to teach her the same things I taught my sister! Well, if no one told you they love you today, I will. I love you yesterday, today, and tomorrow.

Love Always,
Jarelle

PS: Don't forget those pictures when you get a chance!

8/25/2010

Sweetness,

    Glad to finally start getting mail once again. I just received a letter dated August 15, so I'm answering that right now with this one!
    That's pretty interesting that you have a pet rabbit and he likes chewing things, which could become expensive if it chews the wrong things! You'll be using your teaching supplies very shortly, so you might as well put those things out of storage. I'm happy I decided to call you this morning before your interview with the detention center. I felt you needed that 'cuz I didn't like the way you got off the phone yesterday when I told you I had to go. You have to remember that when I'm inside calling you it's going to be a fifteen to twenty-minute call, but when I'm outside we will have until 10:00 p.m. to talk. It will get better once I'm sent to a medium. A lot of other things will open up to us too, so continue to be patient and don't get discouraged.
    That was nice of Nicole to hold a candlelight vigil for the victims that got killed back home. It's quite ironic that I'm

looking at the news right now, and they said the dude that's supposed to have killed them people turned himself into a radio station today 'cuz he didn't want to be on the run. If convicted, he's never going home. That's something I could never be without, freedom! I'm glad to hear that you texted Brooklyn to see what she would say about the Frank situation and about the phone. And she knows me like a book. And I was on some thinking you was playing games, but on the other hand, I knew in my heart that there was more to the situation.

You don't have to worry. I know you're not playing games, so don't get stressed over nothing. But like you say, you have me 100 percent, and I'm not going nowhere! Your next paragraph blew my mind, literally. You feel the need to share every encounter with the opposite sex to keep me interested in you! Wow, that's crazy. 'Cuz you don't need to tell me about that stuff to keep me, you already have me lock and stock and barrel. And I'm interested in you 'cuz you are pure and you need someone in your life that's going to love you for you, and that treats you like you should have been treated a long time ago. And the way to my heart and to keep me interested is to keep being about your business and always keeping your word with me. And stay honest 'cuz once the honesty goes then there is no trust. And with no trust there can't be an us!

And you can't put me in a category with your ex 'cuz it would be unfair to me. 'Cuz he never got the chance to love you like I'm going to love you. My love will be an unconditional. I'm here to make your weakness into strengths. Your insecurities will become your strength. And he don't need to know how desirable you are to me 'cuz there is no other man. The same thing he tried to hold against you happens to be the exact same thing I love, a thick woman, just like my pockets thick! See, he told you, you was beautiful only to get what he wanted, and that was to fuck and keep you stagnated, not uplift you and elevate your spirit. Trust me, I love the power between your legs, but I'd rather have your heart first so I can recreate it and get all that bullshit and impurities that was placed there by a man that pretended to love you.

    I want to ask you something. How can you truly love your children if you don't love and treat the woman that brought those children into existence well? Please answer that question 'cuz I really want to know the answer! And seeing me get angry should not make you confused but make your heart melt 'cuz I'm with you for all the right reasons. And although your intention wasn't to get me upset and jealous (never), you get a rise out of me 'cuz my feelings are pure and real, and I will never let no one put me in game! I don't know what I must do to make you believe that I'm past interested in you. This is the love stage and I haven't even touched you, tasted you, explored you, held you, kissed you. So that should tell you something.

    And you don't have to worry about my looks as far as when I come home 'cuz looks don't last longer than love does. And yes, all eyes will be on us 'cuz you'll be right beside me, glowing like the queen you represent. So I don't shine unless you shine. Don't allow your insecurities to rob you of the love you know you need, want, and crave. And daydream 'cuz you can feel it and you don't want to fall so fast, but you and I know it's too late. Oh, I have lockjaw on your heart and I ain't letting go. You know why I won't get bored with you 'cuz we have too much life to live and we have a job ahead of us, raising two and maybe three children. So how can I get bored with that? And our love will be more than just making love. I want you to reach your full potential career-wise and be the best wife you can be! And no, I don't know the effect I'm having on you, why don't you tell me!

    Okay, so you say you can cook. We will see 'cuz I like to eat a lot! If you have two closets full of clothes, that's crazy. But you have time to create some space for my things. Of course, my things will be few considering I have to start all over from scratch. But that doesn't bother me 'cuz I always had, so there's no reason I can't get again. And once again, I'm not reading too much into your letters. I know it's not something I can just say to relieve your insecurities. I don't care about your weight. There's nothing wrong with you being healthy, you're not obese. I can't change what happened to you in the past but I can help shape your future if you allow me to. But we'll start today by facing the issues at hand and not run from them!

And you tell my sister even though I combined letters into one that's still no reason to be slacking on letters, so you tell her to get out the kitchen and get in the office and handle her business! And she should be happy she has all the kids out of the house. That should give her time to start concentrating on her career path and making some money to put away for them kids! Yes, I can believe that we've been writing each other for five months. And yes, this last year will go faster than you think, and our love for each other will continue to get stronger and stronger. Just don't stop loving me 'cuz now that I have you it doesn't stop there, it just keeps getting better and better!

And since I've been talking on the phone you haven't talked about the gym in a while. I hope you're not slacking! I just worked out hard today and it feels like I've been in a bar fight. I'm so sore. I hope you know how to give massages! Last but not least, make sure you send me the pictures ten at a time. That way they should not give me a hassle. I'm glad you didn't put them in the package 'cuz these crackers would have found a way to send them back!

Well, my love, once again it's getting late. So I will end this for now. Please know that I love you. I love you. I love you. And I pray you have a beautiful day. Tell the kids I said hello and I'm thinking about them also.

Love always,
Jarelle

8/26/2010

Hi Honey,

Yes, I'm including a short note for you this time. I got a letter today at the house but nothing at the old apartment yet! This is irritating the hell out of me. But oh well, what can you do. I'm hoping this is as close to twenty pounds as possible, and sorry if I forgot anything. Since your birthday is ten days from today, you can count this as an early (or on time) birthday present. So happy birthday, Jarelle. And know that I love you!

Love,
Janae

PS: Don't worry, this is only part one of your birthday gift. I'll make sure I send a part two as well.

8/27/2010

Dearest Jarelle,

I can't believe I missed your call yesterday! Of course I wasn't expecting you to call at 5:56 either. I was thinking it would be much later in the evening, like your normal time. When you called I was actually at the gym. I had been seriously slacking with the whole moving thing, going to Buffalo. And the new gym is not near the new house, so I only was going if I had to be on that side of town to save on gas. Now that school is in and I have to be there to drop off and pick up the kids, I plan to get back to business. I did body pump class, and oh my Lord, my muscles are aching, LOL!

Well, so far it looks like the mail may be back on track with the new letters. I got one at the house and the PO box. Luckily they arrived because you had the address wrong. My house is in Charlotte and the PO Box is in Mint Hill, not Mint Field! LOL. Sometimes the phone connection is just so bad like our last conversation on Wednesday. I know you were frustrated. And then I missed yesterday's call with the better sounding phone, so that really ticked me off. But I know I'll be hearing from you today.

I just got Jordan off the bus, so me and Justine are sitting in the car writing you while we wait for her bus. Her letter to you will be very short because one of her friends just came to the bus stop. She is a fifth-grader and very sweet. She kept Justine for me yesterday because the bus was very early. It's supposed to come at 4:14 and came at 3:55! I hadn't got there yet, but Lanice called me to let me know she was with her, then she called her mom and asked could she stay. And they both didn't want her to leave. She may be a good babysitter for Justine when I have to work late.

Now, to answer your two short letters, which mostly were inserted through our phone calls. No, I didn't realize that you were tongue-tied at first. What was going through your mind? How do I sound to you if you had to describe it? I know you think I sound white (like whatever! LOL), but other than that? My mother is better. Bottom line, her blood pressure was extremely low because of some medication that she either was or was not taking, combined with the fact that she never eats and is always stressed about my grandmother. And I know it seems doubtful that Que didn't try to get none of my goodies while I was in Buffalo, but you have to also realize that the opportunity just wasn't there. My mom's house, his house (mom's house) full, and he still fucking with the youngest child's mother. And she came by literally two minutes after we got back from the beach, so he knew if I was really down we would have made an arrangement somewhere, but I wasn't. Plus the fact that I guess he knew he was going to pop up in Charlotte when I didn't know, so he figured he could make up for it then. And, man, he was persistent! But that's a dead issue and he'll never have a peek, touch, or nothing again.

Yes, it's the absolute highlight of my day when I get to talk to you, just like going to the mailbox and having letters from you was and will be once we get our letters flowing again. I hate when that stupid lady's voice comes on and says, "Sixty seconds left!" I never want to hang up either. I just wish that when I missed your calls you could call back later. And please know that if I am able to answer I will 100 percent of the time, but sometimes things happen where I can't. Open house is a two-hour time frame before school officially starts where you meet the teacher, see the classroom, check out the school, sign up for volunteering, etc. At Justine's school it was quick because they were there last year, so I only went to meet her teacher. But Jordan being in a new school, I had to meet his teachers for each subject, so it took longer. I'm actually home now and Justine managed to write two sentences before wanting to stand outside with the other kids. She said she will finish it later. And she really doesn't like writing, so hopefully you will get it before October!

I came home and all of the running around, braiding, last-minute this and that, and adjusting to getting up earlier than normal finally hit me and I fell asleep. That nap felt great. And I can never nap for long because I always feel like it should be something to do. Like I have laundry to do, not having a washer in the house sucks! Still need to put the canopy together on my bed, more cleaning. Now I'm ready to eat some lunch and then I need to clean Neva's hutch.

Oh yeah, how about I got busted getting mail from my old box. Damn maintenance guy saw me and I don't know where he even was, but when I came back he told me he had to change the lock. So I still have not got all of those missing letters. So hopefully the new tenant won't throw them out and at the very least mark them "Return to Sender" so that you can send them back. Or if my mail forwarding finally kicks in, then they will be forwarded to the PO box. But now that the mail issue seems to be resolved, I want you to send my mail to the house. That way I just have to go outside to the mailbox at the end of the driveway instead of the post office.

I sent you some pictures in a separate envelope and have a few that I'm including with this letter. The two with the yellow shirt are from

July 1999, and the red dress was from Nicole's wedding. Your mom designed the bouquet, so I thought you might like that one. Sorry about the scribbles or spilled stuff. I don't know which child to point the finger at, always in my stuff! LOL. So I hope you enjoy, and I will have recent pics coming your way soon! In the meantime, take care, stay blessed, and know how much I love you!

Love you mucho!
Janae

8/29/2010

Hi Baby,

You just don't know how disappointing it was to know that you were calling me this morning and I couldn't accept the call because the phone account has run out of money already! Damn, that went quick. But it was only like $17, and they charge tax on each call. Greedy crooks! So a thirty-minute call with tax is $1.77, and we've been talking a lot! I mailed a money order on, like, Thursday, so I'm guessing it should be added by tomorrow.

Well, I will be interviewing two ladies tomorrow at the library to discuss possibly becoming my troop assistant. One lady was a Girl Scout from Daisy to senior, and earned her gold. And the other is a pre-K teacher with CMS.

I'm so sleepy but not talking to you today has me yearning to hear your voice. I feel like tomorrow I will officially get the call to accept the job at the detention center. I can't wait for them to call!

That doggone child of mine Jordan! When you call again you can talk to him about lying. On Saturday night we went to bed around 10:00 or 10:30 but I wasn't asleep. I heard his door open and close a little bit later. I took a shower, then went to check on them. His door was locked. I've told him repeatedly that ain't no locked doors in my house because you're not grown, but more importantly, if something happens and I need to get to him I can't. So I had to use a skinny stick or something to pop the lock open, but before that I saw that the laptop was not on the couch. When I opened his door he was asleep, so I woke him and asked why was the door locked and where is the laptop. He was half sleep and incoherent, so I decided I'll get him in the morning. On Sunday morning I hear his door open, then a few moments later it closes. About fifteen minutes later I get up. And sure enough, the laptop is on the couch and plugged in. I went in his room and asked why was he on the computer last night, and he straight denied it twice until I told him I knew he got up early and put it back. And the door locking thing, he's been told before but he would always be like, "Oh, I didn't even realize it," or "Justine must have did it," or "My finger must have accidentally pushed in the button when I closed the door." So he is banned from my laptop for at least the next week for lying and the fact that he asked me that evening and I said no because he had been on earlier that day and didn't need to get on no more!

I've been checking the phone account all day and the money is still not showing! It says it takes two business days to post once received, which is some bullshit. That's just to make people use a credit card and pay a $7.95 transaction fee each time they make a deposit, and then the money is applied instantly. When I get my first paycheck I'm going to put a large sum on so that we won't have to worry about that for a while. But at least I should get some longer letters in the mail because of it.

I've missed talking to you so much! Until I officially start my job, I hate to say it, but maybe we need to cut down on the calls to every other or every few days. You should probably have your package on Tuesday. I just tracked it online and it hasn't arrived yet. It will be time for me to pick up the kids in about thirty minutes. Justine is still on her little crutches but her leg is a lot better. She just overdid it yesterday walking around because of that birthday party at Monkey Joe. It's a bounce house type place, with lots of inflatables and slides, so she was taking it easy but at the same time trying to keep up with the other kids.

Rhonda made it back to Charlotte last night and brought me back the pizza logs and my food stamp card. My mom drives me nuts! I told her she could take the rest, which was almost $250. Then later she says her and my dad won't hardly eat that much and she will only use about $150 and send the rest back. I asked, "Are you sure? Because it's for you," and she says yes. So when Rhonda gives me the card I called to see how much is left, and the balance is zero damn dollars! I'm pissed as hell because I asked her was she sure, and since she insisted she wouldn't spend it all, Here I am expecting to go to the store to buy necessities and stuff for their school lunches since I have to wait until the eighth to get stamps again. Now I have to spend cash I don't have. And since I bought some school clothes, supplies, and the clarinet, I really don't have extra. I would have waited on the clothes until next week if I knew I had to buy food because I have to pay the rent this week and I'm using a lot more gas taking them to school. So I've been thrown for a financial loop this week for real, which is why I can't wait to get back to work! And idiot me, I mailed the free reduced lunch application for the kids late because we were moving. I had misplaced it. So hopefully that will kick in soon.

Damn, you just called, and it kills me to not be able to accept your calls! But I mailed a $25 money order last week, so any day now! Well, it's time for me to get the kiddos from the bus stop, so I'll end this for now and hopefully we will pick this up on the phone tomorrow!

Love you!
Janae

9/1/2010

Hi Jarelle,

I was so happy to finally hear your voice even though we only had two days of not talking. Didn't it seem longer? My poor Justine, she is so frustrated that she is not 100 percent recovered yet. The healing seems to be taking longer than I thought, and I think I'm going to follow up with the orthopedic doctor. They said she had a contusion but it never looked bruised, as far as turning black and blue. The swelling is gone for the most part but she still can't fully extend her leg. I'll keep you posted.

Evening . . .

My intention was to finish this letter in the car while waiting for a Justine's bus this morning, but the time went by so quickly. So glad I got to talk to you twice today and twice yesterday! But we are going to have a big problem when that money runs out too fast. I only paid $25 on it, and I feel like we're stuck between a rock and a hard place because now that I've heard your voice I don't want to be without it!

9/3

Why can't I get this letter to you finished? I'm in the car with Justine waiting for her bus, and Jordan just got on his. My hair is half braided, half out, and I'm looking crazy because it's too thick to fit under a hat! LOL. Actually, I only have about a third left to unbraid, so by the time I have to pick them up I will have been done and we will have leftovers for dinner. I have to baby proof the house all this upcoming week since Michael will be staying with us next weekend. He can crawl fast and pull himself to a standing position. Hopefully he won't start walking with me and wait for his mommy and daddy. Justine took her first steps at daycare (at nine months!), so I was sad to miss that because they wrote it on her daily sheet. When I worked in daycare and if a baby took their first step, we didn't tell the parents so that they could experience that moment for themselves.

I'm laughing at the radio this morning, playing a booty-shake mix, this early with Luke, 69 Boyz, etc. Reminds me of back in the day going to the clubs in Canada at nineteen 'cause you could drink. But I was always with broke-ass females that didn't have a car, so I was the designated driver all the time. One trifling chick, Cory, ended up fucking my boyfriend, and of course denied it. But the crazy way I found out it was true was we both ended up with a damn STD! And his cousin was the one who broke into my house back in 1997! I learned a hard lesson about the company you keep!

Justine is finally writing you a letter. She can't write in pen very well and she's not on a flat surface, so please excuse her handwriting. It's actually something she really needs to work on because overall her handwriting is not good, and the main thing is to slow down and take your time. When Jordan was in first grade his handwriting was amazing! Literally perfect, and that was when we first noticed his drawing skills. But he hates to read. Justine loves to read but her handwriting is a mess. Oh well, nobody is perfect, except me! LOL

I told you he took that cake and I think you just thought I was targeting him, but I know my kids as far as the silly things they do. The stolen jewelry though, I would have never thought! That's one of the great things about a two-parent family, so you can balance each other out. Her bus should be here any minute now, so she finished the letter and kept saying she didn't know what to say. So when you write her back, if you can, ask her some questions that will give her something to write about. I sit here listening to the little girls at the bus stop and the stuff they talk about, like what people wear and other gossip! These are second, third, and fourth graders, doggone shame. Okay, the bus is here, so I'll continue this at home.

Man, that ride took forever! Brooklyn called me while I was driving home. She wanted to know what you thought about the picture. And I told her about the cake incident, and she said Nana would have beaten his butt then made him eat the whole cake! Jordan got off way too easy. And then you told me to let him have a can of pop and not pay for it, but you never mentioned any type of consequence for him lying about that cake! After school yesterday, on the way home, he had the nerve to say he can finally get a piece of cake, knowing he had, like, the night before over and over, then admitted it to you last night. I'm just saying, one minute you think I'm always nitpicking with him, then you say I don't whoop him. But then he gets caught in a bald-faced lie and nothing. So I'm saving the last big piece for Justine. But when is the lying going to stop? Because little lies become big lies, then he will steal (which he has already done). So I'm at a loss right now. Enough of this topic. So moving along!

I'm glad it's a three-day weekend because I was so sleepy this morning. On Sunday we will be going to the Curtises house for a barbecue, and Justine should be 90 percent or better by then. And the temperature will only be in the mid-eighties most of the weekend, which is perfect. These high-nineties are killing me. Mainly in the afternoon while waiting for Jordan's bus for almost forty damn minutes.

I ordered cushions for the nook, finally, from the Montgomery Ward catalog because I can finance it and the price was pretty good. I also ordered a breakfast-in-bed tray because I always wanted one, and I know we will be spoiling each other with that!

I'm looking at the clock and I need to get this out today so that you get it on Tuesday, since Monday is the holiday. So again, happy birthday. Glad you enjoyed the pics and package, and the rest of your gift will be in the upcoming weeks.

Love always,
Janae

9/4/2010

What's up love,

    I'm just sitting here on a Saturday morning looking at your pictures and listening to some music, as well as writing you. Also, I called you yesterday and I didn't get to talk to you 'cuz the voice mail came on. Why, I don't know. I guess you were busy, so I came back to the cell and went to sleep for the rest of the night. It's frustrating not being able to talk to you when I want to, but I understand this is what makes us stronger.

    I have been having some rough days like I told you the other day. These crackers are something else. They talk really dirty and they know they are cowards. Only thing they are going to do is gang up on you and stomp you until you can't take it, and then say you assaulted them. These guys are nothing but racist faggots. And what kills me is you get these fucking kiss-ass inmates that suck up to them but don't say nothing when they whipping someone real like me or a handful of other people that feel the same way. Then you got these punk-ass gang bangerz going around cutting people in the face over dumb shit. Half of them are just scared punks that can't stand on their own and need a crowd to act or appear tough. Forgive me, I'm just letting out some steam in order for me not to do something stupid to one of these fools. I hate to see the weak picked on. It's like, what pleasure do you really receive from doing such a thing?

    Well, I didn't write you to talk about this aggravation, I miss you and love you all in the same breath, but I have a question for you. Is it easy or hard for you to tell me you love me so soon? And no, I'm not questioning your love for me, so don't read so deep into this. Another thing, how do you stay focused? Meaning, you're a woman and women have needs that sometimes it's hard to go without. How do you do it? 'Cuz I know you want to be held, kissed, loved in a physical way. How do you resist temptation every day? 'Cuz I know people say all kinds of things to entice you! Just some questions I wanted to ask you and didn't get a chance to. I'm flattered that Justine enjoyed her present and said the things she said. You are extremely welcome 'cuz you can have two fathers. We already know that she has a biological father, now she'll have an actions-speak-louder-than-words father. And I like my position better 'cuz it doesn't promise anything, it just produces with no excuses. And that's very sad to know that all he got her was a card. That's so not cool, but I'm not going to worry about that 'cuz I'll do my part and that will increase as time goes on.

You tell Brooklyn yes, the kids are getting bigger and looking more like me every day. I forgot my little sister is so sensitive when I don't comment on things she says or sends me, and I don't want her to get stressed out over me. Sometimes I don't write back about the kids 'cuz it gives me flashbacks of my daughters 'cuz they were the same size when I left them, and that's not a good memory. I would give anything to rewind time and make some major adjustments to life. I definitely wouldn't be sitting in a cage like some zoo exhibit. But I'm here and I'm learning from my experiences, as well as the consequences brought forth through ignorance about certain situations that occur beyond your control. But through all I've been through, look who I had the honor of meeting, you. I come to not just love but to nurture you back to the original person you were robbed of when being hurt and lied to for so long, and I pray you're here to do the same thing. I also pray that you help me restore some of the joy and trust that was taken from me at a time in my life when I thought I was on my game but actually I was being played to the fifth degree.

That's what happens when you focus on too many things at one time, also doing things that you think go unnoticed by few but seen by many! I'm just retrieving some things that was renting space in my head and heart for a while. And being that I'll be forty tomorrow, now is the time to let it go before it weighs me down for life. Also, you called me an old man. I'm more flexible and carry more energy than anybody you've ever been with, young or old. But like I said on the phone, in due time I'll make you regret calling me old. And I'll bet I'll teach you a thing or two while I'm at it. And I'm not just talking about in the bedroom either, that's minor. I'm talkin' life in general. Trust me, love!

We have a mountain of things to learn together and I'm sure you're going to teach me some things I thought I knew but didn't so we have so much in front of us to achieve together, I just pray I keep you interested enough to do it for life. I want you so much I can taste it! So I hope you continue to feel the same 'cuz here in your voice, your laugh your drive is a turn on like no other, please don't change nothing about you 'cuz it's everything I've wanted and you're right I am older that means I don't have time to find false love 'cuz I have real love right here with you, so allow me to love you the best way I can until I can do it face-to-face!

On that note I am going to leave for now only to return again may your day be blessed and filled with thoughts of love to be had! Tell the kids hello and I send my love.

I love you, woman,
Yours 4 life,
Bryan Edwards

9/3/2010 (finished on 9/7)

Hi Baby,

I can't believe I missed your calls! I was in my room on the laptop, then Justine asked me to help her heat up her food. Seven minutes later, when I came back to the room I saw the light flashing on my phone and saw four missed calls. You had to literally call when I walked out. Of course I was hoping you would call one more time, but I knew you wouldn't call a fifth time. Then I hoped you would call around 9:00, but no call. Oh well. Honestly, we need to cut back on the calls for the sake of money. But it's so hard to do that because I've waited so long to hear your voice! Once I'm working it won't be an issue, but in the meantime we will have to slow down.

9/4

Good evening, Bryan! Yes, I called you your first name. Just got off the phone with you and we'll have to wait all the way till Monday. But we did it four months, so why does it seem like *ugh*? So I look at your picture all the time on my nightstand, and I can't wait to get your picture, and freshly shaven! I'm thinking of what to wear to church tomorrow so I can take a picture with a new hairdo and a sexy outfit to make you smile! I checked on the kids, and Jordan had that book in his hands with a flashlight resting on his shoulder. He asked could I read with him, I said no, not tonight. He has to learn I will read with him any other day but he just wanted me to breeze through it.

9/5

Well, I fell asleep quick last night! Ugh, why do my kids try to annoy me on a regular basis? I swear they like it when I yell and fuss because they keep doing the same dumb stuff. I'll start with last night. I didn't cook, so it was a Chef Boyardee night. Justine only likes Beefaroni and Jordan likes ravioli, SpaghettiOs with meatballs, and Beefaroni. So when I buy a case of twelve I get six Beefaroni and three ravioli and three SpaghettiOs to even it out. There were two cans of Beefaroni and two cans of Spaghetti Os. Jordan never gets Beefaroni but for some reason decided to get it just to spite Justine, so now there are two cans of Spaghetti O's left, which she don't eat. And if they want

Chef Boyardee, it means she has to get something else. Minor issue but totally unnecessary!

Then this morning I get up at 7:30 to prepare for church. Justine was up at 7:45 fully dressed, which was great. Since we don't leave until 8:45, I thought we would make great time. I made the cookie dough for this afternoon's barbecue, and then Jordan woke up. I told them both to take care of business—teeth brushed, bodies lotioned, breakfast eaten, wash faces, make beds (not in that exact order, LOL). Then I figured I could take my shower, get dressed, and have time to eat. Yeah right! Jordan had to be told to lotion, wash his face, but Justine literally did nothing! She brushed her teeth and nothing else. Her waffles were still in the toaster, ashy legs, didn't wash face, neither had their Bibles! It's like if I don't stay on their asses and tell them to do this, this, they just don't do it. So I take my shower and stuff and spend the last fifteen minutes yelling and fussing! Justine was watching TV, so my new rule is the TV does not turn on at all until teeth are brushed, faces washed, bed made, dressed, and breakfast. I asked Jordan what was she doing, and he had no clue. So his rule is to monitor her if I'm not right there. So of course we left fifteen minutes late and I didn't get to eat, so I knew I would be hungry!

After church Jordan wanted to go outside, so I told him he had to get his reading done first and finish cutting the grass from last week when he cut three-quarters and never finished. He gets mad and goes in his room. So when I asked what's the problem, this clown says that every time he wants to do something I start making him do stuff to prevent him from going! Are you freaking serious? So I remind him of the reading that he swore he would do at night instead of getting it over with during the day, then he was too tired to read at night. And the grass, I always tell him to cut it early in the morning or in the evening because it's too hot during the day and afternoon. Plus, if it gets too high, then you have to push extra hard, which is even more tiring. It was only going to be in the low eighties all day compared to the high nineties, that's a huge difference. He said he never finished the grass because he said it's always too hot, yet he plays outside all day long. So I said enough of the excuses, you know what you have to do. And compared to all that I do around the house, I don't expect a lot from y'all. Then he claims that he will be about to do dishes but I'll start doing them, or when he asks do I need help I say no. So I said you can always say, "Mom, I got the rest," and take over doing the dishes. Or just take the garbage out when the can is full, or just pick up the whatever that's on the floor even if you didn't put it there. Just be more proactive. So he shut up then and did his reading and cut the grass.

We went to the Curtises house about 3:30 or 4:00 and just got home. We had a good time with food and just hanging with friends. I like how they just open up their home to so many of us, and seeing all they have is motivation for me. This one lady brought sugar-free homemade chocolate chip cookies and they were so good! My cookies that I made were not my best, but everyone liked them. I tried using clear vanilla extract instead of the regular, and to me it changed the taste. So I won't try that again.

It's getting late and I missed hearing your voice today, my sexy baritone white guy voice! Lol. I don't know, maybe instead of no call at all we can just do a short ten-minute or less call just to say hey, I love you. But then we both probably won't want to hang up. So maybe no call is best, and just every few days. Oh well, I'm going to sleep to dream about my man, continue in the AM!

9/6

Good morning and happy birthday! It must be a bittersweet moment for you. I'm not going to mention the bitter, but the sweet part is that this will be your absolute last birthday in prison, and you have me. And your family, God, and your own strength. You went through all these years of incarceration and you overcame it all. I'm very proud of you, and I can't wait to wrap my arms around you!

This has been an interesting morning so far. Jordan has been a little busy bee cleaning the living room and kitchen totally on his own. Washing the dishes and organizing things! I guess he was listening to me yesterday when I told him to be more proactive! Of course, it didn't last long, and now he's outside. But I let him know how much I appreciated what he did, especially since he wasn't told.

It's now like 1:00 p.m. and I'm so bored! I really want to take them to the movies since it's $0.75 on Mondays and we all want to see *Eclipse*. But the gas it will use up driving to Matthews, and my service engine light has come on, so I don't want to do any unnecessary driving until I know whether it is a minor problem or major problem. So of course I can be organizing all of my Girl Scout paperwork for tomorrow's meeting. I'm going to send a reminder text message today, but one of my Hispanic parents I am going to call her because she never answers emails or texts and I need to make sure she does in the future. Because I'm not wasting time calling anyone. I made a meeting calendar for the whole year and filled in all the Girl Scout events from the leaders' meeting.

I keep thinking about that job at Stonewall Jackson. I feel in my heart that it is the job for me and they will call me, but I hate that I keep letting doubt creep into my head when I know that God has everything all worked out in my life.

Almost 5:00 p.m. I've been watching a lot of TV, did some cleaning, writing this letter in, got online a little. In other words, it's been a lazy, boring day. Mainly because all I wanted to do was go to the movies and can't. So tonight I'm watching either *Twilight* or *New Moon* and pop some popcorn. Then you haven't called yet! Am I like totally addicted to hearing your voice or what? I know it's better when you call in the evening, with more time to talk.

Yay! Finally you called. I literally have had you on my mind all day. How did I get here? Meaning, feeling so strongly for somebody I have yet to see face-to-face and touch, feel, smell, embrace, and make crazy love to. This is definitely going to be a long drought for me, but I've put that out of my mind. Reading your words and hearing your voice are enough to satisfy me for now because I know I will have all of you in the very near future. I wish I could have given you a big hug tonight because I can tell your brother had you heated! The choices grown-ass men make. But like Kimberly always says, common sense is free but the sad thing is how many people just don't get it. I get annoyed because he tells Brooklyn all the time that she needs to move back home, when the reality is that he just don't want the responsibility of helping out your grandparents to fall on him. So if Brooklyn is there, he knows she will take care of business. Wow, it's getting crazy late, so I better catch some z's.

9/7

I bet this is a new record for me as far as how many days I've been writing this letter! LOL. I dropped the kids off and just left Office Depot after printing stuff for tonight's meeting of Girl Scouts. I am starving! I was in there for like an hour. This lady had crazy stuff to print, and I already know that if I waited until later I would be running late. So I'm handling business early and now about to find some food. Can't wait to hear from you tonight. I love you very much!

Love,
Janae

PS: MUAH!

9/8/2010 (finished 9/12)

Hey Bryan Jarelle Edwards,

How are you doing and feeling? I'm okay, but I've been really missing your voice today more than usual, especially since I had two missed calls from you yesterday, but actually that was your fault. I guess you don't remember me saying that my first Girl Scouts meeting was Tuesday evening. We will be meeting the first and third Tuesday of each month, from 6:15 to 7:45. So 6:00 to 8:00 p.m. During those times I won't be able to talk because I'll be setting up, then cleaning up.

Of course I would love to talk to you, but you will have my undivided attention afterward.

It's now 7:16 p.m. on Wednesday, and I thought I would hear from you by now. You should know by now that at any given time when you call, if I can, I will always answer, so I hope you're not sitting with your lip poked out because I didn't answer yesterday, LOL! You better not be. Now I bet you will call when my favorite show comes on, *America's Next Top Model*, it's the season premiere. As much as I like that show my love for you beats that, so when you call I will be so happy. In the meantime, I'll keep writing.

I haven't got a letter from you in forever! The last I got from you was dated 8/25, the day of my interview. I actually called the Department of Juvenile Justice in Raleigh to ask about that position, and they said they have not received the paperwork to fill it yet. Meaning, I'm still in the consideration phase, which is good. They haven't hired anyone yet because it's <u>MY</u> job! So I emailed Mr. Brown today to follow up, and if I don't hear by Friday early afternoon I will call him again.

But how about I only found out last night (because I didn't read all the papers) that the kids don't have school on Thursday or Friday because it's a damn teacher work day! CMS never has scheduled teacher work days in September when school only started two weeks ago and they just had Monday off. Usually the first teacher work days are in October for parent-teacher conference, but whatever. So now we have a four-day weekend. But since Michael is coming on Friday, at least I can get my sleep now because he's teething and Nicole said he has been cranky at night.

It's now after 8:00 p.m., so I got to assume that you are planning to call after 9:00? I think we need to go ahead and make a phone schedule because hoping and waiting for you to call is actually driving me crazy. And I'm sure when you call me and I can't answer it drives you crazy. And I miss the volume of letters we used to exchange before we started calling. And the amount of talking we do is making the cheap calls turn into not so cheap. That's why I can't wait to start my job because then we will talk daily.

Okay, it's 9:30, and I guess you're not calling. And yes, I'm pissed the hell off because the last time I missed your calls you said you almost weren't going to call the next day, probably being a brat! Or maybe the line was just long. Oh well, I guess I won't know until I talk to you again. Nicole just texted me and asked do I want to go to Club Allure, so I asked her is it free because I don't have extra money to be wasting on cover charges. But at the same time, I haven't been out in over a year, which is almost pathetic. I deserve to have a break once in a while, and I guess I'm not getting a call from you tonight. Now I'm just waiting for her reply. Part of me is dying to go out and the other part just wants to go to bed. Oh yeah, my nook cushions came yesterday and they look real good and feel a lot better to sit on. The breakfast-in-bed tray came today and that piece of shit is going back today. It looks like someone else owned it and sent it back and/or there are some tacky details like it was a slightly defective one. I'm mad because it's cute! But I'll just request another. But then I have to pay shipping to send it back. There's not even a packing slip inside the box, which is weird. Oh well, I'm going to pause for now and finish tomorrow. Love you, boo boo!

9/10

I didn't even bother to write yesterday because now I'm really annoyed. I haven't heard from you in days—letters or phone calls! My hope is that everything is okay because I hate the idea that something may be wrong. But my gut is telling me that you got my last letter saying we need to talk less to save money. But before you just up and stop calling, we need to create some type of calling schedule! I wonder if you can sense just how much I'm missing you! Then I'm thinking about the last mail issue when our mail disappeared for two weeks, but at least you got yours. My missing letters, I guess, will never be seen. And I hope that's not about to be a problem. Even the kids are missing their stepdad! Every time the phone rings they are asking, "Is that Jarelle?" And they both are waiting on the mail, just like Mama!

Well, today is Friday and Michael will be hanging with all of us. The kids are really excited, and I'm kind of excited myself. I wonder if I had met you in my twenties and we fell in love and got married how many kids we would have had. I always wanted a big family. I have a cousin pregnant with her second child and she is thirty-eight or thirty-nine, so I guess I can't put an age limit on how old I want to be still having a baby. But I want to have a baby very, very soon! How soon would you want to start when you come home? I don't know how forward I'm being, but being 100 percent honest, I would literally want to be planting that seed the day you get out! Do you realize our birthdays are pretty much nine months apart? So if I got pregnant on your birthday our baby would possibly be born on my birthday! How cool would that be?

Later that evening

What a day! Michael is here. He is such a sweetie and doing quite well for not being with his mommy and daddy. It's like 12:30 a.m. and I've calmed down now. I was so fuckin pissed off! I have had it with Tracey and braiding her girls' heads! Done. Of course, that bright highlight of my day was getting to talk to you, but I couldn't talk to you the way I wanted.

To make a long story short, she texted me on Thursday evening about braiding the girls' hair. I replied today and said Saturday was not possible, but Sunday after church or Friday before 5:00 p.m. because I would have Michael. We agreed on today anyway but she wouldn't get off until 4:00 p.m., then had to get the girls and come shortly after. I texted her at 4:45 saying I was getting Michael and would be home by 5:15, and she said okay. Never mentioned she was running late.

I'll actually be talking to you in the morning, so this will be redundant. But at 6:09 she texted me "on the way." At 7:00 p.m., I texted her, "Never mind, let's reschedule," and she calls and says she's close. So my overly accommodating as says okay. We don't start braiding until almost 7:30. Her younger child is overly tender headed. Then you finally called and I've been waiting to hear your voice <u>all week,</u> so I talked to you but couldn't talk like I wanted to. Maybe I have been having all types of sensual, freaky thoughts involving you, but can't say stuff like that with an audience, LOL! I don't even know if I should say it to you on the phone and have you standing there poking out your pants!

But anyway, when I finally couldn't take the noise of all the kids or them stupid-ass beads, and poor Michael was sleepy and congested. So I told her I would finish the braiding tomorrow because it was a very important call, and this inconsiderate bitch went on to say I should have been braiding faster if I knew I was getting a call when she came late! I was still way too polite when I told her she was the late one. But as she was getting her stuff she said she hated to start and stop stuff and not finish, but right after she said she knew it was her fault. So I grabbed Michael then went to my room just for our time to be up! So I wasn't mad at you. I was really mad at myself for yet again agreeing to do her girls' hair when I told myself I wasn't messing with her no more. Moving on 'cuz I done wasted enough ink on her!

I like that latest picture! You're still looking deep in thought, but slowly looking like you're bringing your sexy back! And you look like you got big strong hands, good for grabbing and squeezing. Hey, sometimes I like it rough! But please be gentle with me those first few times! The first page of that letter definitely pissed me off and saddened me. Please just continue to be strong, and I know you always pray. Them officers and their shitty ways. Just remember we are counting down, and it will soon be a part of your past that you will never have to revisit. So let's get to the questions at hand. Actually, it's 1:30 a.m. and Michael is sleeping good, so I need to at least try to get some sleep in case he decides to wake up mad early. So I'm going to pause here and continue tomorrow. I love you so much!

9/11

Good morning! You have a very backward woman because at 7:30 I was wide awake and Michael is asleep still now at 8:10. But his eyes are somewhat open, which is so creepy, LOL! Justine used to sleep with her eyes partly open, so I would close them. I'm going to have to change his diaper because I know he's soaked and that will surely wake him up. And why are they playing games with our mail again? All together I think you should have three to four letters, one from Jordan and two or three from me, and one of those has a letter from Justine.

I just changed the baby and he lay there for a while just staring at me, and now he's snoring again! Too cute. The kiddos are still sleep too, so I have a quiet moment to just think of my man, and damn, now would have been a perfect time for you to call! But anyway, back to your September 4 letter.

Evening

It's 11:00 p.m. and I'm feeling great! Got to speak to my boo three times today! Got a little tied up earlier, but back to your letter. You asked was it easy for me to say I love you so soon. Honestly, saying I love you is something I rarely did with anyone. Only four boyfriends in my life have I said it to. The first, my senior year boyfriend, and I didn't mean it, just something to say. Then Quincy, then Donald, then you. Que was the worst at communication, so we rarely said it to each other anyway. Donald was long distance over the phone, and we only said it once in a while. I love my kids, so I say it to them probably every day. But outside of that, I was never comfortable saying it. Brooklyn would say it on the phone, and that's how I got into saying it more. But with you it feels very natural to say.

I look back at my past relationships, and with every single one there was a sign or clue or hint that it was not meant to be, yet I ignored the sign and forced it to work until it fell apart. But, Bryan, with you, every indication has been that it will all work out. And it flows so naturally, and I'm at the point where I have to hear from you every day and I have to hear and say I love you! And yes, I have needs and want to be held and kissed and all that physical stuff. But I never had that in a consistent way to where I missed it. It was very sporadic. Having someone spend the night was one thing, but I've never had a live-in boyfriend. So like I said before, I will have a whole lot of firsts with you.

9/12

Sunday afternoon. Actually, it's almost 5:00 p.m. the kids are outside, and Nicole should be here any moment to get Michael. Overall he was a very good baby, but not having a playpen or walker or a crib at night made it harder on me because being a crawler, he can get into absolutely everything. Even right now I have to pee but he's wide awake, so it's not urgent for me to risk leaving him unattended.

We went to Sunday school and the normal teacher wasn't there, so one of the guys filled in. And I'm sure he did his best, but I couldn't honestly tell you what the lesson was about.

I'm just ready to have my house back. Friday was a house full of kids and some damn braiding. Yesterday Jordan had company for a little while and we had Michael, then today. So I want just me and my two. This baby knows he's funny. He pees like crazy, and every time I change him then he shits. I changed him twenty minutes ago, so his mama better hurry up!

Anyway, enough of that. I'm writing this letter way longer than I intended. I finally bought envelopes but used my last stamp the other day, so I'm going out after the baby leaves to buy some more. I've had my cell phone glued to my hip all day so that I don't miss your call. Man, the anticipation of waiting to hear from you is crazy! It's kind of like waiting on the mailman, hoping to have a letter, but times ten. And since we talked last night you already said you were calling today, but damn, I wish I knew when! I keep trying to figure out how did I get <u>here</u>. What I mean is having feelings this strong for you and we haven't physically met. I know I said that already in a recent letter, but it really trips me out. But I already know why because I finally stopped thinking that I had all the answers and could convince a man that I was a good woman, and decided to just be me, stopped trying to force love to happen and just having faith that when it's right I will know it in my spirit.

Ugh, doggone black folks! Nicole called at 3:00 and said she was on her way and leaving Stanfield. Then she called at 3:30 and asked would I mind if she went to the grocery store first or should she come get him.

Michael was just waking up, so I figured I would feed and change him. So I told her to do her thing. Then at 5:30 she said she was in Walmart and did I need anything, so I told her what she could bring. It's now 6:30! Michael fell asleep at 6:00 and I let him because, dang, I'm ready to be baby free! Me and Jordan going to have some crab legs later, I can't wait. I'll get some butter. Justine don't eat them because she is so scared and reluctant to taste anything. So Nicole is buying us more crab legs and some stuff for Justine. I told her to bring some wine too, but she was only trying to spend food stamps. So now she can do my hair because it is now 6:45! At least the baby is sleep. And since she hasn't seen him all weekend she shouldn't mind him keeping her up all night, LOL!

Well, I'm going to fix Justine's food and I have to do her hair for next week. And you'll probably be calling soon, so I want to be done fussing around with the kids so my man can have my undivided attention on the phone. I will make sure I get those pictures to you this week. And I'm calling the administrative office tomorrow to find out what the hell is the problem with the mail. Why, it seems like someone is just hating on our relationship! Too bad they would have to try a hell of a lot harder 'cuz it ain't messing up *nada*! So take care, stay strong, stay blessed, and I love you very much!

Love you!
Janae Edwards (I just love how that looks!)

9/14/2010

Hey love of my life,

Jarelle, you just don't know how much I've been missing you! The last time I talked to you was Saturday evening, and I didn't even realize you called Sunday evening. I went outside to let Nicole and the baby out and had a missed call from an unknown, so of course I didn't think it was you. Then yesterday (Monday) another unknown call but it was you, and I still don't know why they said it was insufficient funds. Yeah, it was crazy low, $1.37, but that was enough for a call! And yes, I definitely have a virus on my computer. I can't get into anything, so I couldn't add funds online. So I tried to do it by phone when you called, but the address on my bank account didn't match the address with the Kinect. So it declined and I was so damn frustrated, so I had to hang up. I wanted to talk to you so bad! But I called them this morning and added money, so we're good for a moment.

I'm taking the kids to see *Eclipse* right after school and my phone will be in my lap on vibrate. So if you call, I'll step out and talk to you. I refuse to miss another call from you. I haven't got any mail from you but I also don't remember if you even said you sent me something. I even called Great Meadow yesterday to see what the problem is with them. Of course they said that they are short staffed in the mail room and had backlogs. And I asked about my five missing letters and she couldn't answer that, and said they don't hold inmate's mail. Whatever, I just want you getting my mail and me hearing your voice.

I'm going to keep this letter short and sweet so that I have time to get these pictures printed and included with this. I'll also send these with delivery confirmation so that no one else is looking at my pictures! We have to take Neva to the vet in the morning because this poop is clumped up under her tail and has been getting worse. It looks disgusting, but the vet said her butt could be raw and bacteria can accumulate, so got to handle that ASAP. Poor bunny! The funny thing is that he sounds black and I literally never heard of a black male vet that specializes in rabbits!

It's almost 3:00 p.m., so I better grab my big purse for the movies. You already know! LOL. I like movie theater popcorn, but hell no, I ain't paying $3 for each drink! Then Jordan has Boy Scouts, which he hasn't been to since June. He was on punishment in June, then we kind of just let it go. But now that my girls are meeting every other week I'm getting him back in as well. I hope you remember that my troop meets twice a month so we can still talk tonight and really on meeting nights after 8:00 p.m.

Well, my love, my heart, my soul, I need to get going so that you get these pictures this week. Can't wait to hear your voice tonight, love you!

Love always,
Janae

9/14/2010 (finished 9/17)

Dear Jarelle,

I am so sad right now. I can't believe you didn't call today. And all that trouble and aggravation to get money put on the phone account. I can't keep track of the schedule anymore, but I'm pretty sure today would have been an inside call. So maybe you thought I had Girl Scouts. Of course I didn't. So, baby, you need to pay closer attention! Or something maybe came up or a long line. Bottom line, another restless night of sleep. What the hell kind of spell did you put on me? On the days when we don't talk on the phone I literally toss and turn all night! We just have to figure out something because I am so in there like *prego*!

We made it to the movies after all. Jordan's bus was only six minutes late! It would normally be twenty-five to thirty minutes late since school started, but two days in a row it was close to on time. The kids loved *Eclipse*. I can't wait to watch the *Twilight Saga* with you. When you get out, the fourth movie will likely still be at the movies. They seem to come out in June every year.

I'm so glad I'm getting Neva to the vet tomorrow. That clump of shit looks so grotesque, especially since her fur is white. Hope it won't cost an arm and a leg. I called Raleigh again about that job because they posted another position on their website for educational development aide 1, and I applied for the same thing but 2. The lady said it is a separate position and the other is still under consideration, so I asked how long does it take. She said it takes a while, so I have to keep waiting and trust in God that he has reserved that position for me!

It's about 11:00 p.m. right now and I'm sleepy and restless, staring at your latest picture. I want to put it in a frame but it's an awkward size picture. And I just love staring at it. So sexy! Yesterday morning I was on the phone with Brooklyn and she had me cracking up about the stuff y'all did to each other growing up! I hope Jordan and Justine and our third (or fourth!) child are close like you two were. Me and my brother were never close like that and I admire you two. I'm going to call it a night, my dear, and pick this up after the vet appointment. Goodnight, my love!

9/15

Hey, sweetie. I'm kind of sad this morning but for a different reason. I just took Neva to the vet and they have to keep her until this afternoon to clean all that caked up poop off her butt. They gave her antibiotics and sedated her so it doesn't hurt. Poor fur ball. It's going to cost about $170 for everything they need to do, and thank God I have a CareCredit account, which is like a credit card.

9/16

Well, you already know what has been going on since yesterday since you called. I miss that rabbit so much. (Unfortunately, the poor bunny died at the vet office. She went into cardiac arrest after they sedated her. I received the call while the kids were at school, and had to break the news to them when I picked them up) Every morning I get Justine up first, then go to the room to wake up Jordan. When I open his door Neva would hear me and scratch at her hutch door, then I would open the latch and say, "Hi, bugga bunny!" This morning I went to the latch to open it and had to stop myself. I'm surprised I never decided to go to school to be a veterinarian because my love for animals is so deep. Even seeing roadkill makes me sad, and hearing about animal abuse cases makes me want to murder somebody.

But enough of the heavy stuff. As always, hearing your voice is so uplifting! Of course I wanted you to call back, but I really didn't want to be so selfish to have you standing, freezing in the rain for thirty more minutes just to hear your voice. I think our new phone schedule will work out. We just have to be patient and most definitely increase the letters in the mail. Once I'm back to work and have much more freedom with money, I'm going to need to hear your voice every day. I keep thinking about our first hug and kiss and how intense it will be feeling! Not going to want to let you go! I hear the frustration in your voice and I want you home so much. I tried to block out of my mind what you must be going through on a day-to-day basis because the thought just is hurtful. All the time I'm praying for you.

9/17

Good morning, love. I fell asleep sorta early last night. Jordan slept with me because he was feeling a little sad. I'm glad it's Friday. I don't know what the last letter you wrote me was, or when, I should say. So I don't know if I should be expecting any mail this morning but I'm going to take a nap this morning even though it's 11:00 a.m. I came home after dropping the kids off and decided to get Neva's hutch out of Jordan's room. As I was clearing a little stuff off the top, the emotion was just overwhelming and I broke down. Damn, I miss that little bunny! But I decided yesterday we were getting those kittens anyway, so I bought a food dish and litter box today and let the lady know yesterday that we were taking the two girls.

The crazy thing is that Kathryn knows about Neva, so I asked her would they reconsider about the no-pet thing and she said no <u>still</u> because her husband put a lot of work in the house. My thing is <u>their dogs</u> were the ones that chewed up the blinds, the bottom corners of the cabinets, dug holes in the carpet. And cats, when they do damage, it's to the furniture (which is mine), not the house. So what is the big deal? Then she said she hopes the kids don't hate them for it. So Nicole said I should sneak the cats in like she sneaked hers living in New York! And considering we will have one or two dogs at some point, I already knew this living situation was temporary. So it's cool. I'm getting the girls because boys spray! Yuck. I know cats aren't your favorite, but I'm sure we will adapt. And I definitely don't like animals that tear it up, so they will be well-trained, especially about not being on the furniture. I can't stand having pet hair on my clothes.

I'm sorry that I didn't get to the post office yesterday, so your pictures will end up in today's mail. So I'm guessing you will have them on Tuesday. Next week will be our first week of scheduled calls, so this would be interesting. But we did go five months without talking, so it's definitely doable. My next focus is where will you be transferred to so that we can plan our first visit. Probably the only visit before your release. But if we can do something during Jordan's birthday it would be sweet because it's a four-day weekend. I'd really like to take an Amtrak train to New York, then maybe rent a car while there. I hate the idea of driving twenty plus hours to New York and back, but I like to come and go when I'm ready and hate depending on people to drive me around. But the cool thing about Buffalo is how easy it is to get around using the metro bus. The buses in Charlotte and other cities, from what I've heard, they are not as convenient. That's why Brooklyn ends up having to take Robert's sister to work and school, since there are no buses there that are accessible.

I'm about to take my nap. I'm pretty sure you are calling tonight but you will be inside, so that will be a short and sweet call. But that means on Saturday I can talk to you a lot more. I love those days of two and three calls. The weather better be good for you so that you don't freeze or get drenched. I have to admit I really miss getting all those letters. Before our Buffalo trip was really the last time I got those nice, meaty letters, so I can't wait until that starts up again! Next week will be a good week for you because you'll have this letter and your pictures, and I'm sure more letters from me. So until then stay strong, stay sexy, stay blessed and focus. I love you and keep loving you more and more every day!

Love always,
Janae

9/16/2010 (finished 9/19)

Dear Love,

"Raindrops Keep Falling on My Head"

    I'm just sitting here trying to get warm and going over in my mind about the conversation we just had before I went into the building. I wanted to call you back so I could relieve the pressure from the gut shot you hit me with when you said that you're frustrated and you usually lie in bed and have sex. I'm frustrated 'cuz I can't fulfill that void in your life. And to hear you say that you have a couple people that are trying to get at you was mind-blowing. When I say I'm secure I mean that, but the first person you mentioned was Frank. You know what I said in my mind, that's why I say him first! We have some time now before I can see you, touch you, and so on. How long before those frustrations turn into temptations? You are human and you have wants and needs that all women deserve. And I don't ever want to be the one that stands in the way of fulfilling your desires. I can take whatever you dish out, but my biggest fear is that you will encounter someone that will pique your interest over mine, being in the lonely state you're in right now. It feels like you're my wife and I'm your husband and I'm on the verge of losing you due to the fact that I'm not doing enough mentally to keep you satisfied for the time being. Right now I'm competing with the outside world due to the fact that you have everything at your disposal to fulfill your womanly desires. The flesh is weak, as we both know, and I trust you more without having been with you more than I trusted the women I had children with. But will that be enough for the time we have left to go? Will my trust in you make you stronger or hinder you?

    Don't worry, I'm not reading too much into our conversation tonight. It's just you hit a sore spot when the frustration sex topic came up 'cuz I instantly pictured you with someone else and I lost my breath for a second. Oh, I don't know if you caught it or not. I wanted so badly to call you back, but I honestly let my pride get in the way. 'Cuz when you said your booty call was good too, I wanted that to be me. I'm a man's man if you understand. I'm not a jealous person, but I'm still human. I've lost so much, Baby girl, that I don't want to lose no more. And I'm willing to go through great lengths to secure what I love and cherish, and you're definitely in that equation. It's so crazy that I don't even want to write no one else or call unless it's you. I've been sold so many dreams that some nights when I'm asleep it feels like I'm awake! And that's literally every night. I haven't had a good night's sleep in a long time. Please promise me you won't stop telling me things 'cuz you think it might upset me or be a burden on me 'cuz that will be selfish on your part in that it won't allow me to know your inner thoughts. And if I can't know those things, how can we grow, stand the test of time 'cuz you were hesitant to tell me the things you told me tonight. That hesitation scares me also 'cuz I thought we was past the pump faking, but I see we still have some work to do. Always remember, baby doll, people can teach you two things: what to do and what not to do. What are you going to teach me?

Now to the children. I know you're doing the best damn job you can considering you're a single parent, and I pray for your diligence and strength. So don't beat yourself up 'cuz things will go your way soon. And I know you're probably tired of waiting, but the Bible says wait on the Lord and be of good courage! When things like locking your keys in the car, the IRS letter, and so on happen, you should turn to God and say thank you 'cuz things could be worse and you have to take the good with the bad and be grateful for both. Also, you have two beautiful, healthy kids that are going to rise due to your guidance and love, and me!

I'm happy to hear you're back doing hair. I just got off the phone with you and you sounded a little disappointed 'cuz the call was so quick. I apologize for that 'cuz I know how much our phone calls mean to you. And I will totally try and stick with the setup of the weekends and Wednesday. Although it will be hard, I still must try. The reason I didn't call you yesterday is I didn't avoid reacting to indirect statements. Cowards speak in sweeping terms, men address issues directly and without an audience. You always have one person out of the crowd that has a chip on their shoulder and wants me to knock it off, but I remain humble 'cuz I'm striving to get home to you. Prison is a place of unsaid rules firmly entrenched like the barb-wire fence that gives it structure. Ever present and menacing. Some rules are revealed only after living and experiencing the mistakes of not knowing them. I have to walk away from a lot of shit due to the fact that what does one say to someone whose continued existence promises not a ray of hope, and yet every day for decades they've managed to find a meaning. That's why every day I change my mind so I don't come home useless.

From beginning to the end of this letter I hope and pray none of my words cloud your comprehension. To me there's no reward in second-guessing and inaction because once the act is committed the only logical course is to follow through. It is what it is and I can never be anything else. Now you're probably wondering what I've been talking about most of the letter. It's just a better look into what I go through every day and try to avoid every morning when I wake up until I go to sleep at night. You know what I learned a while ago was this small passage, "you can't figure out why a snake moves the way it does—the key is to recognize and accept the snake for what it is. Avoid it, but never try to befriend or reform it."

Well, my darling, I hope I didn't bore you with my insight tonight 'cuz that's not my aim. I'm just talkin' about different things that give you a better aspect and not TV or sitcoms. I'm fighting every day for you, for us, for our families. So with that said, may your day and night be blessed and visions of *me be many! Tell the kids I send my love and Janae, I love you like no other, and it's an honor and blessing to do so!*

Love always,
Bryan Jarelle Edwards

9/18/2010

Good morning Baby,

Cannot believe I've been awake since 6:00 a.m.! I think I just was overly excited about your call this morning. I love the weekend days when you can talk outside because that means we can talk longer, and it makes the day just go better. There are times when I have so much I want to say to you, but then I hear your voice and my mind just goes blank from what I had plans to say. And all I can think about is how happy I am to talk to you. The letters will definitely help out with that, and I'm glad I can expect more. The best way to get you to write more is for me to just bombard you with letters so that you have no choice but to write me back. Justine is so anxious to get her first letter from you. I'm sitting here watching *Cujo*, of all movies. I got the mail and there was a card from the vet's office. That was a really nice gesture. I keep wondering how much longer Neva may have lived with that heart defect since she was already five. But I know I can't dwell on it. And since all dogs go to heaven, I'm sure bunnies do too! Damn, could you look scary as hell from them rabies! I'm thinking I may just change the channel, LOL! Yes, I'm a scaredy-cat.

The kids are supposed to be going to a skating party at 3:30 with Logan, one of our neighbors. I may tag along since I don't really have anything to do. I do need to get out to Mount Holly so that Nicole's friend Evelyn's husband can fix the laptop. Waiting for her to get back to me to let me know when he is available. I went ahead and enrolled the kids in the morning ASEP starting Monday. I haven't officially been assigned a job yet at the temp agency but they often call the morning of and want you to be ready or it will be the first to call back gets the better jobs. The good thing is that if I don't get an assignment this coming week, the director of the ASEP is willing to push the fee to the following week, and I'm sure they will have something for me by next week. And the fee for before and after school is $146 for both, which is less than I thought. So even if I'm forced to pay that amount, at least I don't have to worry about trying to get the kids home or finding someone who can keep them. Plus, that will be temporary until I start at Stonewall Jackson and that salary will cover the fee easily. Damn, *Cujo* is off the chain! I vaguely remember watching this when I was young and I thought that was scary, but stuck in the car with your child that can't breathe and no cell phones back then, well. That dog looks scary as hell, whoever trained him. You sure you want a Mastiff? I'm cool with any size dog, but like I said before, you will be cleaning up the shit and walking the small horse, LOL!

I think I'm going to look for some Halloween decorations this afternoon. I really am so bored. I went to Lane Bryant to see if they had bras on sale. I haven't bought new bras in way too long. I tried to buy some cheap bras before but they don't hold the girls up, or the back strap rides up my back or the shoulder straps dig, and it's not worth the hassle. So I can only get bras from Avenue or Lane Bryant and they're usually $30 to $35 each. They are always buy one, get one half off, but that's still $45 for two. Back when I worked at HSBC I had a Lane Bryant credit card, so I stayed in that store and always had to match the bras to the panties. My so-called collection of undergarments now—let's just say you won't be seeing any of this crap. It will all be brand new. But before you try to rip my clothes off, remember, those are $30 bras, LOL!

I've been having a lot of sensual dreams lately, but the crazy thing about my sex dreams, the guy involved is usually some unknown guy, but lately the dreams are with you and I can clearly see you. Those are the days I want to take my alarm clock to the damn shooting range! But like I told you, yes, I'm horny. But no, I wouldn't compromise myself or what we've built just for some dick. I am more than willing to wait for yours! When you are transferred and I can visit you, how long do they allow for a visit? Is there a time limit on the hug or number of hugs? Do they limit the type of kissing and/or for how long because I'm going to want a deep and long kiss! Is there a limit to the number of visits, like if I were in town for a four-day weekend could I only come once or could I come a few times? I'm trying to get every bit of you that I can until you come home!

I forgot I still have to get to the music store to get Jordan clarinet reeds, and I will get those keys made <u>today</u>. Seventy-nine dollars for a lockout. Why are life's lessons so expensive! Oh well. The kids are outside and the kittens are taking another nap! These babies sleep so much, and Pooder is so whiny. She wants attention at every moment. But they are adorable, and unlike Neva, they don't mind walking on the hard floors. So I need to get a squirt gun so that the first time their claws hit my furniture they get blasted! It's getting close to the skating party time. I just realized that my Sunday school teacher owns a Liberty Tax Service, so tomorrow I'm going to ask him what would be my best course of action. Our phone schedule is right on time for next week because Monday is Girl Scout recruitment night at Crown Point, Tuesday is our bi-weekly meeting, Thursday is recruitment at Merry Oaks Elementary, and Saturday is the parade that my troop is participating in, so it's a full week. I have to buy my patches for my leader's vest, and I hope the Girl Scouts store is open today because I may get called for work on Monday then we won't have time to get the patches and iron them on. Dang, I wish I would think about stuff earlier because I always seem to remember at the last minute.

Well, my love of my life Jarelle, I guess I can try to put thoughts of you temporarily to the side and handle business, as since you will be calling tonight I'm cheesing all day! So take care for now and I'll be writing you again tomorrow. I love you!

Love,
Janae

9/18/2010 (much later in the day)

Good evening Jarelle,

Aww, I didn't get to talk to you this evening. But you already told me about the line situation and how it can be, so I understand. We both want to talk to each other more than anything, so we already know when it doesn't happen it was out of our control. That's why I'm thankful I got my two calls in this morning. And I love that you can hear in my voice when I really be wanting to keep the call going because the first thirty minutes just wasn't enough!

Today was a completely unaccomplished day. I didn't do a doggone productive thing. Well, I cleaned the bathrooms, washed dishes, played with the babies, and braided Justine's hair. When the kids went to the skating party, I didn't know Jordan had left the lawn mower and hedge cutter out and I don't know where he put the lock for the shed, so I didn't want to leave that stuff out. Just my luck it would be gone. And the Girl Scouts store was open but had closed at 1:00 p.m. He is spending the night at Logan's house, so I asked Justine did she want to sleep with me and she said, "That's okay, maybe I'll come in the middle of the night." My big girl! We tried to watch *Transformers* but the damn DVD is all messed up!I'm replacing it with a Blu-ray when I get a Blu-ray player. That movie was off the chain, loved it! We saw it at the theater when it came out at the 11:00 p.m. show, and usually I'm asleep that late but I was loving that movie. Set me back to my childhood! But *Transformers II* was a little too grown up to me for the kids. Way too sexual, and too much cussing.

I rolled my hair for church, so I'm going to turn off the AC and call it a night. Maybe I'll break out my "toy" and think about you . . . like that, huh? Love you, baby, goodnight!

9/19

It's like you have a radar that tells you to call me every time I'm braiding! I was like, really? LOL. That's why I figured, hey, let this call be all about the kids and Jordan and this damn book! But I blame me for giving him so many excuses and letting him slide. But he got a decent chunk done today but still days behind, so there will be no outside for the next few days. That call tonight was such tease! I know we set the schedule but I'm glad you will call tomorrow since technically we didn't talk. The little girl's hair turned out cute and her mom is nice. I told her my price range is $20 to $35 for cornrows, depending on size, length, and if here is beading added. And she said give her a $25 style, so I said cool. I don't mind when a client is up front, but don't be like Tracey and tell me what you normally pay the last chick! I hooked her up and it was probably more a $30 style, but that's my hook to get her to come back. Plus the little girl's hair was so broken off in the back, I had to give her a few more braids to make it look good. Her daughter is Justine's age, so depending on how close she lives, maybe they can hook up and play together. Because this little girl on our street, Trinity, is a little too young and a little too annoying and sneaky, so I limit their playtime.

I'm wondering will I get called for a temp job in the morning. I have so much Girl Scout stuff to finish, and these broken laptops are slowing me down, so I really need one more day to get everything in order. Monday is only school night recruitment, so I do have a little wiggle room just in case I'm working. I just hope that if I'm working I happen to be on a break when you do call at 3:00-ish. You should get your pictures tomorrow that were sent by priority mail. I hope you enjoy them! I can't wait to dress Justine up in that new dress. It's so damn pretty, and she looks gorgeous in it! It's big enough that hopefully when you get out she can still wear it that far so we all can take pictures. The father-daughter dance is in January and I wish you could be the one to take her. But the dance in January of 2012, you will most definitely take her on. It's getting late and I want to make sure I'm well rested for tomorrow, so I'm going to pause here and pick this up tomorrow. Goodnight, love!

9/20

Good afternoon Jarelle. I hope you are doing well today and every day. This evening I have Girl Scout recruitment and I have to iron on these doggone patches. Fun, right? LOL. I rarely use an iron anyway. My thing is to dry clothes and try to quickly take them out the dryer and fold them or hang them, and not even bother with an iron. I'm cracking up looking at these kittens. Pooder is always trying to jump on White Boots to play, and she has learned to climb up on so much already. They have very different personalities, it's so cute. Luckily I wasn't called for work this morning, so I could get stuff done. And you will be calling at 3:00, so that makes me smile. I'm annoyed because my hole puncher keeps sticking and WD-40 would help, but do kids ever put stuff back where they got it from? And it's always stuff they shouldn't have.

Rhonda emailed me today and said she wants to come over tomorrow to make phone calls, so I get to chill with her for a bit. She's really going through it living with that dude, and I know every woman has their breaking point and I really feel like she's depressed. The hardest lesson to learn as a woman or even as a person in general is that people treat you <u>how you allow them to treat you!</u>

Enough of that. I'm so happy and blessed to have a good man. No, a GREAT man! The fact that I feel and sense how genuine your love for me is from a distance, it's hard to imagine how spectacular it will be in person. And I plan to show you every day how much I love you in return.

Well, it's getting a little late. I better get it together so I will be ready for recruitment night. So I must get going for now. You should be calling, like, in an hour, so I'm all excited already. I love you, Bryan Jarelle Edwards! I'll chat with you soon!

Love always,
Janae

9/21/2010

Hey Baby Doll,

    I pray this letter reaches you and finds you in the best of health and enjoying life as best you can. I'm just sitting here cheesing, looking at your picture and wondering is that all mine 'cuz that back shot of you standing by the door on the way to church has me feeling really, really blessed. I can't wait to make love to you. It should be a curse that the men you've had didn't know what they had or what to do with it. But their loss is my treasure 'cuz I don't lose and I love like I work, very hard! And the day I don't work hard is the day I can't fulfill your every need or wish and elevate your well-being as your better half. I apologize for my timing when calling you. I wish I could call you every waking moment just to hear your voice, your laugh, your rambling, your fears, your desires 'cuz I can never get enough. The fulfillment I get from that can't be measured!

    I wish you would have gone out that night to Club Allure 'cuz you deserve a night out and shake loose and enjoy yourself. Glad to hear your cushions came in. As for the breakfast-in-bed tray, I guess you're not going to really need that anyway until I get home, so don't fret about that. 'Cuz I plan on finger-feeding you anyway. You deserve to be fed until you can't eat no more. I'm following your letter as I write. Please know that when you don't hear from me you're on my mind, my heart, my everything. Even though some days are better than others, your man is focused. And yes, I can sense how much you miss me. You show it just by speaking my name!

    I'm sorry you didn't get those letters. Maybe they were not meant to be read. So I will make up for them somehow, some way. I'm glad to hear the kids miss their stepdad, and it's a blessing that when the phone rings they ask is it me. That's a feeling I've been waiting on fifteen years. You just don't know what that means to me, it's priceless! That's awesome you got to babysit Michael. If you would have met me at twenty with an ass like that, I think we would have a basketball team, with cheerleaders! And I have no problem with planting a seed in you on the first day I'm out. And you're not being too forward 'cuz I want you to tell me what's on your mind and heart. You're always talking about telling me all freaky thoughts in your letters, but when I'm on the phone you never tell me any of those things. At least give your man something to go to bed with on my mind instead of this jail shit. These cats in here gossiping like women if you know what I mean. You have no idea. Sometimes it's nerve-wracking to the point I would love to start punching people in the mouth, word! I'm glad you like the last picture, and I'm always in deep thought. And I'm bringing my sexy back 'cuz it looks good on me! Yes, I have strong hands and a strong back, so my pump power is crazy! Sometimes I like it rough also, but I don't know if the first few times will be gentle. Come on, fifteen years. I will continue to be strong, and yes, I always pray. But I could also use some prayers, awesome!

That's crazy to hear that the only time you really said I love you it wasn't given back to you equally. And that's important to tell your kids you love them every day and throughout the day! I'm glad it's natural to say to me 'cuz it feels appropriate to say to you. I feel I don't say it enough! And yes, every indication is telling me to give you my all, so that's what I'm doing. My heart is yours without even having such yet! And yes, I have to hear from you also every day, and I'm saddened that you haven't been loved consistently the way you deserve it, that you don't miss it, sporadic, I won't be consistent. I will be, please believe me 'cuz I didn't know points for sounding good. Trust and believe I'm that good. Every day will be different and enjoyable, and I take suggestions also 'cuz I want you to show me how you want to be pleased so I can be about my business! And I don't want to spend the night, I want to spend my life with you. And this is not jail talk or a good line! You've opened your heart and family to me. I will treat that like a precious stone that can't be bought anywhere in the world, and I won't allow it to become colorless either. And don't try to figure out how you got here, enjoy it, love it, and embrace it. Pray for it because God allowed it to happen. Nothing goes on in this world without his hand in it, please believe.

You're right, you don't have all the answers and you don't have to convince me about what Janae does. Your inner love will balance your outer love, where you will shine without having to be polished. I'm yours. Just cherish me like you want to be cherished! And as you can see, our love wasn't forced because any time you can walk away if you choose. But remember, you'll be walking away with the heart and soul of Bryan Edwards! On that note, I'm still sitting here looking at your luscious lips, woman, you just don't know! And don't worry about anyone hating on our relationship 'cuz what we create, let no woman or man destroy!

So with that stay strong, stay blessed, and I love you all so very much. Tell the kids I love them also.

Love you, Mrs. Edwards
Bryan Jarelle Edwards
And it don't just look good, it is good!

9/21/2010

Hi Jarelle,

You didn't call yesterday, mister! So of course there could be a few reasons. One, you remembered that our phone schedule is Sat/Sun and Wed. Two, long line. Three, you want me to pop you upside the head! And since you said you would call at 3:00, I was all anxious and ready. In the evening I had to go to recruitment night with Justine, so I left

Jordan home with my cell phone and told him if you call to tell you to call back at 9:00 if possible. That clown was texting some little girl in his class almost the whole time we were gone! He finished all his homework but didn't do any of his reading from that book, and tried to be slick about it! Each time he reads I tell him to give me a summary, so I asked him how much did he read and he said ten pages even though he's thirty pages behind. So I told him to summarize then get back to reading. So trying to be slick, he says he will read now then summarize all of it afterward. I said hell no, you need to summarize what you so-called read while I was gone. So he got the poutiest attitude look on his face, and I said, "Just admit that you didn't read." So he admitted it, yet he had time to send all those damn text messages to some little chick in his class! The book is 223 pages, he left off on 165 when we finished reading together on Sunday evening, and managed to get no reading done last night, and it's due back at the library on Thursday and you told him to be done by Wednesday. So he would not be going outside at all. And tonight, at my Girl Scout meeting, his little ass will be sitting right there reading. Why do I have to constantly deal with him always half-ass doing stuff in laziness?

    I was sitting in the car all that time writing this letter and waiting for the music store to open so I could finally buy Jordan's clarinet reeds. I got there at 9:00, they open at 10:00, and I didn't want to go all the way home. It was $24.95 for a pack of ten reeds! What the hell! And I forgot the cork grease because the price shocked me so much. I made him save that money and it wasn't near enough. At least that's done.

    In the meantime, the guy from Aerotek temps (Buffalo guy) called me for an assignment to start on Monday, $11.50 an hour, 8:30 to 5:30. Oh, and all the way on Billy Graham Parkway. I wanted to take that one so bad, but ASEP ends at 6:00 p.m. and traffic from the airport to Matthews to pick them up would be insane and I would likely be late picking them up every day. Plus, $11.50 an hour would be $460 a week before taxes and I get $454 a week right now in unemployment, then paying $146 a week for ASEP. The numbers just weren't working, so I told him my situation and reluctantly had to pass that one up. But he said he would take care of his fellow Buffalonians, and that particular job only came up because the person who it was for failed the drug test. When you're looking for work, you need to put the weed down until you're hired!

If the hours were better I would have taken it anyway because this tax situation of mine is going to be a mess. Since I haven't worked at all in 2010 and I had taxes taken out of my unemployment at one point for like four or five weeks. But they take 10 percent flat and 5 percent state, so it cut my benefits down by $70 a week or $280 a month, and I had to switch back. Therefore, since I haven't had taxes taken out this year, paying $146 a week for child care is tax deductible and will offset the fact that I haven't paid taxes. I just need to climb out of this damn sinkhole of bills that keep piling on, good grief!

Then drama last night about the kittens. My priority is to find out which neighbor is all up in my damn business to be texting Kathryn that we have kittens. And I'm pissed that Kathryn has someone checking on me. I'm definitely letting her know I'm a grown-ass woman and don't need nobody fuckin' spying on me. So I already see we will not be staying in this house past August 2011, if not sooner. Can she really come after me for breaking a lease that legally she had no right to even do? She would have to pay HUD back $30,000 if she moved before living in the house for three years.

10:30 p.m.

Damn it! LOL, I was trying to so-called take a nap before it would be time to get the kids. So I was going to finish this letter then sleep, and I heard the doorbell. It's Rhonda. I forgot she said she was going to come over. I wanted to say go back home, but I figured oh well, I have all of Wednesday to chill. I'm guessing this will be my last week to chill because I think Aerotek will have work for me next week. The kids have dentist appointments Thursday morning, and Thursday evening is another recruitment night.

I've been thinking a lot about when you're released and the issues that will come up. In my last apartment a guy who was a registered sex offender moved into the development and he ended up being kicked out. And I know many communities make such an issue about sex offenders living near them, so they try to get them evicted or whatever. I'm just wondering how do you plan to approach the situation? Would you want to be completely open with people like neighbors, who may act afraid or angry toward you? Would you want to have something like a homeowner's association meeting to clear the air and get it out the way? Or would you want to be silent about it and let people speculate? Just wondering so that I can be prepared for whatever. I'm so sleepy now, so I'm going to call it a night. Tomorrow is phone call day and you should be outside so we can catch up on the past three days. I can't wait. And I hope I have letters from you coming in. And it better not be no one letter! LOL. Well, *buenas noches* for now, my love.

9/22

Happy Wednesday! It's going to be very happy for me since I know you will be calling, and we survived two days of not talking! But as I was checking my phone this morning I saw that I missed your call last night at 7:30! I was still in my Girl Scouts meeting, and ironically I got like six missed calls between 7:20 and 7:35 as I was speaking to my two new parents. And as I glanced at the phone I saw Patricia, Mint Hill Middle, and some other number, so I was like whatever. But dang, it would have been nice to hear your voice. But I would not have been able to answer it anyway since it was my two new parents.

So I have twelve girls registered so far, five Brownies and seven Daisies. And a diverse group to, Hispanic, White, Black, and one girl that's half Black half Asian. The funny thing is a White single father joined with his two girls, so one is in my Brownie group and the other is a junior in Jane's troop in the room next door to mine.

Now, remember the little girl I said Justine was texting for two hours on Monday? She is the junior in Jane's troop! When she and Justine saw each other I was like, "Oh, you to go to school together?" And they said yeah. And when she said her name was Madison I had to laugh! So now Jordan said he ain't never missing a Boy Scout meeting! The dad, at the end of my meeting, said he felt much better about joining my troop because at his school's recruitment night he was having doubts, I guess. But with his daughter liking a little Black boy, that was so funny to me!

Basically, for last night's meeting I wanted to see how the girls interacted with the two new leaders while I discussed business with the parents. Kids are hilarious because they made way too many bathroom trips and we're a little more rowdy. But one thing I was pissed about is a toilet wasn't flushed and tissue was on the bathroom floor. That happened once last year because I forgot to do a bathroom check when I locked up and the light was left on. I got an email from the pastor of the church where we meet, which was so embarrassing to me. So I ripped those little girls apart and their parents. That's just nasty to not flush. And I've had to tell the girls many times to wash their hands after seeing them use the bathroom. So just because I didn't meet with the girls they want to forget the basics. He'll know!

But other than that, the banners that they made for the parade on Saturday came out really cute. My White assistant called me last night to discuss meeting stuff, and she said it's sort of bothered her how it seems like the little girls segregate themselves at the tables so that the Black girls sit together and the White girls sit together. Or when they have to take a partner to the bathroom they picked the same race. I wanted to laugh because it's a familiarity thing that we do throughout life, but last night they were mixed together pretty well. And when we do group activities I mix them up and they all get along great, and most of them go to Crown Point. She must not have been looking when they were hugging each other and talking. I just told her they can sit wherever when they first come in, but when we break up in groups it's up to us adults to place them with different girls at each meeting so that they work with everyone.

And damn, she is long-winded! You think I talk a lot? LOL. I was like, I got to get up early tomorrow! But overall she seems like she will work out well. And the other assistant seems a little more passive, but I think she was more quietly observing the girls to check out their personalities and get a feel for everyone since she missed the last meeting.

Well, Justine's bus has left, so I'm going to head home so I can get this in the mail to you. I better have my letter from you today! I can't wait to talk to you tonight. I'm, like, so in love with you! Until the next letter, take care, stay strong, be blessed!

Love you,
Janae

9/24/2010 (finished 9/28)

Happy Friday Jarelle,

I hope the past two days have gone well for you considering the circumstances. It's definitely an adjustment not being able to talk to you every day, but at the same time I'm much more at ease. When the phone rings on our "off" days I'm not racing to see if it's you. And if I leave my phone in another room I don't have to worry about missing your call. Once I pay off the AT&T bill then I can get the internet back on and then the house phone, which rings throughout the house. Then I would only have to turn on the call forwarding when I leave out. Can't remember if I told you about that prepaid phone from HSN, but I ordered it and it came in, like, two days, so that will give me peace of mind when I either have to leave the kids at home or when they are at school.

I'm at the dentist with Justine right now. Unfortunately she has a cavity, so that's getting filled today. I was glad it was only one cavity! Jordan's teeth were perfect, so he's in school. The funny thing is that he knew I had to pick her up from school early to get to the dentist, and usually he would have been begging me to get him too. But he didn't even ask! He is really loving middle school, and so far has all A's, which is fantastic.

I called the animal clinic to see about getting the kittens' shots, but damn, it cost $75 a piece! So hopefully I won't have to put that off for long. Them two rascals are so busy! They just play and play, then fall asleep, then do it all over. And they eat and drink a whole lot. That water dish be bone dry in the morning!

I washed my hair this morning but didn't have time to do anything to it before it was time to get . . .

9/25

As you see, I didn't even have time to finish my letter to you during Justine's filling. They were done in like fifteen minutes! Our first conversation today was so nice. Those two days of not talking to you weren't so bad I guess, maybe because I was so busy. If I didn't have anything to do, I would have been miserable. And I was thinking you wouldn't call until the evening, so that was a pleasant surprise to be woken up from my nap and you to be calling.

I hate those heat headaches, and that parade did it! Out of my twelve girls only eight showed up at the parade, which is a good turnout but annoying when the four no-shows don't call me or nothing to say they're not coming. I'm going to send you a pic that I took when the first six girls arrived.

So you think I have a sexy "just woke up" voice, huh? It was very flattering to read the last letter. And I'm cracking up that you love that backside picture of me going to church because at first I wasn't going to even send that one. Being a woman that still struggles with self-esteem issues, all I focused on in that photo was my huge arms. So then I tried to look past that and I knew you'd like an ass shot, so I put my insecurities to the side. I already know you're saying you don't care about my size and all that, just keep in mind I am a <u>work in progress</u>. It will take some time to eventually let all that negativity go. And you are really helping that process along. Keep the positive feedback coming! So I was loving talking to you, but I felt so helpless when you called the second time. I can't even comprehend what your days are like, but to see you get through them every day and know how many years you've had to deal with the bullshit.

9/28

Why is it taking me so long to finish this letter? I was going to finish last night but Jordan was being a brat over nothing. Just one of them days for him, I guess. Then the writing mood kind of left me. It's Tuesday evening and I'm chilling with Justine while Jordan is at his Boy Scout meeting. Nicole and Melvin brought the washer and dryer over today that they are selling me. Now she told me I can have the washer and to just pay her the $75 for the dryer when I get it. That was truly a blessing and will help out so much!

And I guess I just have the Midas touch because something told me to just try to turn on my laptop again. And sure enough, it booted right up. So as soon as I got the internet up I downloaded a free trial of antivirus software and ran the program. It's found nine viruses and one threat! So those are gone and today I was able to get online and apply for more jobs! My little laptop still is not booting up. Ironically, the last time I was able to get on it was when Que popped up that day. He's so corny. He called like two days after Justine hurt her leg and was on crutches, and wanted to know why didn't I tell him she hurt herself. But did he do a follow-up call at any point to see how her leg was doing? No! Then when my bugga bunny died I did text him and he asked how we were, but did he call to console his kids after their first pet died? No! And it was hard on them, as you know. So literally the last time he called was the day he questioned me about not telling him about Justine's leg. I'm so grateful for the father role you are providing for the kids, and I know they are too!

Well, it's almost 8:00 p.m. and Jordan's meeting should be wrapping up, so let me get going. Yay, tomorrow is Wednesday! Phone day! Dang, being broke sucks because I'd talk to you every day if I could. So I'll pass for now and start a new letter tomorrow because I just love you so much! Stay strong, stay blessed, stay sexy!

Love you,
Janae

9/30/2010

Hey Love,

    I'm just writing while I have some downtime at work. I know I said I wasn't going to write you for a couple of days until I take care of this problem, but as we both know, trials and tribulations will always come our way. But we must not allow those distractions to take away from our love or the things we do to keep each other in love. You always write me letters, so I must do my part so you constantly have love in your mailbox instead of bills and junk mail!

    Our conversation last night really touched me. And the way you describe your love for me and the children's love for me is something I've been searching for, for a long time no. Like I told you, I prayed for you back in 1999 to 2000, and you came to me in 2010, ten years later. That's why I truly believe when they say God may not give to you when you want it, but he's right on time. And like I said, I give God the glory for bringing us into each other's lives and aligning me to love you the way you should be loved.

    And the realest part of all is we haven't even touched one another and we're in love. I just pray I can fulfill your every need and be the man/husband/father that I was put on this earth to be. And WHAT WE HAVE CREATED, LET NO MAN OR WOMAN TEAR IT APART.

    Now, to answer your question about how I'm going to handle the situation with addressing the neighborhood about my case. I will sit down with any and everyone and explain the case and assure them that I'm not a threat, nor am I a repeat offender. I simply want to put everyone at ease. I made a mistake by getting myself in a situation that was ugly, but it made me a better person. And I don't expect everyone to have open arms or be understanding, but I can handle that with your help. But to start out, I would want to wait and see if some people will inquire about it, then we will proceed with a discussion! So with that, I hope you are prepared for the situation in which we will proceed! And if you have any more questions about that situation, feel free to ask any questions!

Today is Thursday. I'm about to go outside and see what the fuss is about. Your man is not a coward, and will never be one, but I will approach with caution. But please understand that it's rules and guidelines in prison, but intelligence plays a part on my behalf 'cuz your man is a thinker. So I will think before a reaction. Just like the street watches what goes on around the streets, the inmates are watching how I handle this!

I'll start this letter again once I come from the yard. Hope you prayed for me 'cuz I'm about to say a little prayer. I love you, Baby Doll. You have me so gone. How you did it still has me scratching my head. So until later, kisses to you and hugs galore!

Well, I'm back from the yard and nothing has happened yet. I see the group of people that are saying things, but they haven't made a move yet, so I'm constantly praying and continuing to do what I'm supposed to do: watch my back, my front.

But moving along, I'm glad to see that your troop is coming along. You have to continue to monitor the Black girls and the White ones so they learn how to intermingle and learn different things about each other!

Now about that one father thinking it's cute for his young daughter to be liking Jordan, make sure he's not on no bullshit. Make sure you keep an eye on that situation 'cuz in our world that's not normal for a White father to be okay with that, especially down South!

Getting to Kathryn and having the police come to the house, it's not a good look, for the simple fact that I don't know no bill collector sending the regular police to ask about a debt unpaid. They have collection agencies that do that type of work. I don't know what to tell you, my dear, but something smells real fishy. Either the neighbors are calling the police 'cuz you're living there or Kathryn is not being up front with you about something. And that's not a good situation to be in! But you let me know what you come up with and we will come up with the best course of action to take.

I'm sorry this is somewhat sloppy, but I'm listening to Donell Jones and he has me feeling some type of way right now. Oh, I wish I could hold you and sing to you right now. You talking about what I've done to you, what the hell have you done to me? I had a fucking wet dream last night. I haven't had one of those since I was a teenager. And the crazy part is it felt real, too real! Are you that good that you're entering my dreams now and leaving me smiling all day?

Well, my dear, I know I have a lot of letter writing to do, so I'm going to cut this short so I can ease your worrying 'cuz I know you're probably a wreck right now. I hope you enjoyed your card. It was something I picked up just for the time being to brighten your day. I hope I have accomplished that, sweetheart. I will be writing again tomorrow. Until then, may you continue to be in my dreams and me in yours. Please know that I love you and you're worth the fighting to get to you. Tell the kids I love them and to continue to do good in school. And tell them I want to see report cards also! Until then, stay blessed, stay focused, stay gorgeous, and stay my better half!

Love always,
Your better half
Bryan Edwards

10/1/2010

Jarelle,

This has literally been torture waiting to hear from you. When you called me on Wednesday and hit me with that news, I realized again how important you are in my life and how much I love you. I truly hate that your prison sentence is associated with such a heinous crime that you didn't commit, and I know how inmates are treated because of it. I understand your need to stand up for yourself in that environment and not wanting to go into that protective status. On the other hand though, my only concern is for your well-being, you not getting physically hurt or worse, and you coming home! You have absolutely nothing to prove to any of those inmates, COs, or anybody else up in there. And once you are released, you will never see any of them again. So if you decided to go into the protection program, please know that it will not make you any less of a man! You've been in jail too damn long, and I don't want anything to happen that could potentially give you any more time! You are my future other half and I won't feel complete until my other half is home with me!

Enough of that. I just wish you would call me because I swear I told you to call me that next day. But maybe you didn't hear me, or maybe since you promised me you weren't going outside on Thursday then you couldn't use the phone? I am dying to know how your meeting went with your counselor and what you were referring to when you said that it was possible that your status could change, or something like that. It's Saturday morning now and I'm just praying for the phone to ring since the weekend is our talk time! The phone schedule isn't as bad as I thought, but these past two days I wanted to say forget the schedule, just call. But since I mailed that money order late, it may not be posted for this weekend. And I'm not sure if you will even call, so I'm not going to do it by phone unless you actually call. Waiting sucks! LOL.

I have been thinking more and more about this house and what you said to me about praying to God once and not about the same thing over and over because that shows you don't have faith in Him. So I prayed about the situation, and if it's meant for us to live here in the house, He will work it out. And if it's meant for us to leave this house, then he will make it happen. So I thought of Stacey, who officially has moved to Charlotte as of this past Tuesday. She loved the house, and coming from Buffalo, was not used to these higher rents in Charlotte. So I asked her would she consider taking over the lease here, and she was very happy about that idea. Technically I could just break the lease and bounce, but I would like to leave on amicable terms with Kathryn, so we shall see. Of course Nicole is not happy about me possibly moving back to Matthews. You know Nicole and Stacey have officially fallen out and are not friends anymore, so she thinks we're about to be all buddy-buddy. And hell no! For me it's all about trying to make this house situation work, so that's the bottom line: what's best for me and my family. Another reason I need you home.

Oh, there are so many reasons why I need you in my life! I'm just tired of doing everything alone. Not just the stuff like cooking, cleaning, and disciplining. But bigger decisions like buying or renting. I'm getting a second vehicle, which we will definitely need, and I hope you like the 2011 Honda Odyssey because I have fallen in love with that minivan because it has style like an SUV.

I think I jinxed myself when I said my periods were very light! I just had to rush to the bathroom because they ain't light no more. I guess my body is getting ready for August or September 2011 when you plant your seed! When we buy a house, I want a flower garden and a vegetable garden. And I'd love an inground pool and high fences, or those landscaping-type trees to block out nosey neighbors because I plan on us getting our serious freak on in the pool!

I was just thinking back to my pregnancies with Jordan and Justine. Most of the time doctors prefer to do C-sections on bigger women because of the so-called high risk factor, but I delivered both of them naturally. Of course rockhead Jordan caused me to get seven stitches, which is really low for a first-time delivery. And with Justine, I had no stitches at all! That's because I did my Kegel exercises regularly and massaged the area where women normally tear. The Kegels, to me, are the most important so that the sugar walls can bounce back to regular size. I can't wait to practice my Kegels with you when you come home!

Man, I swear all I think about lately is sex with you! But not only that, I think about what color we will decide to paint the walls, where our first road trip will be to, you teaching me how to bake a cake, and watching you interact with the kids. You are being so much more of a daddy to them than their own father. I gave him the cell phone number so that he can call the kids whenever. So far he has texted to them good morning once and twice "goodnight, love you all." Now Jordan is starting to say you're more his dad, being tired. It will be very interesting to see how he reacts when he sees us together! I'm cracking up thinking about Jordan's female classmates when they see you for the first time. There're going to be some serious crushes! I used to have to peel my male students off of me. They always wanted to hug me, and their heads always were right at my breasts! So teaching higher grades would mean no more V-cut shirts for me.

Okay, it's almost noon and I haven't heard from you yet. Some Saturdays you call bright and early at 8:00 or 9:00, and other times at noon. Then random times in the afternoon or evening. So I don't even know if I should be concerned. I think you are outside today, which has me worried as hell because I know issues don't just blow over. All I can do is wait and pray. I wanted to get this out in today's mail, so I'm going to pause for now so that you have mail on Tuesday. Then I'm going to try to write every day. And you owe me some letters big time! Now that I have a washer and dryer in the house, I have four days of laundry to catch up on before I start the next letter tonight. In the meantime, stay strong. Please make wise choices, and I support you whatever you decide to do. And I love you more and more!

Love always,
Janae
Xoxoxo

10/2/2010

Dear Jarelle,

I am not a happy woman right now. It's almost midnight on Saturday and I didn't get a call from you, so there are a million thoughts going through my mind. The timing sucks big time because I already have so much on my mind already with the house, the kids, the job hunt, my two furry wild babies (so adorable but they are busy like toddlers!). Oh, and I think I was having an asthma attack all day on Friday. I woke up in the morning and my chest was feeling tight, but I was thinking it was heartburn. But the only time I recalled having heartburn was when I was, like, eight months pregnant with Jordan. So I was trying to remember how it felt. All I knew was that it kind of hurt, and bending down made it worse.

So we all got ready and I dropped the kids off to school, then stopped at CVS and bought some Tums. On a scale of one through ten, it relieved the discomfort to like a six or seven, so I figured I would go home and eat something to neutralize the acid, and drink milk. So I felt a tiny bit better for about an hour. I talked on the phone to Brooklyn and the feeling was coming back, so I decided to take a nap. But sitting and lying down made it worse to the point that I couldn't lie on my back, only my stomach. And after eight Tums I didn't think it was heartburn anymore. I slept for almost two hours, and when I got up I felt completely normal—for about five minutes. As I was bending over to pick up stuff, the tightness started to come back. I looked online and tried to diagnose my symptoms, and ruled out the serious threats. And my heartbeat rate at rest was 146 beats per minute. So then it hit me. That's how I was feeling when I had that asthma attack when I turned thirty. But I have no health insurance, so I was going to try to just be easy for the day, pick up the kids, and monitor myself. So here we are late Saturday evening and I feel slight tightness, so my lungs are not 100 percent. And I can always use Jordan's inhaler if needed. And if it gets bad, then I'll just have to suck it up and have a ridiculous medical bill.

My main concern right now is <u>you</u>. I'm not sure if I should be pissed with you if you took your behind out on Thursday. But even if you didn't, I know you will have to go out eventually, and I've been praying for your safety! I would be thrilled if the line was just long and you couldn't call, but I know better. My gut tells me you're in the hole. So that makes me wonder, does that mean you're stuck at Great Meadow even longer? Will you have to remain at a maximum facility? Did you do something that could possibly add time to your sentence? I know you don't want to, but I wish you would just be in the protection program. Because you will never see any of those clowns again, so who gives a fuck what they think? But I won't know anything until you call or write. I'm going to sleep for now and I will continue in the morning. Goodnight, baby!

10/3

Sunday evening and feeling much better for two reasons. The tightness in my chest is finally gone, and even though you didn't call, I got a text from Brooklyn that you called. And so I found out that for whatever reason my Vonage account is all screwed up again so my calls have not been forwarding. Just knowing when you called means that you're not in the hole, thank God. But I'm still dying to know how the conversation went with your counselor. I know you're not supposed to call again until Wednesday, but with this screwed-up phone situation I know you better be calling me tomorrow!

This weekend flew by and dragged along at the same time, which is so weird. I braided three heads today. This time I did Justine's first and for my other coworker from Devonshire, Deborah, I did her daughter's and her niece's hair. I had to run to Home Depot earlier to get clamps for the dryer vent that I bought yesterday. That stupid ass thing had me so aggravated because the clamps that came with the vent just didn't work, and yesterday I tested out the washer and water leaks from one of the hoses and somewhere else that I couldn't determine, which pisses me off as I was cleaning up water off the floor. But when me and Jordan couldn't get the dryer vent on last night, I was frustrated and just said the hell with it and left the wet clothes in the dryer. So this morning we went to Home Depot to buy better clamps, and Jordan put those on. So I washed another load, and this time a lot more water leaked out, all the way through the laundry room to the pantry and into the kitchen. I was like, what the fuck!? Did Nicole realize this old-ass washer was leaking that bad? I mean, yeah, she decided to give it to me and only sell me the dryer, but give me some warning before I ruin this chick's hardwood laminate floors!

It's been such an emotionally draining weekend. I really was worried about you, and I thank God my worst fears were not a reality. I'm calling it a night, and this will be it for this letter because I want to write the next one after I hear your voice. Because I was feeling empty like a gas tank, and I'm hating this feeling but it just makes me know how much I'm loving you! Wow! Don't have me worried like that again! So goodnight, and I'm looking forward to hearing that sexy voice! Love you so much!

Love you!
Janae

10/4/2010

Hi Baby,

I just got a letter! I Just got a letter! (singing in my *Blues Clues* voice). It's been a minute, so that totally brightened my day. Five days have passed since we talked and my last letter was even longer than that, so I'm glad you changed your mind and wrote me anyway. I just mailed two letters this morning, so I want to try to load you up again to the point where all you can do during your downtime is try to catch up on letters to me.

Yes, I was praying for you as I always do. And I'm so grateful that nothing has jumped off so far, and hopefully nothing will. I know you are smart and strong, but you're surrounded by men who have lost hope, lost faith, and some are just assholes with a chip on their shoulder. So when they see you, your presence alone and the light that shines within you (not the light that radiates off that bald head, LOL!), they envy that. So it doesn't matter what you're in there for. Eventually they will find an excuse to attack that. And you're right, how you handle the situation will be viewed by other inmates and respected. And I can't wait to rub my hands all over that bald head and the rest of your body! And when you do get out, I am by your side 100 percent. So if questions come from neighbors, I'm there right with you to answer anything. And people will see how you interact with Jordan and Justine and me, and eventually know that there is no need for concern. Once I decided that I wanted and needed you in our lives, I knew that it would come with issues. But we will get through it all because of our love for each other and our faith in God and love for Him.

Tomorrow is my Girl Scout meeting, so I will be getting Aaliyah from school, and Justine. Since the kids acted up last night about doing homework, we will be going to the library until our meeting. I think you slightly misunderstood about Jordan and the little White girl. I wasn't saying her dad thought it was cute. I just think he didn't have an issue with her talking to Jordan knowing I was his mom. I doubt the dad realized they were calling each other boyfriend and girlfriend. And I told Jordan before I met her in person to calm all that down because he was calling her *sweetie* in the text message and saying I love you and asking does she think they will be married. So I reminded him, "You are eleven, just keep it at a child's level." So in your next letter, do him give him some advice as far as not being so deep so fast, so young.

Still undecided about this house situation but I hate the idea of having to move so soon. And so far the sheriff has not come back, so I'm window shopping for apartments and continuing the job hunt. And I'm praying for God to show me the best option for us. I'm really shocked that they were in debt, considering her mortgage was less than my rent and they had no kids and two incomes, while I was making slightly more than her with two kids, higher rent, etc. And I managed much better. But I realize that if you've never been broke or been taught how to budget then you can blow through a large amount of money and be wondering how the hell that happened? Luckily I'm a pro at making a dollar out of $0.15, LOL!

Wow! A wet dream! I'm flattered, really. So am I that good? I guess you'll find out soon enough because I can't wait to find out how good you are. I don't even think *intense* is a word strong enough to describe what our first encounters will be like. With that thought, I want to take a nap now and dream about you going deeper and deeper, in and out . . . damn, it's getting hot in here! I'm going to finish this letter later, hopefully after you call later on. I need to hear your voice!

11:15pm

Aaahh! That's always how I feel after we talked. I'm needing that hug as much as you, for real. I know I said I wasn't driving to New York, but once you transfer I will be making my way up there some type of way.

On my way to pick up the kids from school I was listening to Melvin's mixed CD, *Pillow Talk*. He got his music thing going with DJ-ing and mixed CDs, and he's pretty good. But *Pillow Talk* got some nice slow jams. And Ginuwine came on, "So Anxious." Love, love, love that song. And damn, that's how I've been feeling for so long! I already know I won't need to fake anything with you, and I promise I won't. I should be asleep but just the thought of you has me more wired than usual. I've a big barbecued chicken, which I love. And I heated it up after we hung up and had, like, two bites and my appetite was gone. I just keep smiling. You ever get the feeling like something is about to happen that's big and a good thing but you don't know what and you're almost scared to speak on it for fear of jinxing yourself? I don't know what it is, but I have this feeling all over me. I'm so happy I have a card coming. And I will have the kids get right on writing you back. I'm glad Justine's picture made you laugh, and they both have been referring to you as their dad. Looks like our phone schedule for this week went right out the door, LOL!

OMG, I have thought of the perfect gift for you for Christmas. But of course it will have to wait until you are transferred. But I know you will love it, and I'm horrible at surprises, so moving on before I ramble on and say it out loud! My interview is at 1:00 p.m. by phone, and the job pays great but it's not full-time hours. It would be awesome if, like, three or four jobs offer me something at once and I can actually choose who I wanted. That's what's up!

I'm getting a little sleepy now, finally, since it's 11:45 p.m. I'm glad your wet dream felt so real because I'm looking forward to making your dream a reality. You are so good to me and the kids, even from a distance. And I thank you and thank God because I was at a point of being ready to settle for the sake of just being with someone. And not only do I not have to settle anymore, I've let go of literally the biggest burden of trying to be with Que and trying to understand how he could not want me. And now I can say with 1,000 percent certainty that I am so, so over him. It's an incredibly liberating feeling. My next step: covering up that tattoo! It just has "Q," so it will be easy to correct, and I can't wait!

Okay, it's really late now and I'm so consumed with you. Wonder what freaky stuff you'll do in my dream tonight . . . ! I love you, Jarelle Edwards, and I want you to continue to be strong, encouraged, and blessed!

Love you, baby,
Janae Edwards

10/6/2010

My future hubby,

How are you this Wednesday afternoon? I'm feeling pretty good today. I swear you have been on my mind constantly to the point of distraction. Luckily I'm not involved in anything that requires a lot of attention to detail or something, but from the time I wake up to the time I go to bed, you consume my thoughts. It's crazy in a good way. I wasn't expecting a call during my troop's meeting, but I'm so glad my phone was out and that you decided to call. Anyway the girls were occupied with their activity, and I'm glad I traced the last girl on the *Banner* paper. That took longer than I thought it would, and my other assistant hasn't called, emailed, nothing! I've been regularly including her in emails and I've called her twice, and so far nothing. I don't want to worry but it's a little late, so I'm going to give it a few more days, I guess.

As far as the troop's first overnight camping, that is on Friday until Saturday at noon. So when you call on Saturday, try to call after 12:00 p.m. so that you have my undivided attention. Originally there were going to be eight girls total but now we are down to five. The Daisy parents are required to stay overnight also, so most of them changed their mind after that or never said yes in the first place. I know the girls who can't go are disappointed, but we'll do another day sometime in the future.

Yesterday Jordan was given an ISS (in school suspension) for today, and he's lucky he wasn't given three days' out of school suspension! Basically what happened was, in the cafeteria, he supposedly poured milk on a boy, then the boy smeared spaghetti on Jordan's shirt, then Justine punched him in the face. Justine so-called said he kept telling the boy to stop and he kept on, so he hit him. But the assistant principal said he never warned him. My issue with it was, damn, Jordan, why didn't you just put food back on him? Mint Hill Middle is not the typical neighborhood school that tolerates hitting. And it wasn't that serious. Plus the boy he hit, Spencer, was in his old Boy Scout troop, and he's little! One of those kids that's way smaller than the average sixth-grader. And they were friends in truth.

My biggest issue was would he have hit him if it was a child that was his size or bigger or a Black? To me it was almost like bullying. Even though there are small kids that can whoop some serious ass, this little White boy ain't no fighter. But am I being contradictory by feeling like it would have been okay if the boy was the same size? Because, really, a punch in the face is way more serious than a food fight, and Jordan supposedly started it by pouring the milk. See, it's issues like this that I need you here to deal with. And it's a damn shame I can't call Que to get advice because I don't even want his two cents.

The assistant principal said he should have (and will in the future) gotten three days OSS for a hit in the face, but he is banned from all school events for the rest of the quarter. And he's way behind in AR points, so after school we're hitting the library to get all the AR books at once so he can take a test a day. Ugh! Always something, right?

It was chilly this morning! Low fifties, but the temp in the house was sixty-eight. So I told the kids to just get dressed faster because the heat ain't getting put on yet! It's going to be in the upper seventies, like, Friday to Sunday, and it's just a morning chill. I'm still undecided about the house because I don't feel like packing and moving, and I just pray for a good-paying job. But I know for real that I won't be here in August 2011 at all!

I love the card, and I keep reading it over and over. You consider me your dream, wow! That's so deep. And it's so amazing to me and feels so genuine and almost foreign because I've had men tell me they love me but never felt the love until I felt it from you. And I've said I love you before and thought that it was love, but when I say it to you and feel it for you, it's so different from anything I've experienced. And the fact that it's a mutual feeling this time is a true blessing! I wanted to stay on the phone so bad with you last night! I just want you home like now. I know I have it in me to wait patiently, but I damn sure don't want to anymore. I want to feel you, smell, taste you because hearing you just makes the yearning for you stronger and stronger! It's going to be incredibly intense! It's a long shot, but is there any way you will possibly get out before August? Don't worry, I'm not going anywhere and won't ever stray. But even a halfway house or house arrest, but something to cut that time down and I'll be driving to New York every month, for real!

Okay, enough of that because I'm getting myself all worked up, hot and bothered, horny and craving for your touch. But not just the sexual, physical part. When I do hug you for the first time, I may have to be pried off. I want to snuggle up against you and feel the warmth of your chest and arms, and feel your heartbeat and hear your breathing and smell your scent and listen to you talk to me about anything. We're going into our seventh month of communicating, and I can't believe the first six months went by as fast as they did, so I know the rest of 2010 will fly by with all the school days off and holidays.

I can't wait to hear the outcome of your meeting with the counselor. I'm kind of sleepy now because I didn't go to sleep right away last night. Then it did get a little cold in the pre-dawn hours. So when the alarm went off I was thinking, you got to be freaking kidding me! I'm going to take a quick nap. And I'm mad that I told you not to call today and to wait for Thursday, but then it's closer to the weekend and we can talk Saturday after the sleepover, and Sunday. I didn't get mail from you today but I'm good because I know it's coming. Well, Mr. Edwards, Mrs. Edwards is about to snooze for a little and then get this in the mail, get the kids, hit the library, cook dinner, fantasize about you! So take care of my body. Stay strong and sexy, and be blessed! I love you, Bryan Edwards! Muah!

Love,
Janae

10/10/2010

Hey Sweetness,

    I know it's been a while since I wrote you, but I'm back 'cuz I know you need the vitamins I give you to nurture your spirit as well as mine. I know times are rough right now, but the most important part about those times is knowing that I love you and God loves you too, and he's not going to give you more than you can bear! I'm going to answer the other letters, but I just want you to know that no matter what your mother thinks or says, or anyone else, no one is going to destroy what we created. Evidently someone is jealous or envious of your happiness. And as long as our bond is strong, there will be no cracks in our armor. Your mother seems like she still wants to control your life as well as your movements. Oh, now she's trying to play matchmaker, which is very funny to me. 'Cuz I have you and I'm not letting you go. You'll be the one that leaves me 'cuz I will never leave you or give up on the things I know we both can accomplish if we stay true to one another. But can you stand the hate and envy that will come our way, not just from family but friends? Please don't get me wrong either 'cuz I'm not doubting you one bit, but I'm not even free yet and I see the bullshit starting already. I'll let you know now also, I won't bite my tongue either when it comes to telling people to respect my business, especially my woman and what you and I do or don't do as toward what we should do. At the end of the day, I answer to you and God. Not your mother, your father, or your friends, and vice versa. So put your hard hat on 'cuz I sleep with my mine and I wear it daily!

    Well, moving along. I'm happy to hear that you're looking at other apartments 'cause, honestly, I don't think the situation you're in is healthy, due to the fact that something doesn't smell right with the deal that was put in place and police coming by, which in my opinion, the neighbors called 'cause they feel you shouldn't be living there for whatever reason. I'll be happy when you get a job, 'cause a lot of things are gonna open up for you once you do. Also, there won't be so many bills coming your way and you'll be able to breathe a little. I wish there was some way I could help you. It sucks being in here. If I was closer and made a few phone calls, things would be a little better. But once again, that life is behind me and I'm going to make sure it stays there!

Did you call Brooklyn or did she call you with the phone numbers and information on who to call? My counselor's name is Ms. Goodman. And the paper with the movement and control people's numbers on it, Brooklyn has. Remember, you're my fiance and would like for me to be moved closer to home due to travel restraints and not having seen me in a very long time. Also, my grandparents are not in good health, which is all the truth. I'm not asking you to lie for me, just convince these devils to move me closer to home so that I may communicate with the people I love a little better. Also, so I may hug, kiss caress, and love you for a couple hours each time you come see me. I just got off the phone with my nephew's mother. She's going to call also, so make sure Brooklyn gets the information to her also 'cuz the more heads we have calling the better!

Now back to this famous picture I'm supposed to be getting. Why haven't I received it yet? Also, you're buying all these panties and bra sets, you have my mouth watering, LOL! I don't know if you told me or not, but do you wear thongs or boy shorts? Reason why I ask is because I've been watching a lot of shows and movies and all of the women are wearing either one or the other. Even full-figured women are wearing them and looking sexy also. Oh yeah, pump your brakes. They are on TV, so fix your face, LOL! I have a question for you also, since when I get out you want to immediately start on a baby, what's the time limit on us getting married? 'Cuz if it was up to me we would be married right now, and that's not just something to make you feel good or just smile. That's the truth. I feel I know you enough to make you my wife. I'm not saying this 'cuz I'm lonely, desperate to be with someone. I really feel you're wife material and you will enhance my life, as well as my abilities to be successful at whatever I touch or pursue. I'm curious to hear how you feel. I know it's still some things I must learn about you and vice versa, but I feel I know enough to want you for life. Now if I'm getting ahead of myself, tell me chill. I'm too old for games, so please believe my sincerity and dedication. 'Cuz I don't love many people, so when I say I love you, please believe it's <u>priceless</u> and it can't be bargained by no one. So now that you have that blessing, what are you going to do with it, Love?

Well, miss, I have to cut this short 'cuz I want to finish writing your other letter. Plus I'm about to go to the commissary, so let me get ready. Know that I love you, woman, and don't ever want to do without you. It's amazing how close we've become through phone calls and letters. I pray that your love for me will grow and stand the test of time 'cuz the devil stays busy but he's a liar! So my pen reaches this paper again. Allow me to be your dream as well as your vision. Tell the kids I send my love, and *chao* for now.

Love always,
"Yours"
Bryan Jarelle Edwards

10/10/2010

Hi Hubby,

It just totally made my morning and my day to be able to talk to you! I was really stressing over the balance on the VAC account because it was something like $2.49 and our thirty-minute calls are $1.77 with tax (their tax rate is crazy!). And one time, even though there was money left, it wouldn't let the call go through. Last night I was trying to add money online but I told you about the address not 100 percent matching. The credit and debit card is such a rip-off, charging $7.95 for adding money. But they take so damn long to post money orders, and it's bad enough it has to be mailed to Texas. But like I said before, as soon as I get some extra money a lump sum is going toward the phone because I prefer not to put a price on talking to my boo. But you know how it is, and I already know it's a temporary thing, so I'm cool.

I've been up since 7:00 a.m., it's now 3:00 p.m. and I never did go back to sleep. My laundry has been piling up like crazy, and I'm not even wasting time with that washer (going to put it on Craigslist if I ever remember to!), so the bathtubs have been the washer all day. The hardest part is wringing them out. And since I can't do it as good as the spin cycle, it takes longer in the dryer. But I love this new Tide with Acti-Lift. I don't even remember the last time I used a name-brand detergent because I have been buying it from Family Dollar or somewhere else where it was cheap. I'm hooked on the Tide!

Justine wrote a letter finally, so I'll put his letter with Justine's and drop those in the mail. He practiced the clarinet for a while and now he's playing with Legos. We went to the mall yesterday to take Shanita (Nicole's daughter) shopping for her birthday outfit, and they have a Lego store! Never knew it existed, but damn, some (most) of the kits are ridiculously overpriced! But it was cool to look at. Shanita just handed down five pairs of jeans for Justine and they fit her so good except for being too long, so I'm having those tonight. Crazy that she just turned sixteen but she's so petite and Justine is so curvy that it works out, so I'm very happy about that. A few more shirts, sweaters, and underwear and she'll be good to go for a while! Jordan's clothes cost more than Justine's, so anything to help is great. He wears a thirty or thirty-two depending on the brand, but I usually get thirty-four and a belt so that he can grow into it, and he likes it baggy. Which is why I have NO understanding for him liking them skinny jeans. But like I said, it will <u>never</u> happen!

Don't be mad but I just texted their biological dad basically to see when the hell I'm going to get some child support. May was the last payment, our court date was June or July. And as much as he was complaining about having to work to pay child support, I'm not reaping the benefit. I want to say fuck him and his money, but hell, money is tight. And knowing all the back-to-school expenses, you would think he'd offer. Yeah right. If he replies while I'm writing you, I will tell you the reply.

Next week I'll be at Justine's school volunteering at the book fair from 12:00 to 3:00, so that will give me something to do. And I'm going to Empire Beauty School. Oh wait. Damn, forgot it's Columbus Day, so most likely the school won't be open. I told Monica if she wants me to take her braids out tomorrow that I'm available because she works for the county and should be off.

I have a feeling Que won't reply until late. I purposely engaged in small talk to make sure he was answering and had the phone, so if he lets a lot of time pass then he's being a prick, which ain't nothing new. But I'm about to become a real bitch and file for full custody of the kids and force him to have to set visitation. The only issue with that is if the custodial parent moves away then they are responsible for the money associated with visitation as far as airfare, gas, etc. But I doubt he will be actively trying to get the kids until you are physically in the picture. Well, his reply was "I'll see what I can do." He just doesn't get it. You are <u>ordered</u> by the court to pay a little funky $20 a week. Let me get off this topic and get to my favorite subject, <u>me and you</u>!

I thought you would have gotten three of the four letters I sent you by Friday, but they are moving slower lately. I'm washing my hair in a little while and doing a braided wet set to see how it will look tomorrow when I take the braids out. If it looks good, then I'll work on those sexy pics for you. And Tuesday I will be calling your counselor if Brooklyn got the letter. She is usually busy on Sundays with hair and bath but I told her the two oldest should be good doing baths alone, but four heads full of hair, that's work! I'm about to wash Justine's now as I get dinner done and will continue shortly . . .

10/11

Hey, love of my life! I'm so sleepy but I wanted to get this letter done so that tomorrow

10/12

Wow, I guess I was really tired! I don't even remember what sentence I was going to write, LOL. It's about 9:30 in the morning and I'm trying to get this in the mail before the mailman comes.

I went to Empire Beauty School yesterday to check out the school, and wow, the tuition is $20,000 with fees. And since I already have a master's degree I'm not eligible for grants, so it all will have to be loans. When I originally wanted to go to hair school when Jordan was, like three, the tuition was close to $8,000, but the admissions lady said all schools have drastically gone up. The field is always in high demand and the program is forty-four weeks full-time or twenty-four months part-time. I can't see going to school from 6:00 to 10:00 Monday to Thursday for two years, and full-time is like 9:00–4:00 Monday–Friday, so I'd have to either work part-time evenings and weekends (teaching online college courses would be awesome) or take out additional loan money, or a combination of both. Decisions, decisions! But if that path is meant for me, I know it will work out. So I'm going to check out some other schools in the meantime.

Empire is the largest chain of beauty schools in the country, so I think they probably have the highest tuition. Robert's sister's tuition there is only $16,000. But Empire is so close to the apartment I want to move to. We'll see how things go, and I want your input also. But in the meantime my furry babies are officially gone. I can't afford to pay any pet deposit here at Kathryn's house or anywhere else. Plus, this house is just too small for any pet right now. I'd prefer to have a house when I finally do have pets. I put an ad on Craigslist and this guy called, so I asked him who are the kittens for and he said him and his girlfriend. I made sure he understood that they are sisters and need to stay together. And after talking to his girlfriend, she sounded so excited and she said she'd had cats all her life. So they came by at 6:30 and they were a middle-aged couple. They picked up the kitties and she was just giving them kisses and hugs, and you could tell she really likes them. So that put me at ease because I wasn't going to just let anyone have them, and make sure they were well taken care of. I really didn't want any pets at this time, and having them did help with the passing of Neva. But the kids were actually okay with letting them go, but you already know that was more because they didn't like cleaning the litter box. So we ain't getting no more pets until you come home and we have a house.

I most likely won't be volunteering at the book fair for the rest of the week. They seem to have enough people. But the other reason is the one chick had an issue with me being behind the table at the cash register. I was sending a message on my phone and she tells me, "You can't be back there, only so and so." And I'm looking at her like, "Don't you see I'm busy?" So I told her when I'm done I'll come out to the front. I was always the fastest at the register at the two book fairs from last year, so why would you put the slow chick on the register? And I totally understand not having everyone have access to the register, but it's the way you talk to people and how you choose your words. So I was like, whatever.

I'll be doing Monica's hair tomorrow and now that Pooder and White Boots are gone I can do her girls' heads again. Dang, I swear I just heard the mail truck, so I better have some mail from my man in there. Guess this one can go to the post office with me later. I'm going to get some breakfast and take care of some household stuff, so I will talk to you probably tomorrow and hopefully be reading a letter shortly! I love you, Jarelle. Have a blessed day. Stay positive, stay strong!

Love you!
Janae

10/11/2010

Baby Doll,

    As you put it, I apologize for the torture I've caused you and keeping you waiting for some letters from your better half. It is never my intention to keep you waiting 'cuz I have so much love to give you and share with you! I also realize how important you are in my life and how much you give me to look forward to. It's life-changing to be able to come home to someone that's willing to grow with you, as well as learn!

    About my prison sentence, I take it as one of life's biggest lessons. And of course, not inmates, but people in general treat people based on what they think they know as toward actual fact! And I'm happy that you understand I will never go into protective custody. It will go against everything I believe in, and I wouldn't be able to look myself in the mirror if I did otherwise! And on the other, and as you put it, I know you are worried about my well-being. And I'm not going to get physically hurt 'cuz I know my limits and my strength. And you're right, I'm coming 'cuz I have something to come home to! You're right, I have nothing to prove to anyone, but I will not decide to go into protective custody. So please don't ask or suggest that I do 'cuz it's not going to happen, not today, not tomorrow, not ever!

    Nothing's going to happen to keep me in jail any longer. And I feel the same way, I need my other half also. You are my future as well. I know what's awaiting me. That's why I move with caution in here, and my street instincts are in overdrive 'cuz I trust no one! The reason why I didn't call you the next day was 'cuz I did go outside. I let my pride push me outside. I just wanted to look in people's eyes. I do that, by the way, a lot 'cuz the eyes are windows to people's souls and also reveal your tendencies. So I basically see who's who. And the cowards wouldn't say anything face-to-face. They wait until they are locked in and say indirect comments.

As of today I still haven't seen my counselor or talked to her, so that gives you more ammo to get on your job and find out what's up with the transfer and getting close to home! As of now my status should be medium eligible. Before I got here I classified maximum security. When I received a letter from the counselor, she said that Albany automatically reclassified me after six months. I'm working on my seventh month right now. So if you hear something before I do, let me know, and I will also let you know, babe! I think our phone schedule is working out very good, although I won't say I won't cheat and call you on the days in between. But I won't interfere with your Girl Scouts. And pretty soon you'll be working, so I have to get all I can for the time being! Even though I know it wasn't on, I even tried to call you tonight just to hear your voice, but of course it didn't go through!

I'm glad you've been thinking more about the house and praying to God once and believing in that prayer and letting it be 'cuz without faith you're nothing. And how you come back from adversity shows the true character of a man or woman. So you must keep striving and God will guide your steps on what to do concerning that house. Whether you stay or leave, I'm behind you 100 percent. As far as putting Stacey in the house, it's up to you, but you have to live with that decision. So your next move, make it your best move! If you decide to break the lease, make sure you have all bases covered so nothing will affect you in the long run! About people being happy if you move back to Matthews, you have to do what's best for our family, fuck what everybody else thinks. Feelings come and go. And yes, that's another reason you need me home 'cuz a lot of decisions we'll make together and then some I'll make for us with your naive ass! LOL!

And you say there are so many reasons why you need me in your life, you care to tell me some more? 'Cuz I would love to hear them all. So why haven't you asked me any more questions pertaining to me or us? And I know you're tired of doing things by yourself, but maybe you can run some of those decisions by me so I may give you some insight on what you could do. And I love the Honda Odyssey. I see now I'm really going to have to do some serious hustling. You just make sure you keep my oven warm to put this bread in!

Wow your period is getting heavy again? What, you making sure it's purified so when I do plant my seed it will have a safe passage too? 'Cuz it's going to find its way home no matter what. You make sure that thing is tight and warm. And I hope you're doing your vaginal exercise 'cuz I plan on hitting it at very different angles. Also, I pray your legs are flexible 'cuz I plan on bending those things back so home plate is exposed at a degree where entry at any position will be pleasurable!

Yes, we will have to have a pool and a Jacuzzi. And I don't mind two gardens. That will be your thing. And yes, we definitely have to have a high fence 'cuz I'm very spontaneous when it comes to getting my freak on. Anywhere and everywhere suits me just fine. I'm pretty sure you will have another natural birth 'cuz I don't want no one cutting my baby's stomach. At the same time, I don't want to see your pussy wide as a basketball either. That would do some shit to my mental, LOL! I can't wait to see how tight those sugar walls are! I myself have been thinking about sex with you also. I also can't wait to see how our road trips will be, teaching you to bake a cake. And my interacting with the kids will be a ball 'cuz I'm a natural-born leader and I was raised with love around church folk! You're right, I'm being more of a daddy than him 'cuz I know what you possess. And I won't allow no one to steal that from me or interfere with how we raise those children. Oh, they will know both sides of the coin, the civilized and uncivilized! As far as you giving him the cell phone number, that was a waste 'cuz he don't give a fuck about those kids 'cuz he doesn't have control over you or what's between your legs. The novelty has worn off, you know and I know it! And you let Jordan know I am his dad if he allows me to be his dad!

And what do you mean it will be interesting to see how he reacts when he sees us together? It better be respectable 'cuz I ain't for that ra-ra bullshit. He shot his load, and I'm not an Indian giver, so I ain't giving shit back, LOL! Well, you know, what can I say. There will be some crushes from teachers too, not just Jordan's classmates. But if you know like I know, this thing got Janae James written all over it just like that triangle between your legs better have my name written on it! That would be cool to have my name tattooed right over the top of your pubic hair. But of course I would have to be there and a woman would have to do it!

Well, my darling Janae, I must end this for now so I may get ready for work in the morning. But I'm back on my job, Ma, so don't fret! Also, it's about time for some more pictures, mamacita, back shots too. Please know that I love you and need you, and I also support you in everything you do. So stay strong and stay focused. Be blessed and stay loving your man! Tell the kids I love them and be good. Stay on that counselor and keep looking sexy!

Love always, your better half,
Bryan Jarelle Edwards

10/12/2010 (finished 10/16)

Dearest Bryan,

No mail! So you better be writing me at this very moment, and tomorrow I expect to have two letters or a very thick one in my mailbox. It's about 11:00 p.m. and on the news they just showed one of the Chilean miners has been rescued. Sixty-nine days of being trapped so many feet below the surface. It's crazy because until this happened I would have never imagined that mining was down that deep! Then there's this poor ten-year-old girl that was reported missing on Saturday. She has a prosthetic leg because of having cancer previously. And now the AMBER Alert has been changed to a homicide case because the mom admitted to writing a fake ransom note. And it came out that besides family, no one has seen this girl in a month. So it doesn't look good. Such a tragic damn shame!

Okay, new topic. I called another hair school in Rock Hill, SC, and their tuition is about $17,000, which is cheaper but their full-time is Tuesday through Saturday instead of Monday through Friday. And 9:00 to 3:30 instead of 9:00 to 4:45, and the program is twelve to thirteen months instead of forty-four weeks. Plus, Rock Hill would be a forty-minute drive each way, so the $3,000 I've saved intuition wouldn't really be worth it, having class every Saturday for a year and the other stuff. I'm still waiting to talk to you to get your input. But in the meantime I will apply for financial aid to see if they will cover me with loans 100 percent or some out of pocket.

Yay, tomorrow is Wednesday, so I hope you will be outside so we can talk longer. In the morning I'll be taking Monica's braids out, so I'm working toward that $125 to shop at Lane Bryant. Jordan has only eight school days to take these AR test, and two days in a row he has wasted the opportunity. Yesterday he said the computers were full (so he should have just waited) since it looks like a lot of kids waited till the last minute. And today he said he forgot! I told him if he don't get them points in time the punishment will be extended to the end of 2010 and I'll add some stuff! Baby, I'm sleepy again, so here's a big, juicy kiss for you . . . MUAH! I love you more today than yesterday, but not as much as tomorrow! Now to begin my sweet dreams of you kissing all over me . . .

10/14

Good evening, I'm sitting here waiting on your call and hoping at the same time that you actually do call tonight since it's not Wednesday, but our call was so short yesterday and so much of it was spent discussing Jordan. I'm mentally drained with him and this fucking AR point thing to the point where I'm like if he pulls it off, great, but the odds are so against him. He needed to take six tests this morning but managed to take one, so he has to take seven tomorrow to catch up, and he likely won't. Six school days left until the deadline, and these books are only half a point and he needs 9.5 more points. That's almost twenty books, twenty AR tests in six days. Trick-or-treating is out if he don't get them points.

Just got off the phone with you. I was doubting you would call since it was 9:27. Sorry you had to stand in the cold rain. Hopefully thoughts of me kept you feeling all warm and fuzzy like I felt when I saw I had two letters today. Justine is too much. She really was not happy that I said she couldn't talk, and walked away with her head down! You are so much the favorite dad now to both of them, and she is definitely a daddy's girl and will have you wrapped around her finger like she has my father!

I think Brooklyn finally read your letter today, so I will get the info to call the counselor, hopefully tomorrow. I will be so excited for that first visit. Jordan's birthday weekend (2/17–2/?) will work out great since there's no school Friday and Monday. I hope there is no time limit on the hug because I will be hard to pry off! As far as marriage, I literally would be willing to go to city hall and marry you when you got out! But I'm also traditional and want to be officially proposed to on bended knee and be engaged for a while to plan a beautiful wedding, and say "my fiancé," because it sounds so nice. Or maybe both, get married at city hall then have a wedding later so that we are married when the baby comes. I want to just go with the flow and let our love guide us.

With that thought in mind, I'm going to call it a night and finish this in the morning. I love you, Jarelle! Before I go, tattoo above the pubic hair line! Ouch! LOL. Your name can go on my lower back (perfect doggystyle start!) because I've always wanted one there, but the hair line sounds painful! LOL, goodnight, baby!

10/16

Good morning, baby. It's like 7:30 a.m. and I'm anxiously awaiting your call. I hope the phone rings at 8:00 on the dot. I sure didn't want to hang up last night. Three days in a row of short phone calls was killing me, but I'm also hoping it's not too cold or raining outside for you to be out there for an hour talking to me.

Brooklyn texted me with the info last night to call the counselor. We literally only talked for three to five minutes yesterday, so I know she was busy. But she be doing her thing with those term papers and stuff. One day I might pursue a doctorate after our new baby is in school, but for now the only school I'm considering is cosmetology. I slept pretty good last night, and I know you were in my dream but I can't remember a thing! I do know it wasn't a sex dream but it was a pleasant one.

It's crazy. Not to bring him up, but the only dreams I had of him involved lying, cheating, and any other thing that would have me waking up on the verge of tears or pissed off beyond belief! My subconscious was telling me for years to let it go, but damn, I was stubborn. And now to spend every waking moment and some dreaming nights with Bryan Edwards on my mind feels so right. And I never feel doubt or uneasiness, just happy thoughts. I just wish I could temporarily get sex off my mind, damn!

Well, my dear, it's 8:07, and hopefully the phone will be ringing any moment and I can hear that sexy deep voice that makes me want you to just attack me from behind and pull on my hair while I scream your name . . . aaah! With that thought, I love you. Stay strong, stay blessed, stay sexy!

Love you!
Janae

10/16/2010

Happy sweetest day!

Dang, that's one of those holidays that sneaks up on me every year. And normally I would be single and wouldn't care, but this year I have the perfect man and it slipped my mind! But February 14 was always the worst. Sometimes I would actually wear black on Valentine's Day because it was a reminder of what I didn't have but yearned for so bad! I'm sitting here still waiting for you to call. I mean, I swear you said you were calling in the morning. I am still sleepy and it's a chilly morning, so I'm going to lie down for a little bit and sip on my tea until I hear from you.

4:00 p.m.

Okay, what the hell? I haven't heard from you yet on a Saturday! I even checked my Vonage account to make sure the call forwarding was still in place, so I hope you have a good excuse, mister. I guess I shouldn't be mad until 9:30 p.m. comes along. And if you haven't stopped by then, something is up.

Justine has been playing outside all day, and Jordan played with Legos for a while then I had him read, and now he's taking a nap. It's a lazy kind of day. The temperature is like low seventies, which is the coolest it's been since early April. I love this weather but low on money, so we can't go out and enjoy it. But this won't be the only nice-weather Saturday, so I don't sweat it.

I can't wait to get to Lane Bryant for that sale, but I'm still short on money. Monica had to cancel getting the girls' hair done and said this upcoming weekend will be better for her financially. I'm thinking Deborah and Jackie will call you either this weekend or the following to get their girls' heads done. The 50 percent off $250 is on the nineteenth, which is Tuesday, so I could get it on Monday and hope they call. Some bills just have had to be paid slightly late, but I keep my credit cards on time. I really need new underclothes because it's been years! I've got the six-pack basic cotton briefs from Walmart, but the sexy coordinating panties and bras, or even the basic coordinating pieces, it's been years. So I deserve some new! But the purple and cream set, saving that one for you! I wear thongs and boy shorts, but thongs not often. I have a big booty, so it's almost like it gets lost, LOL! They take getting used to, but if you want me to wear them more often I can do that for you. The boy shorts are cute, but as you've seen, I have bigger thighs. So it's almost like wearing regular panties. Then again, the two pairs I bought, they came from Dots, and it's not like their panties were designed for big asses and thighs. When I go to Lane Bryant I'll get some real ones.

Wow, I sometimes forget that discussing Que with you is still a touchy subject. You obviously know I ain't going nowhere, but it is hard to accept 100 percent that since he can't get no ass from me he's cut himself off from the kids. As dumb as it is not to know, which I do because he has given me support before and I tried to convince myself that it wasn't related to having sex with me. But the last child support deposit was in early May, and before that it was early or mid January. I keep thinking, like damn, I was due to have his child on October 31. How disastrous would my situation be right now if I was having a baby in two weeks or less? No job still, no support from him, and we actually planned a baby! His selfishness with taking all of us to court to reduce his support, me going into labor alone again . . . I was beyond wearing blinders, I was in love with the idea of love and a baby. Thank God that the Lord had bigger and better plans for me and us. I have a new friend, new lover, and a real father for my children, and we've formed a new family. God's grace is amazing!

You asked me in the last letter how come I don't ask you questions anymore. I guess I got so caught up in just hearing your voice that I was semi-content for the moment. I will never be completely content until I'm wrapped in your arms. But also Brooklyn be telling me stories of y'all growing up and it's so cute, except you tearing the head off her Cabbage Patch dolls! I had three, so I know how serious that was! My brother used to throw mine in the garbage! Mean-ass big brothers, LOL! And how you would make her a hotdog or peanut butter and jelly sandwich after school, you hitting her with sweaty socks after playing basketball (just nasty!), her wearing your Red Cross colored pants all the time, or something like that.

Me and my brother were closer when we were younger, like eleven and eight, nine and twelve. By the time he hit high school it wasn't the same, but I remember in the winter going across the street to go sledding. The time I got sick after going underwater on the tube ride at Darien Lake and he had to hang with me for like two hours and didn't go on no rides until I was better, which had to suck for him. I wish our family could have done more outings and vacations. We went to the movies often, but it was mostly movies they wanted to see. I remember *RoboCop* straight up traumatized me. It was so violent! But we did see a lot of sci-fi. Oh, my dad is way into *Star Wars, Star Trek*, but there were movies that were more kid friendly too, *Flight of the Navigator, The Last Starfighter, Labyrinth*. I love going to the movies. That's probably why that was my favorite job from '95 through to '98. Too bad the pay sucks!

But one thing I did want to ask you was how you ended up in the hole while you were in Southport, and is that why you were transferred to Great Meadow? Are you sure you can avoid being put in a situation that could result in you being put back in? I do constantly worry. And I want to know about every detail of your day, and at the same time I don't want to know what goes on because I feel helpless and hate the whole situation! But time has gone by so fast that I know we'll be together in time. I don't know if I can wait much longer and may need to visit you in Comstock without bringing the kids. Once I talk to the counselor, I'll make my plan as far as when depending on when you'll be moved.

Well it's 6:30 p.m. and I'm about to braid Justine's hair, so I can stop staring at the phone waiting for your call! Trying to be patient, baby! Love you very much, MUAH! And I only got two letters this week! You owe me.

Love Janae

10/17/2010

Dear Jarelle,

You know the timing of your kidney stones sucks! Two weekends in a row we haven't been able to really talk, and the last four calls have been short. But the most important thing is that you are okay because I was bugging the hell out! My mind had a ton of thoughts. But the good thing is you were in my dream again last night. Don't remember what it was about, but I woke up smiling. And I know these kidney stones didn't all of a sudden appear, and you probably had some symptoms that you neglected to tell me about! If you had mentioned it before then I could at least mentally prepare for a "what if" situation. But again, the bottom line is I'm so thankful you are okay, and I can't wait for our really long next phone call. I mean, dang!

Saturday dragged along like you wouldn't believe! Trying to refrain from constantly bringing up the AR points with Jordan is killing me. But like you said, he's been warned and told of its consequence, so all I can do is wait. Wednesday night I was ready to strangle that child! The cologne, the bottle of ginger ale (which still has not turned up, not even the empty bottle!), scratching up the phone I just bought, the key ring, and crinkling up the cover of one of my books. That child! Today was a good day and I wasn't forceful in mentioning reading. That took some serious restraint. Well, this is the third letter in two days and I'm getting sleepy, so I will continue tomorrow. Love you, baby! Goodnight!

10/18

Good morning, my dear. You know what's so annoying? I had to pee really bad but didn't want to get up, so I kept having dreams about peeing. So I finally got up and it was 5:26. So I'm thinking, cool, I can get forty-five more minutes of sleep before the alarm. It's 5:48 and I still can't fall asleep. And I know as soon as I do the alarm will go off and put an end to that, so here I am writing to you. I actually slept pretty good.

I asked Tara what I could try as far as the fleas since she works in an animal hospital. (as soon as the kittens left, we learned that they left us the gift of fleas!) And she said to buy a flea collar and stick it right inside the vacuum, vacuum the whole house—rugs, furniture, hardwood floors, etc.—then empty the entire bag afterward. And after reading the ingredients on the bottles of flea removal spray and powders, the active ingredient percentages are very different. For one of the active ingredients it said 0.1 percent, and when I looked on the Raid brand it said 1.0 percent. That's a big difference. And the total percentage of inactive ingredients for the brand I bought was 99 percent, so only 1 percent of the whole bottle had chemicals to actually kill these fleas! But for Raid it was 5 percent active ingredients. And the other stuff was Hartz brand, which is specifically for fleas and animals and cost more. I should have stuck with Raid in the first place, so I'll see if it makes a difference in the next few days.

I sprayed all of us down with some OFF! insect repellent (fresh scent version doesn't have that crazy bug spray smell, LOL!) so I wasn't itchy going to sleep and the kids felt a lot better, especially Jordan, since his room had the biggest problem. But earlier in the day I called an exterminator. Well, I called four, and three of them were only open Monday through Friday, so I called Orkin. The chick was telling me all the additional steps they take to make sure the problem doesn't come back, and it was sounding expensive; $135 for the initial treatment, then $80 every other month for twelve months! I told her I plan on moving in less than six weeks, so she says I can transfer the service. And I said no, I'll be in an apartment complex and they spray for free. So she said a one-time treatment is $275 because they have to use more chemicals and treat for a longer time. I wasn't trying to hear that crap, so I figured I will try everything I can first and see what happens. Ugh, I feel itchy just talking about it, LOL!

So my apartment search is narrowed it down to two places—Mission Matthew's Place, where I just moved from but the problem there is the price! When they have a lot of vacancies it's cheap, but when they don't it's high! The other two-bedroom floor plan that I love is going for $845, which is very high. I was paying $669 for a two-bedroom before and the other was like $740 or so before. He said that the price always changes depending on how many leases are up, who moves out, etc., and last month he said they were $640! The other option is Windsor Landing, and I love that two-bedroom. And the price is $699, but the security deposit depends on my credit and I have to pay $99 just to have the application run. And I hope they don't want an obscene amount. My credit has changed since I last applied for an apartment because of stupid Heatherwood Trace trying to charge me $558 for bullshit when I only owed $200 for the carpet. So they referred me to a collection agency, and that may affect my security deposit. But those two apartment complexes are the only ones that will keep both kids at their same school and I won't have to pay for before-school or after-school care. And if I go to Empire Beauty School, it's right down the street literally from both departments. And if I work they can get on the bus both ways. Mission's application fee is up to $65 right now. And if I'm approved, a $100 holding fee will prevent them from renting to someone else. But at Windsor the security deposit has to be paid within seventy-two hours of approval and it can range from $99 to $1,000. Decisions, decisions! But I'm praying on it!

See, the 6:15 alarm went off like five minutes ago, so it's time to get the kiddos up and ready. You will have, like, three letters coming to you this week, lucky you! I was going to mail one per day but I'm just going to put them all in today so that you have a lot to take your mind off your surroundings, at least for the moment. When you get the pictures, I hope you like them. Because I still have insecurities, and wearing a fishnet bodysuit, I can't cover up what I usually hide. So I'm all exposed. That shows you just how much I love you because I'm letting my guard down. And I just want to keep you smiling until you're here with me. I hope and pray you have a great day. Stay strong, stay encouraged, be good. I love you with all my heart.

Love always,
Janae Edwards

10/19/2010

Hi Wifey,

I'm totally excited that I made your day the other morning. I pray the Lord allows me to make your mornings, noons, and nights unforgettable 'cuz you deserve to be showered with unconditional love. And you don't just make my day, you're starting to complete me! And don't stress when the balance gets low on VAC. When you get the opportunity to replenish it I know you will. hey will give me more reason to pick my pen up. And it is a rip-off when you use the debit card, but that's the reasoning for them lowering the price on the phone call. So their end justifies their means!

And no, you can't put a price tag on talking to your husband 'cuz that's priceless. And you're right, it is a temporary thing but a memorable one that I will never forget 'cuz I've experienced triumph out of tragedy. Did you finally put the washing machine on Craigslist or did you work out something else? I know you probably say to yourself, damn, what's next? But always remember God is not going to give you more than you can bear! And yes, I'm definitely hooked on Tide also. I meant to ask you do you use coupons when you go grocery shopping? Just curious, that's all. 'Cuz I use them and it saves money!

I hope the kids like their letters. Oh, I tried to get them out sooner but you know how these people are here. And as you already know by now, I was in the hospital over the weekend with a kidney stone that I passed through my urine. And yes, it was very painful. And yes, I'm wrong for keeping my hurts from you. I have to learn now that I'm not by myself anymore and I have a better half that I must share with when I'm in pain or hurting. So please accept my apology. It won't happen again. You have to understand that I'm used to people selling me dreams and illusions that it became hard for me to separate the real from the fake. 'Cuz I despise fake and I don't have any tolerance for it! Please know that's not a strike against you. It's just I stay in survival mode being where I was to where I currently am!

I'm glad to hear that Jordan is practicing the clarinet for a while. Now, as far as Legos, yes, they are expensive, but he will soon grow out of Legos and turn to something else! Shanita was nice to hand down some jeans to Justine but there will come a time when we will need no handouts 'cuz your man has hustle skills you wouldn't believe. And don't get me wrong, I don't look down on it 'cuz we need all the help we can get. Just don't get used to it, please! I'm so happy to hear Jordan likes baggy clothes 'cuz that tight shit will not be worn around me. That's gay. And no son of mine will be wearing shit that shows his underwear line!

Next time you text your ex about something he automatically is responsible for doing, I think we are going to have our first argument! I feel if a man doesn't feel obligated to take care of his responsibilities, what on God's green earth makes you think that by you texting him he's going to drop everything and run and do the right thing? Am I missing something here? In the last couple years what has he done but literally fuck you? Now you're not giving him anything, but yet you're still trying to get something from nothing. The only way you're going to get support is through the court, nothing less. And the crazy part, you know all of this already. So why you keep beating a dead horse?

Moving along, this Monica lady that works for the county. She don't have any pull to get you a job? Or you're not that close? You're purposely engaged in small talk to make sure Que answers his text. I'm not going to touch that! As far as him actively trying to get the kids when I'm home, all three of us will have a brief talk 'cuz those kids would not be put in game or used as pawns out of jealousy or envy. Either he's there or he's not. I don't think you have completely come to that conclusion. You've only passed that one test, there will be many more before I arrive. I have total confidence in you. Are you game tight? Don't read too much into that last paragraph. What I'm saying is he's going to try a lot more games than the one just popping up without calling, is all I'm saying. So I hope you didn't start cursing me out before you understood what I said. Enough about that. Moving on.

I meant to say, painting this new hairdo as well as this bodysuit you were telling me about should have surprised me instead of telling me on the phone, but you know I know what you're going to say (you asked me, so I told you). I'll take all the blame. I have a big back, so it's all good! Now about this Empire Beauty School. I think it's a great idea, but don't you at least want to get a part-time job first before you venture into something so time consuming? If that's what you want to do beyond a shadow of doubt, I have your back 100 percent. And you said you're going to have to take out a loan (extra). You going to have me out there hustling for real, huh? But for real, Ma, whatever your heart desires. Follow your goals and dreams, and whatever I can contribute or enhance, just holla!

I'm sitting here listening to Ne-Yo (*In My Own Words*). It's my favorite tape. Trust me, it's fire! Listen, forget those cats. I told you so. Now you have house guests that didn't call before coming over. Reminds me of someone. But I am not going there. You need a real pet, so just wait and I'll get you one. I'm glad you found a nice home for them, but I also don't like you inviting strangers to where you live. I hope you get that out of your system soon 'cuz I'll do. It may have been a nice older couple, you're still a semi-young woman (LOL) by herself with two young kids that doesn't have me home yet, which makes me very uncomfortable. Care to elaborate on that?

About the book, fair that chick was probably trying to steal something, that's why she was so worried about you being around the cash register! What did she say when you told her off? 'Cuz I know she didn't get fly out the mouth afterward. I just heard from the mailman also, but I forgot you just mailed the pictures so I have to be patient. I don't know if I can wait to call you Wednesday. I might sneak and call you while you're at Girl Scouts, so please don't be mad at me. I love you!

You say you're about to do Monica's hair. Since she works for the county, I hope you're charging top dollar. I'm just playing. (I know I'm not. Get that money, woman.) I'm sure you have some interesting stuff to tell me from the people at the Albany office as well as here at the jail. These people are so full of bullshit. Here they just told another inmate's family that he was charged with something he wasn't even in jail for. That's how vile these crackers are. But it won't be long now, so I just grin and bear it!

Well, Baby girl, in minute I'm about to go take a shower and wash this body of yours. So I'm going to have to let you go for now, only to return in another envelope very soon. Please know that I love you more every minute and can't wait to tell you face-to-face. Until then, let me get going. Oh yeah, I just got off the phone with you. I wasn't supposed to call but I had to hear your voice. Please forgive me for interrupting your Girl Scouts meeting, but I love you and can't get enough! I'll be talking to my counselor soon to get to the bottom of this shit about my time, so please don't get *discouraged. I'm on it. Well, love, tell the kids I love them. And you stay blessed, focused, strong, and loved by me!*

*Love you,
Jarelle*

10/19/2010

Hey Baby Boy,

I loved talking to you for so long last night! We had a lot of time to make up for, so that was great. I felt all recharged and refreshed. I was going to start this letter last night but I kind of just wanted to chill and review the conversation in my mind. You really threw me for a loop when you told me you had a dream that we were married while you were still there. I hope my silence didn't give you the wrong message. My first thought was, wow, you seriously can see me being your wife! After so many years of hearing all the things that are wrong with me, that if only I was this or that or had never done whatever <u>then</u> I'd be the perfect wife, and for you to accept and even embrace the things that were viewed as flaws by others. That was powerful to me. Then on the other hand, I had this vision of how our first night of being together would be almost majestic. And that vision, I never considered our first time being with you still not free. But then again, I've had a few dreams of our first time making love and each time you were in jail, and I still woke up smiling!

I had to call Brooklyn to ask her was I being ridiculous with my concern. The way she put it was relating it to her relationship with Robert and her him meeting online, which many people ridiculed back then. Him having a ready-made family of three kids already, being a stepmom before becoming a mom, his age. All of those things ended up making their bond stronger by overcoming the negativity. Our relationship is far from the traditional way I envisioned, falling in love and getting married before even having kids, and we both have kids. So with that being said, I'm going to let my heart and our love guide whatever we decide, and just leave it at that.

And I don't want you to think I fell in love with you out of desperation. I know last night I told you I had reached the point where I was willing to accept whatever came my way as far as staying with Que, and compromise myself in ridiculous ways. It wasn't just about him. I was looking at all my previous relationships and the common denominator with all of them was me being cheated on, lied to, deceived, and ultimately being the guy's second choice or a standby. So I thought about cities like DC where women outnumber men, like eight to one. Cities like Atlanta and San Francisco where too many men are on the down low, and just figured this is the way it is, so why not just stick with the familiar. But on Que's last visit here at the end of March, something in me clicked and I literally was like, fuck that! I was tired of being tired! Then we started writing and our newly formed relationship gave me the strength to stick to it and not regress for the umpteenth time. So thank you for loving me, <u>unconditionally</u> loving me and my—OUR children.

Hate to switch up the mood, but I spoke to that guy today regarding your move. I already know I'll talk to you on the phone before you get this, so you will know my greatest fear. He was saying that you needed to have two years of no tickets before your move to a medium, but I thought you were out as of August? Are you keeping something from me? Could you possibly have another year on top of the one we are counting down? Now that I have totally fallen in love and my kids love you, do we have even longer to wait? Would I be a completely selfish bitch if I decided I can't wait that long? Am I totally jumping to conclusions? I guess for the time being I can't worry about that until we talk and until you talk to your counselor. I'm about to take a quick nap until it's time to get the kids, and I will continue this letter shortly. Love you Jarelle!

10/20

Good morning, love. Let me set the record straight now. Yesterday I was really feeling some type of way about what if you weren't getting out in August, and the thought scares the hell out of me. But I was being selfish because you've been waiting like fifteen years compared to my almost seven months, so there really is no comparison there. Yes, I would be pissed and probably cuss and whine, cry, scream. But eventually I would have accepted the situation and continued working on my patience because I can't walk away from you now! Our souls have already connected, and I can't just break that bond because we can't be physically together when I want to. So I'm telling you now, after I have my tantrum I would stick by my man and we'd get through it! And all of this may be totally premature because I was only going off what the guy said on the phone. And until you talk to the counselor, we don't know anything.

I was pleasantly surprised to hear from you yesterday, but dang, your timing sucks! My meetings are six fifteen to seven forty-five and I'm trying to end, like, ten minutes earlier so that right at 7:45 they are gone. I wanted to talk to you so bad and they don't be wanting to leave! Cassy didn't come last night. She said she was sick, so I asked her what time she is coming, and she's like "I don't know." I said, "Stay home 'cuz I can handle the girls easily since last year that's all I did anyways. Plus, no need to spread germs!" I kind of think she was lying, but I didn't care either way. She lives an hour away, so it is a long drive. And she's long-winded and I wanted to wrap up and leave. But if she was there I could have had her close out the meeting while we talked. It's all good though since today is Wednesday. Yay!

As far as the VAC account, as far as I'm concerned it's a necessity, so I'm going to just start mailing $10 money orders every week. Because I end up letting the account get low, then that forces me to use a debit or credit card at the last minute, which has a $7.95 transaction fee, and that fee alone is for thirty-minute calls! A rip-off! So that's my plan. I'm guessing you might get those three letters in the mail today or tomorrow. Then the car tomorrow or Friday. I can't wait till you call so I can hear your reaction to the pictures! Even if you think I look awful, lie to me, LOL! I feel so exposed in them, but love makes us let our guard down. And I know you already know how much I love my Bryan!

Well, I'm going to make some calls to apartments and stuff, and I look forward to talking to you later! Love you, baby!

Love always,
Janae

10/21/2010

Hey love of my life,

As I told you earlier I didn't really sleep last night, so my eyes are burning. But I had to get this quickly Down before I sleep. Our conversation literally had me at a loss for words—in a good way. I'm overwhelmed with the feeling of being loved and in love. All this time I thought I experienced love before, and none of it compares to what I feel for you and from you! I'll finish this tomorrow. And you should be getting pictures, so I'm super excited about Friday's phone call!

October 21, 2010, is when everything shifted. I took the kiddos to the movies to see Toy Story 3, and during the movie my phone rang and I saw my handsome man's face on the caller ID. I stepped out of the theater so I wouldn't be rude. Even after I hung up I couldn't tell you the exact words he said to me. All I knew was that Bryan Jarelle Edwards asked me to be his wife. I don't know of many other moments in my life up to that moment that brought me more joy. No longer was my plan to find an apartment in Charlotte and enroll in a cosmetology program in Charlotte. I needed to be back in New York, and asap! This is where logical thinking started to take the back seat, and I foolishly and selfishly let my heart make ALL of the decisions to come. Before I continue, I need to share the rest of our letters for the month of October.

10/22/10 (the rest of 10/21 letter)

Slept much better, good morning! I'm sitting here watching *Good Morning America*. Dropped the kids off early because Jordan has some make-up work to do for language arts and it's his final day to get those AR points in. I'm praying he can pull it off. He got three more points in yesterday but I was so pissed with him. Yesterday morning, when I took him to school I spoke to his teacher and she said he could stay after school until 4:30. I get to the school around 4:15 and he's not in the class. Mrs. Dirr said he got on the bus. I was like, WTF! Like did he reach his fifteen points? But he was only at 10.3. So when he called me from the bus stop I asked him why the hell did he get on the bus, and he said he forgot. I said, oh well, you already know the consequence if you don't make those points, and how careless and irresponsible that was to just forget, and I left it at that.

It's noon now and I've been waiting for the Whirlpool tech to come and service this microwave. Kathryn texted me at 11:00 a.m. and said they told her they were on the way. I'm glad I have your support, Brooklyn, the kids, and Shelby about going back to New York whether it ends up being temporary or permanent. I have decided to wait until later to tell my mom. The anticipation may be too much for her! LOL. But she's been saying for the past three years that she will <u>pay</u> to help us move back, so I won't wait too long to tell her! I told Nicole and she hopes I get hired full-time somewhere. But even if I get hired now, which would be fantastic, I am still leaving over the summer and going to cosmetology school. She thinks if I get a job in education it will make me stay indefinitely, but <u>you</u> aren't here, so there's nothing holding me in Charlotte.

10/23

I never did finish this letter yesterday like I planned to. The guy ended up coming to check the microwave, then the mail came at noon, which is way later than the usual 9:30 or 10:00 a.m. I had actually just figured there was no mail, but yeah, I had a letter (see, only one) from you. And sorry, sweetie, but no, we aren't past that! I mailed out four letters and a card this week. And I know you were in the hospital, which is hard enough, thinking of my man in pain, but I should be getting a minimum of two letters per week! You should have asked the nurse to give you a pen and paper and wrote through the pain since you were hiding the pain from me anyway! Yeah, baby, I'm talking it right now, and what you going to do about it? LOL. I bet if I miss a call here and there my mailbox would be overflowing, but you already know that whatever is going on is put on pause when you call. So with that being said, you need to step up your pen game! You know I love you!

Okay, so let me get to answering this letter. No, I still didn't put the washer on Craigslist. I'm considering putting both on. The dryer is a bit small for my liking, and it's the kind where socks sometimes gets stuck in those corners and still be wet. And the inside back plate where the heat emits from gets really hot, which may have been because the clothes weren't as dry as they would be from the spin cycle. But I was wringing them out by hand and when the clothes hit that back plate it was steaming. So if I put them on as a pair for $100 or even $125 I can pay Nicole her $75 and make a little profit because the leaking water may be a small problem and I'm still going to the laundromat anyway.

And yes, I use coupons even with food stamps. But Aldi doesn't take coupons, so I use them everywhere else. I am the queen of living ghetto fabulous, thought you knew! I buy from thrift stores, regular stores, online, wherever the bargain and quality are. I never let the kids go out looking any kind of way. And when me and you are out and about, no one will ever say, damn, how did <u>she</u> get a fine ass dude like that looking like that? I will stay looking good even in T-shirts and sweats. We were just at the gas station yesterday and this chick had a sleeping cap on her head, a tank top with dingy bra straps showing, and some stretch pants looking a mess. And I didn't know if she was with a dude until this guy walked toward her and they left together. He was decent looking, but man or no man, don't go out looking any kind of tacky way. No, I'm not as bad as Brooklyn 'cuz she be at the bus stop with the kids in heels! That's why she get hit on all the time!

Okay, you wasted three paragraphs going off on me about texting Que about support, even though we settled that on the phone and again last night. So that topic is dead, baby, let it go. You are all the man I want anyway. And I look forward to the day when you are holding it down for us and I can tell him to take his little funky ass $20 a week for two kids and use it to buy a clue because he is clueless on how to be a real man and real father.

It always catches me off guard (in a good way!) when I tell you about my wants and goals and you answer me by saying how you have to work to make it happen for me. I'm so not used to that. I've always had to strategize and sacrifice and work hard. But knowing I have your support and drive just makes me think God for bringing us together!

I remember when I brought my first brand-new car, a Kia Sephia, and I was so proud that my credit was good enough to get it on my own. And Que told me that out of all the cars I could have got I picked the worst one, and was laughing like it was a joke. But it hurt to the point where I couldn't wait to trade it in and upgrade it to a 2002 Kia Sportage and added over $7,000 of negative equity to my new loan. And eventually I filed for bankruptcy in 2004 and the truck was repossessed. That's why I love my 2000 Olds Intrigue because I own it 100 percent. I picked out what I like and what I could afford and I paid it off. I still want that 2011 Honda Odyssey, so I'm being patient until I'm financially ready. Which is cool because buying it at the end of 2011 or beginning of 2012 will be the best deals. And like you said, you'll be getting your serious hustle on to better us as a whole family!

For the first time in three years, I'm looking forward to moving back to New York and going to major in cosmetology at 50 percent less than the cost of Empire, and visiting my husband on a regular basis, and pizza and wings! LOL. Yes, I am naive when it comes to inviting strangers into my house regarding the couple getting the kittens. And I have bought and sold tons of things on Craigslist where I've had people come to my house, I've gone to theirs, and we've met in public places. I know some people are nervous about letting their kids go to friends' houses down the street and stuff, but that's just not me. It's not that I 100 percent trust everyone, it's just that I'm not going to raise my family in a plastic bubble out of being paranoid or always on guard. I guess that's where you will balance me out. But keep in mind that when I sell the washer and dryer someone will have to come to the house to pick it up. When it's time to move back to New York, movers will have to come to the house to load up the truck.

Encountering strangers at the house is inevitable. But don't worry, I'm not naive to the point of stupidity, so I'll always be aware and cautious.

I only did that one day at the book fair, and I think it was a race thing. She didn't say anything when I told her I would come out after I was done. The expression on her face was more like, "I can't believe she didn't do what I told her!" She knew better than to say anything else.

And if so, when you call on my Girl Scout nights (first and third Tuesday, 6:15 to 7:45), just try to call after 7:45. I love talking to my man, so why would I get mad? I was mad that they weren't leaving fast enough! I did Monica's hair, I took her braids out for $40, no big deal. She's a regular customer with getting the girls' hair done. And she works at the Social Services office, so she's not thinking, like, crazy! My true parents know my job situation and are always telling me about positions, but it's not in their hands or mine. God obviously is pulling me in a different direction, so I'm working hard on just trusting Him!

Well, it's about 9:00 a.m. now and time to make breakfast, so I'm making the weekend usual—pancakes, scrambled eggs, sausage. I can't wait to cook for you! I'll be waiting for your inside call today. I love you so much, and I pray you're having a great day and enjoying your pictures!

Love always,
Janae

10/25/2010

Wifey,

I know you are in a greater sense of being after my phone conversation while at the movies. And I meant to do that sooner, but sometimes we are not in control of our emotions as much as we think we are! Meaning, I wanted to tell you that the other night, but my inner voice said, "not today." But the day I told you those inner thoughts was a night of short conversation instead of a night outside where we would have talked longer. But I'm happy that we have an understanding of what we both want and need. If you should ever deviate from our plans or have something to add, please tell me so I may make the adjustments that may or may not be needed!

It's really a blessing also that you would choose to move back to Buffalo to be closer to me, as well as pursue a career in hair and cosmetics. I know a word for it, but I dare to be different! And to tell you the truth, I'm happy that it will give the kids an opportunity to be around their grandparents as well as other siblings, and see if their father will handle the responsibility given to him by God. But I'm not holding my breath. And for the remark of me putting a hit on him, that's something I would do myself if it warrants that, but I pray that never comes to that 'cuz I'm not a violent person. All the violence has been brought my way, but I've gotten through them with blessings while learning at the same time.

Your choice of living areas are acceptable. Also, please don't rule out moving to the suburbs 'cuz that's where I really want to live, with very few people knowing where we live. That goes for in the city. I'm just private like that. The streets made me that way, and that's one law I've embraced for life. Now, where do you plan on working while you're going to school, any idea? Have you talked to your mother about me yet? And what exactly do you plan on telling her? What if she doesn't accept it? Would that push you away from her, or does it matter? I don't really care one way or another. 'Cuz what she thinks won't have any bearing on how I love you 'cuz it's just going to make me go harder. I thrive off people that doubt me or my capabilities for success. So actually I need for your mother or whoever to hate me or just like me 'cuz I'll never allow them to really know me unless I truly embrace them, and I don't embrace a lot! Have you broken the news to your friends that you're moving back to Buffalo? And who are you going to get to fill the vacancy at Kathryn's house? That ought to be interesting because if the neighbors were nosey when you was there, imagine what's going to happen when another stranger pops up. They might call the SWAT team in, LOL!

Oh, by the way, I'm at work, writing you, listening to the radio. The closest black music they had played is Mariah Carey, wow!

10/26

This is a continuation of the first page but another day. Yesterday I talked to you on the phone and decided to open up the envelope and throw a page away and start anew. It seems to me that you're worried, which is quite typical, considering you're making a life-changing decision for you, the kids, and me. I felt yesterday like you thought I was misleading about when I'd get out of prison. I have not misled you from day one, nor will I mislead you in the days and months, as well as years, to come. I only went by what my last counselor told me, then Brooklyn told me something that, on which I never questioned her 'cuz she never been not accurate! So in case you didn't hear me on the phone or you're second-guessing me, I come home March 2012. Now, if in between that time you decide you can't do it no more or you feel there's something else that you would like to pursue, I will never hold you back from a destiny of your choice. My intentions for us are pure, with no hidden agenda, as I always say! I know you've been hurt many times by the same person, but please don't allow that hurt to dictate our relationship. You ever want to ask me or discuss with me anything, just say it. And if it's something I don't want to hear or discuss at that moment, then I'll say so. But that doesn't mean I won't entertain your question later 'cuz we are a couple, right?

One other thing, concerning your mother and what I tell you, I don't know your mother but I will respect your mother 'cuz she's a black woman/mother and grandmother. But what I tell you in confidence I don't expect you to tell your mother or anybody else without my knowledge or consent! When I told you I was living in Langfield that was cool, but when you tell your mother that's where I caught my case, that's not something I wanted her to know. That was for your ears only for purposes to be known at a later date if at all. Let me break this down in simple terms. Although I come from a God-fearing, very stable home with 100 percent love, I married the streets, only to get a divorce when I caught this case. I still have feelings for the street, but I'll never love her the same. At the same time, there's rules and guidelines I <u>must continue to obey for life.</u> And if you're going to be my wife/girlfriend/woman there's things I may share and may not share. But regardless of either, they're supposed to stay with me and you unless it's agreed upon to divulge to others. That's why it's so hard for me to trust people 'cuz people have told me things and done things for me that I will take to my grave. <u>That's a code I'll never break!</u>

I'm your man, you're my woman. Let's utilize each other's capabilities to take this family to the top. We must be in tune with each other for it to work! I know you're still green to my life, and vice versa, but I'm eager to be taught. Are you willing to teach and learn? 'Cuz knowledge is infinite! And in order for us to put those kids on the level we feel they should achieve, they should feel confident that Mommy and Daddy know what they are doing. Although we may not be able to teach them everything, it's the basics that a lot of black families have steered away from that their kids end up either dropouts, drug addicts, career criminals, suicidal, or gay! If I have anything to do with it, Jordan and Justine won't be none of those titles 'cuz they will know themselves. And even though having limitations, they won't be scared to push the envelope because Janae and Bryan will be there to continue teaching the why and why not.

I pray you read this letter very thoroughly to digest what I'm giving you 'cuz I stayed up late last night putting this letter in my head to write today. 'Cuz I feel it's appropriate for you to know some more about me so we don't make the same mistakes or fall in the pitfalls other virgin couples have fallen into in the past. And when you write back, please continue to speak your mind just like you do over the phone. And no, I'm not saying you don't speak your mind in letters either, so please don't get that notion. <u>I build, not destroy. I elevate, not hinder elevation.</u> So ride with me while I take you on this love train to mental, physical, spiritual bliss! There will be another letter coming with this letter, answering your last letter dated 10/19/10. I just felt I had to address some things in this letter that couldn't wait. And if you shall disagree with anything I said or explained, feel free to express yourself to the fullest. 'Cuz that's the only way we can grow and become as one!

Well, my love, I must end this in order to get this in the mail and in your system. I want to tell you something. You don't have to be in a classroom to teach. The world is your classroom and everyone you come in contact with is a potential student! Please know that I love you and cherish your presence and ability to love me back. Please send my love to the kids. Tell them to stay strong, blessed, and focused. You as well!

Love always, your better half,
Bryan Jarelle Edwards

10/26/2010

My love, heart, and soul,

If I had any lingering doubt before, I don't anymore. My love for you grows daily. And after a stressful day all I could think about was, "Jarelle, please call and reassure me that everything will be alright and you love me unconditionally." Please forgive me for letting my mouth run like water and still being naïve. I was using my heart more than my mind because it's a hard pill to swallow that my mom envies me to the point where she'd sabotage my relationship with you. But I'm not worried because God has brought us together and no man or woman can destroy that. But damn, they trying!

I hope everything I said doesn't have any detrimental effect on the streets. And from this point I've learned I can't share with everyone, so I'll keep my thoughts between us to myself. I didn't mean to get all emotional on the phone and cry. And I surely don't want you smoking cigarettes! I'll be so happy when you are close to Buffalo, and I can't wait to marry you! I thought about it and I know what I want and need! But that will be between us as well. When you are completely free, then we plan for our official wedding. But what about rings in the meantime? I want an engagement ring and a wedding band. So how would this be worked out? QVC has nice silver rings and their CZ line, Diamonique, is beautiful. And I have no problem wearing something like that because it's not the price or stone or metal, it's what it will symbolize! So should I start window shopping? Is that something you can buy in there? I guess I should be waiting on an official proposal! But I've thought about it and I know what I want: you! Bryan Jarelle Edwards! You make my heart sing, and I smile just at the thought of you!

10/27

It's almost 9:00 p.m., 10:00 p.m. now. I was looking at the pictures stored in my laptop (used to be my parents') and there has to be up to 2,000 pictures on it. I was looking at pictures of the kids and me, and looking at all of our transformations and also the stuff that stayed the same. Then I noticed the hallway bathroom light on, so I go to turn it off and a big-ass spider in there! Now remember, I'm not scared of spiders, but the big, big-ass spiders that look like they can be a brown recluse? Hell yeah! Poisonous! So I sprayed it with some Raid. Then go in the kitchen to get a drink, another one on the counter! But I couldn't get it, it dipped behind the wall. That's what I hate about when it rains, the spiders come in! Normally I love listening to the rain and just chilling and getting lost in my thoughts, but these spiders just fucked up the whole mood!

I wanted you to call so bad! It's Wednesday and I couldn't talk to you. There is like $1.04 on the account, which technically you should be able to call. But the money order I mailed should be posted by Friday, hopefully. I literally be feenin' to hear from you. And when we talk, I guess I can only equate it to a high feeling, even when the conversation isn't always pleasant like last night. But just your voice and your words, my own little brand of ecstasy.

Well, for a change I have good news! Mr. Walker stopped me at the office and told me to come in first thing in the morning so we can get the paperwork done for me to start subbing! I'm sure we'll talk before you get this letter, but I'm very happy about that. Because that would mean no ASEP and half the cost of gas since there won't be two trips.

I'll be doing Nia's and Nyree's hair on Friday since there's no school, and hopefully my two other girls will want their hair done too because it's been four weeks now. Other than that I feel much better, and knowing how much you really love me just feels amazing by itself.

10/28

Good morning. I can't believe I fell asleep before I finished this letter. I think I was a little sad because I was hoping you would call, and disappointed when you didn't. I was managing this whole Sunday/Wednesday/Saturday quite well. Then you were calling more often on off days, and what can I say, you spoiled me! I already know once you're moved and we move to Buffalo that I will be visiting you until the guards know me on a first-name basis.

It's 4:00 p.m. now. I don't know why I can't get this letter done! I went to the thrift store this afternoon to try to find a short plaid skirt for this Halloween party I'm going to tomorrow night. I am going as a sexy schoolgirl! Definitely will have pictures for you! But I checked the time and was like, oh shoot, time to get Justine. So I didn't find the skirt I wanted. So when Justine comes I'll go back to look. And don't worry, the sexy schoolgirl look is just for the party. When we trick or treat I won't be drawing all that attention to your goodies! Just jeans and a Halloween T-shirt.

And I didn't get to meet with Mr. Walker. He came in late this morning, so he asked for my full name and SSIN so he could call the sub office. And I left, so we shall see. I hope the money order is applied to the VAC account by tomorrow because they don't post on weekends and I need to hear your voice so bad!

Well, Jordan's bus is here, so I'm going to end this letter here and likely start another tonight. I love you so much, and I'll be talking to you soon!

Love you,
Janae

10/27/2010

Hey Baby Girl,

Before I answer your letter, I never meant to cause you any pain or to tear up over how ignorant your mother is, as well as receptive to her daughter being with and marrying a convicted felon. But I'm here to tell you I don't need your mother's love, affection, or acknowledgment in anything I pursue. I love myself, so that enables me to love others regardless of one's flaws or insecurities. But I have them myself but I don't allow anyone to exploit me, nor will I allow the people I love to be exploited! That's why, once again, I have trust issues. I was taught in the streets to show no love 'cuz love will get you killed. So I'm here to tell you I'm in it to win it. But once I've won I will continue to enhance our dreams, aspirations, short-/long-term goals, and most importantly, our love for one another.

Now I'm going to get to your letter 'cuz I feel I have touched base with you concerning your mother. And for your ex, he would be quite the intelligent one to know his limits concerning me as well as you and I because ramifications love swift endings. And I'll leave it at that!

I'm so happy that you enjoyed our long talk last week. And it should make you feel recharged and fresh 'cuz I have the same feeling when we build—'cuz that's what we do instead of talk! And I meant to throw you for a loop. You complete me and I always envision us married. Not only do you deserve but you should want the children to see and observe the right way to do things instead of the halfway! And no, your silence on the phone didn't give me the wrong message. Actually, it gave me the right one. You needed some time to digest what I was putting on your heart! And yes, I'm serious. Father Time doesn't allow me to be fake or bullshit around the bush! That's my mission also, to wipe your memory slate clean of all the turmoil in your past life that has scarred you, in order for you to love me 360°— that's a complete circle, Ms. Teacher, LOL!

And the only perfect wife I've seen is on a sitcom, so I don't want a perfect wife. I want a wife that can balance life, at the same time enhance the quality of life for her husband and children! See, people are selfish. They don't know how to bring out the potential in people. When you look at a diamond, you see it in a store or catalog, commercials, and so on. But you don't see that diamond's transformation from muddy waters to sparkling stone 'cuz people will think that will depreciate the value. So I see the potential in you but you must keep that drive 'cuz when you allow things in the past to dictate your life then your vision becomes muddy! And whether our first time be in jail or not, it will start a celebration of many to come. And I'm glad you called Brooklyn but you should have consulted me, for I'm the one who will be your better half! And see, concerning some things I don't like traditional 'cuz that doesn't allow us to grow in some areas. That's why I like going against the grain 'cuz then it allows us to create our own lane and discover many different avenues!

And things don't always happen the way you envisioned them. That's why it's so healthy to take a chance on something different before you miss something that was meant for you and end up chasing that one thing you didn't take advantage of while it was in your grasp! There was never a thought in my mind that you fell in love with me out of desperation. I just showed you something different that you wasn't accustomed to seeing or feeling. And the gravity of my love won't allow you to be released! I don't want you to accept whatever or to compromise yourself. I just want you to hate fake just like I hate fake! And today I want you to stop looking at your previous relationships 'cuz what we have formed is a <u>bond</u>, something better than a relationship. For a bond, I'd rather <u>lose my breath than break it!</u>

And I'm the one that should be thanking you for allowing me to love and embrace you and the kids! Please never ask me am I keeping something from you because I've told you everything, even things you weren't supposed to know so soon! I will be in a medium January/top of February and you wouldn't be a selfish - - - - - if you decide you couldn't wait that long. It would be your loss, my gain that didn't have a price tag or a dollar figure. I don't think you're really ready for me 'cuz you guess for the time being you won't worry about it. I'm not one to worry, I'm confident! And for you feeling selfish the next morning is typical, due to the fact that sometimes we speak prematurely before actually taking time out to ponder our thoughts and feelings, and how our decisions no only affect you but the people around us that we love and are responsible for!

And yes, I've been waiting fifteen years, but life doesn't stop because of the complications of life. You will always have a choice to continue or put a halt to whatever you deem unsuccessful. And I'm happy you're still working on your patience 'cuz I've never stopped working on mine. It's also very refreshing to hear you can't walk away from me now! And yes, our souls have connected. And to hear you say you can't break our bond only contributes to everything I've been explaining to you from day one. Oh, this is not a game, this is life. Us not being together physically is only going to compound our actual day we are together. And when we make love, I'm going to take my time so you will feel every sensation a woman's body is supposed to feel while intertwined in lovemaking.

And speaking of premature, once again, stop believing everything these crackers tell you 'cuz their sole purpose is to deter families from being together or love to prosper. So once again, you want to know something about me, ask. 'Cuz if I have to lie to you I don't need you or can I possibly do anything for you! Now for Cassy, if you think she's lying about her sickness, then you need to put someone else in the position, for everyone is not apt at leadership roles. And yes, it is a necessity to put $10 every week on the phone as long as it doesn't take away from the kids or your everyday needs! And you don't look awful in your pictures, you look finger-licking good! And no, I will not lie to you, so forget it! You shouldn't feel exposed. There is no measurement or limit to pleasing your man. Also love, doesn't make you let your guard down, it makes you strive to keep that love complete and refreshing!

I wanted to leave you with something different tonight. I talked to my grandfather tonight and asked him about a scripture with you and me in mind. Isaiah 54:17, "No weapon formed against you shall prosper, and every tongue which rises against you in judgement you shall condemn. This is the *heritage of the servants of the Lord and their righteousness is from me, says the Lord." So you read that when you think of your mother, ex, or whoever tries to sabotage what we created. Also, I've enclosed a page from my daily reading from yesterday and today. Incorporate these things in your life 'cuz this will sustain us for life! Kiss the kids and tell them I love them, and please know I love you even more!*

Love always,
Bryan Edwards

PS: I'm on my job again, writing things, as we need to survive and grow as one

---

10/31/2010

Hey Baby,

    Happy Halloween! It would be so much happier for me if I had been able to talk to you. It's been like five freaking days, and of course our last two days of conversation were way too focused on some bullshit. So I really don't want to keep talking about it, but the damn drama continues. You know how long-winded I am verbally, and when writing it's multiplied times ten!

    So I was expecting a letter from my mom to come any day but I got an email instead, which we will discuss when you call on Monday (tomorrow, yay). But that's her pattern when I do stuff that she thinks is so wrong. When Jordan was a baby I got a letter because she felt like I was starving him, and she called my grandmother on my dad's side and everything. So to prove my point, I brought Jordan to visit my grandmother. And she picked him up and said, "This baby ain't skinny!" My mom has a bad habit of running her mouth to everyone when I supposedly fuck up, so twenty-five years of built-up emotions and issues came out in my six-page typed single-spaced reply to her email. And I didn't even touch the issue of the favoritism I felt they had for my brother or the favoritism that she showed toward Jordan, or a few other things because I can go on all day, as you know. After her response to my letter I guess all I can call it as closure, but things will be very different from this point on. I realized that one reason my parents have always felt they can butt all up in my business is because I've been too open with them about so much stuff, and relied on them too heavily in the past as far as bailing me out of situations, which was one of the reasons I had to leave Buffalo. I needed to know that I could truly survive on my own and not depend on public housing or who my parents know to get me a hookup, or needing childcare and having to thoroughly explain where I was going in order for her to watch the kids. But you are right, she still wants to control me.

11/1

Wow, yesterday flew by! Went to church then chilled for a bit, then it was time for trick-or-treating. And I will be sending pics. Dang, it's time to pick up the kids, so I guess this letter won't be getting mailed today. I would just send it off but it would only be one whole sheet, and I can hear you fussing like, "What's up with the short letter, Ma?" LOL! I'll finish later.

11:00 p.m.

Daaayum! VAC know they take their time posting money to this account. I was looking forward to talking to you because I mailed that money order on Tuesday, and I bet it will show up tomorrow because I have Girl Scouts, and you'll probably be inside to top it all off. But that means longer conversation on Wednesday, so I'm trying not to fret, but damn!

Okay, so weekend recap. Friday was no school, so it was nice to slightly sleep in. But I scheduled hair braiding for Nia and Nyree, so that took up like 10:00 a.m.–5:00 p.m., by the time Monica came. And since I would have them all day, I let them take breaks. Then Justine went with them to IHOP and Jordan chilled with me, so we went to Party City to look at costumes and I got some black lipstick and nail polish. Yeah, I changed my mind about the sexy schoolgirl and went sexy goth, dressed in all black with two ponytails. I think I was sexy and creepy, LOL!

Friday night was the party, and it was so good to get out and be around adults, music, drinks! I danced with a few random guys but then the DJ switched it up with R Kelly's "Ignition Remix," then "Bump and Grind Remix," then "12 Play Sex Me Part 2," and it was a wrap! I told the guy that I was dancing with sorry but I got to go—missing my man! Crazy part is I was missing everything we ain't done yet! But I dream about it, And even with a few drinks in my system and feeling mellow and relaxed and sex literally stays on my mind, you weren't there. And I'll never be that tipsy! But I guess I haven't been out in a long time 'cuz dudes are way more touchy-feely. But I just pushed the hands off and kept on dancing. Whatever was in that mystery mix huge jug was tasting good but snuck up on me quick! I had fun though, and to be at a house party, oh, it was live as hell. Most people wore costumes and nobody got ignorant.

Saturday was our chill day. Jordan even took a nap. I didn't get home till 4:00 a.m. and slept by 5:00 a.m. and woke up at 10:00 a.m. I was just like, damn, really? But I took a nap later on and Justine played outside all day. Sunday morning I made breakfast. Oh, we went to church. Oh, the kids came home and played outside, then we got dressed for trick-or-treating. A lot of people had an issue with Halloween being on a Sunday, but my thing is if you feel that way you probably should not be celebrating it at all. I dressed up again, but instead of the sexy goth I was just a regular goth, and ended up looking like a dark nun! I'll be sending pics of us all dressed up.

We got home around 9:00, and it was 10:00 by the time the kids went to sleep. And this morning we were all sleepy! I just kept telling myself I could always take a nap. So after doing more errands I waited until the mail ran, and yes, I had another letter from my dearest Bryan! I read it and started to snooze when the doorbell rang! Doggone Jehovah's Witnesses! I did end up getting my nap on, which is why the letter to you never got finished. But then I waited for your call. Got a call from Jackie and she wanted Kennedy's hair braided, so I did her hair tonight. And I was hoping my baby would call, but I know you will soon. I will end here hoping to hear your voice tonight!

Love you lots!
Janae

I decided that February 2011 would be a good time to relocate back to Buffalo, New York. The months of letter-writing and phone calls were no longer enough. My soul yearned for more. I needed something to fill this void. Funny thing is, I was fine before the first letter. In March 2010, I decided in my heart that my previous love was not meant to be after I had a miscarriage, and was at peace with the decision to move on and finally let go. So I really was good. Or was I? I have to wonder if I gave myself enough time to heal from the miscarriage, and the idea that it was time to let him go.

I moved to Charlotte in August 2007. My baby girl had turned four the day we left Buffalo. Poor baby spent her whole birthday on the road. For birthday number six we went all out to make it up to her! I was full of ambition and excited to take on the role of teacher in my very own classroom. But I wasn't prepared for such a drastic change being a single parent in a new city, with no family and friends, and taking on the responsibility of educating twenty children. I was beyond overwhelmed. I cried a few times. I wasn't Superwoman like I thought. I struggled to balance it all, and somehow I survived my first and second year teaching fourth grade. Then I was laid off in June 2009. I gave 150 percent to my job and there wasn't enough of me left to guess. It simply wasn't enough. I decided that moving back to Buffalo would be my best bet. I applied to teaching jobs back in New York and even landed an interview by phone, which didn't go too well. Honestly, I don't think I put forth a lot of effort in that interview because I love everything about the South. My mother constantly pressured me and secretly pressured the kids, pleading for us to move back. But Charlotte felt like home. So I made up my mind that Charlotte was home.

Even when I wrote that first letter to my husband in April 2010 I had no intention of leaving. Six months later, when I was completely in love with my man, I had no intention of leaving. But I needed to see him in person almost as much as I needed the sun on a cloudy day. I attempted to plan a visit to Great Meadow Correctional Facility. After calculating gas, hotel, food, and time away from my kids, the trip just did not seem feasible. Jarelle was due for a transfer to another facility soon, and if that facility was going to be close to Buffalo, traveling would be so much easier.

So when he told me he wanted to spend the rest of his life with me I began to brainstorm. This next parole hearing was in March 2011. If I moved back <u>temporarily</u> I would be back in New York when he got out, help him acclimate back into society, then we could move back to Charlotte sometime in August 2011 in time for the new school year. His parole officer would allow him to relocate with me and all would be great! My parents would be thrilled to get extra time with the kids, no need to tell them this is just a temporary move. I would be leaving behind my Girl Scout troop; new friendships I had formed; a three-bedroom, two-bathroom single house on a cul-de-sac; and a very diverse school. I still had not found a teaching job, but my customer service job from home would follow me to New York and I was still getting unemployment partially. So at the end of 2010 I decided that February would be a great time to move since Presidents' Week is a whole week off from school. I'll have tax money, and I can get to my man as soon as possible. I didn't think this move thoroughly. Love was seriously clouding my judgment. School was out in early June, the weather would be great, and I'd be giving myself sufficient time to pack. And I know how bad I am about packing.

The day we were set to hit the road I was nowhere near finished. I remember sitting against the wall around 1:00 a.m. fighting back tears and feeling overwhelmed and helpless. I was out of boxes and couldn't believe that in a matter of hours the family that was taking over my lease would be here, ready to unload their truck. I swear God saw my pain because my cousin Nicole and Yvette showed up in pajamas to help me in the middle of the night. They were such a big help and I felt so much better, but they could only do so much! I had A LOT left to do even after they went home.

Hours later Stacey showed up with her family, and the look her husband flashed at me when he realized they couldn't start moving in . . . can't even blame him. Who wants to drive over ten hours to relocate just to get there and have to wait on me? I ended up with a nosebleed from the stress. I hadn't had one since I was twelve years old. I also started just giving stuff away. I posted on Craigslist and began putting things on the curb that at that moment were no longer important. I just wanted to get out of the house and on the road! Sometimes like today I'll be asking myself where something is and then remember that day. We didn't get on the road until late morning or early afternoon, and it was a beautiful eighty-degree day.

As we drove farther and farther up north, the weather began to cool. Slowly at first, then as the sun started to go down the temperature dropped quickly. The lovely green treetops that I've always admired on road trips began to be replaced by bare trees and a dusting of snow on mountains. Then it was straight up cold as fuck. New York State was cold and dark and depressing as we crossed the state line. It's funny how that's what slowly began to happen to my relationship.

Out of all the household moves I had done in my life, this one was the worst. Financially I wasn't as prepared as I should have been. Selling all of my large items seemed like the logical thing to do, and the small items could be boxed up. I had found a company that was willing to ship all of the boxes via UPS and sent me shipping labels for each box. I ran out of boxes and labels, and on moving day I left behind over a dozen boxes, totes, and containers in the backyard at Touch Me Not Lane. I didn't know what else to do! The rest of my boxes were picked up by UPS and arrived in Buffalo over a week later. Of all companies I decided to use, I had to pick one that had fraudulent activities going on and my packages got caught up in the foolishness. My brand-new winter boots and my daughter's boots vanished. Quite a few things were broken, and had I realized how packages are thrown and tossed around I would have cushioned them much better. The items left behind in Charlotte stayed outside in the backyard for probably two weeks and got rained on a few times. I had asked Stacey if she could at least put a plastic cover over them, and she didn't want to go into the shed to get the plastic tarp. Thankfully Kimberly came by and covered them, but they had already been rained on at that point. Finally I found someone online who could pick them up and transport them to Buffalo. He saw my post on uShip and felt sorry for me! I was literally begging at that point.

Somehow everything works out and eventually we were settled in our new smaller apartment. The kids were enrolled in school and I was ready to make my first drive to Malone New York and meet my fiancé in person for the first time. Would he look like his pictures? Would he like me in person? Would our in-person connection be as strong as our connection through letters and phone calls? What would visiting a prison be like? I had never been to a prison in my life! I was scared, yet anxious. I was hoping that this first visit will prove that this relocation and all the stress and headache that accompanied it was worth it. I was wrong.

I want to now share with you the very first letter my husband wrote to me after I made it back to New York in February 2011, and the very last letter he wrote me at the very end of our relationship in June 2013.

February 25, 2011

Love of my life,

I don't even know where to begin, it's been a little bit since I've written you. I'm far from speechless, but I'm drawing a blank, my thoughts are frozen. I truly can't believe you're in Buffalo waiting on me. And in another week you'll be in front of me, touching me, kissing me, and telling me you love me. Wow, how did we get here so quick! Is this what the year is going to do, fly by? Like, it is too good to be true. You've been accepted by my grandparents, which is definitely a blessing. 'Cuz if they didn't like you, they would have told me in some form or fashion. I also want you to know a couple of days before you put up I asked my grandmother to give me her opinion of you 'cuz I wanted her blessing.

Moving on, I'm sitting here bumping Jodeci (*Best of*), and for the death of me I can't figure out how you lost your ring. When you took it off before you started cleaning, and all of a sudden you couldn't find it or remember where you put it. Now forgive me for saying this, but that sounds like straight-up bullshit. There's no furniture in the house but a couch, and you mean to tell me that it just up and disappeared? That's hella timing, considering. I know you're going to say, "Jarelle. . ." And I'm going to say absolutely nothing, Janae Edwards, just stay focused. 'Cuz I'm so focused right now. I can taste freedom like I taste the particles in the air. And I'm ready and built for anything, and nothing can surprise me at this point in life. My third eye allows me to travel down roads less traveled by the average person.

I know you're probably saying what the hell I'm talking about. Call it thinking out loud, baby! Maybe I need to take this slow music out of my ear and lie down, but I'm not sleepy or tired, so I'm going to keep on writing this letter! I am deeply touched that the kids are calling me Dad or Daddy. That's shocking and crazy, wondering are my daughter's calling someone else Daddy! Do you think they still see me as their father after being gone for damn near twenty years, of not providing or tending to their needs and wants? Only time will tell on what life has in store for me concerning them! Well, baby doll, the lights are out and I'm staring out the window right now, so I'll pick this up tomorrow. I love you, my queen!

2/26

Hello, my sweetness, up early watching the snowfall and listening to *Donell Jones' Greatest Hits*. I hope your morning is going as good as mine. Don't have any plans. Might go work out or just stay in my cube all day or watch some TV. Earlier in the letter I was just venting, so don't pay too much attention to it. You should know about my thought process by now. It's like day and night it varies. I pray that by the time you get this letter, you have received your clothes and important papers! This letter is not going to be long 'cuz I wanted to start the process of me writing again. And although I haven't written in a while you already know it's a longer letter following this letter. Matter of fact, I'm going to keep going 'cuz you've written two letters, so I'm going to bless my baby with some more!

 You're right, everything happens for a reason. That's why they sent me way up here. Plus every Sunday would have been something else. This distance definitely makes us appreciate the visit, but I would have done that without the distance! And I don't feel any type of way asking you for anything. That letter has been forgotten, but I still keep it! I just want you to be 100 percent at your best, and I know you will always make a way for me to have what I need, whether little by little or all at once. I wonder what's taking little bro so long to write back. That's not like him. Also, I do find it kind of crazy I'm right down the street from him, wow! (Referring to Upstate Correctional Facility.) The counselor probably did that on purpose but all devils lie, so I'm not surprised I got lied to once again. I'm kind of getting used to being lied to, are you? Yes, you owe me some oohs and ahs and all that. I wonder when that's going to take place. Thank you for the cards, those were awesome!

 Now you asking me am I going to be able to contain myself when you visit, sitting so close. The question is will you be able to? Now, on a serious note, I went back and read your letter and you said what really scares you is you may end up sabotaging our relationship because of your deep-rooted insecurities. Are you forewarning me of something I should expect, or was that just a feeling at that time? I'm ready for anything, so give me your best shot! Well, baby doll, I'm going to end this letter for now 'cuz I have to write our kids and do some other things before the day ends. So please know that I love you and cherish you with all my heart and soul. And I can't wait to see you next weekend. Stay strong, focused, loved, and forever blessed!

Love you,
Bryan Jarelle Edwards
(I know I'm due for some pictures, so I won't ask!)

I am always asked whether I saw red flags during the relationship. For the first several months of letter writing my feelings of love definitely blurred any red flags. However, once I decided to move back to Buffalo and started putting things in motion, I did start to see some here and there. As soon as Jarelle asked me to be his wife, I immediately went out and bought a ring. I wanted something to symbolize that I was officially a fiancée! I found a basic cubic zirconia ring set in silver that I proudly wore. Once I arrived in Buffalo, the ring vanished! I now believe in symbolism and believe that may have been a sign, but I will never know.

My new apartment in Buffalo was a two-bedroom upper, and the lower tenant was a middle-aged woman and her adult son. My movers were Shelby's two oldest sons and a friend of theirs. I took the ring off to clean the apartment before we started to unpack boxes. When I went to put the ring back on it was gone, never to be seen again. I was bothered that Jarelle was questioning the ring's disappearance. I was bothered by the method of questioning he would use in many circumstances—asking questions that he knew the answer to. It would often feel like a police interrogation. And any time I would speak on it, his response was always the same: his grandmother raised him to ask questions.
Despite the ring interrogation, that first letter overall was filled with love and anticipation of seeing each other for the first time. In our phone calls we constantly professed our love for one another. I uprooted my family and dove headfirst into the unknown because I believed our love fairy tale would have the most magical happily ever after. Fast forward to June 2013 . . .

June 2013

JANAE,

    I don't know why the first thing you asked me is if I took somebody to a party, as if you didn't know the answer already about something that happened in the past. Is that what's going on now? Y'all sitting around gossiping about me? It's bad enough everything I talk to you about you tell my sister word for word! Then you have BIG BALLS AND HANG UP ON ME like I'm a nobody, no problem.

    Then you send me a picture without your ring on and tell me some bullshit about the color of your dress didn't go with it. OKAY! Since everybody seems to be talking about Bryan Edwards, tell everyone that I'm good and don't worry about me. I'm on some way fall back shit. You've been wanting to do you for the longest, so by all means, Mrs. Edwards, do you with all sincerity.

Love,
ME

PS: I won't call you for I'm not into giving people bills. Also, I've never been one to be a burden on any soul, trust and believe I'll be on the other side REAL SOON!

HOW did we get here?

Stay tuned for part two of *Yours Truly, Your Husband for Life*, which is titled, *Loyalty For Life*

About the Author

JANAE JAMES was born and raised in Buffalo, New York, where she has been an elementary school teacher for the past several years. She is a mother of two adult children and has spent the majority of her adult life working with children from infancy to high school. She earned both her bachelor's and master's degrees from Buffalo State College (now Buffalo State University). Janae's love of reading as a little girl and natural storytelling ability ignited a spark within her to someday become a published author and share her own stories. Janae enjoys spending her summers off by visiting the beach, traveling, and spending quality time with her two young grandchildren. Janae is also a member of Zeta Phi Beta Sorority, Incorporated.